Return

to

Deathlehem

Return

to

Deathlehem

Edited by
Michael J. Evans
and
Harrison Graves

A
Grinning Skull Press
Publication

Return to Deathlehem
Compilation Copyright © 2014 Grinning Skull Press

"The Shortcut" copyright ©2014 Susan Jay
"Bloody Christmas" copyright ©2014 Steph Minns
"He Sees You When You're Sleeping" copyright ©2014 Christopher M. Morgan
"A Merry Little Christmas" copyright ©2014 Rose Blackthorn
"The Wren" copyright ©2012 Kevin G. Bufton
    Originally published in *You'd Better Watch Out!*, Cruentus Libri Press.
"White Christmas" copyright ©2014 DJ Tyrer
"A Labor Dispute" copyright ©2014 Michael Shayne
"The Night Before Christmas" copyright ©2014 Philip Thorogood
"Survival of the Reddest" copyright ©2014 Vicky MacDonald Harris
"Awash With the Christmas Spirit" copyright ©2014 Jordan Phelps
"What Child Is This?" copyright ©2014 Joel Reeves
"Minnie's Christmas Surprise" copyright ©2014 Geoffrey K. Liu
"Secret Santa" copyright ©2014 Chantal Boudreau
"A Christmas Miracle" copyright ©2013 Kerry G.S. Lipp
    Originally appeared on The Wicked Library Podcast, Christmassacre 2
 "A Christmas Remembrance" copyright ©2014 JP Behrens
"No Sugar Plum Fairies" copyright ©2014 Steven Bigwood
"Crack!" copyright ©2014 Gerard Griffin
"Split" copyright ©2014 Jay Wilburn
"Nell's Game" copyright ©2014 Nicole DeGennaro
"Cursed Christmas" copyright ©2014 David J. Delaney
"Ornamentation" copyright ©2014 Alyn Day
"The Trap" copyright ©2014 Mike Pieloor
 "Killing Christmas" copyright ©2014 Mark Parker

The Skull logo with stylized lettering and interior graphic was created for Grinning Skull Press by Dan Moran, http://dan-moran-art.com/.
Cover designed by Jeffrey Kosh, http://jeffreykosh.wix.com/jeffreykoshgraphics.

ISBN: 098902699X (paperback)
ISBN-13: 978-0-9890269-9-4 (paperback)
ISBN: 978-0-9890269-8-7 (e-book)

DEDICATION

This one goes out to all the readers who enjoy taking the holly jolly out of the holidays.

And as with the first *Deathlehem* collection, this one is also dedicated to my mother and father, Eileen and Frank, my sister and brother, Susan and Roy, and my grandparents, Emily and Roy, it's not Christmas without you. Love and miss you all.

TABLE OF CONTENTS

ACKNOWLEDGMENTS

Once again we would like to thank Dan Moran for the fantastic work done on the interior graphic, and Jeffrey Kosh for an amazing job on the cover design. We also want to extend a huge thanks to all the authors who obviously took great joy in making Christmas scary.

Happy Horrordays!

Well, it's that time of year again. The stores and streets are decorated for the Christmas season, carols are blaring over the radio, and the Salvation Army bell ringers are harassing innocent pedestrians on what appears to be every street corner. And it's only September! Well, maybe I'm exaggerating a little, but you can't deny that Christmas is being pushed earlier and earlier every year. Is it any wonder that I turn into Ebenezer Scrooge by the time Halloween rolls around?

Those of you who have read last year's collection know the how and why *Deathlehem* was conceived. For those of you who don't, allow me to summarize. The end of the year is a dark time for me, and if it was left up to me, I'd let Christmas go by and not give it a second thought. My friends, however, weren't about to let me wallow in a pit of darkness during what they considered to be the happiest time of the year, especially not when Christmas meant so much to people I have lost over the years. I tried putting up the tree, but there was no joy in it, so back in the box it went. But still my friends continued to badger me. I needed to do something to keep the spirit alive. That's when I decided to put a little darkness into the holiday. I mean, it was only fair, right?

1

Especially when you consider that Santa's rotund, little face has been trying to steal the spotlight away from jack o' lanterns for years now. And that's how *Deathlehem* was born.

The Call for Submissions went out, and I crossed my fingers. I didn't know what to expect. And… Well, you know what they delivered. They blew me away. What I wasn't expecting, though, was the way it made me feel. For the first time in God knows how long, I was actually enjoying the holiday. I vowed that I would *Return to Deathlehem* again this year with the hopes of recapturing some of that feeling. And once again, the authors didn't disappoint. If you thought last year's collection of stories was dark, brace yourselves.

What can you expect?

We've got Krampus, murderous elves, and a Nutcracker that seems to have a fondness for… well… nuts (cue sinister chuckle). JP Behrens returns with a twisted sequel to last year's equally twisted "A Christmas to Remember".

And since the holidays are all about family, wouldn't it be nice to take a trip to Grandma's house? First-time author Susan Jay opens the collection with exactly that, but for her it's not a simple matter of going over the river and through the woods. Instead, she's chosen to take "The Shortcut." Who would've thought the way would be fraught with such dangers? And Ms. Jay isn't the only one to venture to Grandma's house. In "Bloody Christmas," Steph Minns creates a false sense of security in that the horrors don't start until after we've arrived safe and sound at our destination.

Well, maybe going to Grandma's house isn't such a good idea. How about we just stay home and surround ourselves with our immediate families? Nothing can go wrong there, right? I mean, we're not setting foot outside the house so what could possibly go wrong. If your family is anything like those depicted in Rose Blackthorn's "A Merry Little Christmas" or DJ Tyrer's

"White Christmas", you just might find yourself making excuses and sneaking off to the office. Didn't they have that "Secret Santa" thing going on today? Yeah, they did, and what could be better than presents? Unfortunately, thanks to Chantal Boudreau and her tale, maybe the office isn't such a great idea either.

It looks like nothing is safe in this quaint little town (but then again, we knew that coming in, right?), not even a visit from ol' Saint Nick himself, as Christopher M. Morgan is quick to point out in his story, "He Sees You When You're Sleeping". This particular story reminds me of Robert Deveraux's *Santa Steps Out,* although it's not anywhere near as bawdy.

So without further ado, I bid you welcome…

To Deathlehem…

Again.

Michal J. Evans
and the staff at
Grinning Skull Press,
Best Wishes for a very scary Christmas
and a frightful New Year!

The Shortcut

Susan Jay

ason Parker paused on his way down the stairs and stared into the living room. From his vantage point he could see the empty space in front of the fireplace where the Christmas tree should have been, and a wave of sadness washed over him. The vacant spot was a painful reminder that his parents were no longer with him, and even though he knew it wasn't his fault, he couldn't help but blame himself for their deaths. If he hadn't chosen an out-of-state college, if he had opted to enroll at the local university, maybe they would both still be alive. Maybe. There was no telling with The Fates, fickle ladies that they were; they might have chosen to cut the threads no matter where he had decided to go to school. If he had stayed locally, however, at least he would have had his three best friends for companionship, but they were gone, too. Not dead, at least, but gone, and Jason was alone this Christmas Eve.

Well, he wasn't truly alone; he still had his aunt, uncles, and cousins, as well as his grandparents, his father's folks, which is where he was reluctantly getting ready to go. He imagined the visit was going to be an awkward one. He hadn't seen them since the week of his parents' funeral a little over three months ago. He had been considering not going back to school because he had the "kids"—as his mother had liked to call them—to take care of, but his grandparents had reassured him that they would take care of them. Against his better judgment, he agreed to return to the campus and resume his studies. He should have listened to that inner voice that had been nagging him to stay because not two weeks after he received a phone call from his grandparents. They told him that the dogs were too much for them to handle, and they needed to find another home for them. He had been all set to jump the next bus home, but they told him it would be pointless, as the dogs had already been given away. They wouldn't reveal the names of the new owners for fear the Jason would try to get them back, and they felt his education was more important than a few dogs, but they reassured him that they had gone to a very good home.

Pausing a second longer to wipe the tears from his eyes, Jason plodded down the rest of the stairs. His grandfather would be arriving shortly to whisk him back to their house, which would be filled with Christmas decorations and holiday tunes, relatives he hadn't seen since last year, and memories, all of which he didn't feel he was ready to face. Why couldn't they understand he wasn't ready to deal with the holidays yet? It was the main reason why he had stayed on campus during Thanksgiving despite his grandparents' invitation, and why he had been planning on spending Christmas there as well, and would have if it hadn't been for his grandmother's phone calls. The first one came the day after Thanksgiving, and every day thereafter she was calling him, and she finally succeeded in wearing him down. He caved, and now, as the hour grew near, he was beginning to regret his decision.

He wandered into the living room and spied the gift-wrapped packages on the coffee table. He hadn't intended to do any shopping this year, but since accepting the invitation, he felt obligated to get his grandparents a little something. There were also a couple of boxes marked "X-MAS" in bold, black marker that contained some of the decorations his grandparents had asked for. They didn't have much in the way of décor, as they usually spent the holidays here, so they had asked, if it wouldn't be too much trouble, if he could bring some over.

Flopping down on the couch, he put his feet up on the table. With any luck, he'd be able to drift off to sleep and be deep enough under by the time his grandfather showed up that he wouldn't hear the doorbell.

The ringing of the telephone jolted him awake. He scrambled across the length of the sofa, snatched the handset off the end table, and brought it to his ear. "Hello?"

His grandmother's voice filtered through the receiver. "Hello, Jason, dear."

"Hi, Grandma. What time is it?" He glanced at his watch, preparing to launch into a string of apologies, but he saw he had only dozed for a few minutes. "Has Grandpa left yet?"

"That's what I'm calling about, dear. He was on his way out to the car and he slipped on a patch of ice."

Visions of the old woman calling from a hospital waiting room filled his head. "What? Is he okay?"

"He's fine. Nothing more than a bruised pride, but he's

feeling a little shaky and not up to driving."

"If he wants to rest, I don't mind staying home. "

"Nonsense, dear. It wouldn't feel like Christmas without you. What we were wondering…"

"Yes?"

"Well, we were wondering if you wouldn't mind driving yourself over."

He got up and crossed to the window. Pulling back the drapes, he peered outside, hoping to find a raging blizzard and unsafe road conditions, but the night beyond appeared clear, and while the road had yet to be plowed, it wasn't anything he couldn't handle. He let the curtains fall back into place, then ran his fingers though his hair. "I guess," he said.

"The roads aren't too bad near you, are they?"

"No, not at all. It's just I don't even know if the car will start." And that was the truth. Being a freshman living on campus, university regulations dictated that he wasn't allowed to have a car, not until his sophomore year. And true, he'd been home just shy of a week, but he had never given the car a thought. He had no desire to go anywhere, not with all the stores decorated for the holidays. There had been one trip to the supermarket to pick up the basics, but the temperature had been mild, so that was a trip he made on foot. Dinner consisted of ordering take-out, and the following day's lunch was whatever he hadn't finished the night before. Since then, the temperature had dipped and there had been a heavy snow fall; he had no desire to freeze his ass off, so the garage and its occupant had been the furthest thing from his mind. By his calculations, it had been six months since the car had been on the road, so there was a very good chance it wouldn't start. What then? He could call them back and tell them the bad news, but they would see that as an easy out, knowing full well he hadn't wanted to go in the first place. No, if the car wouldn't start, he would probably hoof it across town. It wouldn't take that long.

"Well, if the car won't start, you just call us back and somebody will come get you."

He said he would, then hung up the phone. He turned and looked out the window again, praying to see that a blizzard had stirred itself up within the past few minutes, but his prayers had fallen in deaf ears.

Rather than put if off any longer and maybe talk himself out of going, he headed out of the room and down the hall to the coat closet. After shrugging into his warm winter coat, he returned to the living room and gathered up the packages he needed to deliver, then proceeded to cut through the kitchen and into the garage. He opened the driver's side door and popped the trunk. After stowing the packages away, he slid behind the wheel and ran his fingers over the sun visor for the key. He wasn't sure if it would still be there, but sure enough, it was. He slipped the key in the ignition, gave it a twist...

And as luck would have it... Nothing. No whine. No cough. Nothing.

With a sigh, he hit the button on the automatic garage door opener attached to the visor before popping the trunk again and getting out of the car. He retrieved the packages, then hit the switch on the wall to trigger the garage doors before stepping outside.

The night was crisp and carried with it that distinctive smell that said snow. It barely had time to register in his brain when he saw the first flurry swirl through the air. He was considering going back inside and calling his grand-mother, but the garage door had rumbled shut behind him.

Looking both ways, he realized his was the only dark

house on the street. All the others were decked out in their holiday finest: twinkling lights, plastic Santas and snowmen, and those tacky inflatable lawn ornaments that made the street look like the launching grounds for the Macy's Thanksgiving Day Parade. A wave of sadness washed over him. When his parents were alive, their house was the envy of the neighborhood. Mom and dad loved Christmas, so they tended to go all out. Nothing too gaudy, but the entire house would be decorated, inside and out. He could feel the tears beginning to well again, and he tried to stem their flow. With a sigh and a quivering lip, he hefted the packages in his arms and started down the driveway.

Just as he reached the road, he looked around in amazement as the first flakes drifted past. A smile played at the corners of his mouth. He looked towards the heavens. "Well, mom, looks like you're finally going to get your wish." She'd always prayed for a white Christmas, but he couldn't remember any time in his life that it had ever happened. Yeah, they had snow before Christmas, as well as after, but never *on* Christmas. He wasn't the religious type, but he took comfort from the falling snow. In a way, it made it feel like his parents were with him this holiday season.

The further away from the house he got, the heavier the snow fall became. By the time he reached the end of the street, the road was covered with a fine dusting and he could feel the weight of it in his hair. He stopped and looked back toward the house, wondering if he should just turn around and go home. His grandparents would understand. They'd be disappointed, but they would understand. Indecision weighed on him, and he was all set to head home when he remembered the shortcut he used to take as a kid whenever he went to visit his grandparents. It would certainly cut about thirty minutes off his travels, so it was worth looking into. But after all these years, was it still there? Or had they repaired the hole in the fence? There was only one way to find out.

Hefting the packages in his arms once again, he continued down the road. At the intersection, instead of making the right turn, he cut across the road to the town dump. He followed the chain-link fence another twenty yards or so until he saw the rusted sheet of corrugated tin that covered a gaping hole in the fence. It was held in place on the other side by two steel drums. BINGO!

Setting his packages down, he maneuvered the tin sheet to the side, then slide the packages through the makeshift entrance before following them into the dump. He brushed the snow from the top of the drums, then lifted the packages from the ground and placed them on top. There was no point in letting them sit in the snow any longer than they had to. After sliding the sheet of tin back into position, he turned to get his bearings. Dirt corridors led through mountains of trash and abandoned cars, and while he couldn't be at all certain the alien landscape was still the same from when he was a kid, he didn't think it could be all that different. All he needed to do was cut across the junk yard on a diagonal and he'd be at his grandparents in no time. It certainly beat having to circumvent the large area of ground that housed the dump. Once on the other side, all he would have to do is slide open the main gate, which was never locked, and he'd be home free.

Taking up his packages once again, he started to make his way through the maze of trash. By the time he reached the heart of the dump ten minutes later, the snow had all but stopped, but that didn't mean a thing; it could start up again at any second. He stood on the edge of a large clearing, at the center of which was a huge fire pit. It had been used recently, as the residue still glowed and smoke rose lazily into the air. Not too far from the pit was a run-down shack, the interior of which was dark. The exterior was alive with the Christmas spirit. White lights framed the building, and a plastic Santa Clause adorned the roof.

Circling around the pit brought him closer to the shack. Just as he was moving past it, a gust of wind buffeted the building and stirred up the snow. Movement caught out of the corner of his eye made him turn to face the shack and the darkened doorway. The door swung wildly on its hinges. Thinking the owner wouldn't appreciate a floor full of snow when he returned, Jason approached the building with the intention of pulling the door closed, but as he reached out to grab the knob, he heard a frantic squealing coming from within. Knowing he should just walk away, he acted against his better judgment. Shifting his packages to one arm, he reached past the door frame and fumbled around on the wall with the hopes of finding a light switch. Finding it, he flipped it on…

… and let out a startled gasp at what was revealed.

Scores of startled rats scurried around on the floor, crawling over a pair of work boots that still had legs and shredded, blood-stained jeans attached to them. The rest of the body was mercifully hidden behind a metal desk, but the piece of furniture did nothing to hide the stench that filled the building. Whoever it was had been dead awhile, long enough for the body to start to decay. Gagging, Jason stumbled backwards, the boxes toppling from his arm. His foot came down on something hard concealed in the snow. It slipped out from under his foot, causing him to lose his balance. The sudden chorus of growls rising up behind him further impeded his ability to stay on his feet, and he went down hard. The breath was knocked from his lungs, and it took him a moment to recover. When he did, he whirled around, fully expecting to see a pack of rogue wolves bearing down on him. What he wasn't expecting was the sight of three familiar faces. Muzzles encrusted with dried blood, the three dogs—a german shepherd, a chocolate lab, and a mutt—were emaciated, possibly on the brink of starvation, and there was a feral gleam in their eyes. If they weren't in such poor condition, Jason would have been excited to see his "kids" again, but the sight of them only broke his heart. Is this what his grandparents considered a good home?

If the dogs recognized their former master, they gave no indication of it. What Jason saw in their eyes as his gazed flickered from one animal to the other chilled him more than the weather itself, for he saw only a hunger stoked by the burning emptiness in their bellies. Their muscles vibrated with tension as they prepared to spring.

"Hey, Sarge," Jason said, holding out his hand toward the shepherd. "Hey, boy, you remember me, don't you?"

The only response he got was an even deeper growl as the leader of the small pack shifted slightly on its feet.

"Don't be like that, boy," he said, slowing getting up, all the while keeping his hand extended. *No sudden moves*, he told himself. *Just keep it slow and steady.* "You remember me, right?" He shifted his hand gradually to the left. "How 'bout you, Chloe?" he said, addressing the lab. You remember me, girl, don't you?"

Despite a brief wag of the tail at the mention of her name, the dog bared its teeth and her growl intensified.

"What about you, Heinz," Jason said, addressing the mutt. Typical of the dog, it looked to the shepherd to see how it was reacting before turning its head back to Jason and letting loose with a warning bark.

Jason took a cautious step to the side as his gaze shifted

from one animal to the next, taking in their abused condition. The two and a half months he'd been gone had taken a toll on the dogs. Their fur was greasy and matted, and they were so thin he could count their ribs. Chloe had a festering wound the size of a softball on her right rear haunch. Sarge's right ear was missing, and he noticed Heinz only had three legs. The front left leg had been severed just below the knee. His gaze shifted back to Sarge. There was something else about the dog, but Jason couldn't quite put his finger on what it was.

Jason slowly backed away from the animals until he was pressed against the wall of the shack. Unable to retreat further, he started to slide along the building toward the corner, slowly sidestepping so as not to alarm the dogs. Once he reached the corner, he slipped around the side of the building, turned, and ran.

A chorus of ear-shattering howls went up behind him. He glanced over his shoulder in time to see Sarge round the corner. In the glow from the light shining through the shack's window, Jason was finally able to tell what else was different about the animal. He only had one eye. Chloe followed almost immediately behind Sarge, and Heinz brought up the rear, limping along at a brisk pace.

Facing forward again, Jason narrowly averted barrelling into a wall of trash. He had to find a place to hide because he knew he couldn't be able to outrun the dogs. Well, maybe Heinz, but certainly not the other two, not even in their weakened conditions. And they had the advantage; they knew their way around this place while Jason could turn a corner and find himself at a dead end. He realized his only chance was to circle back around to the shack and take shelter there. He felt he had a better chance against the rats than he did facing off against the dogs. Once inside, he would be able to barricade the door and wait out the rest of the night until the daytime attendant arrived. It hit him then that he might have an even longer wait, with tomorrow being Christmas day. He could go the day without food or water, but he didn't know if the shack was heated. He might survive being mauled by the dogs only to freeze death within the building's sheltering walls.

While he ran, he stripped off his coat. He paused only long enough to stash it within the rusted remains of a Cadillac, hoping the scent would confuse the animals and buy him some time. He took off again, occasionally climbing piles of trash and walking along the tops of them. Maybe the absence of his scent on the ground would deter the dogs and they'd give up the chase.

The crazed barking echoed in the stillness of the night, the sounds seeming to come from all around him. It was impossible to tell where the dogs were with the way their racket was rebounding against the mountains of debris, but Jason pushed on, following the twisting, turning paths and hoping he was getting closer to the shack. His muscles were burning with the exertion, and his legs felt like they were about to give out. Just as he was beginning to give up hope of ever reaching the shack, he saw it. Filled with a renewed hope, he surged forward.

Reaching his destination, he sagged against the wall and used it as a support as he made his way toward the front of the building. Just as he reached the corner, a menacing growl caused him to stop in his tracks. He scanned the clearing and spotted Sarge almost immediately. The shepherd was about ten feet away, head low, teeth bared in a vicious snarl. Safety was only a few feet away. If he darted for the door, would he be able to fling himself inside and slam the door before Sarge covered the distance and attacked? He didn't think so, but what choice did he have? Another growl, this one from off to he left, gave him his answer. None. He would have to chance it.

The instant he lunged for the door, Sarge was off like a shot. He made it to the door and was able to fling himself inside, but just has he turned to close the door, Sarge slammed into it, sending him stumbling backward. Chloe followed not long after, and Heinz brought up the rear, standing in the doorway to prevent his escape. Sarge had whipped around and was now standing between him and one of the two windows. Chloe had the other window covered. He was trapped.

Chloe inched forward, and with each step Jason took a step backward until he couldn't retreat any further. Moving ever closer and putting herself between Jason and the body on the floor, Chloe bared her teeth and snarled. Jason took it to mean, *Mine. Stay away*. He wasn't about to argue.

While his attention was diverted away from Sarge, the shepherd attacked. Jason barely had time to duck, then he was pushing away from the wall and lunging toward the window. He heard the *thud* as Sarge hit the wall, but almost immediately afterward he heard the scrabbling of nails on the wooden floor. He lifted his arms to protect his face as he jumped for the window. They made this look so easy in the movies, but he knew as soon as his feet left the ground that he didn't have the speed behind him to break the glass and sail effortlessly through the window. Instead, he hit the glass and hissed at the pain as the shards lacerated his flesh. His head and shoulders cleared the frame, but that's about all that did before gravity took hold. He came down hard on the wooden frame, the sharp, teeth-like shards of glass still embedding in the wood biting through his shirt and into the tender flesh of his stomach. The smell of blood sent the animals into a frenzy, and before the pain had a chance to register, he felt the tug on the legs of his jeans.

The pain in his calves and the agony in his gut hit at about the same time, and his own cry joined that of the dogs. He struggled to lift himself off the glass that impaled him, but every time he started to make progress, there came a vicious tug at his legs, followed by a fresh wave of pain that robbed him of his strength. He collapsed back down, and, whether real or imagined, he could feel the glass grinding against his insides. Another cry of pain ripped from him as one of the dogs grabbed hold of his right leg and started to shake its head from side to side. The denim ripped, but still the dog continued to pull. He felt himself moving backwards, but he didn't have the strength anymore to brace himself against the frame and push in the other direction. The glass buried within him started to slice up his internal organs as he was pulled every so slowly back into the building.

His vision started to blur as darkness crept in around the edges. He felt one of the dogs sniffing at his crotch, lapping at the blood-soaked denim, while another pushed its snout into the gaping stomach wound and tried to grab hold of a chunk of meat with its teeth. The third dog was still working on his lower leg, worrying it like it was a steak bone, and he supposed, in a warped, macabre sort of way, it was.

Consciousness was slow in leaving him, and he was still alive when the dogs began to feast in earnest.

B[*]LOODY ⁂CHRISTMAS
Steph Minns

Bloody Christmas. That's what Mum always called it any-way. It was so much hassle, she said, and where do we find money for presents and fancy food? Kids are always wanting everything they see on the bloody telly. In truth, Ben, my six-year-old brother, and I didn't, and we were quite happy with what we were given. But Christmas of '93 really was a terrible one.

It had started with Mum losing it on Christmas Eve when she and Dad had a blazing row and she chucked the frozen turkey at him. He'd ventured into the hellhole that was the kitchen, lair of stressed-out Mum trying to follow Delia's recipes for stuffing and trimmings. I guess Dad had thought he was being helpful instead of interfering. Anyway, he was floored by the turkey, smashing his head into the door frame and knocking himself out as he fell.

"Oh God! No! He's dead!"

Mum, over the top as always, scrambled for a tea towel to stem the ribbon of blood creeping across the lino from Dad's head.

"Dan, don't stand there like a lemon! Call an ambulance."

I did. Dad wasn't dead, but we found out later he was badly concussed and had a fractured skull. Of course Mum had to stay at the hospital, as she was convinced he was at death's door, so Ben and I were dragged along to sit in the hospital waiting room. Mum had called Granny Brent to pick us up. She came sweeping into the room in a battered canvas coat that swirled around her calves and wellies, and she had long, wild, white hair that gave her the appearance of a cross between a mad witch and Worzel Gummidge. Granny Brent was mum's mum, and we didn't see her often, even though she only lived a few miles out of town.

"Get in the car, boys. Mind you sit on the plastic and don't touch the gun," she said.

There was a shotgun across the back ledge of the rusty Volvo. Gran explained she'd been shooting rabbits 'for the pot' earlier, and hadn't expected to get a desperate call from Mum to keep us overnight.

"What's the smell, Gran?" I ventured as we sped off down the dual carriageway out of town.

"Ferrets," she replied bluntly. "In the back. They don't bite."

"Will we have Christmas turkey at your house tomorrow then?" Ben asked warily.

"I won't promise turkey, Ben, but I do have a lot of old chickens, and we could maybe sacrifice one for Christmas Day."

Ben looked at me, his eyes wide with horror.

"Where did you think roast dinners came from, numpty?" I tormented him.

Gran turned the Volvo off the dual carriageway at the next roundabout, then down a side road into dark country-side. We drove in silence for a long time, passing occasional pubs, their Christmas lights reflected onto wet parking lots. Rudolph flashed idiotically on rooftops, and blow-up Santas stomped across the fronts of the big, isolated houses dotted along the road. What fake bullshit, I thought. Everyone feels obliged to be jolly and get into the Christmas spirit. At thirteen, I was just entering that cynical age when the magical facade of childhood drops away and you start to see the world in a colder, harder light.

Streetlights finally vanished behind us and the car bumped around as Gran wrestled it along a dark, rutted track. Ben was fascinated as we drew into the yard. I vaguely knew the house but guessed Ben wouldn't remember it, as he'd been really young when we'd last visited.

"Boys, go in and make yourselves at home."

The yard smelled of pigs and I could hear geese some-where in the darkness nearby, cackling and hissing.

Gran let us into the house, and then went back outside to settle her ferrets in the shed for the night. We sat politely at the table, gazing around the old farmhouse kitchen.

"Wow. It's big. Granny lives here all on her own?" Ben asked.

"Yeah. Grandad died years ago, but she still keeps lots of animals and sells stuff at the market, Mum says. There's fields at the back that go down to the woods. They had a Shetland pony once, called Lawnmower. You were still a baby then. I can only just remember him." I filled him in on the little I could recall.

Gran came back in, shrugging off her big coat.

"You boys must be hungry. I'll get some tea on."

Ben looked at me in desperation, eyes wide, whispering, "Will she make me eat squirrels and rabbits?"

Gran caught our conversation and laughed. "No, we're just having cheese on toast. Do you like cheese on toast, Ben?"

"Yes, thanks." He looked relieved.

"Your mum promised to call before your bedtime to say goodnight and let us know how your dad is doing. I don't have a telly, only the radio, I'm afraid, but there's lots of board games in the back room you can rummage through if you like."

Grans' brisk manner had softened a little and she smiled a lot, which made her look less witchy. We spent the next three hours playing Kerplunk, Buccaneer, and Mousetrap together around the kitchen table, laughing and teasing each other when someone's plastic mouse ended up under the trap. Gran was really cool and let us stay up late, but I noticed she kept glancing out of the kitchen window when she got up to get us biscuits or juice, and then she locked the cat flap in the back door.

"Mind you don't go outside during the night. You boys promise me that? And don't unlock that cat flap, even if the cats are scratching at it to go out. They can use their litter tray indoors tonight."

When we went up to bed, Ben was full of it and excited that Gran had said he could feed the chickens and check for eggs in the morning. I'd spoken briefly to Mum, who'd promised us a proper Christmas Day on Boxing Day instead when we could swap presents. I wasn't really bothered, as the day was always full of Mum and Dad arguing anyway and some part of the dinner was usually burnt. We never went anywhere and no one came to visit us. Maybe the day at Gran's would be more fun. Mum had asked how we were getting on. She'd sounded a bit nervous. I'd replied we were fine and Gran was odd but in a nice way.

"I want to see all the animals tomorrow," Ben told me as he pulled off his jumper. "Gran says she's got some binoculars and we can go down in the woods and look for deer. Why didn't mum like living here?"

"I don't know. Why, what's she said?"

I was curious. He shrugged.

"Only that the house was scary. That's why Gran usually visits us and we don't get to come out here."

"Do you reckon it's scary here then?"

Ben pulled a thoughtful face. "Nah. I like Gran. She's funny and doesn't nag on like Mum."

Gran left us in the big bedroom at the back, which had two single guest beds that she laid out with faded, worn sheets and pillowcases. It was all clean, she assured us, adding as she left.

"If you hear anything in the garden tonight, it will be just foxes. So don't get concerned."

"Sure," I replied, puzzled as to why she should say such an odd thing.

As we'd been bundled off in such a hurry when the ambulance had arrived, we had no pajamas with us, so went to bed in our pants and T-shirts. I was woken some time later by Ben, shaking me.

"Dan, quick! One of Santa's elves is in the garden."

"What? Don't be daft."

"It really is. There's a little man by the pond, eating the fish."

I reluctantly rose, wrapping the blanket round myself because the room was so cold. Snow was floating down outside and our breath misted the glass as we peered out of the window. As Ben said, there was a tiny human-like figure outside in the yard, squatting by the pond and gnawing on something, which looked to me more like one of the rabbits Gran had left to hang on the fence. The security light outside threw its shadow across the yard. It seemed to be wearing old brown trousers, a jacket, and a shapeless beanie hat, a bit like the pictures of medieval peasants in our school history books. Dark hair straggled out from underneath the cap, and I guessed it must have been less than three feet tall.

"Maybe it's not an elf, Dan," Ben whispered. "Santa's elves are jolly and have red noses and green hats. What do you reckon it is?"

I replied I had no idea, and then the back door burst open below us and the flare and crack of Gran's shotgun lit up the yard as she fired into the air. The creature turned to fix her for a moment with black, glittering eyes. Its face was like a shrivelled turnip, horrible and malevolent. It drew its lips back in a sneer, exposing tiny, pointed teeth. Then it was gone, dropping its meal from its gnarly fingers to scamper back down the garden, vanishing into the darkness beyond the hedge. Ben had cried out in fear as it had turned and we'd seen its face properly. I had to admit I was pretty creeped out too, my mind racing to work out what it was we'd just seen. A dressed-up pet monkey escaped from somewhere? Some sort of remote-controlled puppet sent in as a joke by neighbors?

Gran came up the stairs to check on us.

"Are you boys okay? I hope the gun going off didn't scare you. I was just cleaning it and it went off by accident."

She obviously wasn't aware we'd been watching from the window. Ben had calmed down and surprised me by saying nothing. Maybe he was too upset and shocked. Gran tucked him in and left us again, this time with a nightlight that gave the faded room a warm glow.

After a while, Ben whispered to me. "Will it come back do you think, Dan? Is that why Gran locked the cat flap, so it couldn't come in and get us, or eat the cats if they went outside in the night?"

"Maybe. We'll ask her in the morning."

He seemed content at that and went to sleep, but I lay awake trying to figure it out. It must have been the early hours of Christmas Day when I heard something scrabbling in the bushes below our room. I got to the window just as the outside security light was triggered, flooding the yard below with cold, yellow light. There it was again, the small goblin-thing padding across the yard, clutching the ripped-up rabbit and gnawing on it as it scouted around on the ground. I guessed Gran must have been deeply asleep because she didn't rush out to confront it this time. It disappeared from view and I realized it must have gone under the lean-to porch to the back door.

A bit freaked out now, but curious, I crept down the stairs to the kitchen and flicked on the light. The cats were in their basket, but up on their feet, backs arched, and hissing. Heart banging nervously, I went to the window and could see its shadow by the back door. I realized with a start it was scratching and probing at the cat flap. I went down on all fours so my face was level with the see-through little plastic door, and I could make out its shape on the other side, muttering and gibbering. The sound made my blood run cold. It suddenly fell silent and pushed its face up against the clear plastic, and I got a good look at its black, evil eyes peering menacingly through, right back at me. The shrivelled turnip face screwed up in the most horrible way as it bared its teeth and said something in that gibber. Then it scuttled away again. I went back to bed but didn't sleep well. I was worried it would come back and somehow find its way in.

Christmas Day dawned bright and fresh. Ben wasn't in his bed when I got up, and he wasn't in the bathroom either. Gran wasn't up yet, so I dressed and went downstairs, expecting to find Ben having breakfast in the kitchen. The back door was wide open.

Curious, I went out into the yard to call him, guessing he'd gone to check for eggs on his own as he waited for Gran to surface. Ben's trainer footprints were visible in the snow, walking out to the middle of the yard. I could also make out tiny boot prints running determinedly across the yard, something the size of a toddler, heading to meet him. Where they collided, it looked like a scuffle had taken place, and I followed the trail of drag and scuffle marks as they headed down the garden path, across the field, and towards the woods. By the wooden fence at the edge of the field, the snow was churned with blood, and scraps of bloody orange cloth were snagged on the top rail, parts of Ben's favorite T-shirt that he'd worn to bed. I felt sick with concern now, terrified for my brother.

I realized I was shaking as I climbed the fence, intent on following the trail. It led me deeper into the woods, where I began frantically calling him. Only the twittering of birds in the trees broke the silence. I stepped on something and stooped to look at it, jumping back when I realized it was a small beanie hat, just like the one the goblin-thing had been wearing. There was also a clump of ratty, straw-like dark hair in the snow. Ben had put up a fight, I thought. Good for him, but where was he now?

I ran back to the house to rouse Gran.

"A goblin took Ben," I shouted as I shook her awake. "He went outside last night. That thing you shot at has got him and dragged him into the woods."

Her face drained of all color as she blinked at me. "God, no! Dan, go back and keep looking while I get dressed. I'll be with you in a minute."

I did as she asked, and ten minutes later she was beside me with her shotgun. We both stalked the woods, desperately calling Ben. The trail through the snow ended abruptly at a large mound in a clearing, and Gran let out a horrified cry.

"It's taken him into the faery realm, the evil fey! Taken him into the Underworld."

"Why? What is a fey?" I asked, baffled.

Gran was close to tears and suddenly looked a hundred years old, her face haunted and withered.

"There are many creatures that share this world with us, Dan. Some good, some evil. That one has been visiting the farm for years, centuries for all I know, before your grandfather and I ever owned the place. It always comes on Christmas Eve. That's why I called it Jack Frost. So far it's only cost me the odd chicken over the years, but now this!"

"Maybe you should have shot it dead last night," I ventured.

"I don't know if they can be killed, Dan. But I wish I'd tried now."

The police arrived and made a thorough search of the wood. I overheard the crime scene officer telling Gran they'd found a chewed child's finger in the snow near the clearing. She'd started crying and I'd felt sick to my stomach again.

Ben was never found and Mum blamed Gran, furious with her. He was listed as another "missing child," suspected abducted by some pervert or weirdo. I've never had the courage to tell Mum about what I saw in the yard that night, but I suspect she may have had some idea of what had really happened. After all, she'd grown up in that house and must have seen things over the years. That's why she was so scared to go back, even as a grown up.

Every Christmas Eve we light a candle for Ben and think

of him. Mum cries. Dad usually gets drunk. Gran has sold the farm now and moved into an old people's maisonette in town, where she keeps to herself. I visit sometimes, but we never speak of Ben.

He Sees You When You're Sleeping
Christopher M. Morgan

There were no visions of sugar plums dancing in Danny Lundgren's head. He didn't even know what a sugar plum was. Whenever he heard that line from the story, he imagined fat raisins dragged through granulated sugar. He figured he couldn't be that far off and what did it really matter? Sugar plums may not even exist; he simply didn't care.

Danny stuffed his hands under the pillow behind his head and looked up at the ceiling. Christmas Eve was always the hardest night to get any sleep. Ever since he was a little kid he remembers lying awake for half the night, salivating at the bounty under the tree that he would tear open in just a few short hours.

But he wasn't a kid anymore. At fifteen, Danny had been aware there was no such thing as Santa Claus for years now. But that didn't matter either, as long as Tommy still believed.

Having a little brother would keep the "Santa Claus myth" alive for a few more years, and that meant he would still rake in the big loot from mom and dad, who had to keep buying Danny the expensive "Santa" presents to keep Tommy from suspecting anything.

Sleep might not come at all tonight, but Danny didn't care. In just a few hours he'd have his hands on that brand new iPad he'd been asking for since October. Danny couldn't wait. The anticipation was killing him. He thought about how specific he was every time the family went out shopping during the last few months. He made it a point of telling his mother exactly which one he wanted and explaining to her that anything less just wouldn't do.

God, can you just imagine having to show up at school with only a sixteen gig mini? Everyone would laugh at him. Danny knew mom wouldn't let that happen. Not after the iPhone debacle from his birthday. He told his mom exactly which iPhone he wanted, but she bought the older version anyway! Can you believe that? She actually did it on purpose! She said something about how it did almost everything the newer version did, but it was discounted at half the price. Danny was so mad he didn't talk to his parents for an entire week. He threw the iPhone in his backpack and didn't get to show it off to anyone because it was last year's model, not the cool new version everyone was talking about... While small groups formed up and everyone compared their new games and apps, Danny had to pretend he'd left his at home.

After a week of this humiliation, Danny was fed up with his brand new, yet inferior piece of garbage. While walking home from school, he ducked down the alley behind Phillip's Pizzeria and threw his new iPhone down on the ground. When he picked it up, he was disappointed to see that it was still intact. He threw it down a second time and then stepped on it for good measure. This time when he picked it up, Danny smiled. The corner of the glass was shattered. There was a small crack leading from the corner and spread into the display area.

By the time Danny got home he had pressed the screen enough to make the small crack spiderweb across the entire screen. He was even able to remove some small chips of glass from the corner of the screen. He put on his best "worried" face and opened the front door.

It only took about an hour before Danny's mom agreed to buy him a new iPhone. Danny was an excellent liar; he knew enough to make sure the story had some details that made him look good, but not to drop in too many details lest his mother get suspicious, or worse, try to verify any of the facts. The tale involved running to class to ask for extra math problems to make sure he understood the work and getting knocked down by Martha Andrews, the mentally handicapped student, so he stopped to help her pick up her books. It was only *then* that he discovered his precious iPhone had fallen from his pocket and…

If only his mom knew just what he and Joey Devereaux had done to Martha just a few weeks before. Joey began feeling guilty about it, but Danny convinced him that it didn't count because "retarded kids don't have feelings like us, that's why they are in special classes." Joey had had his doubts, but after Martha left school three weeks later, he began to relax. The teachers said she was going to a special school over in Dupree, but there were rumors that she had committed suicide. Danny hoped it for the latter; suicide keeps secrets longer.

But Danny's mother had no idea what her son was up to, and by the time she heard Danny's story, she was proud of her son and was eager to reward him with a replacement iPhone. Danny was pretty sure his father was on to him breaking it himself, but since dad didn't say anything, Danny figured he was safe. Mom said they'd go to the Apple store that weekend, but after a half hour of pleading and careful planning, Danny convinced her that they had to go that very night. Within three hours of intentionally smashing his phone, Danny had his hands on the newest model iPhone, the one he had wanted all along.

Remembering how he had manipulated his mother filled him with pride; Danny smiled at the ceiling and waited for morning. He just knew, without a doubt, that the iPad he wanted was just twenty feet away in the living room. It better be, or there was going to be hell to pay come Christmas morning...

* * *

Creeeeaak.

Danny's eyes flickered open and he turned his head toward the clock. It was just after three in the morning. He was shocked to find that he had fallen asleep after all. He rolled over beneath his blankets and looked out the window. The wind blew small puffs of snow from the roof. Danny watched the small crystallized ice pellets flounder in the wind gust as they flew past his window. He closed his eyes and tried to go back to sleep while visions of iPads, gift cards, and cash danced in his head.

Snick.

His eyes flew open. This time he *knew* he had heard something. It was faint, muffled, but it was definitely *in* his room. Danny looked at the window. Nothing new to see there. He heard the noise again and glanced around the room, the light from all the power LEDs on his desk, dresser, and nightstand perpetually illuminating the darkness as though it were merely twilight. Danny didn't see anything unusual, but he was seized by the feeling that he was no longer alone. He tried to pass it off to what his father called "house settling" noises, but there was something... alive... in that noise, almost slithering. Danny began to breathe heavily, rapid, shallow gulps of air, and looked around the room a second time, this time more slowly.

Finding nothing out of the ordinary, he started to feel better, and then it dawned on him that the noises must have been his mom and dad setting up the presents under the tree. Either that or it was Tommy trying to sneak out and take a look. Their parents had always kept to the tradition of the kids staying in their bedrooms until 6:00 am at the very earliest. "If he's sneaking out, he's in a world of shit," Danny muttered as he rolled over and closed his eyes again.

Snick, scrape.

Danny hadn't fallen back to sleep yet. He held perfectly still and held his breath. With one hand carefully lowering the blanket from his face, the other slowly reached up to the shelf above the bed and the flashlight set there. His hand hadn't quite reached the light when the blanket fell from his face and he saw the figure in front of the door.

Danny bolted upright in terrorized panic. Every muscle in his body contracted and he scrambled backward until he was pressed against the wall. There, just inside his room, was a three foot tall statue of an elf. Red jacket, green pants, white beard... the big floppy Santa hat, ears that came to an elongated point, and a smile that showed years of neglected teeth. In the poor lighting, the happy Christmas elf looked absolutely menacing.

Danny pressed himself against the wall and kicked the blankets down away from him as he began to hyperventilate.

His mouse-like squeals were all the sound he could make and he banged his head against the wall as he attempted to put distance between himself and this unwelcome visitor, but he only succeeded in tearing down his posters of half-nude women and leather-clad rock stars. Just as his voice returned to him, his eyes had grown accustomed to the dim light and he saw the figure was only a statue. He began to calm down and no longer felt the urge to scream.

As he slowly returned to normal, Danny started to laugh, a nervous titter. When the thing didn't move, his confidence grew, and his nervous laughter turned to appreciative chuckles. The damn thing looked so life-like that it had scared the hell out of him. He wondered if mom and dad put it there, or if maybe it was one of Tommy's new toys his little brother wanted to show off. "You really are in a world of shit now," Danny said. He wanted to see this thing up close. Danny moved to grab the flashlight from the shelf, but it wasn't there. He looked about on the floor, then pulled up the corner of the mattress. He pushed aside the magazines he stashed there and felt the small box of weed he had scored from Alex Mason earlier in the day, but the flashlight was nowhere to be found.

He let go of the mattress and flopped back down on the bed. He reached for his table lamp but froze when he saw that the ugly statue was gone.

A frantic glance at the door confirmed that it was still closed. Danny had presumed that the noises he had heard were Tommy opening and closing the door to plant his new toy elf. But this time, there was no noise, and not enough time to move the statue quietly. His little brother must still be in the room.

"Tommy, if you're in here, I'll kill you!" Danny warned the empty darkness.

There was no response.

"I swear, you little bastard, I'll cut you for this…"

Time slowed to a crawl when a stranger's voice responded, "What a magnificent idea."

Before he could register the soft-spoken threat, two hands grabbed his arms and a third covered his mouth. A knife appeared in Danny's peripheral vision.

The knife wiggled for emphasis when the elf's face emerged from behind Danny. "You know what this is, you know the threat, you know the drill. One sound out of you and I'll split you wide open to see where it came from."

❋ ❋ ❋

The Lundgrens buried Danny a week later. There was no sign of a struggle, no indication of foul play. The medical examiner found an enlarged and distressed heart, possibly indicating a rare heart disease, but according to all reports, Danny Lundgren simply died in his sleep on Christmas Eve. His younger brother Tommy claimed to have seen a Christmas elf in the house that night. He said it spoke to him and asked him if he had been naughty or nice, but all too quickly people dismissed the crazy stories from a distraught eight year old.

❋ ❋ ❋

The knife was already pressed to her throat by the time she felt the hands restraining her arms. Unable to swat the knife away and unable to scream, Susan kicked her feet until she felt unseen hands pin them to the bed.

"Susan," began the calm voice of an old man, "I'm only going to tell you this once: you will hold still or I will make you still… Very still indeed. Do you understand?"

Fear of what could happen next forced her to rapidly gain control of herself. She tried to speak, to say she understood, but the old man shushed her, putting a finger to the back of the hand covering her mouth. "No sounds, sweetheart. Just nod if you understand."

Lying completely still, Susan lowered her jaw toward her chest by the slightest degree.

The deranged elf smiled, showing her his dark, decaying teeth. "Good girl. You stay calm, remain quiet, and I'll make this quick."

In spite of the threat and her attempt to remain perfectly still, Susan still shivered at the elf's words.

There was a dissonance between the placid and comforting voice and the jagged and ugly face of her attacker. If she had heard the voice without seeing his face, Susan would have conjured images of a kindly grandfather or a wise old man. But the face hovering inches from her own belonged to a broken, squealing monster. Susan began to feel the walls close in on her and the floor began to spin.

"Stay with me, Susan. Don't leave us just yet, dear." The elf brandished the knife closer to her face, twisting it in the darkened room, trying to catch the stray light from the streetlamp outside her window. He removed his hand from her mouth.

Susan fought the urge to scream for her parents. The knife was a very tangible reminder of what might happen if she did. She held still, hoping this was all a vicious nightmare.

The elf was sitting on her thighs, straddling her chest with his tiny feet. He took off his red pointed hat and revealed a bald head between his large pointed ears. "You have made Santa's Naughty List, Susan. I'm afraid I'm going to have to punish you for that."

He dropped his hat on her chest and reached out to his left. A hand emerged from the darkness and handed him a sack. After looking into Susan's eyes and assessing her stability, he pulled the knife away and reached out to his right, where another hand emerged from the darkness and took it from him. He opened the dirty canvas bag and a small bit of light escaped its rim, lighting the twisted elf's face and making him look more horrible than he had in the darkness. He looked into the sack; after some searching, he pulled out a small, black rock. A lump of coal.

"This is your legacy for the year, Susan. This is what you have sewn with your actions and thoughts." He placed the black rock inside his hat and shook it with vigor. He reached in and pulled out a lump of sparkling darkness. It was a paradox, a contradiction of light and dark, good and evil. Susan watched in fascination as the sparkling lights swam in the small cloud of emptiness confined to the space between the elf's fingers.

"Susan, you will consume this and relive the pain you have caused others. It will give you nightmares, it will make you sick. Depending on just how naughty you have been, it may even kill you." The elf paused at this, waiting to see if Susan would begin to scream at the thought of her own death. When she stayed perfectly still, he smiled contentedly and continued, "If you live through this, you will not remember my visit, but you will remember the pain. I will not instruct you in how to behave, but hopefully the remembered pain will."

The grotesque elf moved his withered hand ever closer to Susan's mouth. She wanted to struggle, to scream, but found she was incapable of any movement at all. The elf had full control of her body and she opened her mouth to receive the sacrament of her evil deeds.

He remained perched on her legs and watched as it dissolved on her tongue. Her face wriggled in disgust. "Stay off that Naughty List, Susan," he whispered, then began his preparations to leave.

From a million miles away, through a delirium of lies and deceit, Susan stammered, "Who—"

The elf looked at her. "I thought we agreed on utter silence from you, Susan. Isn't that what your nod indicated?"

Susan held stock still, not making a sound, not acknowledging the question, fighting off the anxiety and aberration her mind was already experiencing, terrified to even breathe.

"But since you asked so nicely, I may as well introduce myself." The elf stood, donned his red pointy hat, and tossed the canvas sack over his shoulder. "I am the one, the only, the eternal... Santa Claus."

Before Susan could even question her sanity, her eyes closed and she fell fast asleep.

❄ ❄ ❄

The dark house offered no new surprises for the ancient burglar. Santa had seen it all over the centuries. Boarded-up houses, no chimneys, alarm systems, motion-sensitive lights, cameras... He could get in and out of any house on the planet undetected. The only real problems he found were the dogs. He whispered a word to them and they slept through it all, but he had to see them before they got in their first bark, otherwise they'd wake up the whole house and he'd have to start all over.

The dark elf strode directly into the living room and pointed a finger down the hall at the sleeping cocker spaniel while whispering his magic word without even casting a second glance at the animal.

"Alright," huffed Santa as he concentrated on his enchanted knowledge of the Naughty and Nice Lists. This house had only one kid in it: Martin Long. Martin was only mildly naughty and deserved a warning, nothing too major. Santa smiled as he took in the Christmas splendor around him. A full fir tree adorned with glowing, twinkling lights dominated the small living room. The traditional plate of cookies sat beside half a glass of rapidly warming egg nog. Ordinarily he was content to let the parents play Santa and leave the cookies and milk to them, but there was an incredible, irresistible aroma emanating from this batch. One nibble couldn't hurt.

He ate one cookie, then immediately devoured three more. The crooked old elf was overcome with feelings of joy and euphoria. Memories of Christmases long ago flooded his brain, and for a moment, Santa was once again happy. The cookies were so good; it took all of his willpower to leave the last two on the plate. He was licking his fingers when he thought there was something about the flavor… something… wrong?

It was only when the floor rushed up to meet him and his senses went dark that he had identified that one mysterious ingredient. "Mistletoe," he mumbled into the carpet and his tired eyes fluttered shut against his will.

※ ※ ※

Struggling to stay awake, Santa rolled onto his back and reached for his magical bag. He had to get out of here. Children were always attempting to catch Santa in the act; he couldn't let this kid be the one to finally nab him. To his surprise, it was not a child, but an adult, a small frail woman who appeared, emerging slowly from behind the festive Christmas tree. Santa began rifling through his memories of the household. *Who was this woman?* The tainted cookies blocked all his senses and skills. He was trapped and his senses were blind. He watched the shadowy form stalk toward her captured prey. When she finally stood above him, she knelt by his face and peered into his dilated eyes.

Her voice was soft and mellow, not the cracked voice one would have expected from her withered face. "Hello there, Kringle."

The moment she spoke his name, he knew who she was. "Befana. It has been a long time."

❋ ❋ ❋

The woman was remarkably spry for one so old. She plopped down on the floor next to him and sat cross-legged as she assisted the elf into a sitting position. "What are you doing here, Santa?"

Unaccustomed to having his near infinite knowledge and powers held in check, the elf shook his finger at the old woman. "What have you done to me, you old bitch?"

"Now Santa, those are some harsh words to casually toss around between old friends. Relax, I'm not here to hunt you. I'm here to ask questions."

"Then why the poison, old woman?"

Befana chuckled. "Because I knew you wouldn't sit still long enough to answer me." She paused before adding, "Old man. I also knew you couldn't resist my baking. You never could."

Santa tried to get up, but his limbs didn't want to co-operate and he clumsily fell to the floor again. Befana picked him up and sat her old friend comfortably on the floor, leaning his back against the couch.

"You really should relax. Every move you make only justifies my use of trickery."

"Mistletoe?" Santa groused.

She chuckled again. "Yes, mistletoe. I stood behind that tree for hours waiting for you. I had to make sure that dog didn't eat them. It would have killed him. But you, I put in just enough to ensure that you would stick around for our little chat."

Santa threw a disgusted look at the old woman. "You drugged me."

"Don't worry, it will wear off in a little while and you'll be free to go."

Resigned to his situation, Santa settled back against the couch and crossed his arms, still defiant toward his captor, but less angry than a moment before. "So what's this all about then?"

"I'm the one asking questions, if you don't mind, Kringle." Befana chuckled again. "Oh, I just sounded like a movie star cop, didn't I?" Amused with herself, the woman stood and walked to the far wall. She flicked on the light switch and the living room flooded with the glow of warm light from above. "If you don't mind the light, my eyes aren't what they used to be."

With the additional illumination, Santa saw his old friend in her usual garb of rags and patches. She looked like a Halloween witch before they sexed up the image with leather and corsets.

He shot a barb her way. "Still dressing like Baba Yaga I see?"

"And why not?" Befana shot back. "She was as good a friend as any back in the day. I see you're still dressing up as a Coca-Cola commercial?"

"This is the look they expect when Jolly Ol' St. Nick arrives, so I give it to them."

"You're three feet tall and you've got Spock ears! They're expecting a six-foot white man, you idiot."

The venom of the conversation lulled as Santa despondently replied, "Yeah, no one reads that poem closely enough.

Miniature sleigh, eight *tiny* reindeer. Christ, he even wrote that I'm a 'right jolly old elf'. He frigging spells it out, E-L-F... yet they always expect the Coke image."

There was a pause as the two of them laughed in spite of the circumstances.

"What happened to you, Kringle? Why are you back? And why did you switch teams?"

"I never left, Befana. I was just pushed into the background. I'm not part of Christmas anymore."

The old woman thought back to the night she sheltered the three astrologers on their trip to see the newborn Messiah. "That happens to all of us, Kringle. Time moves on without us. You are not the first of us to be phased out of the season, out of the hearts of men."

The elf objected to her speculation. "But the season grew a life of its own. I've been outsourced, old friend. My reason to exist is still out there, only they've downsized my job. I..." Santa paused and directly addressed the old woman. "You and I, Befana, us and the dozens of others like us, we used to deliver rewards to the children of the world, we used to spread happiness and cheer, remember?"

Santa looked into the eyes of the old woman, who was lost deep in the memories of the old times.

"Have you watched the faces of the children today? Have you seen happiness and joy? No, of course you haven't. You've seen greed, you see spoiled brats falling prey to rampant commercialism. We used to give candy, berries and nuts, or simple wooden toys, and the children would light up with surprise."

Befana interrupted. "They still light up, Santa. Not all of them are spoiled like you say they are."

The elf dismissed her assertion with a wave of his hand. "They light up for an hour. Or until the batteries go dead on the newest gadget. On one of the many gadgets they'll get this year. And when it breaks, they'll pine for the newest gadget next year. And they expect it, Befana. They are spoiled! They are being bred as consumers, not people. They don't deserve rewards; they need to be taught a lesson."

Up to this point, Befana's voice was soft, like a kindly old grandmother, but now her voice became stern and authoritative, vibrating with anger. "That was Krampus' job Kringle, *not* yours."

Santa looked up at the old woman's face. "He's dead and gone, Befana. He's as cold and dead as your dear friend Baba Yaga. They took Krampus out of the ever increasingly sanitized Christmas lineup and look what happened to him. They for-got about him and now he's gone. All the old gods are dying off as we are forgotten. One by one, we fade from this world. WalMart has taken over my job of rewarding the good. Krampus isn't here to terrorize the brats, so I'll take over his job of punishing the naughty. If I don't, I'll have no purpose and then..." Santa trailed off.

Befana completed her friend's thought. "And then you'll die."

* * *

Santa watched as a tear rolled down Befana's cheek. It was followed by several more, forming a wet stream down her face. Santa patted down his coat and offered her his handkerchief. She took it and nodded her thanks as she blotted her eyes dry.

"I am feeling rather old myself, Kringle. The end is coming soon enough. Why prolong it? If we are destined to die, how can we fight it?"

The elf smiled in disbelief. "You talk of destiny... Have you forgotten who you are? Have you forgotten that we are gods ourselves? We may be the last remnants of the old guard, but we are still members of an elite class of immortals. I have absolute power. I see all, I know all, I reward, I punish. How is this *not* a definition of a god?"

Befana's aging body was aching as she sat on the unforgiving floor. She shifted her legs and sat back against the far wall as she spoke. "There is a reason they forgot about Krampus. They didn't want him around anymore. He was terrifying. He ruined the spirit of what we were trying to build Christmas up to be."

"They may not have wanted him, but they needed him. They need someone in that role, Befana. Look at what they have become without him. Look at what has happened to your beloved Christmas Spirit. Do you see any shred of it left in the hypnotized faces of the Mall-Zombies? Do you see one shred of it left in the empty coffers of the charity collectors?"

Santa's voice began steadily rising, his face gleaming, his energy pulsing with each word he spoke. "Every Thanksgiving and Christmas churchgoers flood the shelters and carve turkeys in front of the news cameras, but where are they the other three hundred and sixty-three days of the year?"

His voice was now booming from the rafters, bellowing louder than his small body could possibly project. He spread his arms wide and felt his power returning to him. "Where is this spirit of charity you claim to be nurturing?! It has been brutally murdered and they are the ones responsible for it! *I am vengeance.* I will give the naughty children of the world something very real to dread. *I* am Krampus reborn!"

The room shook with Santa Claus' voice echoing like a thunderclap in the silence. Befana stared at her old compatriot with wondrous shame and contempt. "You've gone mad with power, old Kringle."

The elf only responded with a single, "Hmmph."

"Maybe recent years have been unkind to you, but you had a good run of it. Better than most. Now we must make way for the young gods. You don't get to reinvent yourself when it comes time for you to bow out. You don't get to impersonate long-dead gods. We are not immortal. We live in the hearts of mankind. And when they chose to discard us, we die. It is the way of things."

Santa threw a sly smile at the old woman. His voice once again returning to the calm restraint of a wise old man. "Maybe for you, tired, old Befana, maybe for you. But I don't intend to make it so easy for them. They may associate the name 'Santa Claus' with images of a kindly, old, fat man who got rid of his North Pole workshop and now buys his toys at Best-Buy, but they will also remember the name of our fallen friend, Krampus. I will rebuild his cause, I will carry on his legacy. Naughty children will fear the dark hours of Christmas once again." Santa flexed his aching muscles and cracked his knuckles as he felt his full strength return.

The old woman shook her head in disbelief. "What happened to that grateful orphan I once loved? When did you turn so dark? You've become a monster."

The ugly, little elf sighed and stared at the floor. "That's a disappointment, Befana. I was thinking you would join me. We could team up, just like the old days. You rewarding, me punishing, traveling together…"

"Those were your good old days, Kringle, you and Krampus. I've never murdered children, and I won't continue watching you execute innocent children on Christmas Eve."

"Innocent?" Santa called out in mock surprise. "You call them innocent? These kids drive a world economy that is overinflated and ready to burst. They demand the latest toys before the old ones are out of the boxes they arrived in. They cry and complain until their parents, who are just as spoiled as their children are, give in and buy it for them just to shut them up! There's no innocence left in this world, Befana. You know this as much as anyone." After a small pause, he cleared his throat. "And how dare you accuse me of murder. I've never hurt these children…"

Hoping to drive the point home and dissuade him from his plans, she began to assault him, trying to break him down. "No, you absolve yourself from your guilt by forcing them to face their evil deeds all at once. At least your pet Krampus had the nerve to carry them off and kill them himself. You don't have the stomach to take on Krampus' mantle. You're nothing but a neutered, weak impression of him." As soon as the words came out of her mouth, Befana discovered that she regretted turning on her friend. "I'm sorry, Kringle, I… I just don't know anymore."

Santa Claus smiled at her as he stood and brushed off his clothes. "Well… It's been nice chatting with you, old friend. Let's catch up again some time when we're both not so busy. I really would like to see you again. But right now, I've got some work to do…"

With that, he placed his finger aside his nose and simply disappeared in a flurry of snowflakes and coal dust, leaving behind words that echoed in the small room, "Happy Christmas to all, and to all, you better watch out…"

A Merry Little Christmas
Rose Blackthorn

Ethan tossed another log on the fire, ignoring the sparks that flew out and left tiny black smudges on the rug. He rearranged the pile of half-burnt wood, embers, and ashes with one of the fireplace pokers, making sure the fresh log would catch. Then he used the poker to push the screen closed, protecting the rug from any more singe marks.

Before the tall, narrow front window a Christmas tree stood. He'd decorated it with every string of lights he could find in the mismatched collection of holiday décor, but some of the strands remained dark. He didn't feel like going through them, bulb by bulb, to find the dead ones, so he just left it as it was. The lights that worked twinkled red, yellow, blue, and green, catching sparkles from glass, tin, and plastic ornaments. The tree was laden; he had hung every single bulb, icicle, and figurine stored in the boxes labeled *XMAS DECORATIONS*.

At the very top was a decrepit angel with a stained plastic face and clubbed fingers. The ball-gown of white satin and netting had faded to nicotine yellow over the years, and the gilt wings were slightly crumpled.

On the old stereo, Christmas music played, crackling a little through the outdated speakers. He'd never felt the need to upgrade to a CD player or those new-fangled MP3 thingies, so the records from his childhood played the music he'd listened to for decades. With everything in order, or at least as much as it could be, Ethan went into the kitchen to indulge in a glass of egg nog. When Mother had been alive, the egg nog was straight; his first Christmas without her, he took the liberty of adding some of the rum he'd bought especially for that purpose.

After mixing the drink, Ethan stood for a while looking out the kitchen window over the sink. The clouds that had covered the sky all day still sat motionless above, blotting the sunset to a dim grey glow that swiftly disappeared. Ethan had heard a weather report earlier in the day, promising a white Christmas. So far, it seemed the weatherman was misinformed. The cloud cover did not break, but there was no indication of any kind of precipitation. Even though it remained frosty cold, he wasn't going to hold out any hope for Christmas magic.

He took a sip of the doctored egg nog, pulling a face at the unfamiliar flavor, but was determined to drink it. When headlights splashed across the fence, indicating a car had turned into the driveway, Ethan frowned. Who would be showing up at his house on Christmas Eve?

He set the drink down on the counter and walked through the threadbare living room, pausing a moment to try and see past the tree out the front window. By the time he got to the front door and reached for the knob, there was a sharp knock.

He hesitated for a moment, and before he could open the door, he heard his sister's voice, shrill and impatient, from outside.

"Ethan, open the damn door."

Teeth clenched, he took a deep breath. What was Sylvia doing here?

"I know you're home, you've got all the lights on. Let me in, it's cold out here!"

Ethan sighed heavily, unlocked the door, and opened it.

Sylvia immediately pushed past him, saying, "Bring in my bags, would you?"

Ethan saw two suitcases sitting on the top step, and when he stepped out to pick them up, he saw the cab pulling back out onto the street. The headlights washed across the front of the house, stinging Ethan's eyes, and then it was gone.

"Close the damn door, Ethan, it's fucking freezing out there." Sylvia's voice was sharp and irritated, and Ethan did as she said after setting the suitcases near the wall. She was right, it was cold; frigid enough that for a moment, in the glow of headlights, he'd been able to see his breath.

Sylvia was standing in front of the fireplace, her hands held to the screened blaze. She wore a knee-length wool coat, high leather boots, and a long fuzzy scarf wrapped around her throat that might have been angora. Before saying anything else to him, she looked at the tree and made a noise of disgust. "For God's sake, Ethan, did you hang every piece of garbage you could find on the tree? It looks like it was decorated by a hobo."

Jaw muscles twinged, and Ethan realized he was grinding his teeth; less than five minutes in his sister's company and he was ready for her to be gone. "What are you doing here, Sylvia?"

"It's Christmas. Where else should I be if not with my

family?"

"Isn't there someone you actually *want* to spend Christmas with?"

"Aw, look at you, worried about my happiness," she crooned, giving him a cynical wink. "I'm on my own at the moment, and coming here was more important anyway."

He watched as she started picking through the ornaments on the tree, making little sounds of distaste in the back of her throat. She hadn't removed her coat or scarf, only setting her purse on his chair, and the two heavy suitcases still waited near the door. He knew she expected him to take them back to one of the bedrooms, but he was her *brother*, not her *servant*, and she could carry the damn things herself. He took another deep breath, making himself calm down, and went back into the kitchen to retrieve his nearly full egg nog.

When he returned, he stood with his mouth hanging open for a minute. Sylvia had draped her coat and scarf over the back of his chair, and was pulling ornaments off the tree and dropping them on the floor. "What are you doing?"

"You can't have all this junk on the tree at once, Ethan. It looks tacky." She tossed a little ceramic deer onto the growing pile on the floor and turned back to the tree. As she did so, the heel of her boot came down on the scattered ornaments, breaking at least two of them.

"Syl, don't wreck them," he said, grimacing at the whiney tone in his voice. In that instant, he was transported back in time to when they were kids. Even back then she'd been the boss, and he'd mostly tried to stay out of her way.

"They're already trash. I don't know why you didn't just toss them and buy some new decorations." A plastic snowman and two tin stars hit the floor behind Sylvia, and now she moved around the tree to pick through another section.

"Syl, knock it off," Ethan said, trying to put some command

into his tone and not faring very well. "It's my house, and my tree, I can decorate however I want."

"Hah," she replied, dropping a couple of discolored glass bulbs, one of which shattered when it hit the pile of discards. "*Our* house, Ethan. Mom didn't leave everything to you, did she? No, she left it to both of us."

Ethan sighed. When their mother died, Sylvia had come long enough to deal with the funeral and the reading of the will. Since Ethan had lived in the house all of his life, and she had moved out as soon as she turned eighteen, she hadn't said anything about letting him stay there. In fact, he hadn't talked to her since she'd left the lawyer's office with a certified check in her hand. "You said you didn't care about the house. You said the cash was fine with you."

"Yes, well," she said, crossing to her purse, "that was before the money was gone. I talked to a friend who's a realtor, and even in this shitty economy, we can probably get a decent amount for the house." She pulled out a cigarette and lit it, paying no attention to the stricken expression on her brother's face.

"You can't sell the house," he wheezed, feeling as though she'd just punched him in the gut, if not lower. "Where am I supposed to live?"

Sylvia shrugged, exhaling a stream of smoke. "Take your share of the money and buy a condo, I guess. For God's sake, Ethan," and she gave him a mean look, "grow up and be a man. I've been paying a mortgage for the last ten years. Why should you get to live for free?"

"I never lived for free," he began, but Sylvia cut him off.

"I know, I know—you stayed here and took care of Mom. Whose fault is that?" She took another drag off the cigarette, and one-handed began culling the Christmas tree ornaments again. "The old bitch should've been in a home somewhere, and you should've been trying to live a real life instead of cleaning up after hers." More figurines and globes hit the floor, and with complete disrespect for her brother or the house they grew up in, she ashed her cigarette on top of the pile.

"If I hadn't been here, the inheritance you already wasted would've been spent on a nursing home," Ethan grumbled, scowling at the mess on the floor.

On the old record player, the needle reached the end of the grooves and lifted back up into its cradle, leaving only the sound of the fire crackling and the crunching sounds as Sylvia walked across the dropped decorations. She crossed directly to Ethan, pointedly tapping her cigarette again to drop ashes on the faded carpet. "Don't argue with me, Ethan. You won't win. You never have, and you never will." She took one more drag of smoke, blew it in his face, and smiled when he coughed, then dropped the butt on the floor and stepped on it.

Ethan waved smoke away from his stinging eyes and stared down at the still smoking hole in the shabby carpet. "You don't think you're going to make any money on the house if you trash it, do you?" He stepped on the butt, holding his foot in place until he was sure the ember was out. Then he bent to pick up the crumpled, lipstick-stained filter, and went over to put it in the fire.

"How much worse could it be?" she asked, glancing at the glass he still held in his hand. "Do I smell alcohol, Ethan? Here? In *Mother's* sacrosanct house?" Her tone was sarcastic and her expression cruel. He wondered if she knew how much she resembled the mother she had hated.

"It's not Mother's house anymore," he said, and took another swallow, fighting not to show a grimace at the taste of the rum.

"Aren't you going to offer me a drink? You are the man of the house now, right?"

Ethan thought of telling her to just get it herself, but then decided he didn't want her to get the wrong idea. This was his house, he had earned it whatever she might think, and he wasn't going to let her take it away from him. "Fine. Do you want any egg nog in your rum?"

Sylvia laughed, surprised by an unexpected moment of real hilarity at his response. "Just make it like yours." Then she turned back and started picking through the ornaments once more.

Ethan ground his teeth again and went into the kitchen to get her drink.

When she finally tired of removing decorations from the tree, Sylvia sat on the old brocade loveseat and sipped at her drink. Ethan had added another log to the fire, then taken the time to pick up the ornaments she'd discarded. The broken pieces went into the garbage, and he cleaned up the smaller pieces as best he could with a hand broom and dustpan. When he finished with all that, and put another record on, he sat down in his chair.

"Why do you want to stay here?" Sylvia asked, ignoring the music. As always, there was a harsh tone to her voice, ample evidence that she wouldn't change her mind regardless of his answer. "You can't possibly have ever been happy here. Why wouldn't you take the opportunity to start over?"

"I did start over." Ethan sipped his drink, not having to try so hard now to look nonchalant. He was getting used to the taste. "I've spent the last year getting used to doing what I want, when I want."

Sylvia sighed impatiently. "Ethan, *this* is not what I'm talking about," and she gestured around the chintzy living room, with its worn-out furnishings and ancient wallpaper. "You're

51

not too old, or unattractive, to find a woman and start a family."

He stared at her. "Aren't you kind," he finally said. "And where's your husband and kids? Where's your bright and shiny life? There's not enough money in this old house to buy you some happiness."

This time Sylvia's mouth dropped open; in all her life, she'd never heard her brother talk like that to anyone, least of all her. "Y'know what? It doesn't matter. I was just trying to figure you out, but in the end, I don't care. You can stay in this house and rot, just like Mother did. All I want is my share of what the house is worth; so we can either sell it and split the profit, or you can buy me out."

Ethan glared at her. She knew he didn't have the money to buy her out. Like she said, she didn't care. As long as she got what she wanted. She hadn't changed a bit. "Maybe you should get a room at a hotel," he suggested, trying to put some steel into his tone, as well as his backbone, but years of habit put him right back where he'd always been, under her heel.

"I'm not spending the money on a hotel when there's a perfectly good bedroom where I can sleep." She slammed the rest of her drink, setting the empty glass on one of the old wooden end tables. "In fact, I think I'm going to go take a long bath and relax. *You* can put my bags in my old room." She got to her feet, snagging her purse where it had ended up on the floor, and sauntered down the hallway that led to the bed- and bathrooms.

Ethan closed his eyes, clenching his fists as he forced himself to breath evenly. It had taken him months to get used to *not* feeling like this. And now, in just a short time, he was right back to the way things had been before Mother died. Hen-pecked, uptight, and anger barely held in check. He thought about throwing Sylvia's bags out onto the front lawn, and even went so far as to open the front door.

Outside, it was snowing. Huge quarter-sized flakes dropped amazingly fast, and they were already beginning to stick to the yellowed lawn, driveway, and front steps. Ethan watched for a moment, taking in the pristine walkway. Maybe there was a little Christmas magic left, after all.

"Ethan! Bring me my goddamn bags!"

He breathed deeply of the cold, moist air, then closed the front door.

Sylvia came back into the living room after her bath wrapped in a thick, warm robe and her damp hair curling against her cheeks. The fire had died down, but occasional flames flickered before lapsing back into the coals. The tree lights were still on, glittering amongst the tawdry second-hand ornaments. There was no sign of Ethan.

She went into the kitchen, remembering her way in the dark. The fridge was there to the left, and she pulled it open. Bright white light flooded from inside, casting black, angular shadows across the cracked linoleum floor. She found the egg nog, leaving the refrigerator open instead of turning on the overhead light. Glasses were in their usual spot in the heavily over-painted cabinets. She poured the nog, taking a sip to verify there was no booze in it. Checking the freezer, she found the half-full bottle of rum and added a generous portion.

After closing the fridge, she stood for a moment in the black kitchen, letting her eyes readjust. Carrying the glass, she went back out to the living room to sit by the fire. Without paying attention, she walked across the section of scruffy carpet where she'd dropped the ornaments.

"Shit!" Sylvia hopped forward, almost spilling her drink, as something sharp sliced into the heel of her right foot. "God damn it," she hissed, balancing on one foot like a flamingo while she checked the other sole. A sliver of glass maybe an inch long protruded from her skin, welling blood. Ethan had swept up the broken pieces, but obviously hadn't gotten them all.

She limped to the side table and set her glass down, then hobbled down the hall to the bathroom. She removed the piece of glass, cleaned and bandaged the cut, all the while swearing under her breath at the pain, at this stupid house, at her stupid *brother* who hadn't had enough brains to clean up all the broken glass.

When she came back into the living room to retrieve her drink, she was surprised to see Ethan sitting in his chair.

"You did a bang up job cleaning the carpet," she said, limping past him to where her drink still waited.

"You made the mess. You should have cleaned it up," he replied. He spoke in the same low, hesitant voice that he'd always used. But there was something about the way he was sitting, his face half-obscured in shadow with the fire behind him, that made her uneasy.

"It's your house," she said glibly, taking a sip of her drink.

"Not according to you."

Sylvia sat, keeping her wounded foot up. "You'll get half," she said coolly.

"You already took all the money, Syl. Taking half the house isn't fair."

"It'll do you good," she said, leaning back. "You've been cooped up in here for far too long. It'll do you good to get out and meet some new people."

"So being told how to live your life isn't right, but you can do it to me." He sat in his chair and stared at her, or at least she assumed that's what he was doing. She could see nothing of his face. "I had enough of that with Mother."

"It doesn't matter, Ethan," she said, tired of discussing it. "I'm calling the lawyers the day after Christmas and putting the house up for sale."

He shook his head, and something crinkled in his lap, hidden by his own shadow. "No, you're not. I went through too much. I'm not letting you take away what's mine."

Sylvia drank more of her nog, grimacing at the taste. She must've put more rum in than she'd thought.

"Who knows you're here, Sylvia?"

She shrugged, wiping her upper lip with the back of her free hand. It was getting warmer in here by the second, and she was sweating. "I told you, I'm between boyfriends. I don't have to clear my plans with anyone."

"Good." Ethan stood, the odd rustling sound coming again.

"You're not going to change my mind," she said, wondering why her words were slurring. The empty glass slipped out of her lax fingers and fell to the floor.

"I put up with Mother's complaints and demands all of my life. When I finally had enough, I put an end to it," Ethan said crossing the room toward her. "I finally found some peace, some happiness of my own. I'm not going to let you take that away, Sylvia."

She slumped back into the loveseat, unable to hold herself up, unable to do anything. She watched as her brother lifted the plastic bag, and then pulled it down over her head. "Ethan—" she tried to say, but her lips wouldn't form the name.

"No one knows you're here. No one ever will." He tightened the bag around her throat, and waited. The ground-up narcotic pills added to the egg nog, left-overs from Mother's medications, had worked better than he could have hoped. He had used a pillow over Mother's face, but the plastic bag seemed to work just as well.

❄ ❄ ❄

Sylvia had always had a big mouth, but physically she was petite. It didn't take much to wrap her in the shower curtain and stuff her into an old trunk from the attic. The trunk would fit into the eaves, behind where all the Christmas decorations were usually stored. Ethan put the two new suitcases up there as well, after moving her clothes to garbage bags. He'd drop them off at the local homeless shelter on Christmas Day, a heart-felt gift to those less fortunate.

But now he could finally relax. He turned off all but the Christmas tree lights, helping himself to one more doctored egg nog, and watched as the snow continued to fall outside his front window. With the rum filtering into his bloodstream, and peace in his heart, he sang along with the old record player.

"Have yourself a merry little Christmas, let your heart be light. From now on our troubles will be out of sight..."

The Wren

Kevin G. Bufton

The wren, the wren, king of all birds
On St. Stephen's Day was caught in the furze
Although he is little, his family is great
I pray you, good landlady, give us a treat

Nana Bella was a witch.

Ryan McGovern had always known. It was obvious from the first time he had set eyes on her. Her head was large and birdlike, slightly too big for the neck and shoulders that supported it, and her nose was long and crooked. She sported a prominent chin, from which three or four long and wispy hairs sprouted at odd angles. She was completely blind, her eyes glassy and blue like marbles, their sight long since lost to advanced glaucoma, but she had an unnerving habit of staring at you—staring through you—as if she could read any thought you might try to hide.

Ryan loved his Nana.

She was his great grandmother, from his father's side of the family, and had been living with them for the last two years, ever since she had had a fall, and not been found for three days. Every night, Ryan would come home from school, finish his homework and take his Nana a fresh cup of tea, before sitting next to her, taking her wrinkled hand in both of his own, and listening to her talk.

The subject didn't matter. She was a few bare years away from her hundredth birthday and she had a wealth of knowledge and experiences. Whether she was talking about her childhood in the 1920s, or raising a family during the war, or lamenting the fact that she never ran away to marry Conrad Veidt, Ryan found himself enraptured by her stories.

"You shouldn't be sitting here listening to your Nana," she said, one cold winter evening. "You should be out courting at your age. What are you now? Sixteen? Seventeen?"

"I'm thirteen, Nana," Ryan replied.

"Thirteen, is it?" Nana said. "And why aren't you outside with your friends, playing football or singing carols or something?"

"I'm okay, Nana," Ryan said. "I'd rather be at home with you."

There were times, he thought, when he was glad that his great-grandmother couldn't see, so she wouldn't notice the red flush that warmed his cheeks. The truth was, he didn't have any friends; not real friends – not the sort of friends that he could invite round to play videogames or watch scary movies with, and certainly not the sort of friends he would go out and play football with. Ryan was a quiet, studious lad. He wasn't a nerd and he wasn't a geek, but he was clever. His teachers and his parents had told him that he shouldn't hide his light under a bushel but, growing up in a parochial village like Halbridge, you quickly learned to avoid anything that might separate you from the herd. Ryan had learned that lesson a little too late and, though he tried not to show off in public, the fact was out there. People knew—pupils knew—and Ryan could feel their eyes on him, whenever he was in the same room.

"Well now," Nana said, satisfied with his answer, "what is it that you'd like to talk about tonight?"

Ryan's mind drew a blank. He was never normally stuck for a topic of conversation with his nan; she was the one person he felt totally at ease with.

"Ryan?" she asked, cloudy eyes seeking him out.

"Tell me about the wren," he said.

"The wren?" Nana asked. "Now why on Earth would you be asking me about that?

✳ ✳ ✳

It had been about a month ago, Christmas Day, when Ryan had first heard mention of the wren. The morning service had just concluded in St. Michael's Church and the parishioners were milling about outside that fine old building, each wishing to catch a few words with Father Donovan, as though their proximity to him on this holiest of holy days would make their Christmas all the more blessed. Ryan's father looked hot and uncomfortable, in spite of the two inches of snow and his breath condensing on the freezing air. He had been forced into his only suit, the one he wore for weddings and funerals and Ryan could tell that he was counting down the seconds until he could get home and into a comfortable pair of jeans and a sweater.

Ryan's mother had already insinuated herself amongst the

gaggle of women surrounding Father Donovan, he noticed. As he walked past the throng of parishioners, he wondered inwardly how many of them were like his mother—nominally Catholic for fifty weeks of the year and committed churchgoers at Christmas and Easter? He also wondered how many of their menfolk were like his father—begrudging their attendance at church even on those two days of fake piety.

For his part, Ryan was just glad to be out of the musty confines of the church and into the fresh winter air. He wandered away from his parents, skirting a path that led around the handful of his classmates that had been dragged to the service, and headed towards the small graveyard appended to the church.

As cemeteries went, it was not much of one. Small, as befitted the village. Ancient, too, since Halbridge itself was old enough to have been mentioned in the Domesday Book. Still, Ryan enjoyed walking between its weather-beaten and lichen-covered tombstones, trying to make out the names of men and women long since dead. He knew that some of the pupils at the school thought that he was weird for doing this (he had already suspected that the epithet of "coffin botherer" he had heard in the corridors was directed at him), but he could not help his passions.

That morning the graveyard had looked particularly appealing, the tombstones rimed with frost and the whitened grass crisp and crunchy underfoot. Ryan had circled the graveyard once and, his mother having shown no sign of relenting, had started on his second circuit, when he spotted a grave marker that he had never seen before. He ran over, knelt down and, with care, brushed away recent ice and ancient soil from it. He could barely make out the description but, from his position below the level of the cemetery wall, he heard two men talking.

"What are you doing for the rest of the day?" the first enquired. That was Mr Forrester, the village butcher, Ryan thought. He'll have made a few quid over the festive season.

"Oh, the usual," said the second, a voice Ryan did not recognise. "I'll pop in to see my sister, maybe have a spot of Christmas dinner."

"Ah, yes," said Forrester, "she got a good bird this year, did your Anna. One of my best, if I do say so myself."

"I'll trust your judgment on that one," the unknown voice said. "Anyway after the pudding, I'll be down the Green Man for a few pints."

"A few pints?"

"Okay," the voice admitted, "probably more than a few, but it is Christmas, after all."

"True," said Forrester, "but don't forget we have this business with the wren in the morning. It won't do for you to have a hangover."

"Shh!" the voice said. "Not out here!"

"Don't be so paranoid, Malcolm," Forrester replied.

"Paranoid be damned! You know what would happen if it ever got out. You more than anybody!"

"Look around you," Forrester had replied. "There's nobody about. The whole town is swarming around that old fool Donovan."

"That's as may be," Malcolm said, "but it doesn't hurt to be cautious."

"True enough," Forrester had conceded. "My lips are sealed on the matter. Anyway," he continued, "I suppose I'd best be back to my shop."

"You're not open today, surely?"

"Oh no, no," the butcher said. "It's just that I've left our turkey in the big fridge in work, and I promised Gladys I'd bring it home after Mass."

"Right you are, Steven," the other voice said. "Well, I'll see you tomorrow morning, I suppose?"

"Aye, bright and early," Mr Forrester replied, the two going their separate ways a moment later.

Ryan had waited a moment or two long before standing up, the grave marker at his feet all but forgotten, and ran to his father, who had now succeeded in disentangling his mother from the crowd of festive well-wishers. What was all that business about a wren, he thought, and why was that man so angry with Mr Forrester about it?

* * *

"The Hunting of the Wren," Nana Bella explained, "is something that has been going on in these parts for hundreds upon hundreds of years. You do know," she asked, "that this village of ours can date itself back to the Norman Conquest?"

"Of course, Nana," Ryan said. Every child in the village knew that snippet of information; it was one of the first things they learned in school. In his more cynical moments, Ryan suspected that the village took such pride in the fact because it had done nothing of note ever since.

"Well, what you might not know is that there has been a settlement on the site of Halbridge for a lot longer than that."

"I don't understand," Ryan said.

"The church of St. Michael," she said, by way of explanation. "That building has been in the centre of this village since 1245 at least," she said.

"Okay..."

"It replaced an old wooden church that had stood there before, for a few hundred years," Nana said. "That was an old one, of course. They didn't dedicate them to a single saint back then.

"I get it," said Ryan, "the church is really old."

"You don't get it at all, young man," Nana Bella snapped,

"and you won't if you don't let me finish."

Ryan reached out with his hand and covered the top of his nan's, both of his own hands meeting gently on the sides, enveloping her cold fingers in his warmth. "I'm sorry, Nana," he said, suitably cowed.

"So you should be," she said, though the iciness was already leaving her voice.

"The church is old, yes," she said, "but there was always something else there. St. Michael's was built on the site of the old wooden church; the old wooden church was built on the site of a chapel; the chapel was built on the site of a shrine to some pagan god or other…and so on and so on."

Nana Bella paused to let this sink in. Ryan looked at her, knowing that she could not be looking at him, and wondered what she expected him to say.

"I don't…" he began.

"Sacrifice," Nana said. "Human to start with, I'd imagine, though I've never heard of there being any proof of that. The animals definitely came next – the best cow or sheep in the village, slaughtered in the very depths of winter to see to it that the sun rose again and that we'd all see another spring. There are heathen sorts still alive today," she said, "who do that sort of thing. They'll sacrifice the very best their village has to offer to win the favour of one of their gods."

Ryan looked sideways at his nan. He had never seen her like this before, her hands shaking and her voice so animated.

"So why did they stop?" he asked.

"Well, I suppose after a few years of sacrificing the very best animals in the village, people realised that this left them with just the worst, and at a time of the year when they could do with the meat, I imagine. The most religious folks in the world would turn on their gods if it meant that the breeding stock went down each year, don't you think?"

"I don't know," Ryan said.

"Well of course you don't," Nana said. "Why should you? But that's what it's all about—sacrificing an animal to fend off the darkness of winter."

"But why a wren?" Ryan asked.

"You wondered that, did you?" said Nana. "I thought you might. You're a clever boy, aren't you?" She took a deep, shuddering breath, before starting again. "The wren, my boy, is the king of all birds."

"I thought that was the eagle?" Ryan said.

"Eagle?" Nana said, "The people who call the eagle the king of birds are macho idiots, who don't know no better."

Ryan smirked a little at his nan's indignation and she smiled in turn.

"The wren," she continued, "has been the king of birds since the olden times—back when there were no Christians in this country and our priests were all witch doctors or druids or something."

"So he's the king of the birds," Ryan said, slowly. "So I guess that makes him the best thing that the village has to offer?"

"You've got it!" Nana Bella said.

"So what do they do, Nana?"

"What do who do?"

"The men who hunt the wren," he explained. "What do they do?"

"Oh, that?" she said. "How would I know? There hasn't been a hunting of the wren in these parts for about eighty or ninety years, I reckon." Ryan thought that he knew differently, but kept his mouth shut.

"I remember, when I was a girl, they used to kill it—I don't know how—tie it to the end of a long branch from an elm tree and carry it from house to house, asking for money."

"Why?" Ryan asked.

"I never asked," Nana replied. "I suppose since the village no longer had to give up its livestock, the villagers just handed over a coin or two, to show that there'd been some sort of sacrifice made."

"But most of them wouldn't have been farmers anyway back then, would they?"

"No," she agreed. "But then that's the funny thing about tradition. Sometimes you do things because there's a reason and logic to it all and you can follow the thread from one end to the other. And sometimes," she said, "you just do it because that's what you've always done."

"Why did it stop?" Ryan asked.

"Ah, now that I can't answer," Nana replied, "and I don't think anyone else around here could either," she said. "Sometimes you do things because you've always done them and sometimes... well, sometimes you just stop doing them and nobody hardly even notices."

Ryan said nothing.

❉ ❉ ❉

All of that was eleven months ago.

Now, in the heart of winter, it was time for another Christmas and it was going to be a sad one. Nana Bella had died in the August, a victim of old age, as the doctor had said. Both of his parents had cried for nearly a week, which had surprised him. He had always thought his old man could handle anything and his mum had never been close to Nana Bella whilst she was still alive. It just went to show, he thought, you can know somebody your whole life, and yet hardly know them at all.

That was Nana talking, he knew. After all those evenings

spent holding her soft, wrinkled hands and listening to her stories of times gone by, it was no wonder that she was imprinted on him in such a way.

Ryan hadn't cried when Nana Bella had passed away. It wasn't that he hadn't felt sad, because he had. His evenings were so lonely now, filled only with the memory of her tremulous voice as she told him tales that everyone else had likely forgotten. Now Nana was dead too, and that was one less person to remember what had happened. He supposed that he was the only one now. Oh, his dad had probably heard the stories a time or two when he was growing up, but Ryan doubted he had ever felt them the way that he had.

It felt like a great responsibility, to remember those wonderful tales and Ryan suddenly thought about the wandering poets and orators from times long past, who would walk from village to village, to tell great stories that had been passed down through the generations as an oral history. He wondered if they felt the same oppressive weight of duty on their shoulders, or if it was just a job to them.

Ryan had remembered. As summer gave way to autumn, he spent every free evening in the library, making his way through the stacks that dealt with folklore and local history. He filled three pads with notes, all written in his small, tight script that was barely legible, even to him. He followed up on as many of Nana Bella's stories as he could recall, following leads and fresh information as he found them, poring through dusty old tomes and marking down the important footnotes.

When winter came, he started asking questions. He was a good student and, as it transpired, a fine journalist, and he always carried his notes with him. For once, he had decided to take his parents' advice and prove to them—to the whole of the village if needs be—just how good he was.

He spoke to Mr Forrester, the butcher and to Father Donovan. He spoke to his headmaster, Mr Peterson, who introduced him to Lionel Greaves, the head of the school board of governors. As one name after another was added to his list, the whole thing began to take shape in his mind.

✳ ✳ ✳

By the time Christmas Day came around, Ryan believed he had figured it all out. There were twelve men in all, who had a part in the hunting of the wren and that was significant. Twelve seasons, twelve hours on a clock, twelve apostles, twelve signs of the Zodiac, twelve labours of Heracles... the list went on and on. That they were all men was also fitting. They were, after all, reprising the role of the druids and wise men from that long-forgotten time.

Ryan and his parents attended St. Michael's for the mid-morning service. As the congregation went through the familiar motions of the Mass, Ryan looked about the crowded church and made a mental tally of each of the men on his list. They were all there, dressed in their finery—smartly pressed shirts and sober suits; some with their families, some sitting on their own. Twelve pillars of the community. Twelve men of wealth and consequence. Ryan wondered if anyone else present in that comforting old building knew what they would be up to in the early hours of Boxing Day.

When the Mass had concluded, Ryan broke away from his father, who was standing away from the milling crowd, looking somewhat lost. He made his way to the graveyard, to the marker he had discovered last year, and ducked down below the level of the old church wall.

His knee had barely touched the cold floor when he heard a voice from the other side of the wall.

"There's no need for any of that, Master McGovern," it said. "We know you're there."

Ryan stood up slowly. Stood opposite him, the stone wall being the only obstacle between them, were Mr Forrester and Malcolm Potter, the librarian. He had been so concerned with securing himself within earshot, he hadn't noticed the two men standing there.

"Um, hi," he said. "Merry Christmas."

Forrester laughed at that, though Malcolm seemed less at ease. A small, nervous man, he was constantly looking over his shoulder, as though he were sure someone was listening in. Even at fourteen years of age, Ryan thought that the man made a very poor conspirator.

"And a very Merry Christmas to you, young Master McGovern," Forrester said. "Or Ryan, perhaps? Yes, I think Ryan would be more appropriate in the circumstances."

"I don't know what you mean," Ryan said, suddenly glad of the foot and a half of stonework that stood between him and the butcher.

"Come now," he said, "you didn't come over here to check out these poor dead bastards. You came here to find out about the wren."

Malcolm looked as though he was about to have a heart attack. "Somebody's going to hear!" he hissed.

Forrester smiled. "Nobody's going to hear us, all the way over here."

"He did," said the librarian, pointing an accusing finger in Ryan's direction.

"So he did," agreed Forrester, "and here you are, young man—a year older and a good deal wiser, am I right?"

Ryan looked from one man to the other and back again.

"Don't be nervous," Forrester said. "You've done nothing wrong. Far from it. You've impressed us, my boy. Impressed a lot of important men around here." He leaned forward, one hand on the wall, and Ryan fought an urge to lean out of his way. "In fact," he continued, "we'd like to give you the opportunity to impress us further."

"H-H-How?" Ryan stammered.

Forrester grinned, conspiratorially. "Come and meet us here tonight," he said. "Well, four o'clock tomorrow morning. Don't be so much as a minute late, or you'll miss out on your chance."

"My chance for what?"

"Your chance to be a part of something great and good," he said, turning away. He strolled away from the church, Malcolm at his heels. "Four, Ryan," he called over his shoulder. "Don't forget."

❄ ❄ ❄

It was ten minutes past four on a cold Boxing Day morning and, up until now, Ryan had thought that sneaking out of the house half an hour earlier had been the bravest thing he had ever done. Now, as he crouched in the long grass, a catapult held in one hand, a small stone loaded and primed in the other, he knew that this had now usurped that spot. They were on the borders of the village now, in what was known as Tanner's Field. A freezing mist looped and curled amongst the grass.

They were thirteen now—unlucky for some, he thought, but lucky as Hell for him. Today was the day he became a man, and not just any man; a man of influence; a man worthy of respect.

On their way to the field, the other twelve had told him how impressed they had been by his diligence and research. They called him Little King. When he pressed them as to why, they explained that this was what his name meant, when translated from the Gaelic. Little King—he liked the sound of that. And here he was, on his first hunting of the wren. It was a ritual that spanned the centuries, one that brought luck and prosperity to the town and he would be a part of it; a part of Halbridge's great secret.

The thirteen men spread out across the field, each armed with a slingshot and a stone, waiting for the sight of the first wren.

The minutes passed and a chill leeched the warmth from Ryan's bones as he scurried through the undergrowth. He wondered who would be the first to spot it and whether he would be able to get a shot in first. Scoring the kill on his first time would surely prove his worth to the village.

There was a gentle warbling in the trees before him and he saw it. Small and swift, it flew from one tree to the other in a single, smooth motion. Ryan felt his arms go up, as if some ancient instinct controlled them, and he let loose the stone from his catapult. There was the tiniest of sounds as it struck the bird, dropping it in mid-flight, but it was deafening to his ears.

He walked over to where the wren had fallen and stood over it. Glassy eyes stared at him accusingly and he had to look away. As he turned, he saw the other twelve, arranged in a semi-circle behind him. They each had their catapults raised and aimed at him and, in the scant light afforded by the moon, the stones they held seemed bigger and harder than the pebble he had fired to dispatch the small songbird.

"I did it," he said, feeling no pride in the announcement.

"We know," said Father Donovan, as he released his stone.

It flew through the chill night air and collided with the side of Ryan's head. Pain shot through his skull and he fought to keep himself from falling. Another missile struck his chin, another his cheek and then he was unable to distinguish one from the next. He fell to the floor, beside the body of the wren, his head on fire and his eyes watering. From his low vantage point, he could see two of the men digging a hole in the hard dirt with a pick and shovel.

A rough hand turned him over on his back and, with eyes that were starting to swell shut, he could make out the face of Mr Forrester. He was smiling.

"Well now, our Little King," he said. "You wanted to be a part of something special, and so you are."

"Please," Ryan managed, trying frantically to get the words out of his bloodied and broken mouth. "Let me go. I won't tell anybody."

"We know, Little King," Forrester said. "We know." He pulled back the rubber bands of his catapult and levelled it at Ryan's face. At this range, there was no way he could miss.

"You don't have to do this," Ryan blubbed.

Forrester smiled sadly, shaking his head. "It seems that for all of your studies, you really haven't learned much at all," he said.

Ryan's bruised eyes closed over, mercifully sparing him from his executioner's face. "You are the very best this village has to offer."

He fired.

W❄HITE ❄CHRISTMAS

DJ Tyrer

"Do you think we'll have snow?" Ellie asked as soon as she had eaten the last chocolate from her Advent Calendar. It was Christmas Eve and Ellie, at seven years old, was desperate to wake up to a white Christmas.

"Maybe," I told her. I didn't want to get her hopes up; the weather forecasters said it wouldn't be white, but you could never rely on them. I didn't want to get my own hopes up either, although I'd be glad to see a crisp carpet of white upon the lawn when I threw the curtains apart.

"I do hope so," she replied, seemingly happy with the uncertainty. I had to agree with her.

The day was spent in anticipation of the visit by Father Christmas, and with the sun shining brightly, snowfall seemed less and less likely. By the time I tucked Ellie into bed, however, the air was crisp and chill and had to it that tang which precedes snow or frost.

I felt as excited as a child when I retired that night, wondering whether there would be snow. Of course, even if it *did* snow, there was the question of whether or not it would actually arrive before Ellie woke me in her excitement. Last year it had only been mere minutes between my putting a full stocking at the end of the bed and her rushing in squealing, "He's been!"

The chill of the night must have sent her into a deep slumber, for it was a good hour before Ellie dashed through from her room into mine to drag me out of my sleep. I yawned widely as she declared that Father Christmas had been and— more importantly it seemed, given the way in which she shrieked in glee at the fact—it had snowed. She seemed more taken with the frosted rooftops and deeply carpeted gardens than with the pile of presents that I'd placed beside her bed.

Ellie barely paid any attention to her presents, such was the lure of the crisp, white snow. She was determined to make the most of it.

"I wanna play snowballs," she exclaimed, "then I wanna make an angel in the snow, and, the–en, I wanna make a snowman. It'll be the best'un in the whole wi-ide world."

I wrapped her up warmly despite her complaints that the scarf and bobble-hat made her "look like a baby." I didn't want her catching a chill.

Ellie began rolling and shaping the snow in the manner of children down the ages, creating first the lower body, and then the upper. Her efforts were a little crude, yet in a way more endearing than perfect globes would have been. A third ball of snow, slightly smaller still, was placed atop these to play the part of the head. I had to help with this one as she wasn't quite tall or strong enough to raise it up.

On went the scarf and hat, and a carrot formed the nose.

We didn't have any coal for the eyes or mouth—who uses coal nowadays?—but I took a couple of larger pieces of gravel from the drive and used them for the eyes; the mouth I inscribed with my finger. No pipe, of course, but I found a rake to prop up against the snowman as if he were at work tidying the garden.

Ellie squealed in delight at the sight of it before proceeding to pelt it with snowballs.

I left her to it while I prepared lunch, glancing out of the window every so often to make certain Ellie was okay. You hear such stories nowadays that even in a quiet cul-de-sac like this, you daren't leave a child unsupervised for long.

When the meal was ready, I faced a battle to get her inside. Ellie would much rather have kept on playing with her "new friend." When she was finally at the table, she was distracted and not much interested in eating and I wondered if she was unwell. However, when I finally relented and told her she could go back outside and play, she halted warily at the front door and shook her head.

"I don't wanna now," she said. I followed her gaze and saw she was looking at the snowman. In the dusk, it suddenly looked a lot less like a person and rather spooky. I couldn't blame Ellie for not wanting to go back out play with her "friend"; he no longer seemed friendly.

Ellie was subdued throughout the evening and kept glancing towards the door as if she expected the snowman to walk through it. If a new fall of snow hadn't begun, I would've gone outside, found a shovel, and smashed it down in order to set her mind at rest. I should've.

That night I slept badly. Tossing and turning, I dreamt of snowy wastelands in which tree branches clawed at me and icy flakes stung my eyes. Then I woke, or thought I woke, and seemed to hear somebody moving stealthily through the house—moving towards Ellie. I tumbled out of bed and stumbled to Ellie's room. I recoiled in shock at the sight of a figure hunching over her bed, reaching out with long, thin fingers towards her.

Then I woke to find myself back in my bed. In a panic, I fought my way out of the tangling bedclothes. I ran to Ellie's room. She was in bed, half the covers on the floor. I checked her. She looked pale and her forehead felt cold and clammy. She let out a low groan, but didn't wake at my touch. Her bed was damp; she hadn't wet the bed in over a year. I wondered if she was ill.

I couldn't quite shake the feeling that somebody had been in the house, although I suspected I'd just been dreaming. I went downstairs and checked that all the doors and windows were locked. Telling myself that I was worrying unnecessarily, I returned to bed but didn't sleep a wink, straining my ears for the slightest sound of an intruder.

When I woke Ellie the next morning, she was still pale and seemed lethargic. I noticed scratches on her upper arms.

"Ouch!" I said. "How'd you get those scratches?"

Ellie shrugged, then said, "The bogeyman."

"The bogeyman?"

"Uh-huh. He came into my room last night and held me down on my bed. He hurt my arms."

"It was just a dream—a bad dream—honey," I told her, but I couldn't help thinking back to my dream. It seemed too much of a coincidence. Could there have been someone there? I told myself I was imagining things; after all, I was exhausted. It was possible that she'd scratched herself playing in the snow—perhaps somehow scraping against the rake's prongs—yet that didn't seem likely. Besides, the marks looked horribly as if hands with sharp nails had pinned Ellie down. As if someone had held her down on her bed and…

I felt sick as I considered the implications, and asked her, "Did he hurt you anywhere else, honey?"

Ellie shook her head. "No. But…"

"But?"

"He told me he'd be back tonight."

I felt a sudden chill that had nothing to do with the weather outside.

I didn't mention her encounter with the "bogeyman" again. I was still hoping that, despite the sick feeling in the pit of my stomach, the events that had disturbed us during the night were dreams. I did all I could to distract her from any such thought by entertaining her with her presents and putting on her favorite films, but when it came time for her to go to bed, she still asked me if he would return.

I laughed and hoped she wouldn't notice the brittleness. "Of course not, honey. That was just a dream and you're going to have sweet dreams tonight. See, I'm checking in your ward-robe and under your bed and there's no bogeyman there. Now I'm going to fetch some fairy dust from the Christmas tree and sprinkle it over you so that you have lovely fairy dreams while you sleep."

She giggled and was soon asleep with a half-smile on her lips. She looked so peaceful, I was certain she would sleep well. Yet, I still couldn't shake the thought that what I'd heard last night had been something real.

During the day, I'd checked everywhere someone could conceivably hide—closets and cupboards and under beds. I rechecked those that were not too cluttered for someone to hide in now. There was nobody in the house. All the doors and windows were closed and locked. Despite this, I decided to take a knife up to my room, just in case. In case of what, I wasn't entirely certain.

I slept fitfully, my mind full of thoughts of burglars and

child molesters and blood. Suddenly, my eyes snapped open, certain I'd heard the creak of a floorboard on the landing. Somebody *was* in the house!

I tried to calm my breathing, telling myself that it might only be Ellie. She'd wet herself the night before; maybe she'd woken in time tonight and headed to the bathroom. I didn't want to rush out and frighten her with a knife. And yet…

I slipped out of bed and shivered with a mixture of the cold and the fear I felt.

Slowly, silently, I crossed to my bedroom door and eased it open. I saw a shadow move at Ellie's door. It seemed too large to be her. The chill that ran down my spine then had nothing to do with the cold air. I moved towards her room.

Ellie was laying in her bed, whimpering, as a large figure loomed over her, pressing down upon her. Long, thin fingers pinned her in place and I felt a burning rage rise within me. There was something oddly familiar about the figure.

I raised the knife and lunged at the figure, plunging the blade into it again and again. The icy flesh was strangely yielding and I felt my hand plunging into it along with the knife. I couldn't understand what was happening. A large, round face, white in the darkness with flinty eyes, turned to leer at me. I screamed in horror and thought I must be going mad. It was the snowman holding her in place, yet I couldn't believe it.

Ellie was screaming and I could see claws like icicles plunging into her. Warm liquid mixed with the cold that was splashed about. It was killing her! The snowman was killing my baby! I kept stabbing at it, determined to save her.

Finally, it collapsed, still and sagging, then melted away before my eyes. Sobbing, I fell to my knees beside the bed, dropping the knife to the floor. I reached out to Ellie and felt her limp, sodden body. I pulled her to me.

I was barely aware of the flashing lights through the thick curtains, hadn't heard the sirens over Ellie's screams, nor did I hear the sound of the front door being broken down and running footsteps on the stairs. Suddenly, strong arms seized me and pulled me away from my daughter and the bedroom light flashed on, blinding me for a moment.

When I opened my eyes again, I looked down at Ellie. Of the snowman, there was no sign. She and her bed were soaked with blood. The snowman's icicle claws had punctured her again and again. She wasn't moving. I tried to reach out and comfort her, but the policemen held me tight.

"Why won't you let me go to her? The snowman's hurt her!"

"She's dead," somebody said.

A policeman held up my knife and said, "This looks like the murder weapon."

"I didn't hurt her. I was saving her. It was the snowman. It was here..."

Only, of course, it wasn't any longer; it had melted away to nothing, leaving me with Ellie's body and a bloody knife. All the evidence they needed.

A LABOR DISPUTE
Michael Shayne

The primer gray pickup truck skidded around a steep curve in the winding road. Jimmy pressed hard on the accelerator. In spite of its age, the engine was top-notch and responded with a burst of speed. His dad had bought the truck right off the assembly line in '68 and used it for a work truck for the last ten years. When his dad retired last year, he gave the truck, rust and all, to Jimmy.

The grass and gravel on the edge of the ragged asphalt were beginning to turn white from the falling snow. The inclement weather was not the primary reason he was pushing the Ford to its limits. He had promised Vanessa that he would be home in time to watch the kids open their gifts, but they had opened a new break in the mines today, and it had taken longer than expected. As dusk gave way to darkness, he guessed that he was at least an hour behind schedule.

She had been livid when she learned he was called to work on Christmas Eve, but Jimmy knew he couldn't refuse the shift. He didn't have the seniority to pick and choose opportunities. Jobs were hard to come by in these hills and, if you were lucky enough to get one, you would do anything to keep it. In addition, the mine was scheduled to be closed until after the first of the year. Losing a week's wage would make money tight around the house. He was happy to pick up the extra shift.

Jimmy Whitt had worked for the Campbell Creek Coal Company for only two years. His father, a thirty-year veteran of the company, had recommended Jimmy for employment. That's the way things worked in Campbellsville. The coal mine was the only prospect in town, and the jobs were handed down from father to son over generations. This practice resulted in a very tightly knit community and discouraged any influx of outsiders.

He felt the rear of the truck fishtail as he gunned the engine. The temperature was dropping like a rock, and the dark, wet slush on the road was beginning to form into ice. He let off the accelerator, deciding it would be wiser for him to be a little late than to ditch the truck. He pushed the eight-track cassette into the dashboard player and twisted the volume knob. His thoughts began to wander as he sang along to the chorus of "Hot Child in the City", using the steering wheel as a makeshift drum.

He abruptly jerked the truck to the right as a man on horseback suddenly galloped from the brushy hillside into the road. The horse, glowing whiter than the snow falling around it, must have been startled by the headlights of the truck because it stopped right in the middle of the road. The Ford hit a patch of black ice and spiraled out of control. Out of the driver's side window, Jimmy observed the man on the horse as the truck slid toward him. There was no indication of fear, no screams in the night. He made no effort to escape the oncoming vehicle. He was still in the saddle, dressed in what appeared to be a ragged, red Santa suit. And, in his right hand, he seemed to be gripping a pickaxe.

The truck came to a stop, straddling the dividing line of the road, headlights pointing away from home. He jumped from the truck, his heart still pounding in his chest. He examined the body of the truck, expecting areas to be crushed from the collision. To his astonishment, there appeared to be no damage at all. He gradually extended the perimeter of his walk, searching for the man. He looked over the guardrail and scanned the ditch line.

"Hey, buddy," he screamed into the cold night. There was no response.

Jimmy decided the man must have gotten the horse out of the road in the nick of time. There was no sign of the man or the horse. Standing at the driver's door, he gave the area one last scan before pulling himself onto the bench seat of the Ford. He righted the truck, turned the heat to the maximum setting, and continued toward home.

Jimmy pulled the truck into the driveway and shut off the headlights. He gathered the contents of his dinner bucket, which had scattered about the bed of the truck during the incident, and walked up the gravel path to his front door. He immediately initiated the ritual of work boot removal as soon as he was in the house. After placing his light on the charger beside his boots, he walked into the living room and exchanged greetings with everybody.

Jimmy quickly showered and gathered with the family in the living room. Gifts were exchanged, photographs taken, and a wonderful Christmas was had by all. After dinner was finished, Jimmy and his father, Claude, went into the living room, hoping to catch the last quarter of the football game.

"Dad," Jimmy asked as he walked toward the kitchen during a well-timed commercial break. "You want another beer?"

"Yeah, bring me one," Claude replied. "How's work going for you these days?"

"We opened up another section today. Supposed to start mining that break after New Years'."

"Keep it up and, one of these days, you'll have one of these," Claude said. He held up his left arm to display the gold watch the company had given him as a token of appreciation for his dedicated service over the past thirty years. Claude was proud of his watch. It even had his name inscribed on it. After a mocking roll of the eyes, Jimmy handed his father a cold beer.

"Dad, you'll never believe what happened to me tonight," Jimmy said, proceeding to tell his father the story of the near collision with the man dressed as Santa holding a pickaxe and mounted on a white horse.

Claude's demeanor changed as he listened to his son's tale. His face drained of color, and his gaze grew distant.

"Dad," Jimmy said, expressing his concern. "Are you okay?"

"Son, I think I need to tell you a story," Claude responded slowly, placing his beer onto the coffee table. "It's about a man named Elson Finch and something awful that happened years ago."

❄ ❄ ❄

"Elson Finch came to Campbellsville in the summer of '49. It was rumored that he had served with some distinction in the War and had won some medals and such. That was all just gossip, though. Nobody ever out and out asked him about it. What wasn't a rumor was the way the man could ride a horse. He owned the whitest, largest beast of a horse I'd ever seen. And, he called it Solidarity.

"Campbellsville was different back then. Civilization hadn't quite reached us yet. Nobody I knew owned a television. As a matter of fact, the Johnson family was the only people I can think of who had a radio. Not that it did them any good because there wasn't any stations close enough to hear. And, it was very seldom we saw a car. It was still horse-and-buggy days, you know? The only thing about this area that was the same then was Campbell Creek. Elson Finch wanted to change all that.

"You see, Elson was an organizer that John Lewis sent down here to rile up the miners. This area was so isolated by the hills that it had stayed pretty much union-free. Slowly, over the course of that summer, Finch won quite a few converts. He would go from house to house on that big old horse trying to recruit people, telling them about the better life the UMWA could give them. He was always talking about some safety standard act and a wage act and stuff. He was pretty good, using big words and smiling at all the right times.

"By the end of November, he had enough miners on his side that he was able to strike against the company. Now, Mister Campbell wasn't happy at all. Since he owned most all of the town, he kicked just about everybody out of their homes. They all set up camp on the hillside behind town. It was really a sight to see. The whole side of the mountain looked like a big campground with clouds of smoke here and there from the fires they used to cook and keep warm.

"December came in with a blizzard that year. The town was blanketed in snow, and it was bone-chilling cold. Elson still had all those people camped out on the hill. They were running out of food, and Mister Campbell was running out of patience. Campbell sent word that he wanted to see me, so I headed up to his house. Mister Campbell used to keep me pretty busy back then. I did all of his yard work and any odd jobs that needed tending to around his place.

"He lived behind where the library is today. He had the biggest house in town, and he liked to let people know that he had money and power. Anyway, when I get up there to see him, he doesn't want to talk about pulling weeds or nothing like that. He wants to talk about Elson.

"First thing he tells me is that Elson Finch is costing him a ton of money, with the mine being shut down and all. He told me how upset he was that everybody seemed to be turning against him. Mister Campbell said that I'd always been a loyal worker for him and everything. Then, he promised me a job in the mines. No more cutting grass, pulling weeds, painting the shed. A real job I could be proud of, son. All I had to do was get Elson out of town.

"Well, I jumped at the chance. I was dating your momma, and it was starting to get a little serious. I figured, with a steady job and such, I could ask her to marry me. All I needed to do was rough up old Elson for Mister Campbell. You know, scare him out of town. I was a pretty big boy and could hold my own, if you know what I mean. It sounded like a good deal to me.

"Mister Campbell put me on the payroll that very day, sort of a probationary period. You see, he gave me a week to run Elson out of town, but he was looking ahead to us running coal again. That's why he had me and Charlie Hagerman go in at night and get things cleaned up. I think he wanted us up there at night to be a sort of lookout in case the strikers tried to vandalize anything, too.

"Me and Charlie had finished working on Christmas Eve.

We were walking back to town and, right at the train stop, there was Elson. He was dressed in this bright red Santa suit. All that was missing was the belly. I told Charlie to go on ahead, that I was gonna talk to Mister Finch for a minute or two. He was in a hurry to get home, because of the holiday and all, so he took right off.

"I walked over and stood beside Elson's horse. I was all black from coal dust, carrying my shovel and pick, and standing right next to this big ol' white horse. Elson was hard at work, transferring wrapped Christmas gifts from one of the opened cargo cars into his "Santa's Bag". The horse kinda snorted, and it caught Elson's attention.

"I started making conversation with him. He told me that he was planning on delivering the gifts to all the children of the striking miners. I told him how nice that was of him and all, considering their fathers could've bought them gifts if he hadn't've made them lose their jobs. And, I made it clear that he needed to leave town or else.

"Elson pushed me hard enough that I fell on my rear. He let me know that I wasn't the first person to ever threaten him, and he had no intention of leaving. He mounted his horse, holding the overflowing bag of toys over his shoulder, and started to ride off.

"Now there I was, on the ground, watching Santa ride away on his reindeer. All I could think about was having to tell Mister Campbell that Elson wasn't leaving. I jumped to my feet and yelled for him to stop. He wouldn't stop. If only he would've stopped.

"Before my mind registered what I was doing, I grabbed the pickaxe from the gravel and slung it at him. I just wanted to get his attention. You know, maybe knock him off the horse. Let him know that I meant business. The pickaxe flew through the air, end over end, and when it met its target, the shaft of the pick pierced Finch right between the shoulder blades. He collapsed, falling forward on the horse. The bag fell to the ground, spilling a couple of toys. And the horse stopped dead in its tracks.

"Well, I just stood there for a minute. I couldn't believe what had just happened. Then, when I got my senses back, I ran over to Finch to see what I could do to help. As soon as I got beside the horse, I knew it was bad. The white coat of the horse was turning red from Finch's blood. He died right there in the saddle.

"I didn't know what to do. Nobody saw anything. The whole town was deserted because of Christmas Eve and all. I grabbed the bridle of the horse and walked Finch, his body limp in the saddle, up to the only place I knew to go: the mine.

"I went to work. I spent almost all that night blocking up his corpse inside an abandoned section of the mine. Walled him up real good. With the darkness inside, I felt that nobody would ever find him. After I was done with Finch, I walked the horse to the top of the mountain behind the mines. I tied him tight to a big chestnut tree up there. Figured Mother Nature would take care of the rest, you know?

"The sun was starting to come up when I was done. It was Christmas Morning. I took the bag of toys to the hillside where all the striking miners were camped out and let them know that Mister Campbell thought it was just terrible that the children up here weren't having a proper Christmas. The kids were happy, and it helped to win the miners back. By the first of the year, they all figured that Elson Finch had deserted them, and they ought to go back to work. At least Mister Campbell cared enough to give out Christmas gifts to their children.

"I've never told anybody about this before," Claude said, finishing his tale. "But, after you told me about the man in a Santa suit riding a white horse, well, it can't be just a coincidence, can it?"

"Dad," Jimmy finally spoke after absorbing his father's story, shaking his head. "Where did you bury him? What part of the mine?"

"About a hundred yards in, there was a section on the right that they weren't going to mine. The seam of coal was too low over that way."

"Listen to me," Jimmy said, his voice shaking. "I think that's the section we opened today. And, it is Christmas Eve, the anniversary."

"This can't be happening," Claude said. "It was all an accident, so long ago."

"I hate to say this," Jimmy said, composing his thoughts. "We have to go in there and get rid of anything that could link you to the body, Dad. We need to do it before the mine reopens, too. That's the section they're going to start mining after the first of the year."

Claude was silent. He stared at his son.

"I'm going to pick you up first thing in the morning, and we'll take care of this together," Jimmy continued. "Don't worry about anything, Dad."

Finally, Claude gained the courage to utter the words filling his mind. "What if he's not in there?"

❄ ❄ ❄

Jimmy was still in a fog of slumber as the alarm clock blared on Christmas morning. As he progressed through stages of awareness, he realized that the events of last night were not a dream. His father had killed a man, and after all these years, Jimmy was going to help him get away with murder. He slapped the alarm and started to get out of bed.

"What time did you come to bed," Vanessa asked, her eyes still closed. "You must've stayed up nearly all night."

"I don't know, honey," Jimmy responded. "I've gotta go over to Dad's house first thing. I'll be back as soon as I can."

"Merry Christmas," Vanessa mumbled as she burrowed into the covers. She was asleep before Jimmy got dressed.

He enjoyed a quick cup of coffee at the kitchen table as he put on his socks and shoes. After rinsing his cup and returning it to the cabinet, he turned from the kitchen and burst out the front door into the cold December morning.

Jimmy grabbed the gearshift, preparing to throw it in reverse. Out of habit, he glanced in the rearview mirror and froze in horror. The reflection showed a bloody pickaxe, leaned neatly against the tailgate, with a gold watch, his father's gold watch, banded around the handle.

He leaped from the truck and ran toward the tailgate. Snatching the pickaxe from the bed of the truck, he fumbled at the watch until he unlatched it. He could feel hot tears warming his face. Filled with rage, he threw the pickaxe against the house and forced the blood-soaked watch into his front pocket.

As he was getting back into the pickup, a County Sheriff squad car, lights flashing, pulled into the driveway. Jimmy slammed the door of the truck and ran toward the car.

"Help," he shouted. "You've got to help my dad."

The two deputies jumped from their car, guns drawn. Jimmy continued running toward them, blood from the pickaxe covering his hands.

"Stop right there," one of the deputies ordered.

Staring down the barrels of two service revolvers, Jimmy complied. The deputy that had been driving the car walked to Jimmy, putting away his pistol. The other deputy had him safely covered.

"We were coming over here to give you some bad news about your father, Claude," the deputy explained. "But it looks like you already know."

"Know what," Jimmy asked.

"Don't play dumb, boy. You've got blood on your hands, blood on your clothes. I would almost bet that's your dad's blood."

The deputy reached for his handcuffs. Surveying the yard, he noticed the pickaxe leaning against the side of the house.

"And look at that," the deputy continued. "I bet that pickaxe has your bloody fingerprints all over it."

"What," Jimmy struggled for words.

"Get on your knees now!"

Jimmy did not obey the deputy's order. He was in a state of shock. Suddenly, the police officer forced him to the ground. Lying on his stomach, his head was turned to the side and the bloody pickaxe filled his vision. The officer's knee was in his neck.

"You are under arrest," he heard in the ear facing skyward. "For the murder of Claude Whitt."

In the ear forced into the grass, he heard the galloping of a single horse vibrating through the ground and growing more distant by the second.

T̲HE N̲IGHT B̲EFORE C̲HRISTMAS
Philip Thorogood

T'was the night before Christmas
when all through the house,
Each person was stirring to Dolly Wright's shouts.
The stockings were hung by the chimney with care,
But Dolly didn't believe Saint Nick would be there.
And without the children snuggled up in their beds,
All thoughts of Santa and his powers were dead.
So as Mamma and Papa into sleep they descend,
Who then would visit, before the nights end?

I n the living room of their old-style Victorian house, to a background of the crackling fireplace, Dolly's parents were getting exasperated. Dolly Wright's father put on his strongest parent-knows-best voice as he spoke, keeping his care-worn face genial and calm with some effort. "Come on, Dolly.

You've got to go to bed or Santa won't come. Don't you want any presents?"

It didn't wash with his daughter. The thirteen year old sat in her favorite wicker chair, arms crossed in front of her cord dress, with a stern look that he knew she must have gotten from her mother. Fairy lights from the tree illuminated the scene, supported by the light of the flames.

"No, I won't! He's not real, so there's no need to go to bed yet!" Her father's eyes flicked to the clock on the wall before looking back at his young daughter—it was nine o'clock. He tugged on his Christmas jumper, adjusting it so it was more comfortable on his thin frame and stalling for a moment to think. Johnny, Dolly's younger brother, came into the room at that moment, interrupting them. The five year old stood there in his matching cartoon train pajamas, his light blonde hair ruffled from where he had wrestled their mother while she tried to dry him after his bath.

"Papa, are we going to bed yet? I want presents!"

Dolly's father smiled at his son. "Yes, Johnny, we'll get you some milk and cookies and put them on the mantle for Santa, and then we'll all be going to bed." He gave Dolly a pointed look, but she remained closed off in the old chair, arms crossed and face turned away from his. He turned to scoop Johnny into his arms and carry him off towards the kitchen. The little boy giggled as he was 'flown' through the adjoining rooms. Dolly scowled; she didn't know why, but Christmas just didn't seem to have the same magic it had had in previous years. Ever since she had caught her parents hiding away the wrapped presents earlier that month, the magic of the season had evaporated for her.

Weeks before, with the turning of the month, the Christmas fever had caught onto her, and she had helped her parents and Johnny decorate the house inside and out. Together, as a family, they had erected the tree, hung the fairy lights in the windows, and even stuck the "Santa Stop Here" sign out on the front lawn to much ceremony and celebration. Now, the twinkle of lights annoyed her, only serving to remind her how naïve and stupid she had been until now. Maybe it was jealousy of Johnny's continued innocence, whilst hers was cast down and destroyed.

Her father and mother had tried, both separately and together, to convert her to the whole "the magic of the season is in the pretense, in the belief of the morals behind the act," but it hadn't washed with her. Dolly felt cheated, fooled, and she was against doing the same to Johnny in the fear that his innocence would be crushed—and his personality changed— forever. She loved him too much to let him suffer such a blow, and had said as much to her parents. Their words had been understanding, calming even, but in their faces she had seen the truth—they didn't believe that she'd act on her new-found belief in the truth, but they were wrong.

Her mother came in, all brunette curls and understated make-up. It was hard to be mad at someone so beautiful, and who cared so much, but Dolly managed it. She clucked her tongue when she saw her daughter's negative demeanor, and strode over full of intent. Dolly sighed.

"Now, now—don't you sigh at me, Dolores—" Dolly squirmed at the use of her proper name, "—and don't give me that attitude!" She took her time to adjust her own Christmas jumper; Dolly was always surprised at how their father's jumper looked out of place on him, but every year mother managed to coordinate her clothes so that it sat naturally amongst her normal wares.

"Christmas time is a family time, Dolores—" Dolly wrinkled her nose once more, "—and that means respecting us all. Respecting the effort your father and I go to every year to make this time of year pleasant, and to keep the magic alive for Johnny; even if you can't find it in yourself to believe in the spirit of it." Her stern tones struck deep inside Dolly, as they always managed to when her mother spoke in anger—she thought it must be a talent that immediately appeared in mothers when they gave birth—but she didn't let it cow her. Instead, she let it feed her anger—the anger at being lied to.

"I'm sorry I can't find it in myself to believe in the spirit of lying, mother," she used sarcasm to emphasize her point, "but I was raised to be better than that." Dolly finished her tirade by rising from her chair and storming indignantly out of the room. She would act, she thought as she passed through the conservatory towards the kitchen. She would do something, though she didn't know what yet, and someone would pay. She just hoped it wouldn't be poor Johnny. Toby, their German shepherd, sensed something was wrong and got up from his bed by the French windows, following her companionably through the dining room and into the kitchen.

The kitchen, which had just recently been refurbished to modernize it, was their mother's pride and joy. The red-fronted cupboards offset the black marble counter tops and the stainless steel appliances. Cream-colored tiles finished the look and kept the room soft and light, despite the presence of the darker tones. Their father and Johnny had just finished arranging a pile of cookies onto a small plate; a freshly poured glass of milk sat proudly on the counter top beside it. With a jolt, Dolly knew what she was going to do. With Toby at her heels, she strode straight up to the pair, scooped up the glass of milk, and drained it in a swift gulp. She smacked her lips in the face of their shocked looks.

"Ah! That was just what I needed, thank you!" With the

added cheek of the words, their father and Johnny seemed to snap out of their stupors. Johnny's eyes filled with tears, and he started to wail, almost at the same time that father's face flushed with anger.

"Dolores Anne Wright, how dare you act like this! You know what and who that was for, and you know Johnny wanted to put that out himself!" It was one of the few times she had ever heard him actually shout; it was usually mother that put across that side of the parenting scales. But even in the face of her father's unusual outburst, Dolly maintained her own anger, partly due to the use of her full and proper name, which her father hadn't used in years, but majorly thanks to her own new-found lack of innocence. She smiled, and it held no trace of warmth or happiness; she knew it would frustrate her parent further.

"I know it was for Santa," she raised her hands and gestured in the universal sign for quotation marks, "and as I know he doesn't exist, and either you or mother were going to polish it off or tip it down the drain once we're tucked safely upstairs in bed, I thought I'd save you the trouble." Her father's face turned beet red as she picked up a cookie as an afterthought. He opened his mouth, most likely to give her another of his new-found indignation, but was cut off by Johnny.

"What do you mean Santa doesn't exist, Dolly?" His eyes held such confusion and the beginnings of sadness that, for a moment, Dolly felt a twinge of guilt.

Their father crouched down beside him, so Johnny wouldn't have to crane his neck to see his father's face. "Dolly's just being silly, Johnny. She's saying silly things because she's not happy with mommy or daddy, but what she's saying isn't true. Santa Claus does exist, and he'll be dropping off your presents tonight!" He finished with a forced smile on his face that Dolly could see straight through.

"Why bother lying to him? You'll just reveal the truth in a few years' time like you've done with me, and bring it all crashing down about his ears. Save him the pain of betrayal, Father, and tell him the truth."

Their father stood up once more as she spoke, a look of hurt in his eyes. "You feel like we've betrayed you?" He spoke quietly, almost fearfully.

She nodded. "How could I not, having the truth kept from me all this time. Pretending Santa Claus is real, lying to me—to us—all this time when really you're just buying the presents yourselves each year!"

Johnny's eyes were back to brimming with tears and father placed his hand gently on the top of his son's head in an attempt to reassure the five year old. He looked daggers at his daughter as he replied through clenched teeth, a low and dangerous growl that spoke volumes about how angry he was getting. "I am telling the truth, Dolores. Santa Claus does exist, and he is coming to deliver our presents tonight."

"Liar!" she exclaimed, not quite shouting yet. "How do you explain the presents I saw you and mom hiding away last week!?"

"They were gifts for friends that we wanted Santa to deliver. Sometimes he needs some help to get all the presents organized before Christmas day, so your mother and I—"

"Oh please spare me any more of your lies," she cut him off, shouting now to be heard over Johnny's crying as Toby bounded around them, excited by the raised voices. "I've just about had enough of them and you! Why you can't just own up to Johnny, and apologize to me?"

Johnny butted in through his tears. "What do you mean own up to me? Santa's real, isn't he?"

She whirled to her brother, caught up in her anger. "No,

Johnny, he's not real. Not him, not the Easter bunny, not the Tooth Fairy. They're all lies made up by mom and dad."

Her father grabbed her shoulder and pulled her away from Johnny, whose weeping had escalated to a high-pitched wailing. "Don't you speak to your brother like that. Can't you see how upset you're making him with your lies?" His eyes were wide with rage as she squirmed and fought to be free of his grip.

"Why do you have to keep up this, this..." She struggled for the right words before it finally exploded from her "... bull crap!?"

A stunned silence followed her finale, a lack of sound where even Toby seemed subdued, as if he knew something was wrong. It was mother, who had apparently entered the kitchen behind Dolly at some point during her tirade, who finally managed to put words to her thoughts.

"Dolores. Bed. Now!" There was no emphasis, just soft, single-word sentences that spoke more of how badly she'd misspoken than any angrily shouted speech. Dolly opened her mouth to protest, to continue her rant, but was cut off by her mother's arm raising instantly to point in the general direction of the stairs. "Now."

Dolly hesitated for just a moment, until her mother's eyes narrowed; then, with a stamp of her foot and an inarticulate cry of despair, she left the room, leaving her sobbing brother, excited pet, and livid parents behind. Each stair was a booming retort as she ascended to her room, and the slamming of her bedroom door the final rebellious word before she flung herself, crying, onto her bed.

When out on the lawn there arose such a clatter,
Dolly rose from her bed to see what was the matter.
At the window she saw none, but she thought she heard a

sound,
Neither jolly or bright, but mournful and drowned.

Dolly's eyes fluttered open, staring at the swirling patterns on the ceiling in confusion. What had woken her? She hadn't been asleep, not properly, not in the traditional sense. Still fuming from the argument with her parents, she had drifted into a fitful half-sleep; that strange place of semi-consciousness where dreams and the real world collided. Had she been dreaming? She didn't think so. Something stirred in the hallway outside of her room, and she jumped up into a sitting position, flinging the covers off her as she rose. A shadow flickered past the open crack in her bedroom door. Something obscured the light and stayed there.

"Dolly? I had a bad dream..."

She let out a relieved sigh. It was Johnny. He stood there in his pajamas, a damp stain on the front of his trousers. Dolly tutted out loud. "Did you wet the bed again Johnny?"

He lowered his head in mute admission and brought his hands up to hide his face, teddy swinging from one clenched fist. It looked like he was about to cry.

She quickly hopped off the bed and lightly padded across the rug, long nightgown swishing. She crouched down next to him and placed her hands on either side of his head, pressing their foreheads together. "It's alright, it's alright. We'll get you cleaned up, and mom and dad'll never know, okay?" She lifted his chin up with one hand as she whispered, bringing his tear-filled eyes level with hers. He stood there for a second, snivelling softly, before nodding once, a brief back-and-forth bob of the head. She took his hand in hers and led him along the hall to the bathroom. As he sat down on the lid of the toilet, Johnny looked up at her with a face full of sleepy excitement.

"Has momma and papa put out the presents yet Dolly?"

She grimaced a little, slight guilt gnawing at her belly for destroying his innocence so young. After a moment's pause, she gave herself a mental shrug; what was done was done, she couldn't take it back now, so she shook her head and smiled at him pleasantly, preparing to tell him the truth that she didn't know as she hadn't checked. Dolly's mouth opened to answer just as something clanked downstairs. She glanced out of the bathroom door to the hallway stairs before looking back at Johnny. "Did you hear that, Johnny?" she whispered.

He responded in kind. "Yeah. Are they putting the presents out?"

The thought hadn't occurred to Dolly, and she wondered what time it was. She opted for safety. "Stay here for a sec, Johnny. Get your clean trousers on, and I'll go check, okay?"

He nodded furiously, and she stepped out of the bathroom carefully, trying to avoid the creaky floorboards under the hallway carpet.

"Dolly!"

She jumped as her little brother's stage whisper cut through the silence of the house, then took a deep breath as she turned back to the bathroom door.

"You're going the wrong way!"

Dolly shook her head and flapped a hand up and down at Johnny. "Stay there, Johnny! I'm going to see if mom and dad are in bed first. Then I'll check downstairs!"

The clanging noise came again from downstairs, making her jump once more as she turned away from her brother and crept along to her parents' room. Peering through the gloom she could see two lumps under the covers of their bed; they were still sound asleep. So who was downstairs!?

"Mom? Dad? There's someone downstairs..." She managed to keep her voice flat, which was funny considering the terror that was seeping into her mind. "Mom?" she repeated. "Dad?" An edge of panic crept into her voice as she entered the room properly, crossing the room slowly in the dark to avoid walking into any of the furniture. They didn't move, not even the slightest stir; she couldn't even see the gentle movement of their chests from breathing. Her breath caught in her throat as she arrived next to the bed and leant down near her father's face. The most delicate of air movement flowed by her; he was breathing, though shallow to the extreme. A wave of guilt flooded her system as she recalled their harsh words the evening before, followed by a second, stronger wave as another clank sounded from downstairs. There was a stranger in their house… And she had left Johnny on his own. She shook her father's shoulder.

"Dad?"

He didn't reply, nor did he stir in the slightest.

Another clanking sound echoed from downstairs, and she whirled. She half-ran to the hallway and found her brother stood near the top of the stairs, staring down them through the bars of the railing with a beatific smile on his face. "Johnny" she whispered, though it came out as a squeak. "What are you doing!?"

He turned the grin on her, seeming genuinely pleased with himself, and bobbed up and down in excitement. "It is Santa! He IS real!"

The squeal with which he said this set Dolly's teeth on edge, and interrupted another series of clanks from downstairs. The noise stopped, as if whatever, or whoever, was downstairs was listening, then a shadow moved at the bottom of the stairs. Dolly held her breath, standing stock still and mentally willing her little brother to keep his silence. Dolly thought that whatever forces that control the universe were obviously having a night of jokes at her expense, as Johnny chose that moment to giggle loudly in glee.

Whatever was down there moved towards the stairs, the shadow it caused elongating as it moved, and Dolly didn't hesitate to think. She was already moving before her brother's laugh had subsided, and had managed to pull him into the spare room between hers and the bathroom before she heard the first step creak under the thing's weight. Using the cover of the noise of the intruder's ascent, she whispered in his ear, "What were you thinking, making so much noise?"

The fear that she was feeling must have shown on her face, and part of it hushed her brother's response to an actually quiet whisper. "It's Santa, Dolly. Santa Claus. It's really him!"

She stared into his eyes for a long moment, searching the excitement there and seeing only genuine belief, listening to each stair creak heavily, as if a weighty man was climbing them. Could it really be him? she wondered. Johnny was reaching for the light switch on the wall above him, and she grabbed his hand back, shaking her head frantically and making a shushing gesture with a finger to her lips. Wondering if she could trust him to stay still and quiet, Dolly leaned sideways into the doorway of the room, peering out into the illumination of the hallway.

Emerging from the stairwell into the light was a large figure sporting a white-lined red cloak and a similarly decorated hood pulled up over its head. Dolly gasped inaudibly, cautious even in her shock, and the thought returned to her once more: *Could it really be him?* She shook her head and looked harder, even as Johnny squeezed underneath her to peer around the door frame to look himself. For a moment, concern for her brother clouded everything else, but it quickly passed — the way the light fittings were spread along the hall, little light penetrated their room, so it would take superhuman sight to spot them where they were stood. The figure turned as it reached the top of the stairs, and the illusion was broken.

From beneath the hood an engorged, red-skinned goats head leered, complete with a pair of twisting giant horns and a mouth full of malformed, pointed teeth. A hooked nose completed the picture. Grotesquely slanted eyes searched the hall for signs of movement. Rusty, linked chains were bound about its chest and belly underneath the red Santa Claus robe. The thing stalked along the hallway, not seeming to care when its footsteps creaked the loose floorboards. Johnny gasped as the beast turned and advanced along the hallway. With a speed she didn't know she had, Dolly grabbed her little brother and pulled him along the wall away from the intruder, one hand over his mouth. Her breath stilled in her chest as the little light from the hall faded and the beast's terrible shadow cast in the room before them. Tension built in her head as she crouched there, Johnny pressed against her body in mutual fear, and the moment seemed to stretch and last forever. And suddenly it was over. The creature passed the doorway and time returned to normal, the thing's creaking footsteps advancing down the hall towards their parents' room.

Dolly took another calming breath, thinking through the situation. What could she do? What needed to be done? She thought of her parents in their bedroom, the demon-thing coming for them. Should she warn them? What would it do if she called out? She quickly dismissed the idea; her priority was Johnny. With the beast between them and their parents, it was up to her to look after him, and he needed to be away from it—out of the house if possible. As the conclusion formed, it brought with it a measure of calm: she knew what she had to do; now all she had to do was do it. Peering around the edge of the door once more, she saw the back of the beast disappearing into their parents' room. It was amazing, in a morbidly fearsome way, how uncanny it resembled the classic portrayal of Santa Claus from behind.

Shaking off the idle wonder, Dolly pulled Johnny with her—hand still clamped over his mouth—as she edged into the corridor and tiptoed to the top of the stairs. She spared a moment to glance back at her parents' bedroom door, despite being unable to see inside from the angle she was at. Johnny tugged on her arm.

"I want to go to Momma, Dolly. I'm scared." There was a slight warble in his quiet voice, the beginnings of fear.

She shook her head before whispering, "No, Johnny, we need to go and get away from it. Mommy and Daddy will be fine. Daddy will look after Mommy."

She started planning their route down the noisome steps. Years ago, back when she had been a little older than Johnny, her and their father would play games of hide and seek to pass the coldest of the winter days. She had quickly learned the route up and down those steps that made the least amount of noise to use to her advantage, but with a stab of guilt she realized it had been a long time since she had given any thought to them; she wondered if she could still remember well enough.

Her foot crept out to try the first "safe" area on the top step—a slightly frayed patch on the right of the rug—when Johnny hissed in her ear. "Dolly..." He whined her name, elongating it for several seconds as only young children can. "...we can't let the monster have Ed!"

She sighed, keeping it low enough to keep the beast from hearing. Ed was Johnny's teddy; Ed the Ted—an in joke between Dolly and their parents when Johnny was born. He had never gotten the joke. There was a moment, just briefly, when she considered telling him to forget the stuffed toy, but then she thought better of it. Ed was sacred to Johnny, a member of the family just as important as Dolly, Toby, Mom, or

Dad. If she told him to leave his teddy, Dolly knew he would kick up a fuss.

Seeing no other alternative, she placed him gently onto the carpet and looked him straight in the eyes, keeping her voice as quiet as she could. "Stay. Here." She stressed both words, trying to impress upon him the urgency with which she wanted him to grasp the situation. "I'll get Ed."

The phrase "easier said than done" rode through her mind more than once as she padded along the hall, slowing as she reached the end of the bannister that turned into the "L" shape of the corridor. Dolly crouched down, glad that she hadn't worn her new pajamas—they had a host of plastic icons on them that would have rustled like dry leaves with every movement. Peering around the corner of the bannister, she could just make out the silhouette of the creature moving around her parents' bedroom. It seemed to be shuffling in a half-circle about their bed, gnarled claws stretched out as if grasping something invisible in front of it. Confusion blossomed in Dolly's mind as she watched, wondering why the monster hadn't moved forward or hurt her parents yet.

She turned her head further round to the right and peered through the banisters, looking at her little brother. Johnny stood there, exactly where she had left him, looking small and vulnerable, at the top of the stairs. Dolly took a breath and gathered herself, watching the intruder's strange routine as she leaned out into the gap between the banisters and the bathroom. Placing her right hand flat against the floor, careful not press on any loose floorboards, she gave her weight over to it and rotated her body, reaching her left arm out towards the stuffed toy lying on the bathroom tiles. She kept her face directed into her parents' room, determined not to turn her back on it. Her muscles burned as they stretched, and her fingertips barely brushed artificial fur. She froze for a moment as the beast half-turned towards her, then felt her body relax as it continued to turn away from her and the doorway. Dolly risked a quick glance into the bathroom, just enough to give her spatial awareness of the teddy, and struck.

A bellow escaped the beast's mouth, causing her to flinch and pull herself back against the railings. She held the teddy tight to her chest as several seconds passed, then ten, a minute. The demon continued its odd shuffling dance; it hadn't seen her, hadn't discovered her during her teddy-bear rescue operation. She let out the breath she had been holding.

"Dolly!" Johnny's insistent whine sounded painfully loud in the silence of the hall, and she felt her heart plunge into her stomach as the thing in their parents' room snarled. With a low moan of despair, she bounded to her feet and fled along the corridor, scooping up her brother and squeezing him face-first against her just as the not-Santa came out of the doorway. She slid her arms slightly lower, covering Johnny's ears just before the thing opened its mouth and let out a short, sharp grunt. Dolly kept still, frozen once more in the beast's presence, and watched as it raised its snout and sniffed the air. The chains dangled and clinked together as it leaned down, sampling the air near the corner of the bannisters. Her breath caught in her throat. It snorted as if disgusted with the smell. Its head turned ever so slowly in her direction until its eyes met hers. Her mouth opened in a silent moan of terror, and its own mirrored hers in a twisted parody before shifting and molding into a leering grin.

The demon reared up high on its hind legs, gripping the banister with its claws and twisting the wood until it groaned in protest—a horrible shrieking sound that set Dolly's nerves on edge. She winced with the feeling and its grin widened in obvious pleasure at her discomfort. One side of its lip curled upwards further, releasing an undulating growl calculated to scare her and her brother more. She resisted it, but obviously Johnny couldn't—he hadn't even known what was coming. A moan of terror escaped his lips, more felt than heard as his head was pressed into her chest, but somehow the beast heard it and advanced with menacing intent. As soon as it moved, the spell was broken, and she could move and think clearly. She needed to get away. They needed to get away. Bobbing slightly at the knees, she scooped her brother into her arms and bolted down the stairs, arriving too quickly at the bottom landing and skidding slightly on the loose rug there.

Another growl sounded behind her from the top of the stairs, and she turned left into the lounge. Without pausing, she rushed through the room, clipping her thigh with bruising force on one of the armchairs, her progress lit by the twinkling fairy lights strung in the front window. She wasted no time looking behind her to check on their pursuit; instead, she careened into the kitchen and flung open the pantry door one-handed.

"Johnny, let go. I need you to let go." She struggled to pry his grip from around her body, and she was filled with guilt at what she was about to try and do. If it failed, he'd be in danger. His head came up slightly from her chest, and she could just make out his red-rimmed eyes from between the curtain of blonde that was his fringe. There was a dark stain on her top where his quiet tears had soaked into the fabric.

"Come on Johnny, let go. You're going to stay here." His eyes widened suddenly as she spoke, and she knew she didn't have time for this. "You're going to stay here, and be real quiet, okay? I'm going to lead the monster away from you." The fear receded slightly from his gaze, but the intensity was still there, pleading with her, begging her not leave him alone. "You've got Ed with you. He'll look after you."

A mixed sound of snuffling and soft growls echoed from the direction of the hallway, and with it her urgency increased. "Get to the back and hide behind the towels, Johnny. Hug Ed tight and don't come out. Don't even open your eyes, alright?"

He nodded slowly, almost gently. Dolly could see the fear still prominent in his eyes, but his trust of her was overriding it—only just—but she didn't have the time spare to try and reinforce it. She planted a hurried kiss on the hair that matted his forehead. "Love you," she said before shutting the door.

Whirling, she ran to the other end of the dim kitchen, bare feet slapping audibly on the tiled floor. A questioning bellow rang out from somewhere behind her as she reached the basement door. She fumbled with the deadbolt that secured it, unlocking it with a screech of metal on wood, and glanced round the end of the wall to check on her pursuer. The noise that the bolt had made must have alerted it to her location, as it had just turned its face from near the pantry when she leaned to look. With a gasp of fear, Dolly pulled herself back around the corner and wrenched open the door in a single movement. Then she flew down the basement stairs.

The chamber was cold and damp as only old basements can be. The cement floor sapped the warmth from her bare feet with each slapping step as she ran from the base of the stairs, barely remembering to pull on the light cord as she passed. As the bulbs flickered on, the shelves and random stacks of boxes lying around came into focus, though Dolly was already moving quickly past them, using her memory as her guide. She hardly ever came down here—no one did —but because of that it hardly ever changed. She turned a corner at the end of a row of shelves and stumbled as she banged her shin against something very solid—obviously someone had moved something. She struggled to stay upright, but her momentum spilled her across the bare floor and she grazed her palms against the rough concrete. The pain of impact came a moment later. A box lay near her head—one of the largest they had used when they moved in five years ago. At the time, it had held Dolly's rocking horse—now Johnny's—but it was empty now. Father had been meaning to do something with it—either fill it up with useless, but memorable, junk or throw it away—and now Dolly said a silent prayer of thanks for his lack of decision. She pulled herself forward and curled up into the cardboard cube, bending the tabs inward to hide her from view.

And then from above her, she heard on the roof,
The clip and then clop; the turn of its hoof.
And as Dolly was listening, straining for sound,
Krampus came to the basement with a leap and a bound.

Dolly couldn't see anything from the gap between the box's tabs—just a pile of old, mildew-ridden magazines stacked on top of an old record player. Even if she had opened them up more, which she was loathe to do, the angle she was at in relation to the bottom of the stairs was wrong; she wouldn't have been able to see the demon anyhow. Somehow not seeing the beast, and not knowing what it was doing or where it was, was worse than seeing it. She squirmed slightly from one side to another in an attempt to see better, but still she couldn't. The sound of its chains clanging together as it stalked around the chamber echoed horribly, making it seem like it was right outside her box. She could hear the snorting breaths it took through that stunted nose, and trembled silently whenever it growled or sounded like it was getting closer.

Without warning, a shadow blotted out the light from the basement bulbs, and she froze. A snuffling sound quested about the edge of the box, shifting a cloud of dust into her hiding place. Dolly took a quick breath, as silent as she could manage, before the cloud reached her face. A minute passed, and her chest ached. Another went by, and her lungs were screaming for release. Time ceased to have any real meaning as she fought against the natural impulse, but eventually she had to give in. In an inevitable whoosh of let out air, she released the built-up carbon dioxide from her lungs and gasped in an almost full breath of dust. She managed to repress a cough. The sneeze, however, she didn't. It started as a tiny tickle in the back of her throat, and she felt it progress through her nasal passageways, the soft tissues there burning and clenching and rippling with irritation. Even by her girly standards, it was a pathetic sneeze. The tiniest of sounds escaped her mouth, but it was enough.

A more definite snort sounded on the outside of the box before a claw found the opening and pulled open one side of the tab. She shrieked as it opened, and Toby tilted his head to the side in confusion. The German shepherd nudged the box open a little more, and after a moment's hesitation, she launched herself forward to hug the hound.

"Toby, you great beast," she whispered into his fur, "you had me scared witless!" Toby answered with a long, undulating growl that vibrated through his entire frame. Dolly peeled herself partially from her pet with exaggerated care, already dreading what was going to meet her gaze. At the end of the row, the monster stood, watching their embrace with a faint half-grin on that leering demonic visage. It matched Toby's growl with one of its own, and the German shepherd seemed to lose stature a little, as if cowed by the leering demon. The hackles on the dogs back were still raised, as was the fur all over his body, and he vibrated with energy, as if he was restraining himself from attacking. Dolly thought that Toby may have been holding back out of an instinct to protect her; after all, their parents had chosen his breed because of their repute of a family defensive nature.

The demon snarled again, and it was different in some way—a change of tone or something that managed to speak directly to that part of Dolly that remembered a time when primitive man knew the value of fight or flight. A cold shiver travelled the length of her spine, and she flew. Like a runner off the starting block, she bolted for the stairs, and somehow she knew, without a shadow of a doubt, that it was after her. It wasn't coming directly for her, for some reason it avoided Toby, but she knew they were racing each other for the stairs. The light bulb came into view above her, and the stairs beyond it, the doorway at the top beckoning.

She cleared the end of the shelving and caught a flash of red out of the corner of her eye. It was the only warning she got before the demon slammed her into the wall beside the bottom of the stairs. Tiny lights sparked and burst before her eyes, back-lit by one large, constant light that wavered and danced in the background. Snarling, growling, and scuffling sounds echoed off the concrete walls as the large light slowly came into focus. It was the kitchen door at the top of the stairs. Dimly she realized that they must have caught the light cord as they flew through the air. A whimpering whine brought her attention to the floor of the basement and the two figures hidden by the shadows.

Through the gloom she could see Toby laying on his side, one leg bent out from his body at an awkward angle, the demon crouched above him. The dog was still shivering, but now it was a quake of pain. The monstrous creature, breathing slightly heavier than before, glared at her with its leering grin, showing pointed teeth. Its near-smile seemed to taunt her, as if it said, "Choose. Run or stay. Your life or your pet." Dolly hesitated, and that horrid grin spread wider. It took a menacing step forward, and she bolted for the stairs, her head kept slightly to one side to keep a watch on her pursuer. She saw it manage a single step after her before it staggered. Toby had somehow managed to launch himself at the demon and had attached himself to the beast's leg. Dolly used the time he gave her to vault up the stairs, pursued by the sounds of snarling from below, and out the doorway into the kitchen. Tears streamed down her face in silent grief as she shut the door and bolted it.

> Her eyes how they twinkled, so sad and so wet,
> So hard now she prayed for release for their pet.
> That mouth it was twisted, all firm and so tight,
> Up to her, now it was, to save them this night.

"Dolly?"

She shrieked, a short, sharp cry of fear and surprise, and whirled to face Johnny. Relief washed through her, smothering the distress, and she hugged him fiercely. Whilst his face was buried in her stomach, she set her features into a sterner demeanor.

"Johnny," she whispered, "I told you stay in the pantry and hide!" The words came out harsher than she had intended. He withdrew a little, looking ashamed and suddenly very vulnerable.

"I got scared... What was all that noise? Did I hear Toby?" She shook her head, not trusting herself to speak about it. She held up a finger against his lips, cutting him off from asking any more questions. She was determined not to think about their dog down there with that thing. Something slamming against the basement door stopped her from saying anything else. Dust fell from around the frame, messing up the neat tiles, and Dolly thought how mother would be mad about the mess on her new kitchen floor.

The thing hit the door again, filling her with dread and spurring her into action. Grabbing Johnny's little hand in hers, she ran the length of the kitchen and out through the lounge to the hallway. As they passed the end of the stairs, she released Johnny's hand and half-jumped at the front door, landing with both her hands on the handles. As soon as her feet touched down, she pulled, almost wrenching her arms from their sockets when the door wouldn't budge. She knew instinctively that something wasn't right; the handles them-selves didn't move so much as a fraction when she pulled on them. Giving up after one last tug, she turned to grab her brother, and dread turned into fear.

Johnny was halfway up the stairs, crawling on all fours with Ed still clenched tightly in one hand. With each step he climbed, the teddy bear's body was squished to the carpet. Normally Johnny wouldn't let anything happen to Ed, and it spoke volumes of how scared her brother was that it didn't occur to him what he was doing to his favorite toy. A step towards the stairs was all she managed, her mouth open wide to call him back down, when the demon stepped into the doorway. Dolly froze for a moment, her eyes flicking from the monstrous being before her to the small boy half-way up the stairs. Johnny had also noticed its presence and was now turned around on the spot, waiting almost crab-like with all four limbs bent below him, holding him above the step. It took her a second to realize that he was avoiding putting any pressure on the noisy step underneath him.

The creature started to follow her gaze, turning its body slowly towards the stairs, and her fear turned to terror. Desperate to distract it, she shrieked like she had in the kitchen—quick, high, and sharp—and moved backwards towards the living room door. Her ploy worked. The demon returned his full attention to her, the sharp, evil eyes shining with glee. She continued to back up, keeping direct eye contact, her hands spread slightly out to either side to find the living room doorway. It took a step towards her, and she took a step back. Again it followed, and she repeated the movement, her hands finding the doorway behind her. One foot back, he followed, another, and they repeated their dance. She was about to turn and run, sure that the demon would follow her, when a creak from the stairwell brought its head snapping round to stare at Johnny. It turned its back on her, a dismissal of swishing red cloak. The calm that had overwhelmed her terror during their little dance broke, and panic flooded her mind.

"No, Johnny!"

The creature didn't even look up, and desperation added to the panic.

"Hey! Hey! Over here! Over here! Come on! Me! Get me, you want me!" The thing gave no response, and its horned head bobbed briefly with a clanking of chains as it sniffed and snuffled at the air, tasting her little brother's scent. One clawed foot raised up and settled, almost gently, on the bottom step. It creaked ever so loudly, the sound echoing in the hallway as the creature put its weight onto the carpeted floorboard. It shifted forward, lifting its back foot off the floor to take the next step. Conscious thought disappeared, and pure reaction took over. Dolly ran forward and launched herself across the hall at the demon's back, gripping the red felt cloak in one hand and pummeling it with the other. Dimly she felt her hand bruise as it impacted the hard musculature of its back, but it didn't seem to make any difference. It ignored her and took another step up towards her cowering brother.

She added her feet and knees to the assault, driving them repeatedly against the demon's frame, but to no avail. It moved upwards once more, causing her to slip slightly, and she wrapped her feet about its body to keep her place. Johnny whimpered in fear, making Dolly's panic skyrocket. She grabbed the only thing within reach—a large picture frame from the wall—and brought it down on the creature's head. Glass shattered, showering her and the steps, and a roar of pained outrage issued from the demon. It crouched down for a brief second, then bucked violently, rolling its shoulders to shift her onto one side. She ended up braced against its left arm, the bulging, veiny muscles hard and taut beneath the red fabric. With a growl of annoyance, the beast flung her away from it like she was a doll. Her shoulder clipped the wall as she flew through the air, and she spun a full twist before hitting the front door.

Through blurred vision she watched the thing leer angrily at her over its shoulder before it turned its attention back to Johnny on the stairs. Tears stung her eyes as she watched, a deep pain throbbing across her back, head, and neck. She gasped for breath and managed to call out, "Run, Johnny!" Her eyes dimmed as her pulse thudded louder in her ears and the pain grew duller and broader. A sob racked her frame as she heard Johnny's scream from somewhere upstairs. "Please don't hurt him!"

"Dolly!" The cry came from the stairwell, and she heard his muffled footsteps run down the carpeted steps. Somehow he had gotten past the creature. She felt his tiny frame slam into her, his arms wrapping around her; he was shivering with terror. She shushed him and stroked his hair, feeling her hand come away wet. Her vision swam in and out of focus, she was still able to make out that his blonde locks were matted down with a thick, dark red liquid. More tears gathered in her eyes, and she fought not to cry out loud.

"Johnny?"

He didn't respond.

"Johnny!" She shook him slightly, and she felt his head move against her.

"I need you to help me to move, Johnny. Come on, just through the living room. We'll try the conservatory doors."

Dolly moved around onto her knees and, clutching at Johnny to keep herself steady, she got to her feet. They shuffled slowly in what she hoped was the direction of the living room, and soon she could hear the crackling of the dying embers in the fireplace. A loud creak from behind them on the stairwell elicited a moan of fear from Johnny, and Dolly caught her breath, whispering to him.

"Keep going, Johnny. Just keep moving. Don't look back."

They continued onward together, and Dolly staggered briefly as Johnny rebounded off a piece of furniture. The crackling of the fireplace passed somewhere to their left, and she realized she was losing pieces of time—they had already passed half of the living room and she hadn't even been aware of traveling that far. A growl from behind them signaled the untimely arrival of their unwanted guest. Johnny whimpered as something smashed against the wall nearby. Dolly thought it might have been a chair, but the short glimpses that she was getting weren't entirely clear.

She stumbled and fell, but had enough presence of mind to push Johnny ahead of her.

"Go, Johnny! Run! Get to the back door." Her vision was starting to clear, the blackness at the edge if her vision retreating, and she saw him standing before her, wide eyed and scared, unsure of what to do. A thud behind her let her know the demon was close now.

"Run, Johnny! Go!" She screamed the last word, then cried out in pain as the creature kicked her side. She rolled with the force until she hit the sideboard beside the fireplace. Her vision cleared enough to see the intruder facing her brother, who was trapped and cowering in the corner. The image wavered, and her head tilted back slightly. Hung from the fireplace mantle, one of the stockings swam into sharp focus, the greens and whites of the pattern painfully bright in the gloom of the living room. The sight of it brought the thought of Christmas to mind, and the words she had spoken to her father earlier that night came flooding back to her.

"Please," she whispered to the stocking, tears streaming freely down her face, "please save him. Let Mother and Father wake up, let Johnny be okay. Let Toby be alright. Let them all be alright... I'll do anything. Please, just let it go back to how it was... Anything."

His eyes — how they twinkled! His dimples how jolly!
He came from the chimney and stood before Dolly.
His droll little mouth was turned down in a frown,
And his jingling hat sat 'round his head like a crown.
The stump of a pipe he held in one hand,
His belt wrapped about him, like a giant black band.
He had a rosy broad face and a red-cloak-wrapped belly,
That trembled with anger like a bowlful of jelly!

A bright light filled the room, and before Dolly stood Santa Claus himself. There was no fake beard or loosely hung costume, only a well-tailored red suit lined with white wool that fit his large frame. He was not fat, as the stories told, but big—tall and filled out. Anger darkened the handsome brow decorated with a carefully trimmed surround of white hair. He stomped forward, black leather boots traipsing a mixture

115

of soot and snow onto the living room carpet. Santa lifted his arm towards the demon that had Dolly's brother trapped in the corner.

"Krampus!" The word rolled around the room like thunder, echoing and reverberating against the walls with immense power. The demon turned slowly, the evil leer gone from its gruesome face. It tilted its head to one side questioningly, like a dog. Saint Nick beckoned with a single gloved finger.

"Come! He never stopped believing."

Krampus turned his eyes on Dolly, and she quailed beneath its evil gaze

"And she has made her Christmas wish."

The beast snarled, frustrated, and began to turn back towards Johnny.

"Krampus!" Santa boomed once more, and Dolly's brother covered his ears and whimpered at the force of it.

"She has wished for safety for her family. She named anything as her price." The demon stopped and looked at Dolly now. That look of evil was gone, replaced by an innate curiosity directed straight at her. It took a few steps towards her then stopped, looking back at Santa.

The Saint of Christmas spoke once more, keeping eye contact with his devilish doppelganger. "Come, Krampus, let this night be over." He looked to Dolly, still shivering where she sat on the living room floor. "Your wish is granted, little one."

> He spoke not a word but with a twist and he leaned,
> He waved but one hand to banish the fiend.
> And laying his finger on the side of his nose,
> Nodding to Dolly, up the chimney he rose!

Father and Mother were laughing, watching Johnny open a present that he had selected from under the tree. Dolly watched, a slight smile on her face as Toby bounded into the room, prancing and yipping at the young boy's excitement. The fire crackled merrily, and the lights on the tree cast a colorful twinkle across the room and the family gathered about the tree. Snow fell steadily outside, depositing small flakes in the thirteen-year-old's hair. Her smile drooped slightly when she felt a hand settle on her shoulder. She dropped her chin to her chest to keep from crying. She wondered silently at how she could be standing right there, how she could feel the ground beneath her feet and the cold of the snow and ice about them, but not make any impressions in the snow itself.

Gathering herself, she raised her head and took one last, longing look through the window at her family, memorizing the image before her. Dolly Anne Wright sighed, took a deep breath, and turned to Krampus, letting him take her hand in his gnarled claw and lead her away into the snow. The price was paid; her family was safe. They didn't remember anything. Not the demon that had entered their house and terrorized their kids, not the death of their beloved pet, not even their own daughter. It was as if she had never existed, and they were happy. Safe. The price was paid.

S*urvival of the R*eddest
Vicky MacDonald Harris

She looked up from her place at the base of the Christmas
tree, under the boughs and tinsel, raised her head as high as
she could,
and mouthed silently to the ceiling and sky,
"Thank you Santa, this is just what I wanted."

ere hours after Santa delivered the gifts to all the children of the world, one after another, fully formed little elves, tiny as Christmas bells, blinked into being in the air at the North Pole. They fell silently into the green velvet folds of the special birthing basket. Some woke with a twist. Already wearing their red uniforms, they fought upward, past one another to get to the top of the heap, and flung themselves over the side. The drop to the floor was mighty and took out a good half of the newborns.

The remainder got up and ran to the sides of the birthing room, where a wall of green velvet hung, strung with Christmas stockings. They climbed into the stockings and hid. Consciousness took longer to develop in this cold wasteland, so they waited until they knew enough to leave.

Elf #345025251, or more commonly known as 51⁵ woke, popped his head up, and slid down the drape. The others poked at him through the velvet stockings. Every move he made as he worked his way down the curtain helped awaken more elves. When he reached the floor, it became a run or be killed moment for each elf. Their numbers winnowed down to only a few hundred thousand from the Christmas morning birth cycle.

51⁵ wasn't bruised or hurt very badly, as were some of the unlucky others. He didn't know where to run, but saw an open door and hurried through into an entrance hall. He ran into a wall of other elves, all whom pushed forward, positioned around a giant red elf standing at the front of the room. 51⁵ looked up, way up. A noise boomed from the red opening on what the elf thought might be a face. 51⁵ began to understand as the noise became clearer.

His smile glistened. "You will work here. You will make my toys. If you do well, then you will live, you will grow. If you don't succeed, then you will not grow. You will wither and be dumped out in the cold," the red man's voice boomed. "The harder you work, the better it is. For everyone."

51⁵ stood and stared at the unholy red evil in front of him. He didn't know that he could become a Santa if he worked hard and slaved away at the toys, but he did understand that he'd play along for the meantime. The children's gratitude that bore him fed him like colostrum, it seemed. He stepped backward and began to run away from the throngs of little elves.

He hunkered down near a pile of other frightened elves to examine himself. He was not hurt, though the climb down had rubbed raw his hands. His outfit was the same red as Santa's, though his elf hat was green. He looked around the room and saw battles happening all about him. In the center, the upright elves were hitting and slashing at others. There were dead elves strewn all around the room. Some other elves, those fighting, had started growing and were now taller. 51^5 stayed in the corner until his foggy brain cleared. He took several deep breathes and ran to the side, hoping the natural cover of the decorative red and green walls would keep him alive until the numbers of other elves had diminished even further. Waiting had its advantages.

51^5 listened as the cries of the dying elves lessened. Soon there was nothing but silence. The red man had left and the rubble of green and red bodies lay about the room. Then, a much taller elf came into the room and shoveled all of the dead and dying out giant doors, opposite to those that Santa had used. The bracing effect of the cold air lifted both the spirit and the energy of all in the room. The doors slammed shut, and all of the remaining elves looked around. They were mostly conscious now and realized that they were the fittest of the fit. The appreciation and gift of gratitude that bore them now deserted them. They were on their own.

Every year that passed, 51^5 grew a little larger. He learned who the red man was. He learned about the toys and the gifts. The children liked the toys he helped make. Some elves were not as fortunate and did not grow with the Christmas spirit. They withered and died in the snow, locked out of the factory on the barren soil. 51^5 worked hard; his hands were sprinkled with splinters from the wooden toys he carved. His calluses grew as he did. He stuck with the classic toys and felt no need to work in the electronic section, one department that was growing even faster than the elves. Many elves there electrocuted other elves whenever they could. There was a high death rate. In his spare time, 51^5 practiced his carving. He wanted his toys to be special. He wondered why the elves had the lives they did, but it was the only world he knew. He wondered also if one day he'd be allowed to be one of the elves chosen to go on Santa's sleigh to deliver the gifts. 51^5 noticed there were always fewer elves that returned from those yearly escapades, but looked no further into the matter. Some topics were never discussed.

Several years later, 51^5 had grown to be the tallest of those remaining in his birth group. His height reached the bottom of Santa's beard. Santa observed this development and frowned. The next day, 51^5 noticed his number on the list nailed to the door of the workshop. Santa chose him to participate in the gift delivery for that coming Christmas Eve.

On his off time, he started carving wooden swords and short knives small enough to fit in his belt that were strong enough to slit a throat. 51^5 spent much time on the sharpening. He practiced reindeer games with the animals to work on his fitness and flexibility. The reindeer laughed at the pecking order of the elves. They snickered every time one fell out of the sleigh or one was left behind on a roof or stuck in a chimney. Reindeer had a long history of mocking and black humor. Ask Rudolph. Actually, that was impossible, because one year, an elf knifed him during a fight, cut off his red nose, and he was never able to fly again. Santa put him out to pasture.

51^5 sharpened his skills along with his weapons, waiting for Christmas Eve. When the time came, he helped load the sleigh and took the time to check out his competition. He was the youngest and smallest of all the participating elves.

He sat at the back of the sleigh next to the toys during takeoff so he could watch as the other elves sized up each other. Santa sat smugly, knowing all of the drama being acted out behind him, confident they would wear each other out long before they came for him. He'd seen the same story play out every year, for as long as anyone could remember.

Sitting quietly, 51^5 took out his knife. Just as the sleigh was beginning to descend onto the first rooftop, he reached forward, covered the mouth of the elf in front of him, and sliced into his heart. He was dead before he knew what happened. None of the other elves or Santa noticed because of the excitement of the landing. 51^5 tossed him overboard, and he was lost to the trees. He wiped the knife on his red outfit; the stain did not show. Red velvet concealed all the sins of the elves.

Since 51^5 had never been out in the world before, he was happy to see his first real Christmas tree. The workshop had none, as there were no frivolous amenities there. He looked up at the lights and the angel at the top. He wondered what an angel was. He read the smile on its face as hiding some evil intent. There were few smiles at the North Pole, not counting the reindeer's, of course.

While climbing back onto the sleigh, 51^5 saw there were two fewer elves getting back on. Deeds were done quickly, invisibly. He stayed at the back of the sleigh again. Over the next few cities, no elves were lost as they were all jockeying for survival. In a cloudbank over Europe, several elves disappeared. 51^5 didn't know all the methods of dispersal yet; strategies brewed while he looked on with interest. Several of those sitting closest to Santa disappeared over the Atlantic. 51^5 was sure Santa took them out. They were the largest and fiercest elves, and none of the others were strong enough to deal with them so successfully.

The gift giving resumed over North America. The lights below were so bright that they lit the sleigh. No elves were lost there either, as it was too bright. After the turn north over Hawaii, the elves sat back, knowing they had done what they could. No one had taken Santa's place, but there was always next year.

Years passed quickly at the North Pole. It wasn't as if anything ever changed there, though 51^5 was certain that the ice packs were smaller and the shrubs on the south faces of the nearby arctic lands were thicker and greener, almost the shade of their elf hats.

The thanks from the children who received gifts drifted up. 51^5 grew, his muscles thickened, and he had to get a new work uniform several times over the summer. His beard showed signs of whitening. All of these were symbols of his success. By the following summer, he was as tall as Santa's eyes. He would sit behind Santa this year he knew. It was time.

Fiddling with the sharp knife in his belt, 51^5 gave stern looks to the lesser elves, who ran to do his bidding. His wood-working skills scared the smallest elves, as his toys grew darker, more wretched, so they gave him wide berth when he strolled through the workshop. He watched Santa in his overhang office watching him. Santa knew the competition was very specific this year. He stared down 51^5. 51^5 stared right back, and he never blinked. He didn't bother to help load the sleigh when Christmas Eve came.

He was the last to get onboard before Santa. 51^5 took the seat bench behind Santa's. No other elf fit next to him. It was going to be about him and Santa. The elves behind them didn't even try to take each other out. Taking down Santa didn't happen every year, so when it was going to happen, the elves were just happy to have a front-row, high-flying seat for Christmas. 51⁵ had his trusty knife. They flew high and fast. The wind kept the other sounds down, not that there was any conversation. All eyes were forward. Even the reindeer swiped glances backwards. They would know immediately when Santa was gone because the hold on the reins would change.

51⁵ bided his time. He was in no rush. He wanted Santa to sweat. The big guy certainly would. After they swung over Turkey, the moisture from the Mediterranean formed a dense fog bank. He started shuffling his feet and Santa sat up straighter, knowing what was coming. Santa relaxed some as he realized that shuffling tactic in the fog was glaringly obvious. He smiled.

Just then, 51⁵ saw the edge of the grin, so he grabbed Santa's head, pushed him forward, took the rein, and quickly twisted it around his neck. 51⁵ seized Santa's whip and lashed it against the reindeer. They jerked forward, tightening the rein. That compressed Santa's neck, crushing his windpipe. At the same time, 51⁵ pulled back on the reins and slowed the reindeer. He untwisted Santa, who disappeared in the same sort of blink in which he was born. 51⁵ climbed over the seat and sat down. He was now Santa. He didn't even have to use his knife.

The other elves sat absolutely silent, shocked and thrilled by what they just saw. No one moved an extra muscle. Santa turned and smiled a big, red, juicy smile at them and tapped his nose. The elves worked hard for the rest of the night and delivered gifts to all the boys and girls all over the world.

Children were very satisfied with their gifts that Christmas and many thanks rose to the sky. These appreciations, the energy of grateful hearts, were stronger than these children would ever know. The thanks fell like snowflakes on the North Pole in the form of tiny little baby elves, who fell into the green folds the great birthing basket. And one dark Christmas Eve night, in the future, one of them would work to earn the red, juicy smile of the next Santa Claus.

Awash With the Christmas Spirit
Jordan Phelps

"Rather chilly tonight, Mister Corvus."

"Quite, Mister Vulpini."

"Makes me wonder if our visits are still worthwhile."

"Don't be silly, Mister Vulpini. This is what we live for."

"I suppose so, Mister Corvus. I suppose so."

The two men crossed the road to the church, swatting at snowflakes and adjusting their bowler hats over their eyes. They wore matching snow-speckled black suits that blended in with night, except for the red handkerchiefs that sat pressed and folded in their breast pockets.

On the other side of the road stood a man in a Santa Claus suit shivering in the cold. He held a Salvation Army canister in his right hand. The left was jammed deep into his coat pocket.

"Merry Christmas, fellas!" he said. "You look like you could spare a few coins. Let's share the wealth the Lord provided us with."

The two men grinned at each other and stepped up onto the sidewalk.

"What do you say, Mister Vulpini? Should we share the wealth?"

"I don't see why not," he said, eyes crinkled with glee. Mr. Vulpini reached deep into his pocket and held out a handful of coins. White tendrils of steam rose from them, blowing left in the wind past the man's face and away with the snow. He tipped his hand over the canister and allowed the coins to fall in, clinking when they hit the bottom.

"What the hell'd you do to get those coins so hot?" asked the man. "Stick 'em in the oven before you left?"

"I hardly think so," said Mr. Vulpini. "That would be silly."

Mr. Vulpini and Mr. Corvus walked past the man and up the church steps, blending into the crowd that had gathered for midnight mass.

Once they had been inside for a few moments, the man in the Santa Claus suit picked up a handful of snow and dropped it into the canister. As he had expected, the snow hissed when it hit the bottom.

Mr. Vulpini and Mr. Corvus strode into the church as if they had done so every Sunday of their lives, shuffling sheep-like behind the rest of the folks and eventually seating themselves in the back row. They looked casually around the room as the flood of churchgoers washed through the door and into the center pews. Not many sat close to the back. It may have been their unknown presence in the small town was noticed; it may have been their smiles that just weren't quite right; or maybe it was something else entirely, but not a single person had dared to join the two men in the back row.

One family came close, sidestepping through the second-to-last row and taking a seat directly in front of them. The wife took two plastic bags of cheerios from a larger bag and passed them down to their children—both young boys—who instantly ripped them open and started nibbling. The man took off his coat, turned around to hang it over the back of his seat, and noticed Mr. Vulpini and Mr. Corvus grinning at him.

"Shouldn't you take off your hats?" he asked. "You're in the Lord's presence."

They looked from the man to each other, and then back to the man again.

"Well, Mister Vulpini. Shall we?

"I think not, Mister Corvus. That hardly seems necessary. Or wise."

The man looked annoyed. "Why do you say that?"

"Well, Mister..." Mr. Corvus trailed off, willing the man to fill in the blank.

"Mister Nicholson," he said.

"Well, Mister Nicholson. Are we not always in the Lord's presence?"

"Yes, I suppose we are."

"And when we were walking through the snowstorm he created to worship him in his church, he didn't seem to mind us wearing hats. Why should he now?"

"You're in the house of the Lord," said the man. "It's different here."

"Well, Mister Nicholson. I suppose we'll agree to disagree."

"Besides, it's rather chilly in here, don't you think?" added Mr. Vulpini.

Mr. Nicholson shook his head as if he were the only reasonable man there and turned back to his family. Soon he was bending over to pick up fallen cheerios.

"A good argument, Mister Corvus," said Mr. Vulpini.

"Cheap, but necessary, Mister Vulpini. Although I do appreciate the kind words."

They waited patiently, flipping through the hymnals they found in front of them, crossing and uncrossing their legs, and taking swigs from a flask Mr. Vulpini had removed from the inner pocket of his jacket. It wasn't long before a short priest in robes of white and gold and holding a figure of the baby Jesus made his way to center stage. His presence commanded the crowd's attention, bringing the opposing chatter to a buzz as he walked through an elaborate Nativity scene and placed the baby Jesus in the manger. He bowed his head for a moment, and then sauntered over to a podium that came up to his neck. To Mr. Vulpini and Mr. Corvus, it looked as if his head were floating. The priest cleared his throat, waiting for absolute silence, and when this was granted, he spoke.

"In the name of the Father, and of the Son, and of the Holy Spirit, may peace be with you all."

"And also with you," chanted the crowd.

"I welcome you here tonight to celebrate the birth of Jesus Christ, our Lord and Savior. Let us recall our sins and ask for his forgiveness."

There was a moment of near silence during which Mr. Vulpini and Mr. Corvus whispered their own sins into each other's ears. This turned into a sort of competition, and by the time the priest had risen from prayer, they were both trying hard to stifle their laughter.

The priest continued with his introduction, attempting to make the good folks feel at home while readying them for worship. When he was done, the choir started belting out *Joy To The World*. Everyone stood to sing—even Mr. Vulpini and

Mr. Corvus. In fact, they may have been the loudest of all, consulting their hymnal and shouting the lyrics, possibly in jest, but most likely because it felt good to sing. Never had an agenda withheld them from pleasure. What would be the fun in that?

The song came to an end and everyone was seated.

Mr. Corvus leaned towards Mr. Vulpini and, grinning, whispered into his ear. "Would you say it's time for the fun to begin, Mister Vulpini?"

"I think so, Mister Corvus. I'm practically itching under my hat."

The two laughed silently and looked around the room, contemplating where to begin. Their eyes shifted from candles, to light fixtures, to the Nativity scene and every other prospective tool in the room, eventually landing on the floating head at the podium. It had begun its sermon, and the room had settled in for it, with the exception of the two men in the back row, who were now smiling deviously at each other.

Mr. Corvus winked at his companion, and then turned to face the podium. He pursed his lips, blew softly into the air, and then watched as the candle to the left of the floating head flickered and went out.

The priest pretended to ignore the smoke rising in place of the flame, and continued with his sermon, occasionally flaring his nostrils. A second priest approached the podium, relit the candle, and then disappeared silently to his position at the side of the room.

"Clever," whispered Mr. Vulpini. "An interesting trick, I must say."

This time it was Mr. Vulpini who blew softly into the air, causing the candle on the right side of the podium to shudder and disappear.

The priest watched nervously as the second spiral of smoke took to the air, and the children in the audience began to laugh. Parents immediately nudged and shushed them. The two boys in the second-to-last row had their cheerios taken away.

Now the priest was laughing, too. "Such things happen," he said. "The Lord has just decided to demonstrate his sense of humor tonight." His eyes sparkled with contagious glee. "It's Christmas. Let the children enjoy themselves!"

The second priest returned to the podium and relit the candle. The two boys in the second-to-last row reluctantly had their cheerios returned to them, and they continued nibbling as the priest went on with his sermon.

"Shall we blow them both out at the same time, Mister Corvus?" whispered Mr. Vulpini, clearly amused by the display.

"I think not, Mister Vulpini. We wouldn't want our material to grow stale."

Mr. Vulpini nodded in agreement, looking about the room for inspiration and finding it in short order. Patterned wreaths dangled along the walls, hosting an array of bows and ornaments that sparkled under the heavy lighting. Mr. Vulpini began twirling an index finger in circles between his knees, gradually increasing the speed while staring ahead to the front of the room. Soon he had produced a tiny whirlwind.

"Interesting," whispered Mr. Corvus, grinning.

Before the whirlwind grew strong enough to attract attention, Mr. Vulpini flicked it upwards with his thumb and index finger. It curved around the room like a boomerang, sucking up each wreath it contacted, and then moved to the center of the room, where it flung red and green ornaments all over the pews. People screamed and ducked and covered their childrens' heads as ornaments shattered on the floor and benches. Soon the wreaths had been stripped of Christmas spirit—naked now except for dark red bows that, if anything, made them look less festive. Mr. Vulpini took a deep breath, sucking in the whirlwind with it, and allowed the wreaths to tumble down onto the pews.

Mr. Corvus looked delighted, but remained silent as he watched the priest's face change from a look of shock to one of self-imposed confidence—it was a thin layer, though, and the two men in the back row took pleasure in seeing through it.

"I'm sure there's an explanation for what happened," said the priest, "but now is not the time to dwell on it. As long as we are in the house of the Lord, we have nothing to fear. Now if everyone will please sit, we will continue with the celebration."

Hesitantly, people began to settle back into their seats, still scanning the room for the source of the attack.

The priest continued with his sermon, visibly flustered now. His voice carried across the room, louder than before, possibly in an attempt to ward off the unknown entity that was disturbing the ceremony, and certainly in an attempt to ward off any uncertainty felt by his audience. Soon, everyone was listening calmly. Other than some occasional backwards glances, it was if nothing strange had happened.

"An interesting group, Mister Corvus. Don't you think?" whispered Mr. Vulpini.

"Yes, I think so. Although this priest is most certainly a talented shepherd."

"That may be, Mister Corvus, but to direct the attention of his sheep away from such tangible and visible mischief? That hardly seems wise."

"Certainly not," Mr. Corvus agreed. "But who am I to badmouth the man who is so kindly facilitating our game. I wouldn't dare."

Mr. Vulpini grinned. "Perhaps it's time we stopped tickling the flock and got to work. I'm not sure how much more they'll put up with."

"Yes, Mister Vulpini. I suppose you're right."

The two men explored the room again with their eyes, taking mental notes and often regarding the priest just in case anyone was watching them. As the minutes ticked by, the crowd was lulled by the hypnotic tone of the sermon, and they were pulled further and further away from the mysterious events that had just taken place. Fresh food had been offered on the safer side of the field and they had gratefully crossed to eat it up.

The priest's approach changed to mirror the gravity of his words as he neared the finale of his sermon. What he didn't know was that Mr. Vulpini and Mr. Corvus—two names unknown to all members of the congregation—had been whispering this whole time, plotting a finale of their own.

"I confess one baptism for the forgiveness of sins," said the priest, "and I look forward to the resurrection of the dead and the life of the world to come. Amen."

There was a moment of silence during which every-one—except for most of the children—simultaneously bowed their heads. The priest then raised his head and walked offstage, breaking the spell he had on his audience. The choir began singing *For Unto Us A Child Is Born*, and joy spread through the room like wildfire.

Mr. Vulpini had nodded off and was now snoring softly with his chin resting on his neck. Mr. Corvus nudged him awake, causing him to jump.

"I'm sorry for disturbing your rest, Mister Vulpini, but if you don't mind, I'd like to blow out this birthday cake before the Eucharist begins. Wouldn't you?"

Mr. Vulpini cleared his throat, embarrassed. "Yes, of course. My deepest apologies, Mister Corvus." He paused. "I'm getting old, you know."

"We all are, Mister Vulpini, so why dwell on it? Besides, it's show time."

The priests had gathered at center stage with bread and wine, and now they were placing both carefully onto a table as if they were handling rare and exotic bird eggs. The priest who had given the sermon walked to the front of the table holding a large, white wafer, which he was preparing to break.

"Shall we?" said Mr. Corvus.

"I should think so," said Mr. Vulpini.

The two men snapped their fingers simultaneously, causing every light in the room to go out just before the priest began the ceremony. A few surprised screams came from the pews, followed by an uproar of agitated chatter. Wispy trails of smoke rose from the extinguished candles, floating about like ghosts in a dark graveyard, filling the room with a powerful aroma.

"Don't worry," said the priest from the front of the room. "Give us a minute and we will have the power back on."

"But the candles went out, too!" came a voice from the crowd. "How can you expect us to believe that this was just a power outage? Something else is going on here, and I want to know what I'm dealing with."

The crowd muttered in agreement. People rose in the dark and began shuffling past the benches, eventually making their way to the door, only to find that it was locked. So was the emergency exit. People began pulling out cell phones, attempting to use them as flashlights, but their screens failed to come to life.

"What's happening?" came another voice, followed by

many more asking different variations of the same question.

The priest tried to light a match, but it wouldn't catch. Not even a spark. He tried another one and the result was exactly the same. It was as if all of the light in the room had been sucked into a vacuum that was still silently eating up new light before it could appear.

The two men had remained seated in the back row, and now, in complete darkness, Mr. Corvus pointed his finger to where he knew the baptismal font was at the front of the room. The water inside of it began to bubble and churn, as if it were boiling.

The congregation noticed this and stopped yelling. Instead, they just listened. Listened to the bubbling grow louder and more violent, as if these bubbles contained the final breaths of drowning men. They had flocked to the right side of the room where the exit was, and from there they tried to determine where the sound was coming from. Many of them were aware of the baptismal font, and that it was the only significant source of water in the room, but nobody spoke or moved towards it. They waited like nervous students, hoping someone else would provide the answer they already knew.

Mr. Vulpini and Mr. Corvus whispered to each other in the darkness, their voices cloaked from the congregation by the bubbling water, which was growing louder with each passing moment. The two men came to an agreement, removed their shoes to make sure they wouldn't be heard, and then got up and shuffled down the row to join the congregation on the right side of the room. They didn't want to be singled out before the end of the show.

Mr. Vulpini laced his fingers together and raised both arms, connecting them horizontally in front of his body and imitating a wave, moving one elbow up as the other went down in a smooth, continuous motion that caused the water in the baptismal font to jump at the edges of its confinement like rabid dogs. The congregation listened as the water splashed onto the ground, still not daring to move. Now Mr. Corvus raised his hands above the wave that was Mr. Vulpini's arms and moved them about gracefully like a fortuneteller's over a crystal ball. This caused the water to glow red, faintly at first, illuminating the horrified faces of the priests and the choir as it did. But soon the saturation deepened and grew darker and darker, until the font looked like a pot of churning blood and the illuminated faces had faded into the darkness once more.

Mr. Corvus swung his arms upwards, and with them flames leapt from the wicks of every candle in the room. It was as if they had been there the whole time, but hadn't made themselves available to human perception. And now Mr. Corvus had willed them to share their light. He returned his arms to his sides as the light spread across the room, bringing with it a dim, eerie image of the blood-red water that was churning in the stone font, splashing against the sides and trying to escape.

The priests' mouths hung open as they watched the font, not daring to look over to the answer-hungry congregation. They had given up looking for answers. They just wanted the nightmare to be over.

Mr. Vulpini had lowered has arms along with Mr. Corvus, and now he was re-creating the wave-like motion in his head where it couldn't be observed or questioned by the congregation. He focused deeply, increasing the speed and power of the waves until he could feel them crashing against his skull. The water in the font was now matching his thoughts, rising over the stone walls and cascading to the floor in a constant blood-red stream, as if the font contained an infinite amount of it. And now, fuelled by Mr. Vulpini's mind, maybe it did.

The water spread out across the floor in all directions, sizzling against it like acid on flesh, eating up the church's carpets and turning it into a sea of red, and still more of it gushed from the font, hitting the floor and forming great waves that swept over the pews. The choir screamed as one of the waves washed over them, burning the identity from their faces and then dragging them under its current. Members of the congregation, who had pushed themselves as tightly as they could into the far corner, saw this and cried out in terror. The scent of putrid flesh rose from the water's surface and permeated the room in a grotesque mist, containing the final whispers of those who had once worn it.

The waves grew higher and more violent, overtaking the front of the room and making their way to the back. They washed over candles, dissolving the wax upon impact and steadily eating away at the dim lighting until only outlines could be seen—outlines that were being eaten up by the sea that was moving closer and closer to the back of the room. Upstanding citizens screamed for help, pounding against doors that refused to budge. And now, in these last crucial moments, Mr. Corvus spoke.

"Well, Mister Vulpini, I don't suppose you'll be wanting to get your feet wet, will you? I happen to be wearing a new pair of shoes, and let me tell you, they weren't cheap. It would be most inconvenient for me to have to make another trip to the store so soon."

"It certainly would, and I *do* hate when my feet get chilly," said Mr. Vulpini. "Shall we?"

The people nearest to them had heard this and turned to stare at them through the dim light provided by the remaining candles. Now even more turned as the two men linked hands and floated upwards, as if they were in an invisible elevator, not stopping until they reached a giant cross that had been fastened to the wall high above the door. And that's where they sat, one on each arm of the cross, and watched as the waves drew nearer to the congregation.

Everyone stared at Mr. Vulpini and Mr. Corvus, the collective terror on their faces morphing into confusion, and then plummeting back to terror again once they realized the corrosive, blood-like substance had arrived, and was melting their leather shoes. People hopped up and down in a feeble attempt to preserve them, but the water continued to rise, setting pants and dresses ablaze and causing the back of the room to light up like a morbid Christmas tree. Screams filled the air. Articles of clothing were consumed one by one, leaving nothing but burning, shriveling flesh to fend off the corrosive liquid. The liquid's surface gleamed and shifted as clothes went out and darkness set in, and slowly it began to rise above shoulders. Children screamed as it climbed up past their necks and ate away at skin, revealing rotting bone, muscles, and cartilage.

From his perch, Mr. Corvus snapped his fingers. The action caused nothing at first, but soon a faint rumble could be heard coming from underwater, a rumble that grew louder and more ominous with each passing second. It felt like an approaching train, the tracks for which were suspended over miles of sky. And the entire congregation was seated on those tracks with nowhere to go. Suddenly, a giant wave climbed up from the water at the front of the room and started rolling towards the congregation, eating up the surrounding water until it was twenty feet tall.

"Quite the show, Mister Corvus. If only you knew what I'd give for some buttered popcorn and a cold Pepsi right now. I think it might frighten you."

The two men laughed, watching the wave as it picked

up speed and moved towards the congregation of rotting bodies that were now struggling to tread water at the back of the room. Most of them no longer had the energy to scream, and when they tried, only desperate moans escaped. Together, they were a symphony of tortured souls.

And now the wave was there, opening up like a gaping, watery mouth and swallowing the congregation like a handful of Gummi Bears. It slammed against the back wall and dragged the dying churchgoers further down into the pool. Soon, only a few heads could be seen floating above the surface.

"I do believe I got sprayed," said Mr. Corvus, standing up on his side of the cross and wiping his pants. He moved his feet up and down, hearing a wet squelch each time he brought them down.

"I can practically hear your money drowning, Mister Corvus." Mr. Vulpini put a hand to his ear and leaned his body towards Mr. Corvus' shoes. "No, certainly."

Mr. Corvus sighed. "Well, Mister Vulpini, I'd say these people have suffered enough. Shall we send them down to the boss now?"

"Yes, I should think so, Mister Corvus."

Mr. Vulpini twirled his index finger in the air, just as he had done to summon the whirlwind, but this time something different happened. The blood-like substance began to empty from the room like water from a bathtub, leaving red stains on the walls as the liquid surface crept closer to the ground. It looked as though Mr. Corvus had pulled a stopper out from the ground, and in a way, he had. The liquid above the baptismal font twisted together, turning into a miniature cyclone and sucking the rest of the water towards it. Slowly, the remaining water was swallowed up by the font, taking with it as many free-floating objects as it could. This included the congregation—now nothing more than a collection of rotting bones with strips of flesh and muscle dangling haphazardly from them.

"Not a bad haul, Mister Vulpini. And certainly not a bad show." Mr. Corvus sat completely still, smiling faintly as he watched the last of the churchgoers get sucked into the vortex; he looked much like a child witnessing fireworks for the first time.

"Quite, Mister Corvus. But we can't leave the place looking like this. That would be rude. Irresponsible, even. Would it not?"

"Yes, Mister Vulpini. I think so."

Mr. Corvus snapped his fingers and a blinding light overtook the room. They squinted for a moment, and then, once the light had disappeared completely, the room was back to the way it had been before the flood: the corroded pews, the torn carpets, the stained walls, all of these were now sparkling and ready for a lovely Christmas Mass. Everything would have been perfect, if only the congregation had reappeared. But they hadn't, and they never would.

"Ah, beautiful work, Mister Corvus. They'll never notice a thing."

"Thank you, Mister Vulpini. I should hope not."

The two men each took a step off the cross and floated down to the carpet. They walked to the door side by side, and Mr. Vulpini opened it, allowing a great gust of wind and snow inside. The bowler hat blew right off his head to reveal two ebony horns. Mr. Vulpini snatched his hat off the floor and placed it back on his head in one swift movement. The street outside appeared to be deserted. Anyone left in town was either sleeping or watching Christmas specials with a big plate of sugar cookies and gingerbread.

"Not a creature was stirring," said Mr. Vulpini. "Not

even a mouse."

The two men looked at each other and burst out laughing. Just as they were about to step outside, Mr. Corvus turned and walked to the table the priest had been preparing for the Eucharist.

"No sense leaving good bread and wine, Mister Vulpini. That would be wasteful, wouldn't it?"

"I should think so, Mister Corvus."

Mr. Corvus reached the table and immediately began stuffing tiny wafers of bread into his jacket pockets. Once they were completely full, he picked up the priest's wine chalice, took a chug, and rejoined Mr. Vulpini at the door with the goodies.

"Thou shalt share with thy neighbors," said Mr. Corvus, holding out a huge handful of wafers to Mr. Vulpini. "Did that sound right?"

"Quite so, Mister Corvus. You're a natural herald of the good word!" Mr. Vulpini snatched the wafers from Mr. Corvus' outstretched hand and began tossing them into the air and catching them in his mouth like popcorn.

They sauntered out the door and into frigid night air. The wind still blew, viciously stirring up the snow, but that did nothing to kill their good cheer. They looked like two men just off work and on their way to the pub, and in a way, they were. Neither of them mentioned the weather.

"Say, Mister Corvus. I wonder if we could find some cheese to go with this. That would really hit the spot, don't you think?"

Mr. Corvus took a deep breath through his nostrils and let it out slowly, a smile forming on his face as he did. "Yes, Mister Vulpini, I think it would."

The two men walked down the empty street and away from the church, adjusting their bowler hats, flicking wafers of bread into their mouths, and passing the chalice of wine back and forth. Their cheeks grew rosy as they drank the last of the wine, and when it was all gone, Mr. Vulpini tossed the chalice to the curb. Somewhere along the way they draped their arms over each other's shoulders.

Mr. Corvus looked to his partner and smiled. "I know we aren't supposed to say this, Mister Vulpini, but the thought has crept up on me like a warm kitten and refuses to go away. So here it is." He coughed, looking from left to right to make sure they were still alone, and then he leaned into Mr. Vulpini and whispered, "Merry Christmas."

Mr. Vulpini smiled and flicked another wafer into his mouth. "I say, on a night like this, it doesn't matter who you are. That kitten is going to find you one way or another, and when it does, it's not going to let you go until your stomach is full and your face is as bright as sunlight on snow. Merry Christmas, Mister Corvus. You are a great man and an even greater friend."

"As are you, Mister Vulpini. As are you."

Indeed, something special was happening that night. It wasn't something you could reasonably explain (especially not if you were Mr. Vulpini or Mr. Corvus), but instead, it was something you could feel. Something that appeared mysteriously and filled your entire body with warmth, like that first shot of whiskey, but without the drunkenness. It was something that made you feel meaningful. On that night, accomplishments were shoved into a deep hole and sealed away, and existence was enough.

As Mr. Vulpini and Mr. Corvus continued down the icy road, further away from the church and the small town, they felt the warmth just as much as anyone else. And together they moved on until they were just two more dark figures cloaked by the swirling snow.

W⁂HAT C⁂HILD I⁂S T⁂HIS?

Joel Reeves

Steven and Allison Wilmot watched and waited for a shopper to approach the apple-cheeked bell ringer and drop coins into the red donation can. Taking advantage of this opportune diversion, they rushed past, slipping into the throng of holiday shoppers, swept along through the automatic doors and into the landscape of artificial Christmas trees, strings of colorful electric lights, and rows of plastic reindeer and elves. They navigated the corridors of the Littleton Super Mall, ogling the shiny new cars, boats, and travel trailers placed on display by local dealers. A few steps behind them their eight-year-old son, Billy, eyed the line of children queued to see the mall Santa Claus.

"Can I sit on Santa's lap?" Billy inquired, looking hopeful.

Steven Wilmot peered into the front passenger-side window of a sleek sports car. Billy could see by the dreamy look on his father's face that the old man was lost in his usual fantasy: Driving down the freeway at high speed with the automobile's top turned down, the last wisps of black hair on his forehead snapping like a kite's tail in the summer breeze.

Mr. Wilmot gazed at the price sticker on the window and frowned. "I will never be able to afford this car," he lamented. "It costs more than our house. Where do people find the money?"

Billy studied his father, feeling the old man's disappointment. He loved his father very much and wished he could do something to help make him happy. But the car was very expensive, and he was a just a child. Even all of the money in his piggy bank and the small fund his grandparents had set up for his college education wouldn't begin to cover the cost of such a vehicle.

Mr. Wilmot walked around the outside of the car, running his hand in dazed delight over the spoiler. "This is a real beauty."

His wife rolled her eyes. "Don't even think about it," she warned. "No new car for you until we completely remodel the kitchen. For starters, I want all new countertops and state-of-the-art appliances."

Steven averted his eyes from the expensive vehicle as if he had been caught doing something very bad. "I was just looking." He glanced down at Billy, always competing with his wife for their son's allegiance. "It doesn't hurt to look, does it, son?"

Billy hated when they fought. If only he could figure out a way to give them both what they wanted, then their family could be happy like the ones on television or in the photos that appeared on the covers of his mom's magazines.

❄ ❄ ❄

Going to church wasn't something that Billy's parents did on a regular basis, but as soon as Thanksgiving ended, every year like clockwork, they started playing Christmas music, attending services, and making him go to Sunday school. And as December 25th loomed closer, their fighting escalated. Billy stopped making snowmen and going sledding. There just wasn't time for frivolous activities. All of his thoughts, all of his energies were expended in a state of high anxiety, thinking about his parents and how he could get them the things they needed to be happy.

The church was made of stone blocks and had two big stained glass windows in front that looked like a giant's eyes. Billy felt like he was being watched by God as he and his parents and several other churchgoers crept carefully along the icy sidewalk toward the steps that led up to the front of the building.

A life-sized Nativity nestled in the snow drew Billy's attention. As his parents started up the concrete steps toward the front doors of the church, Billy hung back, gazing at the masonry statues. He studied the three wise men clothed in the colorful raiment of kings. Except for a small chip out of Joseph's bearded chin, the figures were perfect, their expressions so lifelike that Billy found himself scrutinizing every line and detail of their faces.

He slipped between the shepherds and their sheep and around an angel of the Lord dressed in shimmering blue robes, its wings extended, one tip touching Mother Mary's shoulder. Billy peered down at the baby Jesus. The child, true to the Bible story, was wrapped in swaddling clothes and lying in a manger; it peered up at him with blue eyes, its face seeming to glow just a bit. Billy reached out his hand, touching the little halo on top of the figure's head. He was surprised. It didn't feel cold like stone.

Sacrifice.

Billy pulled back his hand, startled. "What?" He looked about, puzzled. "Is someone there?"

He studied the statue of the Christ child. The figure's shiny blue eyes stared up at him, its cherubic pink mouth pressed tight as if hiding a secret. Billy drew back a step.

Billy. Sacrifice!

Billy felt his blood run cold. He stared down at the baby Jesus, so filled with dread he was unable to move.

Gift for gift.

Trembling, Billy reached out to touch the statue. Despite his fear, he also found himself drawn to it.

"Hurry up, Billy! We'll be late."

Startled, Billy pulled back his hand and turned quickly. His parents had reached the top of the stairs. They were waiting for him, their faces red and cross, as if they'd been fighting again. Billy rushed up the steps.

Inside, the parishioners were settling into their pews. The minister stood at a podium, a towering Jesus looming behind him stretched on a wooden cross that reached nearly to the ceiling. Billy gazed at the pierced hands of this giant symbol of sacrifice, the sad, upcast eyes, and the thorny crown. It distracted him from the sermon and Sunday school lesson, both of which dealt with the sighting of a special star and how three wise men followed it to Bethlehem. Billy didn't understand why they would give gold to a baby and was unfamiliar with frankincense or myrrh. When he tried to ask his mother about them, she glared at him, annoyed, and told him to hush.

The guest speaker, a tall, slender fellow with a pale face and large, gray eyes, went up to the platform and stood behind the podium. Billy guessed he was some sort of missionary. He spoke about helping a tribe in Africa to find salvation by building a sanitation system for the village. The choir sang a hymn and then a group of children dressed in costumes performed the Christmas story. To end the service and tie everything together, the minister resumed his position at the front of the church. He reminded the congregation that, like those who followed the star and gave what was most precious to them in service to the Lord, all people must be willing to sacrifice in order to lead fulfilling lives and enter the Kingdom of Heaven.

After the service, Billy's parents remained inside the church, shaking hands with people they hardly knew and catching up on the latest gossip. Bored, Billy slipped outside and down the stairs to stand in front of the Nativity. He studied the stone figures a moment, puzzled.

The scene looked somehow different then it had only an hour or so earlier. All of the wise men and shepherds and their animals had been pulled back, as if on purpose, to give the bystander a better view of the Christ child. Perhaps Mr. Davies, the custodian of the church, had changed their positions during the service.

Billy kneeled a few feet from the Nativity, his small, gray eyes fixed on the stone baby Jesus. An inch of snow had fallen. It sparkled, making his eyes hurt. Tracks, several sets of human footprints of various sizes, had left their impressions in the fresh covering.

Show your love. Sacrifice.

Billy gasped. He stood up quickly. He stared at the statue, trying to think what to do. The minister had said that God sometimes spoke to people. Maybe He was talking to Billy now.

Give them happiness. Sacrifice.

"All right, Billy, we're leaving."

Billy spun about. His mother and father stood behind him at the bottom of the stairs, peering past him at the statues, curious.

"Did you move those statues?" his mother demanded. "They don't look the same."

Billy shook his head, frightened. "No, I didn't touch them. Honest."

Mrs. Wilmot glanced at the statues, then at Billy. "Just see that you don't," she warned. "The minister said someone has been messing with the Nativity. He comes to work and the statues are never where he left them. That's vandalism."

Mr. Wilmot scowled, irritated. "It's not really vandalism. Nothing broken. No damage. I bet it's just a few teenagers moving them around for kicks. I can see where that would be amusing. You pulled pranks when you were a kid, right?"

His wife glared at him. "No, I did not. Pranks are bad. People get hurt."

Mr. Wilmot sighed, frustrated. "Why do you always see the bad in everything?"

"Like that car in the mall, you mean?" she fumed. "You know we can't afford that. Besides, why should you get your car if I can't have my new kitchen?"

Billy looked up his parents, his forehead wrinkled in worry. He reached for his mother's hand. "Please don't fight."

She snatched her hand away, looking down at Billy, annoyed.

"Tell that to your father," she snapped. "I can't get anything through to him. All he wants is that car."

Mrs. Wilmot pulled her scarf up tight around her neck. She stomped off down the sidewalk, leaving Mr. Wilmot and Billy behind. The rest of the congregation was leaving, too, getting into their cars or walking, disappearing like ghosts into the falling snow. After a few moments, Mr. Wilmot told Billy not be too long, and then hanging his head, trudged through the snow and cold toward home.

Billy returned to the statue. He gazed at the baby Jesus and was soon lost in concentration. Sacrifice equals happiness. The message seemed clear enough. That was how he could give his parents what they needed. But what could he give up that would be enough for God to make his mom and dad happy? He reached into his pocket and dug around. He pulled out one of the plastic soldiers his uncle had given him for his birthday. The soldier meant a great deal more to Billy than its face value. Uncle Walt had been his favorite relative, a gentle man with always the right words to cheer up a person, even in the worst circumstances. The good man's sudden death in a car accident only a year ago made the soldier even more precious.

He eyed the soldier fondly, then placed him into the open arms of the baby Jesus, hands trembling. The halo atop the cherub's head suddenly glowed softly and the infantryman disappeared. Billy watched, horrified and elated, waiting for something more to happen, but when no obvious sign acknowledging his small sacrifice appeared, he bowed his head, disappointed.

"I don't understand," he said. "Did it work?"

He rushed home through the falling snow, hoping for all the world that his parents had undergone a transformation. That somehow, through the magic or miracle contained in the infant statue, his dream of family bliss had been realized at last.

But when he pulled open the icy outside door and entered the warm coat room, his parent's latest argument was already in full swing, except even more heated than usual. He crossed through the dining room and stopped when he reached the entryway to the living room, peeking nervously around the big bookcase to see into the room.

His mother stood in the center of the room facing the wall. His father stood behind her, pleading with her.

"You've done some pretty selfish things," his mother shouted. "But this is by far the worst."

"I'm telling you, Allison," he pleaded. "I did not buy that car. I found it inside the garage with the keys in the ignition when we got home from church."

She spun about, her face a mixture of fury and incredulity. "Don't you mock me," she screamed, breaking into tears. "A lie is one thing, Steven. But don't demean me by trying to make me believe this ridiculous story."

He brought up his hand a little as if to touch her shoulder, but then seemed to think better of it as she drew back, furious. That's when Billy spotted the set of shiny new keys cupped tightly in his hand.

"It did work," Billy whispered, elated. Or almost. God had given his father the car, but maybe the sacrifice hadn't been good enough. His mother still didn't have her new kitchen. When she had that, everything would be perfect. His parents would have their dreams. The fighting would finally end.

Billy knew what needed to be done and there was no time to lose. He sneaked back through the kitchen, pulled open an old storage drawer, snatched up the rest of his soldiers, and slipped out the door, too much in a hurry even to zip his coat or put on his hat. He ran out into the cold, the bag of soldiers tucked under one arm, the wind driving the snow in swirls and squalls across the icy sidewalk.

The wind continued to increase as Billy ran in the direction of the church. When his face grew numb, Billy turned away, walking backward against the storm. Although the whole walk took longer than he'd anticipated, before long he came to the drive leading up to the big stone church.

The lot was empty except for the minister's black car. Billy kneeled down in front of the manger and wiped away the soft layer of snow that obscured the angelic little face of the Christ child. He laid the soldiers inside the manger so that they were touching the open hands of the holy infant.

The halo glowed, a bit brighter this time, and Billy's gift disappeared.

He jumped up and ran all the way home, barely noticing the cold in his excitement to see his mother's new kitchen. But when he reached the outside door, he could already hear the sound of his parents arguing within.

He cleared away a fine layer of snow and peered through the glass of the kitchen window. He gasped, his eyes growing wide. The kitchen was like nothing he had ever seen before, everything new and of the highest quality: refrigerator, oven, stove, mahogany cupboards and matching kitchen table and chairs, a stainless steel sink and countertops, and a very expensive set of iron skillets, pots, and cooking utensils.

And yet, something still wasn't right. His parents were fighting, louder than ever. He slipped through the door and into the kitchen. He listened to the fury, could imagine in his mind's eye his mother's bugging eyes, that ball of spit gathering on the corner of his father's lips as the two spewed out terrible, hurtful words.

"The kitchen makes the rest of the house look small and shabby," Mrs. Wilmot complained. "We must build on."

"You want to talk about shabby," Mr. Wilmot fumed, eyeing his clothes in disgust. "Just think of how I'm going to look at work when I get out of an expensive new sports car wearing these rags. Not a decent shirt or pair of pants in my whole closet. What I need is a whole new wardrobe."

Billy felt a heaviness in his chest. His parents were more unhappy now than ever. But what could he do? Why, he decided, there was really only one solution. The soldiers had been a good start, but it was obvious he needed go one step further. He decided he would give up all of his most prized possessions—an antique glass angel, a rare magic set rumored to have once been owned by Harry Houdini, his remote control car, and several other personal belongings he held closest to his heart. He ran to his room and packed them all up in a box. With night already beginning to fall, he rushed outside. He found his sled, placed the box atop it, and pulled his load as quickly as he could along the icy sidewalk through the dark and lightly swirling snow.

His body felt stiff, every step an effort. He wondered if the cold was creeping into his bones and whether he might be freezing. He quickly pushed the thought out of his mind and pressed on. Like a junior Santa, he had a package to deliver aboard his little sled, a gift that would bring happiness to the two most important people in his life.

The Nativity was breathtaking, the faces of the stone statues lit by an electric footlight that shone upon them through a fine layer of snow. Billy pulled his sled up close and pulled open the flaps on the box. He reached inside and pulled out each special object, his hands trembling as he placed the first of these—a rare glass angel he'd found in an antique store a few years back—into the baby's open hands. The object disappeared, but to Billy's surprise and disappointment, the halo did not glow.

It's not enough. Sacrifice!

Billy gasped. The little baby sneered up at him, its soft blue eyes hard and hungry. Billy felt a chill fill his whole body, not from the winter night, but like an icy hand that crept into his chest and lungs and squeezed his heart.

He pulled the rest of the contents out of the box and placed them in front of the Christ child. The objects disappeared. The infant shook its head, displeased. Billy dropped to his knees, exhausted.

"It's all I have," he cried, tears running down his cheeks. "I've sacrificed everything. Please."

The infant shook its head, unconvinced.

No, it hissed. *Not everything.*

Billy gasped. His eyes grew wide in terror as the baby sat up and slid down from its makeshift crib to the snowy ground. It sneered and extended a groping hand, the tiny fingers squeezing into a tight fist. It took a quick step toward the stunned boy, clutching him in its icy grip.

Billy screamed as a jolting chill spread through his body. He tried to run, horrified to discover that he could not move. Paralyzed, he could only watch as the infant snarled and climbed up his leg, clawed its way like a wild animal up the front of his coat to his face.

The hungry creature wrapped its arms around his neck, tipped its head slightly to one side, studying him, and stared into Billy's eyes. Its mouth stretched open, much wider than seemed possible, bearing a mouthful of small, pointed teeth. It pried open Billy's frozen jaws. Billy felt the creature's icy breath against his face, filling his mouth and nostrils. Felt its thoughts inside his head.

It smiled, satisfied.

I commend you, Billy, and accept your gift.

❄ ❄ ❄

The next Sunday the minister gave his annual sermon on how to set reasonable spiritual goals in the New Year. When the service finished, the congregation filed out the church door quickly, busy with their thoughts of Sunday dinner. Steven and Allison Wilmot hurried down the stairs, pausing at the bottom, watching as Mr. Davies, the church custodian, unlocked a pair of steel storm doors that led down to the church basement.

"Where's Billy?" Mr. Wilmot asked.

Mrs. Wilmot shrugged, annoyed. "I don't know," she stated. "I've got too much on my mind right now to go searching for him."

The elderly custodian began carrying the Nativity, a piece at a time, through the wet snow. Mr. Wilmot watched the frail man stumble and fall once, get up, and continue dragging the heavy statues, stopping often to catch his breath.

"Let's go," Mrs. Wilmot urged. "We'll be late for the party. I've invited twenty guests to the house. I can't wait to show it off. Come on."

"We'll go," Mr. Wilmot assured her. "But I'm going to give him a hand first. It shouldn't take very long."

"Steven, no," she insisted. "This party is very important."

Mrs. Wilmot watched, irritated, as her husband helped the old custodian carry the remaining Nativity pieces through the storm doors. When the final piece had been carried down the stairs, the two men stood for a few moments in the basement of the church, shivering.

"Thank you, sir," Mr. Davies said, shaking Mr. Wilmot's hand. "That's a job well done."

He did a quick count of the pieces because he knew the minister would require an inventory. When he was done, he counted them once more, perplexed.

"Is something the matter?" Steven asked.

Mr. Davies stroked his gray whiskers, irritated. "I would have bet my right arm this collection had fourteen pieces."

Steven counted. "There's fifteen."

Mr. Davies raised his eyebrows, stumped. "Yes, well, my wife was right then, I suppose," he chuckled. "I guess I really am getting forgetful."

The two gazed upon the silhouettes of the statues for a few moments more before turning away and heading back toward the stairs. The statues peered back at them as the steel storm doors swung shut and locked, officially marking the end of Christmas for yet another year.

There in the darkness, where no one was left to see, a tear slid down the cheek of the boy shepherd, the newest addition to the Nativity family.

Minnie's Christmas Surprise
Geoffrey K. Liu

T'was the night before Christmas, when all through the house,
not a creature was stirring, not even a...
Bump. Shuffle. Ga-lump!

Minnie Koch's eyes popped open in the dark. Her mind was on high alert. She had never quite fallen asleep. She had only lulled herself into a state of half-consciousness by repeating the first line of the poem over and over again, "*T'was the night before Christmas, when all through the house not a creature was stirring, not even a mouse.*" She waited and listened, warm in her bed, toes twitching slightly. Tonight was the night, the most magical night of all.

Ga-lump!

It was what she had been waiting for all along; of that she

had no doubt. The sound of boots on the roof. After eight long years of waiting, she would finally be successful—although, admittedly, she was only eight years old and only remembered a handful of those years, but that didn't matter. He was here, and she was finally going to see him.

Santa Claus.

Ga-lump!

The sound was moving across the roof towards the chimney. They had a big house, and she was thankful for that. She had checked to make sure their chimney was big enough for a full-grown man to fit down, even a fat man burdened with presents. Santa had magic to help him, of course, but he wouldn't need it at their house. They were rich; Santa didn't need magic at rich houses.

Ga-lump. Ga-lump. Ga-lump.

Slow, careful steps crossed the roof. Next to her bed, Minnie heard a soft huff as her dog, Plump, raised his head and sounded a quick, and not entirely urgent, alarm. There wasn't much the big galoot did that was urgent.

"Shush, Plumpie, it's okay."

There was a grunt and a wet snort as he put his head back down. He was a good dog, a loyal rescue pup that listened to her every word. He wouldn't be alarmed until she was alarmed, and she was nowhere near alarmed. She was excited and triumphant. It was only a week ago at school that her friend Melissa had tried to convince her Santa wasn't real. If Santa wasn't real, Minnie had asked, then who the heck brought all the presents? *Your mommy and daddy, stupid,* Melissa had replied.

Who's stupid now? Minnie thought as she swung her legs out of bed. Another long snort indicated that Plump had lifted his big head again. Minnie couldn't see him in the dark on the other side of the bed, but she didn't have to. She knew his noises better than anyone.

"Stay, Plump. There's nothing to worry about."

There was a groan followed by the immense *thunk* of his head against the floor. Minnie went to her bookshelf and took down her Fisher-Price digital camera. If Melissa needed proof that Santa Claus existed, she would get it.

* * *

The suit was warm and smelled funny. He liked it. The beard made him itch and he didn't like that, but it was part of the suit, which was part of him now. He walked across the roof towards the chimney. This was the best way down, and he could fit. He had watched the house for weeks, and he knew as the weather got colder, they always kept a fire at night until it burned down and wisps of smoke drizzled up from the chimney. The flue would be open. This would be easy.

He stopped at the chimney, preparing himself for the short descent. He wouldn't have to come back up; when he was finished with his work, he would leave by the front door. He would make the man turn off the alarm. He had ways of making the man do anything. A man would do anything to not watch his wife and daughter get hurt. Anything.

He took a deep breath and could practically smell their scent coming up from the chimney, mingled with the scent of the smoldering fire. He liked their smell, especially the two girls.

* * *

Minnie crept down the hall, her camera clutched in her hands. She stopped at the doorway to the big den where the three of them, Mom, Dad, and Minnie, had spent the evening decorating the Christmas tree. Decorating the tree on Christmas

Eve was one of her Daddy's traditions. He said he didn't like doing it too soon because seeing Christmas decorations beforehand cheapened the season. Minnie didn't think this was true; she thought she could be happy looking at Christmas decorations all year. But it had become an activity they cherished, one of the few times of year when none of them were too busy to just sit and be together. Daddy had to work most other holidays, but Christmas was the one he refused to give up under any circumstances.

She stayed close to the wall and peeked into the room. The noise on the roof had stopped, but as she looked into the fireplace, she could see a light sprinkling of soot falling over the few glowing embers left. Her timing was perfect. She looked down at her camera and turned it on, and while she fiddled with the settings, she whispered the words that had allowed her to stay up for this unforgettable Christmas moment.

"T'was the night before Christmas, when all through the house... t'was the night before Christmas... t'was the night...."

✳ ✳ ✳

Climbing down the chimney was more difficult than he thought it would be, but he was strong, he was in control. He pressed his back to one side and his heavy work boots to the other, and slowly 'walked' down the inside of the chimney. He almost slipped a couple of times, and to do so would have meant a broken ankle at least, and probably discovery. Discovery could get messy. Discovery meant people had to be silenced sooner than he would prefer, and he wanted to draw this out. He wanted to take his time with the girls.

He made his way slowly and steadily, keeping his breath under control, relaxing his muscles in alternating groups as needed so that he did not strain any of them more than the others. He would need all of them for his work.

Besides, he was Santa Claus. His magic would help carry him down.

* * *

Minnie waited with her finger on the camera's shutter button, forcing herself not to take the picture too soon. In a few moments, a pair of black booted feet appeared in the fireplace, crunching heedlessly over what remained of the embers burning there. Minnie's heart sped up. The red pants with white fringe, though caked with soot, were unmistakable. She shifted slightly where she stood, not allowing her finger to press down any harder. If she took the picture too soon, then Santa would know he had been discovered and he would be back up the chimney in a heartbeat. No picture, no presents. If she caught him in the act, however, he had to speak to her. That was the rule.

A figure bent down in the fireplace, his hand swiping the air, trying to chase away the puffs of soot, and at the same time, his boots crushed out the last of the embers. Crouching down, he emerged from the fireplace and then stood on the hearth, dusting himself off. Clouds of black soot billowed off his big red coat. Minnie hadn't imagined Santa Claus would be so dirty; she thought his Santa magic would keep him clean on his trip down the chimney.

Still, he was *here*. She stood for a long time, rooted to her spot, mouth agape. Then she remembered why she was there, and raised her camera. As Santa stopped cleaning himself and looked around, her finger pressed down on the shutter button, and the room was momentarily filled with a blinding flash of light. Santa's eyes whipped suddenly to her position, and she couldn't help but notice how sunken and black they were, not twinkling like in the poem. He had no dimples and no rosy red cheeks, either. He looked, Minnie thought, like a regular man, and a slightly ugly one at that. He still had his white beard, but it was crooked and tangled and full of soot. She had always thought it would be more curly and silky.

His eyes narrowed and he stared at her for a long time. She stepped into the doorway, knowing she had been discovered, but satisfied with the picture she had taken.

"Hi, Santa," she said.

"What the fuck do you think you're doing?" Santa asked. Minnie gasped loudly at his use of the most forbidden of all forbidden words.

"Santa! You can't say that!"

He seemed to remember himself. He looked around the room, his eyes resting on the Christmas tree. His hands slipped down over his belly, though it was not as jolly and round as Minnie had expected.

"*Shit*—ho, ho, ho, little girl." Santa's voice was coarse and cold. "Don't you know you're supposed to be in bed?"

"I stayed up so I could see you," Minnie said. "Melissa at school—you know Melissa, she's a bad little girl and you probably have coal for her, she lives down the street—she said you don't exist, and I told her that wasn't true, you *do* exist, and I was going to prove it to her. But don't worry, Santa, I won't tell anyone else."

Santa looked at her for a long time, then back at the fireplace as if deciding whether or not to try to make his escape. Minnie placed her hands on her hips like adults did when they were serious.

"I caught you, Santa, you have to stay. Those are the rules.

Where's your bag of toys?"

"Bag of what?"

"Toys. Presents for good little girls and boys. And you can't tell me you don't have presents for me because I was a very good girl this year, I tried really hard, and I got all good grades and did my homework and didn't bother Mommy when she was trying to get stuff done and didn't bother Daddy with my in-*cess*-ant chatter as soon as he got home, I always waited five minutes or more like he told me to."

"Where *is* your daddy?" Santa asked.

Minnie asked, "Why?"

"I need to see him."

"Adults don't get to see Santa. It's the rule." Minnie frowned. "Shouldn't you know that already, Santa?"

* * *

This wasn't part of the plan; the tiny bitch wasn't supposed to be awake. This wasn't how it worked. He always went to the father first; the man of the house always proved the greatest danger. He threatened the father with the life of his family, and made him do what needed to be done. Usually it was turning the alarm off if there was one, sometimes it was showing him where the gun was kept if there was one. Not that he liked using guns in any way, they scared him too much, but he didn't like the thought of one in the house behind his back while he was working.

So the father went first. Once he had outlived his usefulness, his throat would be cut. It was a quiet death, and afterwards, he would position the father so he could watch everything that happened. Dead or not, he liked when the father watched. Then he would wake up the girls. But this girl was already awake. He had to change his plan, and he didn't like changing his plan. It made him frustrated and angry. Worse, she had taken his picture. He would have to destroy that. Even in costume, he didn't like his picture taken.

Now he had to convince the little girl not to put up a fuss. Not yet.

"Little girl, you should go back to bed."

"What kind of food do your reindeers eat?"

"What room is your father in?"

"I know you have magic so you can go all across the world in one night to give presents to the good Christian children, but does it feel like one night to you?"

"I need you to show me your mommy and daddy's room."

"Did you bring me an Xbox?"

"Little girl!"

"Shhhhhh! You're going to wake Mommy and Daddy, Santa!"

He reached beneath his coat and extracted a long knife with a flat black blade. The only part that shined was the tiny, sharpened edge. This was the tool of his trade, the only one he needed—well, not exactly the *only* one. He held it up for the little girl to see. Her hands went to her hips again.

"You know," she said, "you shouldn't play with that. It's dangerous. You could get a cut."

"Take me to your daddy."

"Why?"

"I'm going to kill him. And if you scream, I'll kill your mommy too, do you understand me?"

The girl frowned again. "That's not very nice to say, Santa. I don't—" her voice cut off suddenly, and her eyes widened just a bit. "You're not really Santa, are you?" To his surprise, she actually came forward a few steps, her eyes gazing into the relative darkness of the room, examining him. "You're dressed like Santa, you have a beard like Santa, but you say nasty things."

He held up his knife and took a step forward, but paused when the little girl held up a hand like a crossing guard at an intersection. He was so taken aback by her bravery when so many others would have dissolved into tears and begging. She was ruining everything; he could see he might have to get rid of her first, which was like eating dessert before the meal.

"Stop, Santa," she said, her hand still up. "Or whoever you are. I'll call my dog."

"You don't have a dog." And she didn't, he knew. He had watched this house for too long, learning the family's patterns, their schedules, down to the minute. He had never seen a dog here, ever, not even to visit. She was bluffing, no doubt ready to fabricate some massive guard dog like a German Shepherd or Doberman, the kinds of dogs kids thought were scary, but that he knew could be turned away with a well-timed boot to the head. He had no fear of animals, and they knew it. No dog, big or small, had ever stopped him. They were animals, not worth the oxygen they consumed, and if he had to, he'd kill a thousand of them before being afraid of one.

"Yes-huh, I *do* have a dog," the little girl said. "His name is Plump. He's sleeping by my bed. All I have to do is call him."

He gritted his teeth and took another step forward, his knuckles turning white against the handle of his knife. The nerve of this little girl to impede his work in such a manner.

"If you call your dog, I'll kick him until he's dead. I'm not afraid of dogs."

He thought this might be enough to shut up her little mouth, but instead, she *laughed*. His blood turned hot in his veins, his ears burned. How dare she laugh at him. Every woman that had ever laughed at him was dead.

"You won't kick my dog, Santa. He won't let you."

"And what kind of scary, scary dog do you have, you little shit?"

"A rescue dog."

"A rescue dog?" He could barely believe he was standing here having a conversation with this girl, but it was the way she approached this, so matter-of-factly. Something about her earnest demeanor held him to the spot. Her sassy mouth, he thought, might actually be buying her a few more moments of life. And who ever said these things had to be done quickly? The only thing he had to be concerned about was if the girl started screaming or the dog started barking. So far, it seemed like neither one would happen. He was close enough to the girl that if she started screaming, he could stop her in a second, and still have the mother to play with. And there was no dog. He knew it.

"Plump is a rescue dog, which means he's special. He was mistreated, and we saved him."

"You can't mistreat a dog, they don't have souls."

"Yes-huh, they *do*," the little girl said. "Plump has a soul, and he loves me and I love him, and he'll do anything I tell him to, except go get the newspaper because rescue dogs are special and they shouldn't have to do work like that, but it doesn't matter because Plump would just ruin the newspaper before Daddy got to read it. Daddy didn't like Plump much when we first got him, and Mommy said he was gross, but they don't really care about that now because I love Plump and he protects me. Are you really Santa?"

"You don't have a dog. I've never seen a dog at your house."

"Plump doesn't go out much; he doesn't really like the sun."

"What kind of dog doesn't like the sun?"

"A special dog. Are you going to leave presents? Did you bring me the iPad I asked for? The 64-gig, not the 32-gig?"

"I didn't bring shit," he said.

"Santa, that's awful language!"

"I don't give a fuck. I'm going to cut your tongue out, then I'm going to kill your mommy and your daddy."

For the first time, the little girl looked nervous. Her eyes widened slightly, and she took a step back, until she wasn't much more than a light figure in the darkness of the doorway. Now he had her attention, and he waited anxiously for her to start screaming. He was ready to pounce at any second.

"Plump," she said, barely loud enough to be heard. Her voice wavered just a little.

He could feel the smile spread across his lips. There was no dog here. The little girl was in a fantasy world, and that would make it so much easier to—

The movement was barely noticeable behind her, except that his senses were always heightened when he was working. There was a flash of movement first, and then the smell. It was a distinctly animal smell, one he was very familiar with having grown up on a farm. A livestock smell. Beneath it, however, was something more disturbing, more sinister. Sulfur. What in the world could possibly make that kind of smell?

The thing moved behind the girl again, and from what little he could see in the darkness, it was at least as tall as the girl herself, and three times as big. Maybe she had not lied about the dog. Maybe they had gotten it today, an early Christmas present. No matter. He wasn't afraid of dogs, and this one wasn't a barker. If it became a problem, he would simply put it down and go on with his work. So often he had encountered a dog that hadn't done a thing, even as he slaughtered their owners. People thought dogs were loyal and protective, when really they were just animals and could be bought with a treat or a friendly voice. Or put down with the boot.

The dog moved again; it appeared to be pacing behind the little girl. As it passed, it bumped her and she rocked forward slightly on her toes. She smiled and glanced back at her dog.

"That's Plump," she said, her voice still maddeningly calm. "Do you want to meet him?"

"No."

"Did you bring me any presents?"

"No."

"Are you really Santa Cl—"

"*NO, I'M NOT FUCKING SANTA, YOU LITTLE—*"

"Plump, go!"

The thing emerged from the darkness next to the girl, a horror born of the black depths, and suddenly he *was* afraid, very, very afraid; he had never been so afraid. It was a dog only in that it was dog-shaped, its enormous head tapering into a pointed snout. Hanging, leathery jowls pulled up slightly to reveal pointed, yellowing teeth, so many more than a normal dog, it seemed, maybe hundreds. Malicious black eyes glittered in the multi-colored lights from the Christmas tree, and between them, sharp ridges of bone stood out from the skull. On top of the head, two shafts of bone protruded from the skin, each half-covered in matted, greasy fur. Horns. The goddamned thing had *horns*.

The dog—or whatever the hell this abomination could be called—was easily three feet tall from head to long-clawed toe. Those claws were talons and he had never seen anything like them on a living animal. They clicked against the hardwood floors as the awful thing approached, its stench burning into his nostrils with every step, worse and worse.

Never in his life had terror like this touched him. He had always been in control, from the very first day he could remember. Every moment, every second, every situation compartmentalized to perfection in his mind. It was how he was able to do his work, have his fun, and get away with it for so long. And now all that was ruined. He had no preparation for this, no instructions, no plans. Only terror.

Plump. Plump the rescue dog. There was a reason he hadn't seen it during the weeks he had stalked this house, and it was because Plump the Rescue Dog was a sin against all that was good in this world, an abhorrence, a repugnant, festering gash on the face of mother nature. It reeked of hell, a creature hand-crafted by Satan himself.

He wanted to scream, but he couldn't. The thing approached him without haste, and almost casually stretched its awful neck, opened its jaws, pressed its muzzle into his crotch, and clamped its jaws closed again. Paralyzing pain surged through his entire body, and there was a terrible ripping sound as something down there ruptured and separated. Uncontrollable nausea filled him, and he was certain he would spend his last moments choking on his own bile and vomit. He dropped to his knees, eye-level with the awful creature, staring into the glittering, malicious black orbs. Then the thing clamped onto his neck, and he could feel those horrific bony teeth sink into his flesh with crushing pressure. Thankfully, the pain from his ruined genitals masked the pain of his throat being torn from his body.

He blacked out and fell forward hard onto his face.

Then he died.

❋ ❋ ❋

Anja awoke when she heard the loud *thump* come from somewhere in the house. She sat up immediately and jabbed her husband in the side. He kicked and groaned, barely waking.

"Mark, wake up! Did you hear that?"

"Mmmph... *wha?*"

"I heard a noise in the house."

"It's nothing. Probably just Minnie getting a drink."

"Go check!"

"Are you serious?"

She jabbed him again, harder this time.

"Okay, okay."

Mark slipped out of bed, rubbing his hand through his sleep tousled hair. Anja slipped behind him and pressed herself close. *Suburban battle formation*, he thought, and a smile slipped onto his lips in spite of his exhaustion. Together, they walked out of the bedroom and into the hall. Even through his blurry vision, he could see Minnie standing in the doorway to the den. Seeing her standing there seemed to relax Anja, who popped out from behind Mark and put her hands on her hips.

"Wilhelmina, what are you doing out of bed?" she asked.

Minnie glanced back at her parents, then raised her arm and pointed into the den. Her face was neutral, but that gesture made both of their hearts quicken a little. Anja held on to Mark's arm as they headed down the hall, and as they turned the corner into the den, she issued a gasp that was almost a scream. She clamped a hand over her mouth. Mark went rigid.

The man in the Santa suit was face down on the floor in the middle of the den. Leading up to his body were sooty black footprints from the fireplace, where he had broken in. Anja knew there was absolutely no way he could have fit down the chimney, but somehow he had. There was no blood around the body, but she knew he was dead.

Mark turned and squatted down in front of Minnie, who eyed the scene casually; her neutral expression never changed as her father rested his hands gently on her shoulders.

"Minnie, what did you do?" he asked.

"I didn't do it," she said. "Plump did it. Santa Claus tried to kill us."

Mark glanced back and saw the thick Boxer dog sitting a few feet from the body, looking back at them dumbly the way he did. Mark hadn't liked the dog much at first; there had been so many better looking dogs at the rescue, but Minnie had fallen in love with the thing upon first sight, in spite of a drooling problem from a poorly set broken jaw and the rather disgusting snorting sound he made for no reason that they knew. Plump wasn't pretty, and he certainly wasn't the brightest of pups, but he was a good dog—the best really— and he loved Minnie.

Anja took her hand from her mouth and sighed. "Wilhelmina, not again."

"Plump did it," Minnie repeated.

"Now, Minnie," Mark said, "you and I both know that's not exactly true." He reached up and gently cupped his hand under Minnie's chin, turning her face towards his.

"But Dad," she said, "he was a really, really bad one. He tried to make me think he was Santa."

"Oh, Minnie," Anja said, "you have to stop doing this. It's a terrible way to use your gift, sweetheart."

"But he was really, *really* bad, and he would have hurt a lot more people!"

Plump huffed and snorted in his peculiar way as if to agree with Minnie. Anja looked down at the big dog, and as she did, a long line of viscous drool slipped from his jowl and splattered against the hardwood. She rolled her eyes, but calm flooded her just looking at the big galoot. He really was sweet in his own repulsive way.

"You," Anja said to the dog, "you're supposed to keep her from doing this, not help her."

Plump groaned, snorted, and ducked his head down, his eyes rolling up to look at her. It broke her heart every single time. She reached down and scratched Plump on his chest just below his chin, the magic spot that started his leg thumping against the floor.

"He's a good boy," Mark said, his words starting Plump's tail wagging. "He stinks, though; it's almost bath time again." He glanced at the corpse on the floor of the den, then looked back at Minnie. "Min, honey, you need to go back to bed. Mommy and I will take care of this. Take the Plumper with you, okay?" He kissed her on the forehead and she giggled as the bristles of his five o'clock shadow tickled her skin.

"I'm sorry I did it again, Dad. I was just waiting up for Santa."

He sighed, then pulled her into a hug. "It's okay, sweetie. Go on back to bed. Go with her, Plump."

Minnie turned and disappeared down the hall, Plump following quickly on her heels, a cloud of funky dog scent following behind him. Mark waved his hand in front of his nose and then went to stand next to his wife, who was looking down at the body. He put an arm around her shoulders and pulled her close. She sighed, rested her head on his shoulder.

"What are we going to do with this?" she asked.

"Same as last time. We'll call... breaking and entering. He's got a knife, and he's probably got a hell of a record if Minnie was right."

"Minnie's always right," Anja said, "you know that. But Mark, we can only get away with the breaking and entering story so many times. This is how many? Four? Five? There's not a family on this planet as supposedly unlucky as we are. I understand what she's doing, but we have to get her to stop bringing them here."

"I don't think she has any control over it, honey. And we'll use the breaking and entering story as many times as we need to."

"But if people start to get suspicious, they'll try to take her away. They'll want to study her."

Mark sighed and looked down, his eyes travelling over the body. No blood, but his head was twisted at a most peculiar angle, and his fingers were locked into rigid claws, as if his last moments of pain had been so horrendous he had tried to reach out for hell itself to relieve them. Mark wondered what this one had seen, how innocent, stupid, smelly Plump had looked this time. He decided he didn't want to know.

"No one is going to take Minnie away," Mark said. "No one can touch Minnie without her permission. We never, ever have to worry. There's only one thing I'm worried about."

"What?"

He glanced to the corner, where a present sat on the table, one he had brought home tonight after work and had only wrapped just before bed. The wrapping paper was full of air holes, and a light scratching was coming from inside. The tag said, *For Minnie, from Santa Claus.*

"I'm worried about what she's going to make that hamster do.

S*ecret S*anta

Chantal Boudreau

lle glanced down at the flashing icon that notified her she had e-mail. It had been sent by their floor rep from the social committee.

All those interested in participating in this year's Secret Santa drawing, please gather in the West Boardroom at 2:00 today.

"Secret Santa?" she asked out loud.

Kirsten, a neighboring co-worker, peered around the edge of the cubicle wall. The lanky redhead flashed Elle a knowing grin.

"Yup. We exchange names at random. Then you're supposed to buy the person you drew a gift—some trashy thing under ten bucks. But you're not supposed to tell them who it's from. I can usually figure it out anyway. That's the fun part about it—playing detective."

It was Elle's first year working at Atom Industries, and

her first Christmas there as well, so she had no idea what sort of roles or rituals were expected for the holidays.

"It's the only thing we do for Christmas fun around here other than the office Christmas party, and that's cursed," Kirsten continued.

"What do you mean, 'that's cursed'?"

Before Kirsten could answer, the sound of squeaky wheels announced the arrival of Austin, the shy man who delivered the mail by cart to every floor. He seemed scared of his own shadow, so Elle always tried to say something nice to him as he passed by.

"How about you, Austin? Are you participating in the Secret Santa draw?" Elle asked.

While the mail room was in the basement, he had a station on their floor and was counted as one of the floor employees for social events. Management thought it would be more inclusive for the mail clerks, who would otherwise have been relegated to events involving only the handful of people working down below.

He smiled nervously and dropped his gaze, never meeting Elle's own when she looked his way.

"Yeah... yeah, I do, but it's silly. You're too good for that kind of thing, Ms. Vierra. You shouldn't bother."

Elle detected something unusual in his tone of voice, a strain that wasn't normally there. Maybe he was uncomfortable with the idea that he might have to buy her a gift. Perhaps he worried she wouldn't like it, or that it might even offend her.

"Nonsense, I'm sure it will be fun. And I told you to call me Elle. I don't go in for all that formality."

Austin smiled again and pushed the cart onwards.

Kirsten waited until he wasn't quite out of earshot to share her thoughts on the matter with Elle. "Creepy twerp!

Notice he didn't offer me the same advice. He must be crushing on you. I wouldn't be so friendly with him if I were you. You might be encouraging him in the wrong way and end up with your own workplace stalker."

Elle shook her head, believing Kirsten to be needlessly paranoid and cruel. "What, Austin? He's a sweetheart. He's just shy is all. I'm sure he's perfectly harmless. Besides, I've been chatting with him since I started here. It has been months. If he were going to stalk me, he would have started by now. I think you ought to give him more of a chance."

Kirsten rolled her eyes before sliding back into the shelter of her cubicle. "Suit yourself, Elle, but I'm going to keep my distance. Better safe than sorry, I say. Don't say I didn't warn you."

❄ ❄ ❄

Elle and Kristen stood amongst the others gathered in the West Boardroom, waiting for the bowl filled with names to come their way.

"What did you mean by 'the Christmas party is cursed'?" Elle asked again, intrigued.

"It has been for the last two years. A couple of parties back, one of the guys in finance, Hal, crashed his car on the way home from the party. Died in a fiery, twisted mess. The company had concerns about drinking and driving, but word has it he only had one beer. Whether that's true or not, our generous employer now hands out free taxi chits to anyone who wants to cab home from the party and insists that anyone who has even a single drink arrange for alternate means of transportation home rather than driving." Kirsten smirked, the expression accentuating her pointy chin. "It's a 'cover our asses' sort of deal."

Elle shrugged, craning her neck to see where the bowl had gotten to. "Accidents happen. I don't see why that would label the party as cursed."

"One incident wouldn't, but a death two years running gets people talking." Kirsten's smile dimmed and she lowered her voice. "Last year, at the end of the party, one of the interns, Cassie, wandered into the stairwell, fell, and broke her neck. Atom Industries' Health and Safety Committee kicked into high gear again. They now have a two drink maximum for the party and the stairwells are off-limits during and after any special work events unless there's an actual emergency. But Cassie's fellow intern, Tom, said she was barely tipsy that night. She didn't fall because she was drunk."

Seeing the bowl still had a stretch to go in order to get to them, Elle leaned back with a sigh. "It still sounds like coincidence to me. Only one drink throws me off enough that I don't drive and I try to avoid navigating stairs. People aren't as careful as they should be under those circumstances."

"Well, I don't drink at all at these things. After Karl from accounting got all handsy with me my first year, and let me tell you how much he reeked of alcohol and bad cologne, I haven't touched a drop at any of the work parties. I have to stay on my guard in case someone else decides to get all touchy-feely. Hey! My turn." The bowl had reached Kirsten and she plucked out a slip of paper. She made a dismal face.

The bowl moved on to Elle and she drew a name as well. They both headed for the door.

"I don't even know who this is," Elle murmured as they snaked their way through the remaining crowd.

"Let me see. Oh, that's Lauren, the new co-op student in operations. Nobody really knows her all that well. Just aim for something young adult and you should be fine." Kirsten waved her own slip of paper. "Me, I'm going to try to remember what kind of bad cologne Karl wore. Since he liked to bathe in it, I'm sure he'll need more."

Elle glanced back just before she stepped out of the door and caught sight of Austin drawing a name from the bowl. After reading his selection, he returned her stare, making eye-contact for the first time she could remember. She wondered why he had such a pained expression on his face.

❄ ❄ ❄

Emerging from the bathroom stall, Elle heard Austin's voice on the other side of the ladies' room door.

"Trade with me, Barry, please."

"I don't understand why it matters to you so much." Elle was fairly certain the nasally response had come from Barry in IT. "Anyway, you should be happy you got Elle. If I had her, I'd at least be willing to give her a gift. She's nice to us. I got Kirsten. She treats us like dirt she's trying to scrape off of her shoe. Why on Earth would you want her?"

"It's not something I'm comfortable sharing. If you'd prefer to give Elle a gift, then take her. It's better that way for every-body. I don't mind trading for Kirsten. I'd rather have her. And you'll be doing me a favor, so I'll owe you one. Come on, Barry."

A few moments of silence ensued, followed by a quiet sigh from the techie. "Sure, if that's what suits you. I'm glad to pawn off Kirsten. But if I trade, there's no returns. It's a done deal."

"Of course, of course."

Elle could hear relief in Austin's voice. She wondered what she could have possibly done to offend him so much that he couldn't bear the thought of giving her a gift. As Barry had pointed out, Kirsten treated him far worse. It saddened her and made her feel somewhat guilty.

After the two men were gone, she waited a few moments and then made her escape from the bathroom. She didn't care what gift anyone would be giving her, but because she knew that Austin had traded her away, she had a lump in her throat that stuck with her for the rest of the day.

※ ※ ※

Elle noticed an air of discomfort at the Christmas party. Perhaps it was caused by the whole superstition that the event was cursed, or perhaps it was because some people were unhappy with the two drink maximum. Either way, she found herself looking forward to the point where she could leave, but that wasn't until they were done with the Secret Santa gift exchange. After that, she would happily go on her way.

Kirsten joined her by the bland-looking artificial tree where the gifts were piled. The redhead wore a sweater that matched her personality, with loud colors and obnoxious blinking lights. She noticed Elle eying her attire.

"Oh this? I'm hoping this thing will help me keep Karl away. If I could rearrange the lights to say 'Don't touch,' I most definitely would."

Glancing around the room, Elle decided Kirsten didn't have much to worry about from Karl at that party. He was hanging off of a buxom intern instead, who was awkwardly warding off his advances. If it got to the point where it looked like she had more than she could handle, Elle promised herself she would go over and intervene in her defense.

Kirsten yawned.

"This party is dullsville. I could kill for a coffee. I hope they hand out my gift next. As soon as they do, I'm slipping away to the break room to make some. Black as night and thick as mud the way I like it, otherwise I'll fall asleep on the drive home and wipeout like Hal. My coffee won't be the watery crap the break room club makes."

It wasn't Kirsten's name called out next, but Elle's. She opened the gift bag to find a decorative mouse pad with a kitten in a stocking on it. Not a surprise considering it had come from Barry.

"Lame," Kirsten remarked. "But better than the half-melted chocolates I got last year."

Three names later it was Kirsten's turn. Her package was fastidiously wrapped with silvery paper and black ribbon.

"Sweet! At least it looks nice," she said, but she scrunched up her nose at the contents of the box. She reached in and pulled out a Christmas ornament that looked like a skeleton in a Santa suit.

"I remember someone got one of these last year. I think it was Carol or Cassie, one of the interns. It must be some-body's idea of a joke."

"No, no, not necessarily." Elle pointed at the ornament. "He's a character in a movie... Something about Christmas and nightmares and Halloween. It's cute."

"Bah! Tacky pop culture junk. It won't be hanging on my tree alongside my grandmother's antique glass orna-ments. I have far better style than that." She tossed the box in the trash and dropped the ornament in her purse. "Maybe I can hand it off to my nephew. He likes crap like this. "

Elle glanced around to see if Austin was in earshot and had overheard Kirsten's tactless comments. He was nowhere in sight.

"I'm off to start the coffee. Are you coming along?" Kirsten asked.

"No. I'm done. I'm going to go grab my coat and purse and

head for home."

"Meh, I've got nothing better for me waiting at home. I'm going to see if I can chat up a hot exec before I go. Maybe I'll get lucky."

With that Kirsten flounced away, her gaudy sweater still flickering out of sync with her stride. Elle couldn't help but think she wasn't likely to attract any of the management while wearing that, especially if they hadn't had more than two drinks.

Elle had just arrived at her cubicle and was reaching for her coat when screams erupted from the vicinity of the break room. Elle left her things where they were and dashed towards the sound of trouble. A small crowd had already gathered, grouped beside the door. Elle could smell the nauseating stench of singed hair, burnt flesh, and coffee.

"What happened?" she asked the man closest to her.

"An accident. Supposedly, somebody's been electrocuted," he replied.

"It's the Christmas party curse," someone else in the crowd declared, followed by a murmuring of assents.

A sudden horrible thought gnawed at Elle's stomach and she desperately pushed her way to the front of those gathered. With what she found there, she couldn't restrain a half scream, half gasp.

Kirsten lay sprawled and steaming on the floor in a puddle of watery coffee and broken carafe glass. The little lights on her sweater blinked sporadically as they sizzled and sparked. Kirsten, on the other hand, didn't blink at all. Her red hair was blackened and shriveled in places and her face was set in a surprised grimace, frozen that way upon her death.

"So much for blaming it on the alcohol this time," a woman behind Elle said.

Elle turned away from the gruesome scene, trying not to throw up.

※ ※ ※

For the third year in a row, staff from Atom Industries returned to work after the holidays dressed in black. Management had announced the availability of a grief counselor to help cope with Kirsten's death. Having never seen a dead person before, Elle considered seeking counseling every time she had to pass the mouthy redhead's empty cubicle. Although she avoided looking at the vacant space as much as possible, she had passed it too many times not to notice that somebody had hung up the Christmas ornament Kirsten had been given by her Secret Santa. It dangled from a velcro wall hook beside her computer.

The fourth time the grinning Santa hat-clad skeleton caught her eye, a strange feeling began to niggle at Elle's nerves. Something Kirsten had said when she had opened her gift, that Cassie, or possibly Carol, had received the same present from her Secret Santa the year before. If it had been Cassie, could there be a connection? Was there really a Christmas party curse?

The idea kept eating away at Elle as she tried to do her work. She was relieved by the distraction of the rumble made by Austin's mail cart, when he eventually arrived toting the day's mail. As he rounded the corner, he actually made eye contact with her, an unusual act. He also offered up a small smile to her.

"No mail for you today," he said as he dropped a small stack on Kirsten's desk. A few of her coworkers were sharing out her work and would drop by to pick up her mail later.

When he turned to go, Elle reached out and caught his arm. "Austin, I need to know if I've done anything to offend you. If I did, I truly do apologize. I overheard you and Barry talking about trading your draws for Secret Santa. I know you originally drew my name, but you weren't interested in giving me a gift..."

She was interrupted by soft laughter, low and hiccuplike. Austin turned his cart to go. "You shouldn't eavesdrop," he said. "And you shouldn't make assumptions. I traded your name with Barry because I *do* like you, and not the other way around. I was doing you a favor. Now Kirsten, on the other hand, I didn't like, so I was happy to give her my gift. Same with Cassie last year... and Hal the year before." He paused long enough to give Elle a malicious grin that made her blood run cold before he wheeled away whistling "Santa Claus is Coming to Town."

Elle sat in her cubicle trembling for quite some time after he had gone. She wasn't sure if Austin was serious or just having a laugh at her expense. If he really had been the Secret Santa for all three, she wasn't sure if the deaths had been an unfortunate coincidence, an actual curse, or if Austin had had a hand in orchestrating their accidents, nor could she prove anything if he had. But Elle did know one thing for sure.

Next Christmas, she would be abstaining from the Secret Santa draw.

A Christmas Miracle
Kerry G.S. Lipp

obby Bitchlovich stared at three things at the same time. A triptych of hopeless comfort.

He had a tough time deciding which was the most pathetic. The Christmas tree, which stood only four feet tall and was decorated with nothing but white lights and generic bulbs or the two pictures that flanked it.

One was of his mother, who'd been great to him his entire life. Given him everything he'd ever needed and died unexpectedly a few years ago.

The other was of Chipper Holiday, his favorite porn star, wearing a Santa hat and sucking on a peppermint stick the size of her forearm.

He remembered his mother as an angel who loved Christmas. Always prepared the best meals and wrapped the perfect presents with tight precision.

And now Bobby's tree stood generic and cheap. It was the first time that he'd erected one since his mother died. He'd loved Christmas too, but her death had taken that from him. Even though he was happy to finally be trying again, something was missing.

And Chipper. Chipper fucking Holiday. His queen; his star. God, how he lusted for her. Her pursed red lips, her bright eyes and her succulent cleavage. She looked extra cute with her curves barely contained in sexy Christmas lingerie.

Bobby stood to light a fire and celebrate the holiday alone.

Halfway to the fireplace something crashed down shooting out a puff of ash. Santa Claus, all fat and jolly and a little dusty stepped out.

"Fuck. That hurt," Santa said, rubbing his head.

Bobby gaped.

Santa patted the dirt off his red suit and counted down with his fingers.

3

2

1

Another thump and something else landed in the fireplace.

"Merry Christmas, Bobby," Santa boomed with a grin.

"Santa?"

"Who else Bobby Bitchlovich? It's nice to see you finally celebrating Christmas again."

"I don't even..." Bobby trailed off.

"But look around, Bobby," Santa said. "You're celebrating Christmas all alone and that tree, it's just not ready. That's why I'm here. I've got a present for you."

"A present?"

"Are you deaf, Bobby?"

Bobby's mouth opened, then closed.

"To celebrate you celebrating again, I'll give you a choice.

Would you like an angel, Bobby? Or a star?"

"I… uh, I don't know, a star, I guess."

"Excellent," Santa said. He turned to his bag that had fallen behind him in the fireplace. Only now did Bobby notice that the bag moved just a little bit. Santa opened it and pulled out a star.

A porn star.

Santa pulled out Chipper Holiday.

Bobby grinned but couldn't form words. He couldn't believe his luck.

Then Santa grabbed her by the waist hefted her over his head and shoved her, ass first, onto the top of the Christmas tree.

Bobby cried out as the apex of the tree went straight up her ass and came flying out her mouth in a spray of blood and tinsel that splattered the ceiling. Bobby's star twitched, dying slowly, impaled on his Christmas tree while Santa grinned.

"Wait a minute," Santa said. "I think maybe, we can… let's see. Yep!"

Then Santa grabbed Chipper by the legs and pulled her down even farther as another bag landed in the fireplace.

"It's a Christmas miracle, Bobby. We'll have room for both this year!"

Too scared and shocked to do anything but stare, Bobby watched as Santa hefted and then slammed Bobby's angel, just the way he remembered her, atop the Christmas tree. Santa turned to Bobby and grinned.

"Many deliveries to make, Bobby. I gotta split. Merry Christmas."

Santa left. But Bobby wasn't alone. He spent Christmas with his angel, his star, and a tree connecting them both.

✱A ❆HRISTMAS ℝEMEMBRANCE

JP Behrens

he last thing Wanda remembered was screaming. The scene seared itself into her mind. Nathan loomed over Simon. Blood dripped from one of the tools she and her husband had given him as a Christmas gift. A grateful smile contorted Nathan's face while Simon dead eyes stared at the ceiling.

"What happened? What have you done?" asked Charles. Her husband's voice pulled Wanda out of her stupor.

"Nathan... he..." Wanda's body shook with uncontrollable tremors as sobs erupted from her. She pulled the bloody, lifeless body of little Simon to her chest. She felt exposed ribs poking at her but didn't care. Her baby was gone.

"Nathan is dead, Wanda. How?" He sounded out of breath. His eyes flickered wildly around the room, searching for clues to explain the scene laid out in front of him.

She turned to find her other son on the floor, gazing at nothing. A bloody hammer lay next to him.

"Oh, God..."

"Wanda, we need to call the police. Figure this out."

She said nothing. Rocking her lost child back and forth, mumbling prayers, Wanda begged every power in the universe to fix it all.

Charles went to the phone, dialed two numbers, then hung up.

Wanda snapped her head up. "What are you doing?"

"I don't know what to say." His eyes glinted in the dark hallway. "I picked out the tool set. He used it on Simon, you used it on him. What are we going to do?"

"Jesus, Charles! Call the police! Maybe they can—" Wanda choked on the words and burst into tears again.

Charles hugged her. "We need to clean this up. School doesn't start for another few weeks. We can make it look like Nathan ran away with Simon. Stole him."

"What the hell are you talking about?"

"I don't know, Wanda!" Charles took a breath. "I don't want to go to jail. I'm scared. If we report this, everything Nathan did in those woods, to those animals, will come out. All I see is Simon's smiling face surrounded by tortured animals. Who takes the blame for that? Us!"

"Maybe we deserve it."

"No! We're good parents. Something was just off with Nathan. I know that now. I should have listened to you. He was our son, though. We need to protect him and this family." Charles motioned toward Nathan's body. "You'll go to prison for this, Wanda. Please."

Wanda nodded. The decision made.

She couldn't watch Charles fold the flesh back over Simon's cracked ribcage. He vomited twice before managing to replace the flaps of skin. They carried the boys into the garage. A large freezer stood in the corner. The motor's humming made Wanda think of a swarm of flies coming to feast on the dead. Wanda and Charles emptied the freezer of meat and then placed Nathan and Simon inside. They wrapped the bodies in tarp, covered them with a layer of ice, and then replaced the food. No one would be able to tell the children were there.

Charles sighed, satisfied with the work. All the tension drained from his face. Wanda wondered if without the reminder of the bodies, would he be able to live with the secret? Would he be able to construct a plausible story to live with while his children remained frozen away. Out of sight, out of mind?

They gathered the bloodied sheets and tools from the bedroom and burned them in a fire pit in the backyard before collapsing in bed for the evening. The next day, Charles removed the carpet from Simon's room and waited until nightfall to burn it. Wanda scraped and bleached the subfloor several times. No matter how much she cleaned, it seemed as if more blood oozed up. Charles realized bringing in one room's worth of carpeting would look bad. Not having carpet to throw out for that room would look worse. He tore out all the carpeting in the house, rolled it up, set the piles on the curb, and contracted someone to come in and install the new carpeting. A witness to say nothing seemed out of place if police got involved.

Charles' next project was building a fake wall in the garage. He planned on hiding a smaller freezer with the boys in it. He rented a truck, drove two towns over, and bought one. He used cash every at every step. The new freezer held the boys perfectly.

The work took up their entire weekends. Sleep became

only a word. When out in public, they did their best to act normal. Charles worked, Wanda stayed home "watching the kids," and after two weeks, school started. When the school called to ask about the boys' tardiness, Wanda acted surprised. After all, she watched them walk out the door that morning to the bus stop like always.

Worry naturally colored Wanda's words. Underneath the river of maternal confusion raged an undercurrent of fear and guilt. The school knew. Everyone knew. Charles' plan would never work.

The police investigated. They searched the house, the woods, and the surrounding areas and came up with nothing. Wanda bawled her eyes out, and Charles tried to hold it together, but the stress tore him down. The police declared the case cold within a few months and moved on to other investigations.

Life settled down. The whole town showed support and sympathy. Wanda wanted none of it. She wouldn't even open the door for her parents or take their calls when they tried to show their support. Each time someone offered condolences, the icy grip of her dead son tightened around her stomach. She started taking walks in the woods and found the spot where it all began. Charles went on with his life without her. He buried himself in work during the day and dove into whatever bottle the liquor store put on clearance at night. Wanda witnessed the world move forward, forever aware of the horrors decaying in the woods.

"I can't handle this anymore, Charles."

"Handle what?"

"Don't be like that."

"Our children were kidnapped, Wanda. That's it. We need to move on."

"I can't."

Charles sighed. The fog of bourbon on his breath told Wanda how far gone Charles already was.

"So get a hobby or something."

"A hobby? Are you serious? You can't erase the memory of what we did with crosswords and sudoku."

"I didn't do anything wrong! I protected this family from a shit storm." His eyes narrowed, focusing on Wanda. "*I* didn't do anything."

"Go screw yourself!"

Charles thundered out of the room. Wanda lifted a nearby picture of Simon smiling beside Nathan, dour as usual, and wept.

For weeks, Wanda moved through each day on autopilot. The people in town tried their best not to notice her disheveled clothes and hair. Some offered the occasional perfunctory nod, but most crossed the street to avoid the woman who lost her children along with the will to live. As Wanda hauled a bag of groceries down the sidewalk, her attention fell on the statue of a snarling bear on display outside of a store.

The glistening yellow-white teeth fascinated Wanda. The monster seemed ready to move at any moment. How something dead could appear alive again stirred a long-forgotten emotion in Wanda. Hope. She glanced up and read the name of the store. Marty's Mountings.

She slipped into the store and wandered around, taking in the musty aroma of so much fur. All of the animals stood poised, ready to spring.

"Can I help you, ma'am?"

Wanda nearly dropped her bags. "I'm sorry. I just saw the bear and felt the urge to come in and look around."

"One of my best. Took forever to mount though. I'm sorry for your loss, by the way."

"Thank you. Tell me, is it hard to do this sort of thing?"

The man behind the counter shrugged. "It has its moments, like anything else. Some projects are more difficult than others."

"So anyone can do it?"

"Thinking of taking up a hobby?"

Wanda didn't answer. Possibilities danced through her mind. All these creatures. Dead, but cleaned and repaired. All the violence removed.

Wanda left the store without another word. As she drove back home, the yells of the taxidermist waving her forgotten bags of groceries went unnoticed.

Weeks spent on the internet educated Wanda on the basics of skinning and tanning. Of the two methods, she chose to use the animal's natural attributes to tan the hides. The modern method would raise Charles' suspicions. Explaining canisters of battery acid and boxes of bran flakes would instigate an argument. He did mention she should find a hobby, but if he didn't approve, she didn't want the confrontation. The urge to repair the damage Nathan caused needed fulfillment. Through this, she could save what remained of her family and forge a new path into the future.

It took hours to dig up one of Nathan's victims from the clearing where he performed his "experiments." She found a winter-preserved cat, stiff with rigor and frost. In another spot, she dug up a dog with no legs. She remembered Nathan beating the poor thing. She would keep the dog frozen until she learned a little more about taxidermy. She wanted to do the poor animal justice.

After dragging the two animals home, she placed the

dog into the freezer in the garage and brought the cat to the kitchen. She put the cat on the cutting board and scoured the kitchen for a sharp knife. After washing the cat to remove all dirt from its fur, she dried it and searched for the best place to make the first incision.

With a slit across the belly, careful not to puncture the stomach or intestines, Wanda began. Easing the skin back from the meat turned out to be more difficult than expected. The skin gripped the meat as if super glued on. Sweat soon dripped from Wanda's brow and her arm burned with the effort of peeling back the skin and slicing it away bit by bit. Several times, she needed to stop and force back the bile in her throat. The stench of blood and death reminded her too much of the night she lost Simon.

Once finished skinning the cat up to its neck, she took a rusty pair of pliers and extracted the cat's teeth. Many pulled loose without effort. Others cracked and chipped under inexperienced hands. While she wrestled with one of the teeth in the back, the cat's head ripped away from the torso. A dry heave exploded from Wanda. Sweat rained from her head as she coughed into the sink. It took her several minutes to recover and continue the grisly work.

A mangled skin lay draped across the counter, a furry train trailing behind the dismembered skull. Wanda lifted the bloody cutting board holding the remaining offal and tipped it over the trashcan. The wet plop made Wanda want to wretch again. Only the mission to save her family pushed her to finish. She lifted a small paring knife and, with all the care she could manage, began skinning the skull. With such a small creature, the knife proved too large and she ended up with many small bits of skin to be sewn back together.

She filled a medium-sized pot with water and set it to boil. She cleaned the skin while she waited, scraping away any remnants of fat and flesh. Once the water began bubbling, she lifted the cat's skull. She gazed into the lifeless eyes covered in gore and steeled herself. She gripped the skull and cracked it on the edge of the pot like an egg. A gray lump of meat resembling a chewed up bit of gum splashed into the water. She tossed the skull aside and waited for the mixture to turn into a soupy paste.

As the pasted cooled, Wanda scrubbed the hide and fur again. She used a spoon to apply the boiled down brains to the hide. With plastic cleaning gloves, she worked the mixtures into the skin. After every bit of the hide looked treated, she stored it in a freezer bag, which went into the refrigerator, hidden behind a wall of old, unused condiment bottles. She finished cleaning the kitchen just moments before Charles came in.

"What's that smell?"

"Hmm?"

"Did you put out steaks and they went bad?"

Wanda paused. "Yes. Want me to order pizza?"

❆ ❆ ❆

After Charles left for work, Wanda dressed and went out back. She found the old fire pit, coated in rust, near the back edge of the property. Moldy leaves and stagnant water were plastered to the bottom of the basin but didn't take long to remove. She withdrew a coarse scrubbing pad and began brushing away the rust. Once the fire pit appeared clean, Wanda pulled it closer to the center of the yard and filled it with leftover charcoal. It didn't take much effort to light. She added some of the wet sticks and logs found along the edge of the woods and soon the pit produced a tower of smoke.

The skin in the refrigerator came out of the bag feeling

slimy and smelling rancid. She washed the hide off, readying it to be smoked. A massive amount of the hair came off, disappearing down the drain.

"No, no, no, no."

Watching the hair swirl away devastated Wanda. Her attempt at bringing some kind of life back to the beast Nathan slaughtered failed before her eyes. She took a deep breath and reminded herself of the ultimate goal. Bigger tragedies still required fixing. This attempt provided valuable experience and the knowledge to avoid preventable mistakes when her efforts mattered most. She finished cleaning the hide and found a small sewing kit. Stitching the skin back together took a long time. So many mistakes. Just another skill to hone. Once the skin appeared to be back in one piece, she sewed it two of the sides together then sewed the bottom together to form a kind of bag. The thing resembled a moist paper bag ready to become papier mâché. A plant hanger stood out just outside the backdoor and served as a perfect device for hanging the skin over the smoking pit. The opening filled with smoke.

A strong wind blew the smoke into Wanda's eyes again and again, so she watched from the kitchen window, making sure the fire stayed under control. After an hour, she went out to flip the bag inside out and rehang it until the smoking process finished. Wanda worried a neighbor might call the fire department. No one came. When it was finished, she covered the pit to stifle the fire and smoke.

The end result appeared to be a ragged mess unfit for use as a dust rag. Whole patches of hair had fallen out and bits of the skin shrank or broke as a result of the smoking. Worst of all, the hide became inflexible. The rough texture reminded Wanda of rawhide. After checking the process online, she discovered a skipped step. Before smoking the skin,

it needed to be stretched and broken down to retain plia-
bility.

The deformed skin bag rested on her lap. She considered
it, staring at the two sewn slits where the creature's eyes
once rested and thought about repeating the process on later
projects. Working with the brain matter of a small creature
and concealing the skin in the refrigerator proved possible,
but larger projects would require more secrecy and time.
Turning a larger brain into paste and smearing it over a skin
might be too much to handle. Wanda decided the modern-
ized method would be better.

The clock showed most of the day had passed her by.
Charles would be home soon. She went to the garage and
opened the freezer door. A high-pitched yelp escaped Wanda at
the sight of the legless dog.

"I forgot about you."

Pushing the corpse aside, she reached in and pulled out
some frozen vegetables and ground beef. As she closed the
lid, she wondered if they had the right ingredients for meat-
loaf tucked away in the crisper.

❄ ❄ ❄

Life for Wanda and Charles morphed into something
close to normal over the next few months. She found that
hiding her projects was easier than expected. She stored
everything in the basement, turning the small area into a
makeshift workshop. Taxidermy took over her days. The
food in the freezer disappeared. New projects filled the
space. After attempting to preserve the legless dog she realized the animals brutalized by her son were too far gone to
be of any use.

Wanda carried the mounted, mostly hairless dog torso

into Nathan's room. The space remained unchanged since Christmas Eve except for the new carpet and the addition of Wanda's projects. She set the dog down on Nathan's desk, knocking down the neat pile of notebooks in the corner.

"Damn it."

She crawled onto the floor to gather them. In bold, black marker, animal silhouettes marked each notebook as dedicated to the study of cats, dogs, squirrels, and more. Morbid curiosity forced her to open one with a picture of a dog drawn on the front. Inside, she found notes on musculature, pain tolerance, measurements, and how long it took them to die under certain conditions. Nathan had even taken notes on the level of pain displayed during an animal's final moments. The number of animals necessary to compile so much information weighed on Wanda. Still, the date she found in the books appeared useful. She needed more practice if she wanted to be ready, and the number of suitable, deceased subjects she found in the woods dwindled daily.

At first, strays wandered into the backyard, enticed by the odor of grilled meat, and vanished. But they lived in a good neighborhood. Not a place where you find strays often. When flyers for missing pets littered every telephone pole and street lamp, Wanda became a shut-in. The freezer burst with the bodies of animals. No room for food remained. Still, every night, dinner found its way to the table.

"What is this?" asked Charles.

"Do you not like it?"

"It's fine, just don't recognize it."

"Just something I found in the freezer. I'll try a different way of seasoning it next time."

"Next time?"

"We have quite a bit. You know what they say, 'Waste not, want not.'"

Wanda marveled at how much money they saved by not going to the store. With the additional funds, she went on-line and splurged on a professional set of precision knives, large and small.

She worked in the basement night and day with an increasing quantity of quality tools, perfecting her skills, always moving toward the ultimate goal. As each specimen went up on the mounting forms ordered on-line and delivered to her door, she refined her technique. With every improvement, Wanda knew it would all be okay. The horrors of last Christmas would soon be erased and life renewed.

She carved the fat and flesh off the piece of skin draped over a fleshing board, marveling at how much fat fell away with each slice, when a loud crash echoed from the garage.

"WHAT THE HELL IS THIS?"

Wanda glanced at the clock. She'd lost track of time and forgotten to get dinner ready. Charles must have gone to the freezer to pull something out. She dropped her tools and rushed up the stairs. In the garage, Charles leaned over the freezer, staring at the pile of cats and dogs, raccoons and foxes, all gutted and laid out.

"Close the freezer, Charles."

"What is all this?"

"Mine. Now close the freezer."

"My God, what have you done? What are you thinking?"

Wanda remained silent.

Charles swallowed. "When was the last time you went shopping?"

"I haven't needed to."

Charles paled and went weak at the knees.

"I'm going to fix everything, Charles. You'll see. Just close the freezer and let me finish."

Charles ripped his gaze from the animals and stared at his wife. At first, he couldn't understand, then he glanced at the wall and remembered for the first time in a very long time what they'd hidden so long ago.

"You can't—"

"CLOSE THE FUCKING FREEZER!"

Charles slammed the freezer door closed. "I need to call the police. This has gone far enough."

Wanda stepped forward and pushed Charles back. After months of gutting, skinning, and scraping, Wanda's arms shot out like well-oiled pistons. Charles fell back, tripping over himself.

"Wanda! This is crazy."

"Charles, please, I'm doing this for us."

She reached out for a thick rope hanging on the wall. "Don't struggle, Charles, I don't want to bruise you. This won't hurt. I promise."

Charles fought back with every ounce of strength he possessed, but Wanda had grown stronger. In time, she would fix this, too.

Christmas raced closer. Wanda sat at Nathan's dusty desk, making notations in his journals, adding to the knowledge with some of her own insights. His discoveries made Wanda so proud. Such an intelligent boy, his diagrams of muscles helped Wanda mount her specimens in lifelike ways. All around Nathan's room stood different animals mounted in varying degrees of skill, all special in their own way. Almost forgotten, the first skin she tried to tan leaned in a dusty corner. Falling apart, decaying, she learned from those mistakes, and though a complete loss, she refused to throw it away. It represented a turning point. The moment she knew everything would be okay.

Bills piled up. The television went dark. The phones

were disconnected. Only the electric and gas companies received payments since Wanda still needed them for her work. Her efforts spilled out of Nathan's room and lined the floors and walls of her dingy home. Nothing mattered outside of the ultimate goal. Some of the earlier pieces attracted vermin into the house, which only provided Wanda with more material on which to practice.

Time didn't exist within the house. Only work. She glanced out the window and saw the overgrown garden, the wild grass, and the weed-infested sidewalk. A few notices from the city hid in the pile of unopened mail at the foot of her door. None of it mattered. Time was running out. The sight of snow, however, stirred something in Wanda. She dove for the pile of mail and found a piece with a recent date on it. October. She needed to get ready.

She went over her supplies and made a list of things she would need. The nearest big box store was three towns away. She cleaned herself up just enough to appear present-able and drove for the first time in months. On the way, she passed the mall where she and Charles had purchased the tool kit Nathan used last Christmas to open up Simon. Tears of joy squeezed out of her eyes as hope swelled in her chest. This Christmas would be different. She could fix everything.

The clerk at the store scanned through Wanda's purchases. Four large carts full of bran flakes and battery acid formed a train in front of her.

"You like cereal, I see."

Wanda gazed at the clerk in a daze. "What?"

The clerk pointed at the boxes. "You really like bran flakes."

"Not especially."

The clerk stared at the block of boxes. His face twisted in confusion when he started scanning the bottles of acid. Wanda ignored him and handed him a wad of crumpled bills and tarnished change. One of the workers helped carry everything to her vehicle. Wanda drove the crammed car home with a few bottles of acid on her lap.

Something didn't feel right. Incomplete.

Christmas needed to be a family affair. She drove by her parents' house. She hadn't seen them since last Christmas. They'd left right after dinner and never saw their grand-children again. On a torn bit of cardboard from one of the cereal boxes, Wanda scrawled an invitation to Christmas dinner. After slipping it through their mail slot, she drove home. A great deal of work remained ahead.

❄ ❄ ❄

The aroma of meat slow-roasting in the oven with potatoes, carrots, celery, and parsnips couldn't drown the sharp, acidic odor soaked into the soul of the house. Wanda clicked her tongue, annoyed by the stench of vinegar and musk. She needed today to be perfect. The first good day in a year full of darkness. An over-decorated pine tree stood in the living room. The dining room table twinkled under the soft light of candles. For the first time in a year, her parents were coming over for dinner. Another Christmas had arrived. Time for for-giveness. Time for family.

Wanda hummed to herself as she stirred one of the large pots boiling on the stove. Flashes of that horrible night one year ago invaded her cocoon of holiday spirit, but she shook them off. Everything would be different this year. She pre-pared for this day most of the year. It would be perfect. Charles kept saying she needed to move on, to go out into the world and live again. He never understood. Too much damaged needed repairing. It took a long time to develop the skills needed to make everything just right, but the time wasn't wasted.

Wanda checked the table to make sure everything looked clean and tidy. The roast smelled of rosemary and thyme. Candles flickered in the dark dining room, casting dancing shadows against the cobweb-covered walls. The contrast of the perfect white tablecloth and the dirt-covered floor mirrored the overall state of the house. Large Christmas displays lit up the outside as music played and a plastic Santa waved at passersby. The overgrown, crystalline lawn sparkled weirdly under the flickering lights. A twisted, jagged wonderland of holiday cheer and neglect.

Headlights flashing across the front windows signaled her parents' arrival. She ran to the door, smoothed her best dress, and checked her hair and makeup in the hall mirror. A green, tarnished patina obscured her image. Still, Wanda nodded, satisfied.

"Would it kill Charles to clean up this yard?" asked Wanda's father. His voice sounded muffled by the front door. Wanda's stilted smile never wavered as she awaited their knock.

"Now, Harold, be nice. You know this hasn't been easy for them."

"It hasn't been easy for anyone, Margery. Still—"

"Let's just try and be cheerful. Remember, she finally reached out to us. Now is the time to repair the damage in our lives."

Wanda giggled. If only they knew how right they were.

The knock came. Wanda opened the door and gave her mother a tight hug.

"I'm so glad you both came."

"We're so happy you invited us. We've missed you so much."

"I know. I'm sorry. Tonight that all changes. I promise."

Wanda took their coats and hung them on nearby hooks, clearing away a wall of webbing in the process.

"When was the last time you cleaned, Wanda?"

"Harold, shush. I'm sure she's been busy."

Wanda laughed too loud and too long. "You have no idea."

She led them into the living room and bade them sit on the sofa. A cloud of dust enveloped them.

"Dear God! What is going on here, Wanda?" her father asked.

"You'll see. Just wait here for one second."

Wanda scampered like a child into the dining room. "Charles, could you please get Dad a drink, as well? Thanks."

After she removed the roast from the stove and plated it, she set it on the table. "OK, you can come in."

Cautious, unsure of what they would find, her parents entered the dining room. Wanda stood off to the side like a game show model, holding her hands out to present a prize. The candles didn't offer enough light. The silhouette of Charles holding a glass of bourbon greeted them. Margery let out a soft sigh of relief.

"Good to see you, Charles. How are you?"

Silence.

"Charles?" Harold's voice quavered in the darkness.

"Mom, Dad. Look who else is here! Surprise!"

The two smaller figures sat at the table, unnoticed in the shadows.

"Who—?"

Margery choked on her words.

"Oh my god! You found them! Oh my god! It's a miracle. Where were they?" cried Margery.

Harold gripped his chest. Loud, labored breathing brought on by shock crippled his ability to move.

Wanda leaned in and whispered conspiratorially, "They were never gone. We hid them." She put a finger to her lips. "Shhhh…"

Wanda grabbed her mother by the arm and pulled her closer. "Say hi, Nathan, Simon. Your grandmother is here to join us. We're all going to be a family again."

The light glittered off glassy eyes.

"Boys! I'm so—"

Margery placed a hand on Nathan's shoulder and froze. She touched his cheek. She pressed a little harder. Nathan's entire body tipped like a statue. Margery gasped and pulled her hand as if burned. The boy and the chair, all as one, rattled on the floor for a second before coming to a rest. "What's wrong with his skin, Wanda?"

"Nothing. It's perfect." Wanda's voice fell an octave. A subtle threat mixed into the response.

"But—"

"It's perfect!"

Wanda punctuated the statement by slamming a carving knife down into the table.

Margery fell back a step, crashing into the chair, tipping Nathan over and into Simon. They both collapsed like human dominoes.

Harold grunted and coughed, desperate for air. Margery screamed. Wanda sighed and went over to lift them back into place.

"Now, boys, stop fighting. It's Christmas. I won't have you repeating last year."

"Wanda, your father. He needs help."

Wanda glanced at her father curled up in pain on the ground. She lifted him by the shoulders and plopped him into a chair at the head of the table. "There you go."

"Call and ambulance, for God's sake!" screamed Margery.

"It'll be fine, Mom. Now get into your seat. It's dinner time. It took me forever to cook this roast. It's bone in!"

Wanda lifted Margery off the ground and forced her into a seat beside Harold. "It's remarkable how much this tastes like a beef-pork mix. With the right seasonings, you'd never know what you were eating."

Wanda pulled the carving knife free from the table. "Normally, I wouldn't cook this, but tonight is special." She sliced a thin piece from the roast and laid the serving on her mother's plate. The unique texture and scent brought confused wrinkles to Margery's pale face.

Margery gawked at Wanda, lost in the madness of the night. Wanda continued cutting bits off the roast, placing slabs of meat on everyone's plates. Harold's breaths turned wheezy and shallow.

Margery regarded the smoking meat. "What is this, Wanda? What have you done?"

Wanda slipped a tender portion into her mouth and chewed. "You know the old saying." She ran her hand lovingly through Simon's hair. The candlelight flickered, revealing a taut, smiling face. Bits of string stitching hung loose from his chin and scalp. Lifeless eyes stared at nothing.

"Waste not, want not."

No S*ugar P*lum F*airies

Steven Bigwood

NEWS HEADLINES: DECEMBER 24

NORAD'S SANTA TRACKING KICKS OFF TODAY AT 5 PM MST

The Los Angeles Reporter

EVIL MAY COME YOUR WAY ON XMAS EVE!

The Daily Enquirer

> *T'was the night before Christmas and all through the house,*
> *not a creature was stirring...*

xcept for the twins. Michael, a freckled 8-year-old hellion with red hair to match his temperament, was the elder by 30 minutes. His sister Kelly, also freckled and crowned with fire, was honey and maple syrup compared to his vinegar and hot sauce. Their parents, still asleep upstairs, had instructed them to stay in bed until morning, but Michael, who refused to be refused, had cajoled Kelly into disobeying, and the two now mounted a late-night Christmas Eve vigil for Santa Claus at the bottom of the staircase.

Kelly, dressed in a flannel nightgown decorated with Christmas trees and snowmen, crouched near the bottom riser, timidly clutching Sir Wuffle, a brown teddy bear who had been her companion since birth and was now flattened by years of use as a comfort-giving pillow. Still groggy, she rubbed her eyes with tiny fists, not only to deny sleep, but also to squelch tears that her disobedience was summoning from her worried conscience. Michael wore pajamas patterned with Formula One racers and, like the cars, and in contrast to Kelly, he was ready to speed into the living room adjoining the staircase the instant that the imaginary green flag dropped.

For Michael, who no longer believed in the gift-giver from the North Pole, the staircase stakeout had a dual purpose: first, to prove to his sister that Santa was a fairy tale, and secondly, to feed his own mean streak, which his parents had put on a forced diet that holiday season by threatening to ignore his gift list. Kelly was there for one reason only: her twin brother, who happily kicked cats and plucked wings off butterflies, had essentially kidnaped her into becoming an accomplice. As for Santa, she didn't need to see him to believe in him; she knew that he existed.

Christmas at the twins' house was always a pageant of the five senses: for the nose, the woodsy fragrance of fresh pine, the spicy scent of cloves, nutmeg, and cinnamon in hot apple cider, and the aroma of freshly baked cookies encrusted with crystals of colored sugar, with the cider and cookies serving double duty as purveyors to eager taste buds of seasonal bliss; for the ears, a crackling fire and cheery holiday songs; for the touch, embroidered tableaus on stockings hung from the mantle with care, the texture of silk ribbons and bows on gifts beneath the tree, and the warmth of dancing flames from the fireplace as it caressed the skin; and for the eyes, the blinking of multi-colored lights repeated as happy winks in silver tinsel and as twinkling stars in oval-, diamond-, and icicle-shaped glass decorations as thin and fragile as a dragonfly's wing, and especially in the delicate balls of glass that, like so many convex mirrors, reflected hemispherical panoramas of the entire room.

The same mixture of Christmas magic and merriment is always at its strongest on Christmas Eve, and this wondrous elixir was the only solace for Kelly as she waited for her brother's next defiant move, reluctant even to peer into the living room to see the tree except by extending Sir Wuffle at arm's length around the corner as a periscope, a job Sir Wuffle admirably fulfilled in her imagination, but for which his black button eyes were not especially well-suited.

Michael did not need an extra set of imaginary eyes to observe the layout of the living room. He boldly stood at its entrance with legs apart like a junior version of the Colossus of Rhodes and, from that vantage point, could see that the patterned apron around the base of the tree was no longer visible under the plethora of dazzling presents that obscured it. Some gifts were stacked neatly and others haphazardly, and their acute angles often fashioned colorful hills and unexpected tunnels through which an antique circus train with a cow-catcher slowly chugged as it navigated its way around the perimeter of the tree. Assessing the vista before him, it was obvious to Michael that his parents had not yet substituted in as proxies for Santa, not only because the cookies and milk that Kelly had left for Santa remained on the hearth, but also, and most tellingly, because the stockings, which were a telltale sign of a purported visit from the North Pole's celebrated resident, remained saggingly limp and devoid of gifts.

The still-empty stockings and the knowledge that his parents wouldn't deliver Santa's share of Christmas until sunrise gave Michael the go-ahead to rush into the living room and skid to a stop on his knees right in front of the presents beneath the tree. Kelly cautiously followed her brother, dragging Sir Wuffle by a paw across the carpet. Rather than settling in front of the blinking tree like her twin, she sat on the flagstone hearth in front of the fireplace, where embers still glowed from the yule log that had burned there earlier in the evening. With the beknighted teddy now in her lap, she lovingly surveyed the varied decorations on the tree instead of scanning the presents below it.

Michael was already unwrapping presents indiscriminately, and Kelly wanted to distance herself from such outright disobedience. Even if it meant that she would have to unjustly share blame as Michael's co-conspirator in the stealthy trek downstairs, maintaining her distance from her twin would at least allow her to plead innocent to the premature unwrapping of someone else's presents and the mayhem of ripped paper and frazzled ribbon that the prohibited activity was producing. Still a child, she obviously didn't analyze the situation in exactly that way, but she was nevertheless old enough and smart enough and had enough experience as her brother's shanghaied accessory to know that the parental penalty was always directly proportional to one's proximity to the crime.

Kelly was actually quite happy to simply stare at the decorations, which had entranced her since the tree went up in early December. Her favorite was the large, apple-red glass ball dangling from the edge of a branch near the middle of the tree. It was an antique ornament like those in the beautifully illustrated Christmas storybooks that her parents bought for her. It had a shimmering translucency that she had never seen in any other ornament, and she especially adored the delicate gold design surrounding both poles as interwoven branches and leaves.

Just as a common word begins to sound like gibberish if it's repeated again and again, sometimes our eyes trick us when we stare at an object for too long. At first, Kelly thought that the thin column of pinkish-gray smoke was simply an illusion, as it seemed to curl out of the antique globe hanging on Michael's right, and then she became frightened that the ornately decorated tree had somehow caught fire like trees the News reported every Christmas. Michael was too busy to see the strange cloud spiraling upward past his head. He was still absorbed in ripping open presents that were meant for others and was growing increasingly frustrated when he could find nothing that he had asked for, and even worse, nothing that he hadn't asked for.

The column of smoke that had emerged at first as a pencil-thin stream from the apple-red ball increased in diameter as it streamed into the air, forming itself into a miniature cyclone that was wide at its top and narrow at its point of exit from the decoration. Colors also had begun to coalesce within the cloud. Its pinkish-gray hue became the same apple-red color in some spots as its host ornament, with intermittent patches of white as pure as table sugar and with stripes of carbon black reminiscent of skid marks around its middle and at the bulging apex of the now-whirling column.

These changes in appearance were coupled with a whooshing sound, like a strong wind racing down a narrow passageway. The new and unusual sound that broke the Christmas Eve quiet in the room finally caught Michael's attention, and he looked up from his kneeling position in front of the presents in time to see the rising column loop downward and begin to take form as it contacted the carpet. A moment later, a rotund figure appeared before them. He wore black boots with curled-over rims and was dressed in a red jacket and pants, each trimmed with white fur at the collar, sleeve ends, and pants bottoms. After placing a large sack brimming with gifts down at his side and adjusting his wide, black belt so that it fit more comfortably around the girth of his belly, the white-bearded man turned to Kelly and, with a hearty laugh, bellowed "MERRY CHRISTMAS!" in a voice that was imperceptible to grownup ears.

Michael, a confirmed non-believer rather than a mere skeptic, stood up and glared incredulously at Santa Claus. His mouth was agape and his eyes were beginning to assume the appearance of cartoonish ping-pong balls. His present state would have left him momentarily incapable of speech in any event, but even if his lips had formed words, nothing he could have said would have mattered to Santa, who was now standing in front of Kelly and patting her on the head like a kindly uncle who was very happy to see his niece again.

"Ho! Ho! Ho! Kelly," Santa boomed in a bass voice that once again filled their heads without vibrating even a single molecule in the living room air. "Tell me, Little One, where are the snacks? My belly's begging for a cookie."

Kelly, simultaneously astonished and overjoyed, pointed to a plate on the opposite end of the hearth. The round-bellied man tromped over to the plate in his heavy boots and sandwiched together three of the gaily decorated cookies that Kelly had helped to make; he then gobbled them down with obvious relish. Kelly had left carrots on the same plate for Dancer and the other high fliers, and Santa deposited them into large fur-rimmed pockets on either side of his red jacket. Then he wiped cookie crumbs from his white moustache and ample beard and turned back toward Kelly.

Before he could speak, Kelly said in her tiny voice, "I thought you'd be coming down the chimney, Santa."

"Ho! Ho! Ho! The embers from your yule fire are still hot, Kelly, so I took a different route. Not every house has a chimney, or even a tree with decorations, particularly a special decoration like the red one, so sometimes I just come in through a crack under a window or through a leak in the roof. A smoke wisp can slip in just about anywhere."

By this time, Michael had tolerated enough of Santa's inattention and tried to force the spotlight back onto himself, believing, as always, that circumstance had somehow anointed him as the darling prince of the house. Not only was his self-assessment completely erroneous—as evidenced by the entries in Santa's Big Book of Good and Bad—but he also made the mistake of drawing attention back to himself in the worst possible way that a child could before Santa had reached into his bulging sack to pass out presents to one and all.

"Where are MY PRESENTS!" Michael wasn't asking a question; he was making a demand, and it would have been an impolite interjection even if it had been directed at a mere mortal.

Kelly cringed when she heard the words come out of her brother's mouth. She hoped that he wouldn't ruin this miraculous visit for both of them with his usual unpleasant behavior. Santa, however, appeared unperturbed by Michael's outburst. He turned toward Kelly's twin and, standing with arms akimbo, simply stared at Michael as though he were contemplating the best way to deal with a fly buzzing annoyingly in his ear.

"I said 'WHERE ARE MY PRES...!'" Michael was unable to complete his renewed demand. Santa had placed a gloved finger to the mouth that had just made three Christmas cookies disappear in a flash, and Michael may as well have had a zipper on his mouth, because Santa tightly sealed it. As it were, he contorted his mouth in a futile attempt to make sounds emerge and looked like a dog who was trying to dislodge a glob of peanut butter from the roof of its mouth.

"Ho! Ho! Ho! Presents, you say!" Santa replied to Michael. "You have unwrapped gifts that were not yours to open. You have ruined Christmas for everyone else. You are not just a bad boy; you are a mean and selfish boy and a terrible brother. This year, even coal is not enough of a punishment for you."

Looking past Michael at the opened boxes and litter of wrapping paper and ribbon under the tree, Santa waved his hand in a full circle and the gifts returned to their pre-Michaelian state, reassembling themselves as if in a film shown in reverse. When everything had been returned to its original state, Santa reached into his bag, and with a wave of his other gloved hand, gifts for Kelly magically appeared under the tree beside and on top of those already arrayed there. Then Santa turned his attention once again to Michael.

"And now, Michael, my gift to you," he boomed in a voice meant for minds, not ears.

With a wave of his hand that traced a downward spiral, Santa began to transform once again into a column of smoke. The first tones to appear were the red, white, and black that had formed his Christmas clothes; next in order was the pinkish-gray that had originally colored the column. Then, swirling faster, the smoky column turned a menacing dark gray with tones of deep black and murky brown. As the spinning slowed, a new figure coalesced on the carpet where Santa had previously stood.

With few exceptions, Santa is seen as a plump and jolly grandfatherly figure who can bring happiness to children just through his appearance and demeanor. Add presents, candy canes, elves, and flying reindeer and Santa Claus has no peer; he is the epitome of generosity and, as the arbiter of childhood behavior, the paradigm of what is just and good. His *alter ego*, however, was the horrific opposite of the jolly soul headquartered at the North Pole.

Twisted into a permanent stoop because his human-like torso was melded with a goat's hind-quarters as its bottom half, the newly formed creature stood on cloven hooves; its head was crowned with a billy goat's backswept horns, and also featured snorting, heart-shaped caprine nostrils. Its fiery red, almond-shaped eyes, however, were clearly the devil's contribution, while its snarling mouth was studded with sharp, pointed teeth that were bared and ready to rip and tear. Santa's red outfit was trimmed in soft white fur, but the creature was completely covered in an unhealthy looking pelt that ranged in color from jet black to various shades of sickly brown.

Like Santa, the creature grasped a large sack but held it in a clawed hand rather than in the grasp of a soft white glove. From time to time bulges appeared on the surface of the sack. They were clearly not caused by presents shifting around inside. Instead, the bulges seemed to be caused by something that was trying to get out. In its other claw, the creature gripped a bundle of birch switches bound at one end with a leather thong and, in perverse mockery of the holiday season, tiny bells attached to thatches of fur tinkled sonorously whenever the creature moved.

"Ho! Ho! Ho! *Gruß vom Krampus!*" the creature bellowed in a guttural language that sounded only inside Michael's head. "The Krampus greets you!" the voice gruffly repeated.

Whether it was just fear or some form of insidious magic, Michael was frozen in place by the sight and the voice of the Krampus, and he was still unable to move when a hideous claw tipped with knife-edged nails snatched him up by the back of his pajama top and hoisted him into the air as if he were a puppy being lifted by the loose skin at the nape of its neck. Still immobilized, Michael could not even kick or scream as the Krampus shoved him inside the dark mouth of the bulging sack that the creature held in its other claw.

Once inside the sack, whose interior was barely illuminated by the meager light of blinking bulbs on the Christmas tree, Michael understood why it seemed to bulge so unnaturally: it was filled with young children like himself, and the bulges were caused by the flailing elbows, knees, and feet of those who vainly tried to escape.

To preserve her belief in a benevolent Santa, Kelly was mentally shielded from witnessing the unfolding drama, and simply stood frozen in the same spot clutching Sir Wuffle to her chest. Michael, however, was experiencing the futility that the other children felt as captives within a sack that was inexplicably bigger on the inside than the outside. Then, without warning, the situation got worse: a harsh thrashing delivered painful blows to every part of his body that was unfortunate enough to touch the sack's inner surface. Had he been back on the outside and able to see what was happening, he would have witnessed the Krampus beating the sides of the sack with his bundle of birch branches.

Thwamp! Thwamp! The awful sound echoed coldly inside the sack again and again as the Krampus' swats seemed to find their mark everywhere on Michael's incarcerated body.

Finally, with the same alacrity that had marked his insertion into the sack, Michael was plucked back into the world of colored lights blinking on the Christmas tree and was dumped unceremoniously on the carpet, with the Krampus staring down menacingly at his supine body. And just as suddenly, another transformation occurred: Santa reappeared, replacing the Krampus.

"Ho! Ho! Ho! Merry Christmas, Michael!" Santa said, his voice jolly again. "Now you understand that Christmas is not just wooden soldiers and sugar plum fairies. I bring gifts for good children and leave a lump of coal for those who have been naughty. But everything has a price, even lumps of coal, and there are certain economies that must be met in this Christmas commerce. That's where my alter ego conveniently fits in. Returning to the North Pole with an empty sled is bad business. Happily, there are children who are bad beyond naughty. As Krampus, I give them a final chance at redemption before they become part of my other Yuletide delivery work. Let this be a lesson to you, Michael, or next Christmas I will drop you off in hell on my way home like the others in Krampus' bag."

NEWS HEADLINES: DECEMBER 25

UNEXPLAINED CHRISTMAS EVE DISAPPEARANCES WORLDWIDE

XBC TV Nightly News

PROVEN: SANTA HAS MULTIPLE PERSONALITY DISORDER

The Daily Enquirer

THE JINN THROUGHOUT HISTORY

Professor Rolf Bagelman, Ph.D., Gandalf University Press, Vienna, Austria (2013)

"Known as *jinni* in Arabia and before that as *tribicenas* on the Canary Islands, there is no longer any doubt that the Easter Bunny, Tooth Fairy, Santa Claus, and other magical creatures, perhaps even Mary Poppins, are actually *jinn*, or in today's vernacular, genies."

CRACK!

Gerard Griffin

rack!
Winter logs popped in the hearth like a gunshot, waking Angie from her dreams of trees and tinsel. She sat up, blinking in the firelight, and took stock of her surroundings. Paper chains festooned the walls like gaudy cobwebs and a shanty town of Christmas cards crept across the mantelpiece. The firewood had been ill-stored and the thick smoke had already made Angie drowsy; a stiff brandy had helped to finish the job. She lifted the bottle from the table and refilled her glass. Christmas Eve, a roaring fire, and a fine glass of Courvoisier. What could be better?

She looked over at the Christmas tree that stood in the corner of the room, then at the solitary gift beneath its branches. *Thomas*, she thought. *That's what could be better*. The present was from him. He had sent it from Germany, where he was barracked with the 20th Armored Brigade. The Iron Fists, they called themselves—a stupid bloody name, she thought. One to crush her heart.

She wiped away a tear as she knocked back the rest of her drink and looked at the carriage clock above the fireplace. It was partly obscured by greetings cards from family and friends, filled with their wishes for the festive season. Angie had replied to each of them, penning her own message of seasonal cheer from a heart ill-suited to the task.

This was her first Christmas on her own—no husband, no son. Four dozen cards from her nearest and dearest attested to the fact that she still had people thinking about her, but they brought her no spark of joy. She didn't expect a lot—no invitation to Christmas dinner or anything like that—but where were the expressions of concern for her, all alone at this time of year? Not festive enough, she supposed. That's the sort of notion that might ruin somebody else's Christmas.

It was half-past eleven—nearly Christmas morning—and she had but one present to herself. Two, if she counted the bottle of brandy she had bought, but that thought was so depressing that she pushed it aside. Perhaps she hadn't been a very good girl this year. She wanted to laugh at that, but there was nobody here to share it. She picked up the present and turned it over in trembling hands. It was around three feet in length and heavy, too. It had sat under the tree for the last week, and every day she had picked it up, tested its weight, and read the label.

Mum,
Happy Christmas.
Love Tommy.

Five words shouldn't make her this sad. She was so

proud of him—Thomas Michael Harton, a soldier in Her Majesty's Armed Forces. Another tear trickled down her cheek and she brushed it away, chiding herself for her foolishness. She tore off the paper where she stood, casting it into the fireplace where it flared briefly before being consumed. Within there was a plain box made of lacquered cardboard. A sideways glance at the clock confirmed that it was still twenty minutes shy of midnight, but what the hell?

She took the lid off the box and saw a thin sheet of parchment laying atop a pile of packing peanuts. After a few seconds of trying to manipulate both box and lid, she gave up and threw the lid into the fire. In an instant the smoke turned thick and black, flames licking at the treated coating, and Angie started to cough. She retreated to the comfort of her armchair, filled her glass again, and started to read.

Dear Mum, the letter said, *I'm having a great time here and being looked after really well. I know you wish I was at home with you, so I've sent you someone to stand guard over Christmas. All my love, Tommy.*

Tears that had nothing to do with the smoke blotted the paper as Angie pulled out handfuls of polystyrene lumps and dropped them on the floor. She laughed as she uncovered the gift—it was an old-fashioned wooden nutcracker in the shape of a soldier. Its uniform was painted in red and white, and its face was adorned with a lustrous, black handlebar moustache. It held the butt of a rifle in its left hand, the muzzle leaning against its shoulder, and it sported a small sword in a scabbard slung at its waist.

It was a heavy thing, well made, and Angie wondered how much Tommy had spent on it. The eyes fascinated her— just two dots of black paint, but they stared *through* her rather than at her. The mouth housed two serrated metal plates for gripping and cracking nuts and was operated by a handle set in the back of the soldier, painted to represent the strap of its rifle. When pulled, the action caused the jaw to dislocate and drop into the figure's chest like a ventriloquist's dummy.

She placed the nutcracker on the table next to her brandy. *Quite the haul this year,* she thought as she gathered the packaging from the present and threw it on the fire. She considered doing the same with the letter, but decided against it. Instead, she ran a single, neat crease lengthwise down the middle of the paper and propped it up against the soldier. The box was already smoldering in the hearth, but it would clear by morning. She finished the rest of her drink and raised a lazy salute to the infantryman.

"At ease, soldier," she said, suppressing a titter, and left the room for the sanctuary of her bed.

❅ ❅ ❅

Crack!

Angie wondered if she had really heard the noise—sharp and sudden, like a pick driven through rime ice—or if it had been part of her dream. Gooseflesh crawled up her bare arms as she lay beneath the bedclothes and listened. The only sound was the howling of the wind around the eaves daring her to leave the comfort of her bed. No wary foot-steps, no muffled shouts; not even the sound of sleigh bells on the roof.

She marked off five minutes on her alarm clock before getting out of bed and creeping onto the landing barefoot. She looked over the balustrade, straining to see the tell-tale flickering of an intruder's torch in the hallway.

"Hello?" she called. "Is there anybody down there?"

And what will you do, she thought, *if someone answers?*

She tiptoed down the stairs, conscious of every creak,

and gasped at the chilly parquet flooring against the bare soles of her feet. The front door was shut and she could see the security chain from the foot of the stairs. Nobody had entered the house that way.

She went into the living room, where the last dying embers filled the fireplace with a sullen glow. It was warm and cozy in here and she felt the tension leaching from her body. She looked around the room; everything seemed to be in place.

No… not everything.

The nutcracker lay on the floor, face-down in the carpet, the wooden rudder of its biting mechanism pointing sky-wards. Angie relaxed. Just a decoration falling to the ground. No wonder it had woken her, with that kind of weight behind it. *The little sod must've been at my brandy,* she thought, smiling. *So much for standing guard.*

She bent down to pick up the soldier. As she stood up, somebody grabbed her arms from behind, and she dropped it again. She opened her mouth to scream but was spun around to face a wiry redhead who clamped a hand across her face.

"Don't even think about it, bitch," she said, holding the business end of a knife to Angie's throat. "My friend, Jon is awfully big and he wouldn't think twice about snapping your fucking arms."

"What the fuck?" came a deep voice by her ear. Angie stared at the woman in front of her, not daring to blink. She had cheap whiskey and cigarettes on her breath and madness in her eyes.

"What?" she said, casting a glance over her shoulder.

"Why did you just tell her my name?" Angie could feel his breath, hot and damp against her neck.

"Who cares?" the woman said. "It's not like she's going to be telling anybody."

"Then why don't you tell her your name?" the man asked.

The redhead smiled. Whoever was holding her stood a good few inches taller than her and had some serious strength to his grip. Her arms were already numb below the elbows, but she would sooner face a dozen of him than a woman who smiled like that. It was like a slit in her face, lips peeling back to reveal crooked teeth stained by nicotine, and God knew what else.

"Fine. My name is Gill—the big prick you already know," she said, nodding behind her.

"For fuck's sake," he said.

"Now we've got to know each other," she said, pressing the blade tighter against Angie's throat, "I'm sure you realize only two of us will be leaving this house tonight. Right?" She tilted her head to one side. "No, no, no—don't answer. I can't hear you through my gloves and I really wouldn't shake my head if I were you."

Angie was shaking and she felt the knife rub against her neck with each tremor that she fought to suppress. The madwoman with the flaming hair was right. The names probably weren't enough to go on, but she'd already had a good look at her face—more than enough to describe to a police artist.

"Now," Gill said, "Jon is going to set you down and you're going to stay exactly where he puts you, understand? You might be a big, old bitch, but Jon's bigger than you and I'm faster. Isn't that right, Jonny-boy?"

"That's right."

Gill took a step back. Angie managed a single deep breath before she was shoved onto the couch. She twisted round, struggling to right herself, but froze as she saw the knife mere inches from her face. She looked over Gill's shoulder and saw her partner. Jon was huge; he towered over the two women and his face bore the scars of countless fights. His nose was lumpy and misshapen and Angie instantly regretted wondering how many times it had been broken and rebroken.

"Now," Gill said, the knife drifting to point at one of Angie's eyes and then the other, "where are the presents?"

"Presents?" Angie asked.

"Presents," Gill repeated. "It's Christmas, you stupid bitch. Where are the presents?"

"There aren't any," Angie said.

"What?"

"Th-there aren't any presents."

"What do you mean, there aren't any?" Gill said. The knife flicked from side to side in front of Angie's face. The woman was losing patience.

"I didn't get any presents," she said. "I'm the only one in the house."

Gill stared at her. "You're lying," she said.

"I'm not," Angie said. "I swear to God I'm not. The only present I got was from my son."

"Ha!" Gill said, hopping from foot to foot. "And where's that?"

Angie nodded in the general direction. "On the floor," she said. "Behind J—" she faltered. "I mean, behind him."

"Do you think I'm fucking stupid?" Jon asked.

"Just look," Gill said. "This bitch isn't going to try anything, are you?"

"N-no", Angie said.

Jon picked up the nutcracker. He turned back to the women, brandishing it. "Is this it?" he asked.

"Yes," Angie said.

"This?"

"Yes!" Angie shouted. "That's it! That's all I've got! Please, just leave me alone... I won't tell anybody, I swear."

"We know that," Gill said, walking over to join her partner. The knife pointing in Angie's direction served as both warning and threat.

Angie sat where she had been thrown, watching the two intruders argue with one another beneath their breath. She wondered what her chances would be if she tried to make a break for it. She might be able to get past Jon—big as he was, she didn't think he would kill someone for the sake of a decorative nutcracker.

The woman was different, though; she looked like she would kill her for the fun of it. Angie had already let slip that she was on her own, that she wouldn't be missed until after the holidays. Gill might decide that she had nothing to lose.

As if reading her thoughts, the pair of them walked over to the couch, the dying fire casting their shadows long before them.

"Kill her," Gill said.

"Please don't," she said.

"Do it," Gill said. "Beat her to death with that piece of shit. It might get into the newspaper, a thing like that."

Jon looked at Gill with something approaching disdain, but there was something else. Even through her tears, Angie could see that he was terrified of her. Angie could understand that—being held at knifepoint did that to a person—but what did this man, this behemoth, have to be scared of?

Jon raised the nutcracker like a cudgel, testing its weight, and looked Angie square in the eye. *I'm sorry*, he mouthed as he tensed his biceps and brought the ornament down with all his might.

Crack!

There was a terrible scream that did not come from her. "Jesus, fuck!" Jon cried, dropping to his knees. Gill was standing next to Angie, waiting for the killing blow, and turned her attention to her partner.

"What is it?" she said. There was a shrillness there that Angie hadn't noticed before.

"My ear!" Jon said. "Bastard's got my ear!"

The women looked at the nutcracker Jon held and saw the lump of flesh caught in its mouth. Blood trickled down the wooden jaw and more of the same flooded from the ragged hole on the side of Jon's head.

"How did you manage that?" Gill said. If Jon responded, Angie didn't hear him. She glanced at the small end-table, at the letter that lay flat on its surface without the soldier to support it.

I've sent you someone to stand guard over Christmas.

As Jon clutched vainly at his ruined ear and Gill stood over him spouting a spittle-flecked tirade into his face, the smallest of movements caught Angie's attention. The nutcracker's jaw was opening and closing, the rudder in its back moving in and out with the motion. *Chewing*, she thought, *it's chewing his ear*.

Gill smacked Jon across the back of the head and he dropped the wooden soldier. Angie saw it tumble, head over heels, landing head first between his spread knees. She screwed her eyes shut, fearing what was to come.

Crack!

Jon's scream became a howl that, loud as it was, could not mask the terrible crunch of metal against testicles. His tracksuit bottoms proved no protection against the insistent attack and each rise and fall of its serrated jaw was met with fresh cries of anguish. There was a final, meaty *pop* and Jon lost consciousness.

The silence didn't last. Gill replaced her partner's scream with one of her own, but her's was not born through agony. Anger and madness combined into something dark and terrible. She picked up the nutcracker in both hands, tearing it away from Jon's crotch, leaving him prostrate in a pool of his own blood.

"What is this!" she said, brandishing the nutcracker in Angie's face, the mouth still opening and closing, dripping with blood and flesh.

"It's from my son," Angie said.

"Look what it's done to him!"

"Good!" she said. "I hope it does worse to you!"

Gill held the ornament at arm's length, her eyes growing wide, a desperate clarity eclipsed the madness that lurked there. Was it fear, she wondered, relishing the possibility that it might be. Whatever the impetus, the redhead took control soon enough, hurling the nutcracker into the fire, where dark red embers blistered the varnish and paint.

"No!" Angie could see the soldier's free arm pin-wheeling as the flames engulfed it. Its jaw was moving up and down, as if trying to tell her something. "What have you done?" she said.

"You're next, bitch!" Gill shouted, thrusting at Angie with an empty hand.

The knife, Angie thought. *She's dropped the knife!*

She saw it on the floor and made a grab for it, but Gill was half her age and at least half her weight. She sprang from the fireplace, reaching the knife in one fluid motion and kicking it from Angie's grasp. She pounced on the older woman, pulling her hair and scratching at her face. Angie may have had the weight advantage, but the redhead fought with a strength born of insanity. She rolled Angie onto her front and looped an arm around her neck, pulling back with all her might. Angie choked, struggling against the smaller woman to no avail. Dark lights danced across her eyes and, as her vision clouded over, she saw something emerge from the fireplace at great speed.

Right arm pistoning like a steam engine, stiff legs moving back and forth, the little soldier rocketed across the carpet, leaving burn marks in its wake. As she wavered on the cusp of oblivion, Angie heard a scream and felt Gill's arm go slack. She hacked and wheezed, pulling the air down her bruised windpipe while the screams went on and on.

Crack!

Her vision started to clear, blurry images coalescing before her. She could make out Gill spinning around in circles and clutching something red to her face. *No,* she thought, *not* clutching *it—trying to push it away.* The smoke and the heat overcame her and, as she passed out, a single thought penetrated her mind.

Not red, she thought. *Fire.*

❄ ❄ ❄

Crack!

Winter logs popped in the hearth like a gunshot, waking Angie from her dreams of blood and fire. She sat up, blinking in the firelight, and took stock of her surroundings.

Blood?

The word resonated with her for a reason that she could not place.

Fire?

Gasping, she drew her arms across her chest, anticipating an attack. After a few seconds, she lowered them and looked about the living room. Everything was as it should be—Christmas tree sparkling in the corner, fire burning in the grate. There was no blood on the floor, no soot discarded before the hearth, and no unpleasant lumps of human flesh glistening in the firelight.

The smoke from the fire was thick and black and settled

in her chest. Was that all it had been? No terrible night-time visit, no wooden protector from overseas—just a stiff brandy and a smoky fire leading to a broken sleep and a vivid dream? Everything was accounted for, even the pain in her throat.

Jesus, she thought, *I could have died from smoke inhalation.*

She stood up on unsteady legs and took a look at the clock. Half-past one in the morning. Christmas Day. *Time to go to bed*, she thought.

As she turned to leave, she tripped over something large and heavy. She knew before she reached for it that it was the nutcracker. She cradled it in her hands, turning it over and over, looking for any evidence of the night's activity.

Nothing. No scorch marks, no blood, not even a bit of chipped paint.

Everything was as it should be.

Not quite everything. She fiddled with the rudder that worked the nutcracker's jaw, but it would not move—the soldier's jaw remained open. She held it closer, looking for any obstruction. She could see something right at the back, where the mouthpiece joined the rest of the figure, something blocking the hinge mechanism. It was some sort of dark lump, but she could not make it out in the shadowy living room. She tilted it towards the fire for the benefit of the illumination it provided. There was definitely something there; she could see it glistening in the firelight. Something dark, wet, and shapeless nestled in the soldier's maw.

Angie slipped a finger into its mouth, sliding the tip over its serrated metal plates and probing for whatever was stuck there. When she touched it, she found that it was not only dark and wet, it was also still warm.

Crack!

S*PLIT

Jay Wilburn

"You can't have the dining room table."

The two men looked at each other and then back at the man standing between them and the door.

They're both just boys really, Justin thought. *If they believe half the stuff she has told them about me, they won't fight me on it. They aren't even looking me in the eye.*

"This belonged to our mother," Charity's brother said with his hands still on the table.

The other fellow, a friend of a cousin or some such nonsense, had released the table and had nearly backed into the antique pie cooling rack. He had surrendered this argument. He was young and helping a friend in distress. He had "no dog in this fight" and Caleb could not carry the table by himself.

"Our mother," Justin said.

He suppressed his smile as Caleb's nostrils flared and

his knuckles went white on the stained oak.

"The table is the reason we are here," Caleb spoke quietly.

Justin took a deep breath and looked at the cousin-friend by the pie cooler. The kid folded his arms and found something to stare at on the floor of the kitchen behind him.

Already surrendered.

"Well, Caleb," Justin sighed, "this was a really long way to travel for a table. You picked up her clothes and the kids' things... my kids' things."

Now Caleb found something to stare at in the carpet of the dining room. There were plenty of stains in the thick, white carpet that was older than anyone standing in the room.

Why did their crazy mother put white carpet... any carpet... in a dining room?

Caleb's knuckles regained their color and his hands slid from the edges to the polished top of the table. He rested his palms flat on the surface. Justin's nostrils flared now. He yelled at his own kids all the time for doing that, but Caleb had let go at least.

That a boy, Justin thought, *you're getting the picture here.*

Caleb spoke softly. "We're supposed to come back with the table."

Wives aren't supposed to run off with the children while fathers are at work.

"No," Justin answered flatly. "This is the table I'm going to have to use to eat alone on Christmas. I imagine this will be the first Christmas in generations where a family didn't gather around this table for the holidays. Am I right?"

"She wants the table, Justin," Caleb said. "We both know you don't really care about this table."

"No," Justin answered, "I care a great deal, Caleb. The table is staying in the house. Anyone that wants to eat at this table on Christmas—or any other day—comes to this house to do it."

Caleb slapped his hand loudly on the table. Even Justin jumped. Cousin-friend nearly tipped the pie rack.

Caleb said, "Mark, grab the shelves out of that rack."

"No, Mark, go on to the truck," Justin ordered.

Caleb turned toward Justin. "Are you cooling pies this Christmas, Justin?"

"Are you?"

"You knew why we were coming."

"You have a pretty full truck," Justin said. "If she wants her clothes and my kids' things until my lawyer has them returned, fine. If she wants to clean out the house and move in with a boyfriend or a girlfriend or a cousin-friend for good, then she can get a lawyer and we'll decide which half of the furniture she gets before we sell mother's house and split the money."

"This is a family home, Justin," Caleb's voice was shaking.

"For better or for worse," Justin said.

They stared at each other without looking in each other's eyes.

Caleb said, "Let's go, Mark."

Mark was already in the foyer before Caleb started walking.

"Close the door to my house on your way out, son," Justin called.

The door slammed and Justin sat in one of the chairs in front of the empty table. He listened to the cargo door roll closed and bolt shut. He heard both doors to the cab open and slam. The truck started and idled for a few moments.

He's going to come back in, Justin thought.

"I hope you do."

The transmission made a grinding noise underneath the truck twice. He heard the engine noise modulate, and then the sound faded off down the street into the other background noises in the neighborhood.

Justin's chest hitched as he sucked in air suddenly. It surprised him. He wasn't much of a crier. He was a screamer. Occasionally, he was a shover. Rarely, was he a hitter. He was nothing like what Charity made him out to be.

I don't deserve to lose my kids.

He dropped his chin to his chest and bit hard on the inside of his mouth. His body bucked a few times and his vision blurred, but he did not allow himself to sob. Even in the house by himself, he did not allow it. After a few moments, he sniffed air through his stuffy nose and wiped his eyes on his sleeves.

He looked around the table that he had managed to keep for himself. He had kept it from her. She would either find out when they drove all the way there or they would call her and she would know that she wouldn't have it for Christmas. Even though his lips quivered, he smiled.

"Serves her right," his voice came out hoarse.

"No one deserves to be alone on Christmas," he heard the voice from inside the dining room. It sounded familiar to him.

He looked out the window in time to see a bundled woman walking along the opposite side of the street holding her child's hand.

Justin whispered. "Mind your business."

He looked down at the table. There were two sets of hand prints. One set was complete palms on both sides of where his place setting would normally be in front of him. The Christmas place mats, napkins, and table cloth were still boxed in one of the closets. The Christmas glasses were on the top shelf in the cabinet above the coffeemaker. The china, crystal, and their cabinet rattled in the back of a truck going to wherever his wife had taken his kids to hide.

His eyes started to blur again, but he blinked it back and took long, slow breaths. He looked out the bay window. It looked strange with the deacon's bench missing. It made the wall under the windows seem too big and too white over the spotted carpet. The window seemed deep and distorted without the bench that had been there since he had started dating Charity.

It was like the house mutated without its furniture. Pieces that were a part of the fabric of reality in this old house suddenly vanished and the house felt wrong without them. Even the carpet sunk in four deep indentions where the rough legs had rested since time out of mind. The wife, the kids, and the deacon's bench spirited away.

I should follow them, he thought.

The idea made his legs feel weak and his groin tingle. He pictured his keys on the counter in the kitchen. He'd tail them. She'd be surprised to see her stupid brother had brought him and not the table.

He smiled as he stared out the window, but he stayed seated.

She'll call when she doesn't get the table.

He looked down at the table again. He hadn't even remembered placing his hands on the table. The other set of prints smeared around the edges on one end where Caleb had attempted to claim the table. Justin wished now that he hadn't polished off the kids prints from the last time they ate.

He just had his own tiny handprints now. He squinted his eyes at the small, white palm prints with thin fingers spread open. He held his own hand in the air above one of the prints. His broad hand and thick fingers enveloped the prints. He moved his hand to look again. They faded. As he drew one finger in a squiggle through the palm print on the surface of the wood, his fingertip left a dark trail through the cold moisture.

The prints finished evaporating, leaving Caleb's paw prints at the end and the squiggle smudge in front of him.

Justin stood up, bumping the table with his hip. He saw the cabinet above the coffeemaker had been left open and the glasses from the top shelf were missing. He shook his head as he wandered into the kitchen to close it.

"I'll wipe down my table later," he muttered, "and I'm calling in sick for a few days."

❄ ❄ ❄

The phone always sounded like he was talking through a tin can. She could have called him on his cell phone, but she had called on the house phone.

"It's good to hear from you," he said softly.

He heard his own voice ring back at him. The plastic piece felt weird against his ear. He always had to hold it awkwardly to keep from pushing the buttons with his face.

Her voice sounded distant and hollow through the plastic speaker. "You didn't have to be rude to Caleb and Mark. We discussed what they were going to take. You weren't supposed to be there. That's what we discussed."

He never knew what to do with the weird coil of cord that ran from the receiver mounted on the kitchen wall to the handset. It was the extra-long cord, so it always got impossibly tangled.

"I was afraid I would come back and find the place empty."

There was static-filled silence on the other end. He jerked at the coils of the cord, trying to work them free of each other. He suspected this was the same phone that was mounted over the same yellow wallpaper when Charity and Caleb were still hanging their stockings here when their parents were alive.

Charity's tin voice hissed. "I don't want any of this."

Justin's eyes widened as he leaned his free hand on the counter. "There's still time to come home. We can work through everything after the holidays. The kids could be home for Christmas like they should be."

There was staticky silence again.

"… this way," her voice popped in suddenly.

He adjusted the ear piece to the other side. "Repeat that, Charity. This stupid kitchen phone is crap."

"… why it has to be this way," the phone crackled over what he could hear.

Why didn't you call me on my cell phone?

"Charity, I'm not getting everything you're saying," he shouted. "Could we meet somewhere just to talk… somewhere public. We could meet halfway between here… and wherever you and the kids are."

Her crackling voice said, "I don't think that's a good idea, Justin."

Something moved in the corner of his vision. He looked over quickly at the calendar with one page left and the rack of bills that overflowed next to the bags of chips. Each bag was folded and clipped neatly the way he liked. Justin scanned around the bag of cheddar popcorn the kids liked. He expected to see a roach exploring, but he didn't.

"Are you still there, Justin?"

He turned back. "Yeah, so how about meeting?"

"You're not listening to me," she snapped. "You never listen."

"Charity, just…"

He tried to think of the next word and he heard something click across the floor near the refrigerator. He turned sharply and tried to look over the island of the stove. The clicking continued steadily across the tile. He tried to walk over to the edge of the stove to look, but the cord caught on the tight knots, preventing him from going more than a couple feet.

The sound was gone.

"Just what, Justin?" Charity demanded.

Justin turned back toward the counter. "I want to see the kids. I want to watch them open presents."

"I don't think that's a good idea."

Justin gripped the edge of the counter. "How is me getting to open presents with the kids a bad idea?"

There was static and a crackle.

"I'm going to go now, Justin. I'll call you again... sometime."

"Wait!" he said. "What are you saying? You are hiding the kids from me on Christmas? Put them on the phone so I know they're okay."

She didn't call my cell because she's hiding her number.

"That's not happening," she crackled.

"I'm smashing that table into firewood," Justin screamed into the phone.

A dial tone punctuated his threat in his own ear.

"Don't hang up on me," he hollered, making his voice crack and his throat hurt.

He raised the phone to slam it down and rip the plastic piece of garbage off the wall.

"You don't mean that... You're just angry."

He looked around the kitchen and back down at the phone. He brought it back to his ear.

"Charity, are you there? Charity?"

Nothing but the persistent tone with sparks of static remained. He placed the handset into the cradle and leaned on the counter.

"Decorate."

Justin looked up at the silent phone and then around the

kitchen. He walked to the window over the sink and looked outside. He could see the neighbors just over the fence next door.

"They like Charity better," he muttered. "That's not the same nosey-nellie from earlier. You all have the same lecturing voice though."

Trained to nag for generations, he thought.

He walked through the kitchen into the dining room and looked at the smudges on the table again.

I'll need to clean these up, I guess, he thought.

His eyes locked on a single, moist handprint on the surface near the edge where he stood. This time two of the fingers were together forming one thick line with three thin digits in tiny droplets for the other two fingers and thumb.

He started when he heard the muffled voice behind him. *"You'll feel better when you start decorating."*

He looked back into the kitchen at the window over the sink.

"Don't tell me what do," he smiled at the window and the neighbors on the other side. "Although you have a point."

He looked back down and the handprint was gone.

※ ※ ※

He opened his eyes and stared at the dark ceiling. His left hand felt over to Charity's side of the bed. She wasn't there and it was cold. The sheets were turned down on her side. He started to call to the bathroom for her, but then stopped himself.

Justin hated the confusion of falling asleep in the middle of the day.

He looked over at his clock. The bright, blue numbers made his head hurt behind his eyes. It was 4:30, but he wasn't clear on am or pm. His hand came away from the sheets on Charity's side moist. He looked at his fingers in the blue light and rubbed them together.

One of the cabinets banged closed downstairs in the kitchen. His chest hurt suddenly with fear.

Someone's in the house.

He listened. He could see light coming from the stairs through the open bedroom door.

Justin swung his feet off the bed. They itched from sleeping in his shoes. His jeans twisted and he felt sweaty under his clothes.

The bed squeaked when he placed his feet on the floor. There were two pops from the floor downstairs. A plate set down on the dining room table with a crisp clink. Silence followed.

A burglar getting a sandwich? He pictured it in his mind complete with striped prison uniform and raccoon, cutout mask. Then the image shifted to *a crazy, homeless guy coming to eat my face.*

Justin stood. The floor popped under him. The plate shifted on the table downstairs an inch or more across the surface. Justin could feel his heart in his throat.

Caleb has come back for the table in the middle of the night. The thought instantly made him feel relieved and angry. *And he decided to sit down for a snack until I woke up?*

Justin walked across the dim bedroom listening to the floorboards under the carpet announce his every step. The crazy killer would be ready by the time he reached the stairs.

He pulled the door all the way open. Justin expected the hinges to give a slow, haunted house creak, but the doorframe had nothing to say.

It occurred to him, *Charity came home. She slipped the kids into bed without waking me and then she fixed herself something to eat after the long drive.*

He walked down the hall, the floorboards grinding, creaking, until he reached the top of the stairs. From the light in the dining room, he could see the closed doors to the kids' rooms. He wanted to go in to see, but he didn't want to wake them. He stepped on the first step below the landing and stopped. He looked back at the open door to their bedroom. Blue light accented the dark corners of the furniture.

He rubbed his fingers together without realizing he was doing it.

Why did she turn down her side of the bed and then go back downstairs?

He looked back at the doors to the kids' rooms and then back into the dark master bedroom.

Justin walked down the stairs, running his hand along the cold wood of the banisters on each side. He felt his hand slide through moisture in two spots, but he kept looking under the edge of the ceiling as the end of the dining room carpet and the kitchen came into view beyond the foyer.

He walked a few steps and stopped again. He looked through the twisted distortion in the glass on both sides of the front door. Dark trees swirled and separated from themselves through the glass. He did not see her car in the drive or at the curb. She would have pulled up past the house by the garage. He had not heard the car doors or the garage door.

He pulled at the doorknob. The door crackled against the brittle weather stripping, but the lock stayed fastened.

A piece of silverware clattered from being dropped in the sink. He turned to see the very edge of the window, but he couldn't see who stood by the sink in the darkened kitchen. He watched and waited. He heard no footsteps. He didn't see anyone or their shadow.

Who's there?

He couldn't make the words come out of his mouth.

Who is doing dishes with the lights out?

Justin looked down where he still held the knob. He felt the urge to unfasten the lock and run outside into the cold wind. He stared at the door as he pictured himself running through the dark neighborhood.

He imagined the neighbors that liked Charity best looking out their curtains as he fled from his own house in the night. They would let the curtains drop back and then shake their heads at each other. They would make some snide comment about how unfortunate it was for Charity to end up with a crazy man like that, a man running down the street in the middle of the night in December.

It's okay to be crazy, Justin thought. *You just have to keep it hidden from your boss and neighbors.*

He released the knob and let his hand drop to his side, still locked inside the house that should have been empty. He looked around the wood and glass of the door. It took him a moment to realize that he was looking for handprints. He had cleaned all of those off just like he had done the table before his family left him.

Then who is standing in the kitchen dropping knives in the sink?

He walked across the tile of the foyer, deeper into the dark house, until he reached the splash of light coming from the dining room.

How do you know it is a knife?

He lifted one foot over the thick, white carpet, then froze in place. He grabbed hold of both sides of the archway.

A saucer with crackers on it sat at his spot on the table. Not normally a source of terror for him, Justin felt his heart throbbing in his chest as he stared at the crackers with cheese smeared over the tops. The crackers were from the fancy box in the back of the pantry, the ones he was saving for Christmas Eve. The cheese was from the ball that was still wrapped up in the bottom of the refrigerator when he laid down for a nap. Maybe the knife in the sink was the spreading knife from the fine silver that Caleb had taken.

"Charity?" his voice cracked.

He gritted his teeth. He didn't want his wife or a crazy, homeless person hearing that.

Someone started humming in the kitchen. They were beside the sink. He couldn't see them, but that's where the sound was coming from. He gripped the walls tighter on both sides of the arch. At first the humming was tuneless and inhuman. Then, it bled into a melody in a woman's voice. It was an alto, but definitely a woman's hum. He couldn't place the tune or the woman. The tune felt mildly familiar. The woman did not. The hum became disharmonic again, and it seemed to evaporate around the kitchen. Maybe the hummer was moving.

Justin crossed the carpet until he stood just outside the kitchen. He paused again, his breath coming in harsh bursts. He flipped on the kitchen light and listened. No one stood by the sink or the island of the stove. He walked into the empty kitchen and stopped again.

"Who is here?" he yelled with more force.

His voice rang off the light fixtures and echoed out into the living room around the corner. No answer came. The humming was still in the kitchen. He actually looked around the ceiling. No elves that he could see hung in the corners humming at him. He did see cobwebs that had long been abandoned by even the spider.

Noticing the spider webs bothered him. He wanted to get a stepstool and swipe them down despite the odd situation.

"You could have at least cleaned before you left," he muttered.

"I made you crackers."

He turned around in a full circle and then grabbed the corner of the pantry. It was a woman's voice again, but he was fairly sure it was coming from his terrified brain. The endless humming still came from the empty air near the sink.

He walked over and looked inside. The sink sat empty, no knives or any other silverware. A bit a peanut butter and bits of rice sat on the rim of the drain from earlier leftovers. Justin turned up his lip at them.

He looked back at the closed pantry, then through his reflection in the dark window. He pressed his face against the glass and cupped his hand. He couldn't see much, but the neighbors were not humming carols in their yard. No one hummed in his driveway. The hum hung right beside him inside.

Justin looked around the counters. He reached for the socket beside the sink and unplugged the coffeemaker. The humming stopped. He held the cord in his hand and smiled.

Hide your crazy, Justin, he thought.

He dropped the cord on the counter and walked back through the kitchen, but stopped in the dining room again.

A steak knife sat across the edge of the saucer. Bits of rich cheese clung to its side. He looked into the dark foyer and then back at the knife.

"Who is here," he screamed toward the foyer. "Get out here where I can see you so no one gets hurt."

They had to have come back through the foyer to place the knife, but he didn't know where they hid now.

He walked around the table and stood with his back to the table, holding the curved back of his chair. He could see the tile, he could see the stairs, and he could see the light from the kitchen leaking through the side of the living room and out into the hall for the laundry room, bathroom, and storage closets.

He listened to see where the mad cracker maker was going next. He heard nothing.

This isn't Charity, he thought. *Unless she's trying to scare you.*

The thought made him cold inside. Could he have pushed her hard enough to make her want to sneak in during the night… to do this? She wouldn't come in to make him crackers to terrify him.

And then kill me with the knife she used to make them, he thought. *The neighbors will shake their heads and side with her even after she murders me.*

He turned back around and took in air to shout again. He held his breath and stared down at the table. The crackers were still there, but the knife was gone. He breathed out slow and shaky as he waited for the blade to plant itself in his back.

His legs turned watery under him and he dropped into his chair. He stared at the plate and tried to convince himself that the knife hadn't been there.

He tilted his head along the side of the table to see the light striking it from an angle. The thin fingers and small hands were drawn again in moisture on both sides of the plate. He did not believe these were his any longer, and he knew if he touched them, the water would be cold.

"Who are you?" he whispered to the plate of crackers.

He watched the moisture fade as the hand prints vanished from the edges toward the centers. The humming started in the kitchen again. Something clinked in the sink. He sat upright and looked into the empty kitchen. He couldn't place the tune, but now the voice struck him as familiar. Something strummed at the cords in his memory. Humming from the kitchen, this kitchen, was not new. It had not been for a while, but he remembered several Christmases ago. There had been humming by the sink while he had sat at this table. He had not been alone.

The humming stopped. He started to slide out from behind the table.

"I made you crackers."

He hovered above his seat, holding the back of the chair and the edge of the table. He was afraid to look in the kitchen.

"I'm not hungry," he whispered.

And now you are crazy, Justin thought as he hung in space above his chair, behind the table, looking at a plate of real crackers.

He dropped back into the seat.

He swallowed hard. *You made these. You made them before you laid down upstairs and passed out from stress and exhaustion. You don't even remember opening the crackers or the cheese. You were upset when you couldn't find a spreading knife. Only you would use a steak knife to spread cheese. You put it in the dishwasher. It's in there right now if you go look.*

"No, thanks," Justin said to himself.

"I want to thank you for saving my table from those awful people," the voice said.

"I'm going back to bed," Justin announced. "Life will be normal... better in the morning."

"You need your energy," the voice explained. *"We are behind on decorating this year."*

"It's four in the morning," Justin said. "I'm not eating crackers, and I'm not decorating by myself on Christmas."

"Eat your crackers."

Justin lifted one of the crackers and bit through the crisp crust and the thick cheese speckled with shaved nuts. It tasted like Christmas.

I don't remember making these, he thought as he slowly chewed the bite in his dry mouth.

He was painfully thirsty, but he was afraid to say it out loud. He feared that the glass of milk might just appear with no memory of how it got there. Worse yet, it might have a butcher knife sitting in it to stir.

"When you're done, we need to start decorating," the voice added.

The humming started again. Justin held the bitten cracker in his shaking hand. He took another dry bite to avoid hearing the voice again.

What if you look and the knife is not in the dishwasher, he thought as he chewed loudly to cover the humming. *Where would she have put it?*

* * *

"That doesn't go there," she scolded.

Justin breathed deeply as he balanced on the back of a loveseat trying to place a mouse figurine on one of the built-in shelves.

I wonder what she would do if I just dropped it, he thought.

He didn't want to find out. He had looked. There was no steak knife in the dishwasher, but one was missing from the block.

Caleb could have taken it, he thought. *And then he snuck it back in the house so you would think you were crazy?*

"My mother bought that one. It needs to be down lower and closer to the tree where we can see it," she insisted.

Justin climbed down slowly. "All the low shelves are full of... stuff."

"There is always room, if you just look, dear."

Justin stuck it on a low shelf adjacent to the half-decorated tree. Every ornament was placed with exacting instructions from... beyond.

"Move it to the left," she ordered. *"Just a little, mind you."*

Justin said, "There's a Santa Claus and three ceramic reindeer to the left... *Dear.*"

There was a long silence punctuated by two clocks ticking out of time from two different parts of the house. Justin became nervous. He wanted the voice to stop, but he did not want it angry... even if it turned out to be in his head and he was hiding the knives.

He started to reach for the mouse to move it into the line of reindeer. A droplet of water ran down the mouse's tiny face and over the cookie-cutter heart in her hands. The figurine wobbled. Justin pulled back his hand. The mouse tilted but did not fall. Its feet slid loose from where it had stuck to the paint and then the mouse ground against the shelf as it moved just a little to the left. It came to rest facing out at Justin at exactly the right angle.

Please, let me be crazy, he thought.

"Sometimes you have to just do it yourself," she huffed. *"Try to remember that spot for next year."*

Justin shivered. *I'll kill myself before next year.*

He looked down at the shelf and saw a thin circle of mist around the mouse. Justin couldn't forget that spot if he tried.

"I can't believe they painted my fine wood shelves. Why would anyone paint over crafted wood like that?"

Justin looked around the empty living room. He spied the giant wreaths along the wall below each window. He looked up at the nails in the boards at just the right spots where they had been left for generations.

Justin said, "I should go out to the garage to get the ladder so we can start on those wreaths."

"Don't be foolish, boy. The ladder is in the mudroom just past the laundry."

Justin gritted his teeth. *I wonder if she can keep me from opening the doors. I don't care what the neighbors think.*

"I should call and check on your... daughter. See if she and your grandkids are okay," Justin said to the empty house.

There was another prolonged silence with the double clicks from clocks. He looked back at the mouse. The moisture had evaporated. When the voice spoke again, he jolted.

"My daughter is already here, young man... and so are most of my grandchildren... This is a family house."

Justin closed his eyes and swallowed. *I suppose killing myself won't allow me to escape from next Christmas.*

"Who are you?" he whispered.

He realized that he had said this same phrase in more than one way today and he had yet to get an answer.

"We need to look for my table cloth," she said. *"It just doesn't feel like Christmas without it."*

Justin began walking toward the hall storage closets.

❄ ❄ ❄

"Get up."

His eyes opened to the dark ceiling again. *Where am I?*

He reached over to Charity's side of the bed. The sheets were soaked through to the mattress. Someone had spilled something in the bed or had wet it. It was cold.

Justin pulled his hand back to his chest. He couldn't stop thinking about the mouse.

He looked over at the blue glow from the clock. It was 2:15.

"We need to find my table cloth," the voice said very close to his ear.

He put both his hands over his eyes and squeezed at the pain there. "We looked. I couldn't find it."

"It has red birds and bells on it."

"I know," Justin said. "We use it every year. It wasn't in the tub it was supposed to be in, and we looked in all the others... twice."

"Then, we look again," she said. *"It's not Christmas without it. We didn't look in my china cabinet. I always kept it in the drawer of the china cabinet... the one with the fine, curved glass."*

"Yeah, that's not here," Justin said.

"Don't be foolish, boy. Where would it be? That cabinet is a part of the home."

"Not anymore," Justin said. "Your... Charity... her brother took the cabinet. Maybe they took the tablecloth, too."

"They wouldn't dare."

Justin held his breath for a moment.

"Those horrible boys who tried to take my table? They took my tablecloth? My cabinet? Those things are a part of the house. They belong to the family. They can't take them... I will not allow it."

"I'm sorry," Justin whispered, still covering his eyes.

"Get up," she said. *"We're going to look again."*

"I'm not getting up," Justin said. "It's two in the morning and the cloth is not here. The family is not here. I'm alone and I'm sleeping now."

There was a pause. Justin began to doze off. He felt wetness begin to soak into the shoulder of the shirt he had been wearing for a couple days. He woke again thinking about the mouse.

Justin was forced into the air. His hand connected with the side table, dumping it over. The lamp hit the wall and lost its shade. The clock spun on its cord and strobed blue light through the room. Justin slammed into the carpet with the top sheet still wrapped around his legs.

He felt around the table for his cell phone but couldn't find it.

The bedsprings creaked. He held his hands in front of his

face to defend himself in the silence that followed.

"Find my tablecloth."

❋ ❋ ❋

"What are you doing?"

Justin held the phone to his ear and tapped the receiver. "What did you do to it?"

"That monstrosity does not belong to me. Neither does that awful paper glued to my fine walls."

Justin hung up the dead phone. He felt in his pocket for his cell phone and remembered it wasn't there. He picked up his keys and walked toward the side door leading out to the driveway from the kitchen.

"Where are you going?"

He kept walking. "I'm going to get your tablecloth from Charity, and then I'm going to bring it back... so we can have Christmas... as a family."

He breathed slowly as he reached for the lock. He already saw the wet handprints begin to glaze on the surface of the door.

He rested his hand on the knob. "I can bring back the cabinet, the china, the silver, the deacon's bench... and your tablecloth, too."

"That bench is not mine," she said.

Justin watched the moisture build and thicken over the prints. *Her daughter is here and so are most of her grandchildren. How old is this house? How old is she?*

"I'll get everything else, then," he offered.

He turned the lock and the door groaned as it pressed harder into the frame. Droplets began to run down from the prints toward the floor.

"Let me go do this for you," Justin whispered. "I can get

249

them back. I promise."

"*I heard you talking to her on that monstrosity, foolish boy... you don't know where she is.*"

Justin closed his eyes. *I wonder if her daughter and grand-children are here by their own choice.*

"Let me out of this house... please."

"*No one should be alone on Christmas.*"

He turned the knob and pulled. The door crackled but did not budge. He braced his foot on the frame and pulled with both hands, dropping his keys. The knob strained against its screws. The handprints drained into long, shapeless swatches on the door.

He let go and ran.

The humming started again. He didn't know who this was. It was not Charity's mother, but he remembered his mother-in-law humming in the kitchen, too. This was one tradition he was thankful Charity had not picked up from her family line.

Justin leaned over the sink and began banging on the glass. "Help me! Call... Help me, please!"

The neighbors looked up from their backyard. The mother said something. She began shooing her children into the house. He looked at the coffeemaker and reached to pick it up from the counter.

The storm shutters outside slammed closed over the window. Justin stared. He used to brag about living in a house with working shutters.

The humming continued around him. Justin backed away from the sink.

Charity used to hum, he thought.

Now he remembered her doing it when they were first married. He had yelled at her until she stopped.

Justin sat down in the floor against the stove. He pressed the heels of his hands into his aching eyes.

✳ ✳ ✳

"You need to eat more, foolish boy. You are rail thin."

Justin muttered, "You're invisible."

"Stop being silly and eat."

Justin looked around the table covered with plates and glasses... and knives. There was a raw turkey breast still in the plastic. There were ribs that were still frozen with the plastic partially torn. Several unopened cans were stacked around the table. Whipped cream had been dumped out on the table. A mixing bowl full of ice cubes gathered moisture. Raw hotdogs were scattered out from an open package leaking across the wood and dripping on the floor.

Justin had brought some of the food to the table as he was ordered. Other items had found their own way.

The surface of the table was covered with a film of water. The liquid ran down the legs and soaked into the carpet. As it followed the discolored fluid from the hotdog package, the cold water began dripping in his lap.

The tabletop pasted white from the damage.

"The food is raw," Justin complained.

"Eat your food. You will need your energy. We still have a lot to do for the holidays."

Handprints dented into the surface of the water. He could see the impressions of the fingers moving as if alive. More water poured into his lap as it was disturbed. He saw tendrils of ice crystals forming in the indentions as the handprints moved across the table. The package of raw turkey moved like a mouse figurine toward him, pushing the flow of water over ahead of it.

Justin jumped up, knocking his chair over and scuffing the wall behind him.

"Eat up or I'll put coal in your stocking... or worse."

Justin grabbed the wet edge of the table and turned it up, pouring water over the other side. For the briefest moment, Justin saw the water part around the curve of hips, legs, and a frail pelvis. He saw a hint of nakedness, and then the water folded back together in a natural sheet. The food, plates, and knives followed the water as it toppled off the table onto the carpet. The bowl of ice scattered. As the table flipped upside down, Justin saw a puff of vapor, like breath on a cold day. He wasn't sure if it was from the ice or something else.

"Throw your tantrum, foolish boy. You'll be punished soon enough."

"Let me out of this house," Justin screamed.

"How about I spread some crackers to quiet you down?"

There's no spreading knife, Justin thought.

He grabbed up his chair and hurled it to the opposite wall of the dining room. He expected to see it shatter in mid-air around the frail, naked body of his wife's great grand-mother or whoever this was. It scarred the wall and cracked along the back.

"Your anger does not impress me," she said. *"I've watched you throw these tantrums for years."*

Justin stormed to the pie cabinet and pulled it over with a crash.

"You behaved like a foolish boy until my things began to vanish and my house was empty... vacant at Christmas."

Justin ran into the foyer. He unbolted the front door and pulled it open. He felt the natural cold from outside and a wave of fresh air that showed him how stale the air had become inside. The door pulled out of his hand and slammed closed. A spray of mist hit his face with the impact.

He grabbed the coat rack and broke it against the frame

of the door. The decorative side glass shattered outward. Red light from morning was cutting through the trees and over the roofs of the other decorated houses.

Justin screamed, "Someone, help me. She's trying to kill me. Someone, call the police. Help!"

"You are the reason my house is broken. You are the reason my tablecloth is gone on Christmas."

"Let me out or I'll break it all," Justin yelled.

"Foolish boy," the voice hissed.

Justin ran into the living room and pulled the tree over. He stomped on the ornaments, shattering the thin glass under his shoes. He jumped up, knocking the wreaths off their nails, and he pulled at the wreaths with his hands until his fingers were bleeding. He ran to the storage closet and began throwing the boxes onto the floor.

He looked over at the mudroom and saw it in the doorway. He wrapped his hands slowly around the handle and dragged the ax head along the hardwood floor. He buried it into the walls. He swung it into the rare books on the top shelves. He ran it through every piece of old wood he could find.

Then, he stopped and heaved for breath.

He smiled as he stepped over the toppled Christmas tree. He reached to the shelf and picked up the tiny mouse figurine. Justin lifted it in his fist above his head.

He felt the cold, wet spots form on the front of his shirt. He was hit in the chest with sledgehammer force. Justin lifted off his feet and crashed through the top of the coffee table that he had overlooked in his rampage. He held on to the ax but lost the figurine.

Justin stumbled to his feet and ran through the foyer to the front door. He chopped the ax into the wood around the knob until it collapsed out from the frame. Splinters and water flew into his face, but he kept chopping. He started seeing blue light flashing in his face. He thought about his alarm clock.

Justin threw his shoulder into the remains of the front door. As he stumbled out into the cold air on the porch, he started laughing and crying.

"You can't stop me," he screamed. "I'm getting away from you. If I have to kill you again, I'm getting away."

Three police officers approached the house through the yard from their cars and flashing lights along the curb. The neighbors watched.

This can't look good, Justin thought as his smile slowly faded into a grimace.

"You can't go. You don't just walk out on family. You're ruining Christmas."

Justin began to step forward on the porch. The officers crouched slightly and placed their hands on the butts of their guns. They did not draw.

"Don't. Don't. Don't," one of them shouted as he held out his other palm at Justin. "You just need to stay there, sir."

"Don't leave... please," she pleaded behind him, *"this is your home... our home. Come back... just for Christmas. You can't possibly want me to be alone. That's not how you treat family."*

Justin shook his head. He felt the dampness at the back of his shirt as she began to pull. He ran forward. As the police reacted, he realized he was still holding the ax. He tried to let go, but the cold grasp closed over his hand and held it to the handle. Then, she jerked his hand into the air, raising the ax over his head.

Justin closed his eyes as he fell. The pain was horrific, and then there was the cold. He wanted to be gone. He wanted to be free. He suspected he was too close to her house for that. He felt her hands close around him as the sound drained out of the world.

He stared at his own bullet-riddled body on the lawn as she pulled him backward into the house.

"No one should be alone for Christmas," she whispered.

Nell's Game

Nicole DeGennaro

Nell held her breath in the dark, straining to hear even the faintest noises beyond the closed bedroom door. Jimmy, her younger brother, snored gently in his bed to her right. She entertained the idea of smothering him to silence the noise, but she knew the consequences would outweigh the reward.

A faint *creak* in the hall pulled her thoughts away from her brother. After having faked being asleep when her mother had checked in about an hour ago, Nell had been waiting for any sign that her parents had started putting the presents under the Christmas tree. She didn't care about the presents themselves so much as she liked knowing that her parents always gave her more than Jimmy, even though they said she and Jimmy got the same amount. But she had counted the last two years and knew she had received more. She knew exactly why, too, but she kept that to herself.

She didn't remember a time when she had ever believed in Santa, but she had pretended for a few years because she knew her parents wanted her to be normal, and that meant believing in Santa. But now that Nell had turned seven, she didn't want to pretend anymore, so she sat waiting for the right moment to open her bedroom door and wipe fake sleep from her eyes while her parents put out the presents. It would seem like a regular way for a child to discover the truth about Santa, instead of her mother and father realizing that she had always known, that she would always be able to outsmart them.

She heard a jingle from the small bells decorating the Christmas tree, and another soft noise that might have been her mother shushing her father. Nell gripped the doorknob and pulled open the bedroom door, deciding the moment had come. Jimmy continued to snore in his bed.

Darkness blanketed the hallway and rooms beyond, and she hesitated, wondering if she had waited too long, if her parents were already back in bed. A loud *bang* echoed down the hall from the living room, and she jumped. As her eyes adjusted, she saw a shadowy shape moving near the tree. She began her charade, rubbing at her eyes as she shuffled down the hall. She had navigated the house in the dark so often that she didn't bother to turn on a light. The aroma of pine from the tree overwhelmed her as she approached the living room; it felt like another presence in the dark, pressing against her skin.

"Santa?" she asked, suppressing the satisfied smile that wanted to creep across her face at just how groggy she managed to sound.

She stopped at the end of the hall, the entrance to the kitchen on her left and the living room a dark, gaping maw in front of her. The slender triangle of the Christmas tree dwarfed the couch and coffee table and stood sentry in front of the bay window. Moonlight filtered through the branches and needles, reflecting off the gold bells and red ornaments. The shape Nell had seen moving near the tree had disappeared, and she glanced around, wondering if her parents were trying to hide to avoid detection.

As she looked into the kitchen, her gaze lingered on the magnetic knife rack, where her familiar friends hung waiting, their blades gleaming in the artificial glow of a nightlight. The jingle of bells pulled her attention back to the tree, and she peered around as she shuffled into the living room, trying to find the dark shape among the shadows. Nothing moved.

"Santa, are you there?" She rubbed her eyes again, knowing she could outlast her parents.

"*Nell,*" a deep voice called her name, coming from the direction of the tree. She crept forward, her toes sinking into the soft carpet, and tried to spy her father hiding behind the tree. She hadn't expected him to be so reluctant to reveal himself.

"Who's there?" she asked, injecting just a smidge of fake fear into her voice for the sake of her father. A low chuckle came in response. Nell kept her face neutral and sleepy while her mind worked to figure out this new game. Her father wouldn't be able to outsmart her, but she found the notion that he would try intriguing. Her heartbeat quickened with the thrill of competition; whatever game he wanted to play, she knew she would win.

"*Oh, it's a game all right,*" the voice said, smooth like a snake's hiss and unlike her father's in every way. She wondered if her father were like her—different when he thought no one could see him. Maybe he didn't want to hide it from her anymore.

"Then there must be rules," she said, and as she did it

occurred to her that she hadn't mentioned her thoughts about a game out loud. She came to a stop near the couch but kept her attention on the Christmas tree.

"You like to break rules, don't you? The important ones the most. Whatever happened to your brother's hamster, Nell?"

A game of confession, then. She twisted the toes of her right foot into the carpet and put on her best innocent face: wide eyes, slightly open mouth, both eyebrows arched.

"We never found Boscoe," she said in a voice to match her expression. She even wrung her hands in front of her in mock worry, as she had seen her mother do out of genuine concern plenty of times before.

"Good show, Nell," the voice said with a chuckle that sounded like cracking bones. *"But I don't need a confession. I know what you've done, what you will do."*

She kept her expression vacant, innocent, even as inside she scrambled to figure out the game. Not confession—then what? Fear? She took a calculated step back, willed her eyes to start watering.

"You're scaring me, Daddy. I don't like this game."

Now the voice cackled, and the sound thundered through the house, shaking the floor. Nell glanced down the hall, grateful that her mother could sleep through anything but certain that Jimmy would wake up, certain also that the voice did not belong to her father. But nothing stirred, so she turned her attention back to the Christmas tree.

"Your tricks won't work on me, Nell. But you're good; better than most kids your age that I've met." As she watched, part of the Christmas tree separated and solidified, the branches coagulating into a tall, strange shape silhouetted against the window. Two glowing red eyes stared at her, partly illuminating a fur-covered face with a mouth full of jagged teeth and a lolling tongue. Moonlight glinted off of two curling horns coming

from the creature's head; the points almost touched the high ceiling. The rest of the body remained obscured by shadows.

Nell stood her ground, and the creature grinned.

"That's how I know you're the real thing." He spoke, but his mouth did not move. *"There are plenty of normal kids in the world that just have a mean streak. But not you, Nell. Your very core is rotten, isn't it?"*

"Who are you?" She still wanted to win the creature's game, but she needed to know something about him to guess what he might want. If it had been her father, the game would have been over—he had caught her once replacing the carving knife in the kitchen after a night of adventure, had seen the specks of blood on her hands. He wanted to believe that it had been a one-time thing, that she was still innocent and liked horses and Disney princesses and whatever other little girls enjoyed. She could easily manipulate her father, his wants readable on his desperate face. But this creature was not her father.

Again the bone-crunch chuckle; again no movement from the creature as the sound reached Nell.

"If you think it will help you, I'll gladly tell you who I am." The creature turned his large head to the tree and reached a hand toward one of the ornaments. When he moved into the moonlight, Nell saw that the fur covered the creature's whole body, including the long, bony fingers of his hands. He touched a homemade ornament, one she had created in her kindergarten class—she knew because underneath the crudely drawn picture of her family it said *by Nell, age 5*. The popsicle stick frame around the picture began to smolder at the creature's touch. He let the wood blacken and then withdrew his hand, turning his red eyes back to her.

"I am Krampus."

She paused. "I've never heard of you."

"*Ah, and can only things that you know of exist, young one? Do you think that is how this world—or any other—operates?*"

"Why are you here?" She crossed her arms over her chest. She didn't appreciate Krampus calling her "young one," as if she were just another dumb child.

Krampus nodded. "*You are starting to ask the right questions now, Nell. I come to play games with children like you, as Kringle brings presents to those like Jimmy.*"

Now Nell laughed. "Santa isn't real, though."

"*I'll be sure to inform him of his nonexistence.*"

"Why do I get presents, then? And why haven't I seen you before?"

"*Kringle hoped you would come to deserve those presents. Now that we know you won't, I've been summoned.*"

She turned away, deciding that at some point she must have fallen asleep waiting for her parents and had sunk into a realistic but bizarre dream. She just had to get herself to wake up.

"I'm going back to bed."

Krampus lunged at her, ducking down so his large head stopped only inches from her face. She scrunched her nose at the thick stench of rancid flesh and the tang of blood that created a sickening mix with the pine from the tree. Krampus gave his head a slow shake; strands of pale gray fur tickled Nell's face.

"*You think you can be rid of me so easily?*"

She stepped back until she stood closer to the kitchen doorway, waiting for her opportunity. Krampus straightened to his full height again, standing on two horse-like back legs, with the elongated ankles that people often mistook for backward knees. He continued to watch her with his emotionless red eyes.

"I don't want to play your game."

Again Krampus shook his head, as if he saw right through her lie, and then he turned his attention back to the tree. Nell seized the moment and rushed into the kitchen. She grabbed one of the chairs from the small kitchen table so she would be able to reach the carving knife waiting for her in the magnetic rack. When she turned toward the counter, clutching the chair in her hands, Krampus stood in her way. The tip of one of his horns dug into the lower ceiling of the kitchen, leaving a deep gouge in the otherwise flawless dry- wall. In one long-fingered hand he held the slim, perfect carving knife—Nell's favorite. He ran a finger over the sharp side of the blade; she watched it bite into his skin, leaving an oozing black trail behind. When she blinked, the trail and wound disappeared.

"I know you'll like this game, Nell. I designed it just for you."

She released the chair, setting it down against the tile floor in a clatter, and watched Krampus twirl her knife, feel- ing each rotation as a twist in her heart. She took a step forward but managed to stop herself from reaching for her knife.

"When do we start playing, then?"

Krampus flipped the knife into the air and held his hand out; she watched as the knife fell and the blade sank into Krampus' open left palm, sticking clear out the other side of his hand. Then she blinked, and the knife sat blade flat in Krampus' uninjured left hand. He held the handle toward her.

"Soon. So very soon."

Nell couldn't help herself; she reached for the knife, wanted to feel the worn wooden handle against her palm, wanted to be reminded of all she and the knife had done together. Krampus nodded, and his grin widened. Once her right hand touched the wood, her whole body relaxed, as if a missing piece of herself had been replaced. It always impressed her how well the handle fit in her small hand, like the knife had been made for her. She brought her right hand to rest over her heart, gripping the handle tight and tilting the knife blade away from her face. It shone in the artificial light.

"Goodnight, Nell. Merry Christmas."

Krampus stepped away from her, dissolving into the shadows lurking in the nearest corner of the kitchen. For a few seconds his red eyes glowed at her from the darkness. Then she blinked, and they vanished.

Nell woke in her bed, sunlight filtering in through the window. She winced as something on her pillow reflected the light into her face, and when her eyes adjusted, she saw her carving knife sitting sharp and clean next to her head. With a quick movement, she shoved it under her pillow, hoping her parents wouldn't notice it missing before she could return it to the kitchen. She had a vague memory of waking up in the middle of the night and retrieving the knife, but she couldn't recall much else. Still, she tended to be more careful than that — she always returned the knife when they finished their adventures.

With that done, she sat up and, remembering that it was Christmas day, made a show of leaping out of bed and being the excited child her parents and brother would expect.

"Jimmy! Merry Christmas!" She gave him a rough shake as she raced past him toward the door; her hand came away from his sheets sticky, and she wiped it against her pajamas as she ran out into the hallway to wake their parents.

"Merry Christmas!" she yelled, banging on their door. Again her hand felt sticky, and she wiped it against her pajamas without thinking as she continued down the hall. "I'm going to open presents now!" Although she faked the excitement in her voice, she was curious to see what presents her parents had chosen for her; they revealed a great deal about her parents' expectations of her.

Nell stopped halfway down the hall, waiting for a reply from her parents or brother because she knew she would get in trouble if she started opening presents without them. When the house remained silent, she went back into her bedroom and approached her brother.

"Jimmy?"

In the sunlight, she could see a large dark spot on the cream-colored flannel sheets, and when she pulled the covers back, she knew her brother would not be getting out of bed. A memory came to her of Jimmy struggling as she held a pillow to his face, of the carving knife sinking into his chest.

She pulled the covers back over Jimmy and left him there. She remembered playing some kind of game with someone in the night, but the details were hazy. She returned to the hall and pushed open her parents' bedroom door, although she knew what she would find.

They laid where she had left them, stuck in a hideous parody of sleep. The coppery tang of blood permeating the air reminded Nell of something else, but she couldn't recall anything more specific than an image of two red glowing orbs like Christmas lights in her mind.

She remembered killing her father first, then her mother, who had remained oblivious up to her last moment. A few quick stabs in the right place finished them both. Afterward, Nell had wiped the blade clean on her pajamas before returning to her bed and drifting off into an untroubled sleep. Now she stood in the doorway, staring at her dead parents for a few moments in the daylight before she turned and left the room, closing the door behind her.

She returned to her room and retrieved the carving knife, the wooden handle warm in her small hand. She carried it down the hall and into the kitchen, where she slid a chair across the floor to the counter, not worrying about the loud scraping sound that echoed through the house. It would not disturb anyone. When she stood on the chair and held the knife near its empty place on the rack, she felt the magnet pulling at the blade. For a moment she didn't want to give it up, but then she uncurled her fingers from the handle, leaving the carving knife hanging next to its brethren. As she stepped off the chair, a dark spot on the ceiling caught her eye. She stared upward at the deep gash in the drywall, wondering how it had got there.

After she replaced the chair by the table, she exited the kitchen and went into the living room to the Christmas tree.

It stood as tall as ever, still strung with lights and bombarding the living room with the scent of pine. Nell sat on the floor in front of the tree in her blood-soaked pajamas and counted her presents. Fourteen to the twelve that would sit forever waiting for Jimmy. She smirked. Her family had never known that the one thing she always wanted had already been in the house, had been within her grasp from the age of five, when she had first noticed the way the beautiful blade shimmered in the light.

For lack of anything else to do, she began to open her presents. After the first three—a Barbie doll, some kind of bead bracelet kit, and the latest Disney movie—a small parcel caught her eye. The plain, bright red wrapping paper stood out against the busy patterns and giant bows covering the other packages. She reached for it, thinking how much the red matched the two glowing orbs she kept seeing in her memory. After turning the lightweight present over in her hands for a moment, looking for a nonexistent gift tag, she tore off the wrapping paper.

She blinked at the ornament: a crudely drawn picture of her family with the words *by Nell, age 5* underneath, surrounded by a charred Popsicle stick frame.

A hand covered in pale gray fur reached down and plucked the ornament from Nell. She looked up into a pair of glowing red eyes and a grinning mouth full of jagged teeth and a lolling tongue. Two shiny brown horns curled from the creature's forehead. Krampus grasped the ornament in one hand; in the other he held her carving knife. As she stared up at him, she remembered everything from the previous night. She rose to her feet; still he towered over her, peering down with his glowing eyes.

"I won the game, didn't I?" she asked.

"You did. And so did I," Krampus said, his grin widening. He stooped down and held her knife up between them; this time he did not offer her the handle. Nell could see a faint reflection of her face in the smooth blade. *"Now I'm going to collect my prize."*

Cursed Christmas
David J. Delaney

December 21, 1961

Excerpt from The Daily Herald

"... *young man dies during a tragic accident while working on a family Christmas tree farm. The man fell and broke his neck while loading a truck bound for the city's Christmas tree buyers. His mother and father, who own the farm, are said to be in a state of shock. Earl Bradshaw, father to the deceased, has said that the business cannot go on with such loss...*"

❄ ❄ ❄

Present Day

Winter's bite was hard tonight. The radio said minus 5 Celsius and Richard felt every single bit of it. The small amount of heat his car generated and held within its confines caused his windscreen to mist up constantly. He wiped it with his coat sleeve every few minutes, getting more and more pissed off. Traffic was light though. The reason was that it was 9:00 pm. Nobody wanted to share the ice-laden roads with him, and he couldn't blame them.

It was Christmas week, six days from the big day, and Richard was scouring the streets looking for that iconic item of the season, a Christmas tree. The plastic one from last year was in pretty bad shape, barely standing, so Richard told his wife and kids he would get one. There excited faces sealed the deal, and he knew he'd have to find one. A crazy work schedule had stopped him from getting one, and the family had begun badgering him to bring one home. He felt pangs of guilt each time he looked at the feeble tree they had while fobbing his family off with excuses of needy clients from his financial firm.

"God Damn windows," Richard declared as he wiped them for the thousandth time.

He scanned the streets for any store that might still be open. He found nothing but darkened signs and interiors. All that shone into the darkness of night were pubs, clubs, fast-food restaurants, and corner stores, none of which would give him what he needed. He thought maybe being Christmas Week there would be late-night shopping of sorts, but that wasn't the case.

Richard decided to pull off the road he was on so he could check his smart phone for any potential targets. Dirt crunched beneath his tires as he came to a stop. His hands felt like lumps of cold meat at the ends of his arms. He cupped them to his face and blew warm breath into them. He rubbed them together vigorously before taking out his phone. He searched Google for a few minutes before deciding to call it a night. It wasn't going to happen until tomorrow.

"Shit," he said out loud, while the light of his phone illuminated his chilled, wispy breath.

Richard let out a long sigh as he began dialing his wife's number. He looked out the windshield as he placed the phone to his ear and waited for the connection to be made; he was only barely able to see through the frosted glass. His headlights were still on low beams, but he thought he could see something a little ways up the road. He cancelled the call before the first ring.

Wiping the screen and hitting his high beams, he could see what caught his attention. A smile erupted on his face as he saw a derelict sign about 10 yards further up the road. The wood looked rotten, and the paint was chipped, but the message could be made out clear enough. It read, *Uncle Earl's Christmas Tree Farm Next Left*. A faded Christmas tree with a smiling face had also been painted on the sign.

"You've got to be joking?" He wondered if fate was about to slap him in the face.

He drove towards the sign, and then past it, and found himself at the mouth of a driveway. Darkness separated him from the house at the end of it. No roadside light shone the way forward, so he drove slowly, careful not to hit any unseen dangers. At the end of the small driveway, he reached a quaint, single-story, weathered-board home. Its windows spilled yellow light that gave Richard a feeling of warmth. He cut the engine and stepped out of the car. The blistering cold hit him head on. Richard pulled the collar of his coat up around his neck and made his way towards the front door. As he extended his frozen hand, preparing to knock, the door swung quietly open. A small, gray-haired woman stuck her head out through the light-filled crack. "Hello."

"Hello, Madam. I'm sorry it's so late, but I was wondering if you were selling any Christmas trees. I'm a little desperate."

"Oh, well… That's not my domain, young man, but I'll get the very man who can help you. Come in out of the cold."

The woman held the door open a little more for Richard to enter. He thanked the woman, glad of the chance to warm himself. The old woman closed the door, smiled at him, and then walked down the hallway and disappeared through a doorway. He stood waiting by the door, hoping — praying — he'd get what he needed.

A moment later, an old man appeared through the same doorway the woman had gone through. He was tall and lean and had the harsh features of someone who knew a hard day's labor. He walked toward Richard, looking him up and down. Richard, although of a similar height and build to the man, instantly felt intimidated.

"Hello, the name's Earl," said the man as he held out a shovel-sized hand.

"Oh, I'm, uh, Richard," he managed to say as he shook Earl's hand.

When they broke the connection, Earl shook his head from side to side before saying, "Sorry to be the bearer of bad news. Pat told me you're looking for a tree. Now I know the sign, or what's left of it at least, says we have a farm, but we haven't been in that game for a long time."

Richard felt gutted. "Right, that's a shame. I've been everywhere."

"Well, son, as I said, we're out of that game now a long time, and I can't for the life of me think of where you'll grab a tree now, especially at this time of year."

"Yeah, I know. I was hoping to surprise my family, but it's okay."

Richard turned to the front door when the old woman called from the end of the hall. "Earl, come now, let the man have one."

Earl turned quickly toward his wife and said, "Pat, for God's sake, why suggest such a ridiculous thing." He seemed angry at the idea.

Richard felt a little awkward at Earl's sudden harshness. He thought of making an excuse, then a quick getaway, but with the possibility of getting a tree... Well, he had to stay.

"It's been fourteen years. We need to stop being silly. Come on," Pat said, keeping her voice controlled.

"Pat, the last time we—" Earl began before Pat quickly interjected.

"Earl, give the man what he wants. It's Christmas, and he's been driving around in that bitter cold for his family."

"Oh, I don't know," Earl said, bringing his hand to this fore-head and rubbing hard, as if the mere thought of giving this stranger a tree was causing him physical pain.

"Well, I *do* know. Now you know where they are out the back. Give him a nice one and let him get home," Pat said before disappearing back through the doorway.

"Alright, alright."

Richard couldn't help but smile even though Earl looked worried. Earl threw his thumb over his shoulder and said, "Back here, son; they're all back here."

Richard followed Earl along the hallway. Passing the door-way that Pat went through, he caught sight of the old woman and mouthed, "Thank you," to which she replied with a nod and warm smile.

The end of the hallway led through to the kitchen, which in turn led through to the backyard. The cold once more assaulted Richard's exposed skin. As his eyes adjusted to the weak illumination offered by the kitchen light, he could tell he was in a vast space. A few yards from the back door, Earl stopped before a large, black tarpaulin.

"Could you get that end for me?" Earl asked Richard, pointing to the far right corner of the immense plastic sheet.

Richard grabbed the corner as told and helped Earl lift the sheet up and over the contents it covered. Even through the cold night air, a strong scent of pine hit his nostrils. Richard smiled; beneath the tarp were dozens of felled Christmas trees, fallen soldiers long-since forgotten.

"Was gonna burn 'em up," Earl said as he scanned the bounty of trees. "Guess one missing won't hurt."

Earl rubbed his chin as he looked upon the trees. Richard stood silently waiting, wanting to know why the hell perfectly good trees were lying unsold on Christmas week, but he didn't want to disturb or annoy Earl.

"Okay," Earl said, studying the trees. "This one." He reached down and pulled up a six footer with bristling branches full of green needles.

"Here, hold onto this while I get some rope and netting."

Earl stood the tree up and placed the inner trunk into Richard's hand. Even just holding it upright, it was heavy. He was surprised a man of Earl's age was able to pick it up as easily as he had.

Earl returned with white netting and a ball of twine. "Hold the netting open like this and I'll lift her. We'll tie her all up nice and neat for you."

"Are you sure you don't want me to lift?" Richard asked. Earl smiled to himself as he began to lift the tree with ease.

Richard held the netting open as he had been shown,

and Earl eased it in. He slid it up the body of the tree, then tied the twine in three places, up top, down at the bottom, and one in the middle. Earl then heaved the cocooned tree onto his shoulder and said, "Let's get her packed up for ya."

Through the heat of the kitchen and down the hall once more he followed Earl. Out front, Richard skipped past Earl and opened the back doors of his car. Earl expertly maneuvered the tree into place. After a few seconds of fine adjustment, it was secure. Earl closed the door and turned to face Richard.

"Haven't shouldered one of those things in a long time," Earl declared, only a little out of breath.

"Thank you so much. My family is going to be thrilled with this," Richard said as he took his wallet out of his coat pocket.

Earl held up his hand. "Put that away. I don't want any money from you."

Richard looked up, a little dumb struck. "You sure? I mean, this would easily cost a hundred, a hundred fifty."

"No, no money, but do you have a mobile phone on you?"

"Yeah, sure," Richard said at the unexpected question.

"Right. Well, take my number and put it in there." Earl called out his number, and Richard placed it under "Earl Christmas Tree."

"If you come up feeling strange, headachy, or feeling angry or aggressive for no reason at all, you call me right away," Earl said with an emphatic tone.

"Um… Like sick or something?" Richard asked, confused.

"Yeah, sick. Headaches, mood swings, just not feeling right. It can happen sometimes. An allergic reaction… to the tree."

"I've never heard of that before."

"It's rare. Just call me, any time, if you feel like that. Okay?" Earl looked directly into Richard's eyes.

Richard nodded. "Okay." He felt silly agreeing with the

old man, but Earl seemed fairly serious about his warning.

He thanked Earl once more and got into his car, turning the car around, ready to go back the way he came. As he drove down the driveway, he glanced back, but Earl was gone.

The drive home felt quick. The scent of fresh pine needles filled the car, lifting Richard's spirits despite him having to wipe the windscreen a dozen more times. It was 10:15 pm by the time he pulled up in front of his house. The kids and Evelyn would be sleeping. The lack of lights in the house confirmed this. Richard got out and opened the back door. He managed to get the tree out, but struggled with the weight of it. Earl made it look easy. It took a few minutes to bring the tree quietly in through the front door and into the living room. Richard tried to be as silent as a mouse. He wanted this to be a surprise for Evelyn and kids. He found an old stand in the cupboard under the stairs and lowered the tree into it, tightening the bolts to secure it in place. He cut the netting and twine. He gathered the refuse and stood back to view his procurement. Even in the darkened room, it looked magical. Lush and green and full of life.

Feeling satisfied with himself, he stealthily made his way up the stairs. He undressed in the bathroom and tip toed into his bedroom, where the steady rise and fall of Evelyn's chest told him she was in a deep sleep. Richard slowly slipped in beneath the covers and drifted off to a dreamless sleep.

* * *

Light slipping in through the space between the curtains told Richard's groggy brain it was time to rise and shine. Normally an early riser, he didn't mind. He blinked away the sleep, then yawned and stretched. Richard always rose earlier than Evelyn; she wasn't a morning person, as she always told him. This morning, though, all he could find of his wife was her outline and the fading heat of her body beside him. The digital clock on the nightstand blinked 5:07 am. *Weird*, he thought.

With a furrowed brow, he jumped up from bed and pulled a dressing gown from the wardrobe, wrapping it quickly around himself. The previous night's chill hung in the air still. Stepping into some warm slippers, he made his way onto the landing, listening for any of the normal signs that his family was up and about. He heard none.

Charlie, the youngest at four years old, took after his Dad, waking up at first light, while Tom, seven, was his Momma's boy, savoring each moment of sleep he could. Richard walked into Charlie's room first, expecting Lego to be strewn everywhere while he worked on his latest masterpiece. He found no Lego and no Charlie, just an empty bed with *Teenage Mutant Ninja Turtle* bed sheets half on the floor. Charlie's room was the same. No sleeping Charlie, just an unmade bed.

"Evelyn? Guys? You down there?" Richard called out. Nothing.

Jokes over. Come on, he thought as he walked down the stairs.

He called out again as he entered the kitchen. The sun was low in the sky, rising with the morning. It streamed through the large window at the back of the house, blinding him. He rubbed his watery eyes with his knuckles. When he opened them, silence and another empty room greeted him. Evelyn's car keys sat on the table, beside where he had thrown his the night before. Seeing the keys caused an ominous feeling to rise from the pit of his stomach as he tried to figure out why she would leave so early on foot with the two boys.

He turned to the living room, ready to give another call

for his family, when he was greeted with a barrage of, "Surprise, Daddy!" His heart leapt into his mouth. "What the fu…" but he caught himself before finishing that exclamation.

Standing beside the Christmas tree, Evelyn and the two boys grinned widely at his show of surprise. Each of them held tinsel and decorations. The boys held their pieces high above their heads in triumph.

"Surprise, Daddy," the boys repeated in unison before racing towards a startled Richard.

They jumped up at him, hugging him tightly. His stunned face broke into a smile. He looked at Evelyn and then to the tree. He hugged the boys harder.

"Charlie got up real early, and then woke me up, too," Thomas began to say.

"I told Thomas to be super quiet because I saw the tree and wanted to decorate it before you got up. That's when I sneaked in and got Mom."

"And I bet Mom was only too delighted to be woken up by you two rascals," Richard said.

"This morning she didn't mind. Thanks, honey, it's beautiful," Evelyn said as she planted a kiss on Richards's lips. "And then Mom and her little rascals decorated the tree to surprise Daddy when he woke up."

The two boys nodded in unison. Richard put an arm around Evelyn and brought her into the family embrace.

"Hey, I know you're busy, but what do you say about playing hooky today? Call in sick," Evelyn said quietly into Richards's ear.

He thought about it for a moment. If he called in sick, he'd have double the crap to deal with tomorrow. Evelyn could see him ruminating on the idea, mulling it over. He looked at her, into her eyes that asked him to stay home. He couldn't say no.

"You know what? You're right. Let's do it."

He left a voice mail for HR and his boss, telling them he'd be back tomorrow, that a cold had rendered him useless.

After his white lie, he busied himself playing with the kids. He hadn't done this for a long time, and it felt great. Hours swam by as they played with Lego, an array of other toys, and board games.

"Jeez, I'm worn out," Richard said to Evelyn, collapsing onto the couch beside her.

"They're a handful."

"Yeah. Hey, I might take a granny nap," Richard said.

"Go for it. They'll happily watch a movie now."

Richard took his window of opportunity and tip toed up the stairs to his room. He'd crash for a half hour, then get up and start it all over. He dropped his gown, stepped out of his slippers, and crawled under the sheets. It only took a few moments for the warmth to creep back into to clean cotton and duvet. Richard began to drift further and further away the warmer it got. Within minutes, he was out cold.

This time he dreamed. He became aware of his dream state as he stood in a field of turned soil. Death surrounded him. He could sense it somehow. It sent a shiver up his spine. There was nothing but dark earth for as far as the eye could see. A gray sky hung low. It seemed to bear down on him. Foreboding flooded his body. A sudden urge to run from this place took him. His muscles felt sluggish, but he managed to turn. As he did, he saw Earl, his Christmas tree savior. He didn't feel surprised to see him here.

"Where you goin', son? You gotta pay your dues first," Earl said.

"What are you talking about?" Richard asked.

Earl shook his head and replied, "Pay your dues, or you gonna have to pay a higher price."

Richard shook his head. He didn't understand, and his need to leave here grew. Goose bumps broke out all over his body, and the hair on the back of his neck bristled. He turned away from Earl, preparing to head in the other direction, only to find someone else standing before him. Richard, feeling penned in, began to panic.

The other man was younger, but just as big and brawny as Earl. He held a shovel in his hands and was digging in and turning the soil over and over. The soil never seemed to stay turned, falling back into place as soon as it left the shovel. Richard wanted to scream at the man, tell him how pointless his feat was, and to get out of his way.

"Without it, it ain't gonna grow," the young man said as he dug and turned, dug and turned.

Richard's head became filled with fear, confusion, and anger. His feet felt rooted to the ground, but he knew he had to move, needed to get away from this place. His eyes fell to his feet, willing them to move. Then, like a stage show magic trick, a miniature-sized Christmas tree appeared before him. It didn't startle him to find it conjured from thin air, more intrigued him. Its sight was comforting, something familiar among the strange and bizarre. Richard bent down to touch it, bring his finger to the very top of the tree, but pulled it away when he felt a prick. He instinctively brought it to his mouth and was surprised when he tasted something metallic. Pulling his finger from his mouth, he discovered blood gushing from a tiny hole in his finger. His eyes widened as the blood ran down his arm and dripped to the ground. It flowed in a straight line towards the tree.

"Nope, won't do. She needs more," the young man said, now standing up and looking at Richard.

Thunder boomed over head as Richard's blood soaked into the soil around the tree. He felt weak. Using every ounce of energy, Richard tried to move. He made it a mere inch when rain started to fall in blinding sheets. His skin felt slick from the downpour. In his mind he wished for the comfort of his home, his family. He looked to the sky, which had taken on a scarlet hue. In front of him, Earl and the young man stood smiling. Their faces ran red with crimson streams. Richard realized then what the downpour was. It wasn't simply water. The clouds above burst with blood. He held up his own soaked hands, looked at them for a second, and then let out a guttural cry of sheer terror.

"Now that's more like it," roared the young man above the sound of the macabre torrent.

Richard awoke with a jolt, a cold sweat covering his body despite the warmth of the bed. His breath was quick and shallow, and his throat felt tight. He held up his index finger expecting to see blood leaking from it, but it was fine. No injury to note. He closed his eyes as reality began to assert itself again. Within a minute, he felt himself once more. Richard shook his head and, deciding against attempting another nap, got out of bed.

Downstairs, he could hear a conversation between Shrek and Donkey coming from the living room. The boys would be glued to the screen. He found Evelyn seated on the couch reading a book. A deep ache spiked behind his eyes. He went to the medicine cabinet and dry-swallowed some aspirin.

When he returned to the living room, Evelyn looked up. "That was quick. Only gone 10 minutes. Not able to nod off?"

"Yeah, something like that. I have a headache."

"You look a little pale. You sure you're feeling alright."

"Yeah, I'm fine. I might just sit here and wait for the tablets to kick in."

He sat on beside Evelyn, who absently stroked his hair

as she returned to her book. He loved when she did that, but this time he didn't receive the same comfort from it. It irritated him for some reason, but he didn't want to upset her, so he endured it.

"You sure you're okay, honey?"

"Yeah, fine," Richard said, wishing she would just shut up.

Richard looked at the tree. It stood there, decorated as before. He looked more intently at it, noticing something between the branches. Something moved along the trunk. The boys seemed oblivious to it as they lay on their stomachs staring up at the TV. Richard followed the trunk of the tree with his eyes until he reached its base. He gave a start when he saw blood saturated the floor below the tree, blood that appeared to be flowing from his boys to the tree.

He stood up, knocking Evelyn away from him. He started toward the tree but stopped when he noticed the blood was gone. He blinked twice, looking around for any sign of it. All he could see was the two kids and the tree. There was nothing unusual.

"Honey, what was that?" Evelyn asked with annoyance.

Richard broke his search of the living room and turned to Evelyn. *Why don't you mind you own damn business*, he thought, but said, "Um, nothing. I mean... nothing."

He turned back to the tree. It appeared normal again, although, in Richard's eyes, it did appear bigger somehow, more powerful, which was silly because it was only a tree. He was afraid, though; he couldn't quite put his finger on why, but he was afraid. He felt darkness flowing from it, a darkness that seeped into his very soul.

"Honey?" Evelyn said, sounding concerned.

"I'm good. Really, I am. I just feel a little off. I guess its work withdrawals," he said, attempting to make a joke, but feeling none of the joy behind it.

Evelyn nodded and smiled. "Sit. I'll make you some tea."

He didn't want it but said, "Okay." His temper was rising at Evelyn's concern for him. *Why couldn't she just worry about herself*, he thought.

He sat back down on the couch and closed his eyes. Once again, he could see the tree and blood. It drank greedily as the red trails led across the floor from his boys. The fear he felt moments before was replaced by something different this time.

Richard felt solace.

"Hey, Dad," Charlie called as he approached Richard.

Fucking hell, what now, he thought as he opened his eyes. The feeling that had been warming his insides fled. He looked down at Charlie, a frown on his face.

"Can we go to the park today?"

Richard rolled his eyes and said, "What the hell do you think? I'm supposed to be sick. Can't go gallivanting around now, can I?"

"Okay," Charlie said, shrinking at Richard's sudden anger. He quickly rejoined his brother on the floor in front of the television.

"What was that for?" Evelyn said, returning with the steaming cup. "You didn't have to bite his head off."

"Bite his head off? You're being dramatic."

"You know what? You're acting strange, and I don't like..."

Richard cut her off. "Oh, shut the fuck up, will you? I'm going back upstairs."

He didn't look back at his wife to see her reaction, but knew she wore a look of shock. A wry smile crossed his lips as he walked up to his bedroom. He shut the door and lay on top of the sheets. He closed his eyes and smiled as the images of blood came back more vividly than before. He started to drift off to sleep once more.

Richard opened his eyes to the dreary expanse of his previous dream. A nightmare within which he now felt comfortable. The turned soil and menacing sky appeared sinister but welcome. The young man appeared before him, still holding his shovel. He stopped and looked at Richard. The man's eyes were gone. In their place were two dark holes. Richard gazed deeper into the black voids, entranced, unable to look away.

The young man smiled. "Now you're getting it. Gotta pay your dues."

"We pay with blood," Richard said, his voice distant.

"Stop this now, son, before it runs away from you," a voice said from behind.

Richard broke from his trance, centering himself within the field of death. He turned to find the source of the voice, knowing it would be Earl. The hulk of a man wore a concerned expression upon his face.

"The number, son. Use the number."

"Can't," Richard said. "I have to pay my dues." The cogs in his mind were being turned by another now. He could feel this but didn't want to fight it. "I have to pay with blood."

The young man closed the gap between him and Richard. He placed a cold hand on Richard's shoulder and said, "You know what you've got to do."

Richard nodded as the young man turned him and led him away, taking him across the field, further from Earl.

"The number. Use the number," Earl cried out, but Richard heard little of it. He walked with the young man, the one who now led him down a dark path—a path he knew he had to take. Diverting was not an option.

Richard woke up. Night had fallen outside. He threw his

feet over the side of the bed, knocking his mobile phone to the floor. He didn't bother picking it up; he had more important things to attend to.

He walked into the en suite shower room adjoining his bedroom and looked into the mirror. He saw his reflection but knew it wasn't him looking back. He was the vehicle, and somebody else was driving. It felt good to leave his fate in the hands of another. Richard opened the en suite cabinet and searched for an antique box, something he found in his father's basement after he died. He looked for a blade. An old cut-throat blade. One his father used religiously on a daily basis.

After a few moments of rummaging around, he found it at the back of the cabinet beneath the sink. He pulled it out and placed the box on the ledge. Opening the box, he felt giddy when his gaze fell upon the gleaming blade. He took the sharp instrument out and held it in his right hand. The yellow spot lights glinted off the shiny steel as he turned it to the side.

He knew it was now time to pay his dues.

Richard didn't bother creeping around anymore. He walked down the stairs and secured the dead bolt as he passed the front door. He could see Evelyn and the kids in the kitchen. Evelyn was washing dishes while the boys were drawing at the table. He walked through, keeping the blade low.

"Hey, can we have a word with you," he said to Evelyn.

"Yeah, hang on. I just want to finish this off."

"Now, not in a second," Richard shouted, walking towards his wife.

Evelyn turned to Richard with a stern look. She dried her hands on a dish cloth looking like she was ready to argue. "Listen, whatever has gotten into you, it has to stop now," she said. He could see how angry she was.

"Oh, it's going to stop alright," he said. He walked closer to her but could see her eyes widen when she caught sight of the blade. He didn't mind because it would all be over in a few moments.

"What the hell are you doing?" Evelyn said, fear gripping her voice.

"It's okay, honey. Don't worry about it."

Evelyn backed up until she felt the kitchen counter press against the base of her spine. Her frightened eyes darted from Richard to the blade and back to Richard in quick movements. She opened a drawer behind her and fumbled inside it. She pulled out a wooden rolling pin and raised it above her head. "Keep away from me."

He could hear the quiver in her voice. The two boys huddled together and started to cry as they watched the events unfold. Richard had almost forgotten about them.

"What do you plan to do with that?" Richard said, laughing.

He inched closer, readying to strike. He was thoroughly enjoying this moment. He was the Big Bad Wolf about to devour Little Red Riding Hood. He could see her looking for a way out of this madness, but he knew there was none.

Richard had now narrowed the gap to no more than a few feet.

"Have to pay the dues, honey," he said_before leaping towards Evelyn, blade held high. Evelyn simultaneously swung the rolling pin. Richard's blade bit into the flesh of her upper arm while the wooden baking tool smashed into Richard's left collar bone. They both crashed to the floor. Pain surged from where she caught him, but he had to finish what he started. Evelyn kicked at him until she found an opening. She wriggled out from beneath him and dashed for the boys. When he tried to grab her, the pain exploded in his shoulder. He stood up awkwardly as he watched her grab the boys and make for the front door.

"Oh, no you don't," he cried as he followed the trail of Evelyn's blood Evelyn on the floor.

He laughed as she tried to open the front door only to be denied exit by the dead bolt. She then pushed the boys towards the stairs, urging them upwards. Richard sped up and grasped a handful of her hair. She stumbled down the first riser. She screamed up into his face, asking him to stop, but he didn't listen; instead, he brought the blade closer to her neck. Evelyn thrashed about, trying to break his grip, then decided to throw her fist back into Richard's collar bone. It took two fierce blows before he released her. She turned tail and ran up the stairs as he fell back, feeling the searing pain race through him. It took his breath away, and he fell, gasping, to his haunches.

This isn't how it was supposed to go, he heard a voice inside his brain say. He felt stupid just then and knew he had to redeem himself.

Richard stood and raced up the stairs two steps at a time. He pushed his pain to the furthest recess of his mind, trying to stay on task. He heard a door slam shut and a lock turned. They were in the en suite bathroom. Richard followed them. As he prepared to throw himself into the door, he stopped as the screech of tires came from somewhere outside. It was close, very close. He walked to the bedroom window to see a pickup truck parked diagonally across his lawn. The door was hanging open, and the driver had left on the headlights. He tried to spy the driver but saw none. Richard turned from the window, then bristled at the sound of somebody banging on the front door. Evelyn and the boys must have heard it, too, because they started hollering at the top of their voices. He was livid, seething with rage as he stormed from the bedroom to deal with the uninvited guest.

As he made his way down the stairs, he heard an almighty *thump* against the door, followed by the sound of splintering wood. He quickened his pace but only reached the bottom to see the door smash open, swinging back until it hit the wall. Framed photos rattled under the force of the impact.

Richard's eyes widened when he saw Earl standing on the threshold. An angry snarl, almost inhuman, formed on Richard's face, showing his inner hatred for the man.

"Son, put it down. You know you don't want to do this," Earl called from the doorway.

Earl held his hands out before him defensively as Richard approached.

"I've seen this before," Earl said. "I've seen that devil in someone else's eyes before. Now, I don't want to hurt you, but so help me God, I will."

"Is that right, dear Daddy?" Richard said.

Earl's shock was evident. His face took on a deathly pallor as he weakly said, "Son."

Richard launched himself towards Earl, swinging the blade wildly in front of him. Earl side stepped, but the steel bit into his forearm. Blood spilled from the wound and onto the floor. Earl grabbed Richard's wrist, struggling to force him back. Earl pushed Richard against the wall and knocked the wind out of him. Richard dropped the blade. With one massive fist, Earl punched Richard in the chest, then the cheek, and finally the stomach. As Richard collapsed, Earl brought a knee up to meet Richard's face. He was unconscious before he hit the floor.

❋ ❋ ❋

Evelyn sat in the corner of the en suite rocking back and forth and holding her boys tight. They waited for a miracle. She couldn't have put her terror into words even if she wanted to. All she could see were Richard's crazed eyes and the blade that now had her blood on it.

Footsteps. She heard footsteps. They were getting closer, louder.

"Hello. Are you in there? I don't want to frighten you, but you're safe now."

Evelyn nearly jumped at the sound. It took a few second for her to replay it in her mind. The voice sounded calm, re-assuring. It wasn't Richard's menacing growl.

She managed a meek, "Who are you?" before bursting into tears.

"My name is Earl. I can explain everything to you. I've called for the police and an ambulance."

Evelyn could hear the sincerity in his voice, but her nerves were too frayed to trust the stranger just yet. "We'll wait here until they arrive," she called out.

"No problem. I'll wait downstairs then."

She heard the footsteps retreat and steadily descend the staircase. She heard sirens a short while later. Only then did she feel safe enough to unlock the door.

Her world spun out of control as the police took state-ments from everyone. The boys were too upset to speak to the officers, so one of the officers told her that they could come down to the station the next day. She nodded blankly and thanked them. Earl dealt with the ambulance attendants. She couldn't look at them as they took Richard out secured to a gurney. She overheard words like "psychiatric evaluation" and "facility," but she didn't want elaboration on them. As she listened to Earl deal with the paramedics and police, she knew she could trust him. She thanked him when he offered to stay and help clean up. She put the boys to bed. They were both exhausted, physically and mentally. She wondered how long something like this stayed with kids.

He handed her a picture that had been knocked from a table while the paramedics ushered the gurney out of the house. "I was able to salvage the photograph, but the frame is in the bin." "Thanks," she said. "I'm Evelyn, by the way." She held out her hand.

"Earl."

They shook hands, then sat at the kitchen table. "Well, I suppose I should start from the beginning," Earl said.

Evelyn nodded and looked at the man as he began his tale.

"Your husband bought that blasted thing from me," he said pointing at the Christmas tree. "But I think the problem goes back a bit further. See, I bought a Christmas tree farm when I was a young man. Didn't know many of 'em around and thought I'd clean up during the holidays. Me and my wife worked it together, and eventually so did my son, Robert. We did alright with it." Earl nodded his head in remembrance. "But see, Robert was an odd kid. He didn't have friends, kept to himself. He left school at fourteen. Nothing we did could convince him otherwise. He started talking to himself and cussing. We tried talking to him, but he wouldn't listen to us. We thought of bringing him to the doctors, but we were afraid he'd end up in an asylum. Back then they were terrible places." Earl paused a moment and inhaled deeply. He let out a deep sigh and continued. "We kind of hoped he'd come right, eventually. He worked on the farm, ate with us, then disappeared at night."

Evelyn watched the old man and could see the pain in his eyes. She wanted to console him, but he continued before she could reach out to him.

"People started goin' missin'. Twelve in all. The whole city was in a mad panic. We noticed Robert was acting stranger around this time. Leaving the house and not returning for days at a time. I wanted to speak to him but knew it was pointless, so one night I followed him."

Earl squeezed his eyes shut and rubbed at them with a huge fist. When he opened them, they were bloodshot, and tears rolled down his cheeks.

"Those poor people. He killed them. All of them. Robert was a monster. I caught him driving up the highway to this old, run-down garage. It had been closed since I was a boy. I followed him as he went in through a gap in the side. It was like an abattoir in there. He'd butchered those people. The evidence of his evil lay all around the place. Body parts on tables, blood stains, it was unbelievable. Such violence. When he finally saw me, he didn't say a word. He just ran at me like a wild animal with a look just like your husband had."

Evelyn reached across the table and placed her hand over Earl's as he continued his story.

"I fought him off and tried to talk sense into him, but he was gone. Spitting and snarling like something demonic. He eventually told me how he buried those poor people in our farm, said that's what made the trees grow so well. I was blinded by rage. Before I knew what I was doing, I had broken my boy's neck." Earl broke into deep sobs but pushed on through the tears. "Life lost all meaning after I killed my son. I carried his body home. Pat and I learned to live with the truth. I burned that place where Robert committed his evil. A reporter plastered our story in the local rag, but nobody paid it much attention. We tried to move on. Couldn't leave the house, we'd no more money. Couldn't work the farm knowing what lay beneath the soil. One day I tried cut down every last tree. Tried killing the roots and soil with poison. A barren field would have been better to look out on, but they came back. Year after year, they came back. I tried everything I could think of to kill that field of trees, but nothing worked. In my heart I knew never to sell one, ever... and for over fifty years I hadn't... Until your husband."

Earl looked at Evelyn with sad overflowing eyes. "I'm sorry. I knew there was evil in those trees. Robert warned me as much."

Evelyn didn't know what to say. Here sat a man, confessing to something horrendous and claiming it all led to her husband losing his mind. It was a lot to take in, but the sincerity in Earl's words, in his voice, melted whatever coldness she should be feeling towards him. She knew he was telling the truth.

They sat a while longer in silence, allowing time to pass between them. The gravity of what had happened hung in the air. Both had shed tears.

"I might go now. Will you be okay?"

Evelyn nodded. "Of course. Thank you."

She led him to the door. It still locked good enough to keep the evil out, but the tumbler would need to be replaced. As Earl stepped outside, Evelyn stopped him and asked, "I never asked. How did you know to come here?"

Earl turned to Evelyn. "Your husband called me. I gave him my number to call if he felt strange. He called, sounded distant, and said I needed to be here before something terrible happened. He even gave me the address before hanging up."

Evelyn shook her head, wondering what had gone on in Robert's mind before he lost it.

"Goodnight, Evelyn."

"Good night, Earl, and thank you."

Evelyn locked the door. She didn't watch Earl drive off;

she wanted to have a barrier between her and the outside world, a world that now seemed bleaker than before. She walked up the staircase thinking to herself that somewhere deep inside Richard's madness her husband, the man she loved, still remained. She hoped that someday, somehow, he would find his way back to his family again.

⊛RNAMENTATION

Alyn Day

Jim Holiday sat in a shabby brown recliner in his living room. His sweat- and otherwise-stained wife beater clung to his sallow skin like a lizard's skin, peeling away from the flabby flesh underneath like a scab. The garment had seen better days, much like Jim himself. Also like its wearer, the garment was tired, worn out, and derelict. It had grown too small to hold Jim's burgeoning frame within its cotton cage, so much like a prison, and odd protuberances of hairy lard poked out at random intervals through holes in the material. Jim opened his mouth and let out a low groan, drool that reeked of morning breath, nicotine, and old liquor ran over his lip and down his chin like a filthy river. It meandered through the mangy forest that was his 3-, perhaps even 4-week-old beard growth; although, in all honesty, it was far too scraggly and sparse to be referred to as a "beard," and yet too wild and overgrown to be considered stubble.

Jim sat up, adjusting his position as one of his feet had fallen asleep sometime during the previous night. Beer bottles and empty fifths of Jack and Johnnie clattered to the floor in a derelict melody before rolling under the chair and across the carpet in the direction of the Christmas tree.

Jim's eyes shifted as he yawned, yellowed teeth like uneven tombstones pushing up through the pale pink, fleshy graveyard of his gums. The tree stood about ten feet away from where he sat, an ancient monument to a preexisting version of the grotesquery he had become. It had been up for a year, or somewhere thereabouts. He couldn't be sure exactly what day it was, or really what month, though judging by the Christmas music filtering through the walls from the next apartment over, he supposed that it was probably sometime in December. Either that, or they were just plain mad.

The tree had long since gone brown, dried up and desiccated. It had lost the greater majority of its needles, needles that lay undisturbed where they had landed, like an ashy brown halo around the weary old symbol of Christmas past and the unopened presents beneath it. Ornaments sparkled from its branches through a thin haze of dust and dirt and spider webs, which had been woven throughout the limbs like intricate little garlands. They had become sort of a decoration themselves. Atop the skeletal remains of last year's happiness perched a little golden angel, a silent specter. Her tiny blue eyes beat down on Jim as if in accusation—or contempt.

Jim barely regarded the tree any longer. It had become just another shadow in what remained of his pitiful life. Nothing had been the same since his wife had uttered those few heartbreaking words, "I want a divorce." Jim had always given Angie everything she asked for. So when she asked for a goodbye, he had given her that, too.

Jim hadn't been out of his recliner in days. He was beginning to worry that perhaps he couldn't move if he tried. He struggled to sit up, placing both of his hands with their bloated sausage fingers on the arms of the chair and pulling himself forward, the massive bulk of his gut obstructing his view of the ratty brown carpet in front of him. One of his feet, clothed in what remained of a grimy red slipper, slid to the left, knocking over a beer bottle he had been using as a urine receptacle. The foul yellow liquid splashed onto his leg, running down the grungy mat of hair and spilling onto that unfortunate slipper.

"Ahhhh," Jim croaked, the crackley, course tone of his voice sounding alien to his own ears. How long had it been since he'd last spoken? Weeks? Months maybe? When had he last heard another human voice, he wondered? He couldn't recall.

Jim's annoyance at the wet mess on his leg, slipper, chair, and floor fueled him into action. He stood up abruptly, wheezing a bit from the exertion, and grabbed the bottle. He hurled it against the wall beside the doorway, where it shattered into a plethora of sparkling shards. They rained onto the carpet as the remnants of the bottle's liquid contents dripped down the wall. The shape the mess made was almost festive. It could've been a Christmas tree in the right light, with enough imagination. Fortunately, or unfortunately, depending on your perspective, the scent of rancid urine was barely noticeable amid the room's predominant stench of sweat, body odor, and old booze.

Jim was turning towards the kitchen when a sharp, melodious voice stopped him in his tracks.

"Jim," it sing-songed, "Jim, Darling, won't you be a dear and bring me something to eat?" Jim stood stock still for a moment, unsure of what to do. It was the voice of the Angel alright, but he hadn't heard it in… well… nearly a year. He thought perhaps he was imagining things in his deep-seated loneliness, in his longing, but the voice continued.

"I'm so very hungry, my darling. So very, very hungry."

Jim swallowed. He had missed that voice. Missed his angel lo these long months, but now that she was back, he wasn't sure he wanted her. He didn't know what to do, and so he remained stone still for a few lingering minutes, listening to her pleas. He remembered her hunger, remembered feeding her, watching her eat. He remembered the touch of her skin with a shudder that was so close to revulsion and yet so close to elation at the same time.

Jim faltered for a moment before racing down the hall and opening the door to his bedroom, a door he hadn't opened in almost a year. The air inside smelled ancient, reticent with mildew, dust, and decay. Cobwebs clung to everything. The petals of the rose in the little glass bud vase on the night table had long since fallen. That rose had been fresh and dewy when he'd last seen it, and as pink as a newborn's bottom. Pink had been her favorite color, after all.

Jim shoved aside a heavy footlocker and opened the white accordion doors that lead to his closet, ignoring the deep gouges on the inside. One of them still held the remains of a fingernail.

He knelt on the floor, dust and dirt clinging to the sores on the sides of his legs, sores caused by his lack of motion and his near-permanent position seated in his old recliner.

There she was, folded in the back of the tiny space, still wearing her costume, just as she had been when he'd locked her in there, begging her to just take some time and please, please reconsider. He'd never opened the door again. Now she couldn't leave him.

Her white gown had been discolored by time, as well as

by mold and rot, but in Jim's eyes, she was still beautiful. The sequins lining the gown had long since lost their luster, but that was okay.

"Why'd you have to leave me, Baby?" he whined, voice cracking with disuse. "Why'd you have to go and do a thing like that on Christmas?" Jim straightened out the tinsel halo that still clung to the pale blonde wig she had worn that day. The wig had fallen over her face sometime during the twelve months she had been inside the closet. Beneath it, her dried-up flesh had pulled her once-full, pink lips into a gruesome smile.

"Merry Christmas, Angie," he whispered as he leaned forward and kissed her.

T̶HE T̶RAP

Mike Pieloor

The trap was sprung!

David heard the snap of the trigger and the whoosh of the canvas. He leapt out of bed and ran to the stair rail. He could hear the clatter and bang of a struggle in the kitchen, like an animal desperate for freedom.

He'd caught him!

David raced down the stairs, taking three steps at a time, and burst into the kitchen. The room was still in darkness, but he could hear the canvas flapping wildly. He flicked on the light and stared in excitement. The large canvas bag was twisting violently, suspended half off the floor by the yellow rope he'd attached to the closet door handle. David quickly inspected the floor and was relieved to see his circle of white powder surrounding the hanging bag.

He grabbed a broom from beside the cupboard and sat

quietly on a stool next to the breakfast bench, observing the dancing yellow rope and his captive's effort to escape. "You're my prisoner!" he said after a few moments.

The canvas stopped shifting and swung from the rope, the occupant listening to the boy.

"I knew you'd come. I knew it!" David eyed the half-chewed biscuit and spilt glass of milk on the bench above his make-shift trigger. "Set a trap for you. Knew it would work!"

The canvas bag continued to swing quietly.

"Last year it was coal, but not this year. This year I'm going to get what I want!" He eyed the canvas and laughed. "You won't be visiting anyone else until I do."

The prisoner hadn't moved since David announced his presence. He hopped off the stool and approached carefully, holding the handle of the broom out in front of him. "You still in there?" He prodded the bag.

It swung violently toward him as his captive made an attempt to break free.

David jumped clear and rushed back to the breakfast bench. "You can't escape!" he panted, "I've prepared for that. I'm clever, you know." He eyed the swinging bag and sat again at the bench. "Next March I'll be eleven!" He smiled at his own success. It was just like he had hoped: his plan, his trap, and now his prisoner. Better than what Bobby could do. But he wanted to see the prisoner. More than anything, he wanted to see his face and for the prisoner to know who had beaten him. He'd show Bobby afterwards.

He hopped off the stool and cautiously edged his way to the closet. The kitchen table had been overturned when the trap had triggered, and he pushed it out of the way with a scraping sound as he reached the closet.

"I'm going to let you out of that bag now," he said, leaning the broom within easy reach. He placed his hands on the coiled rope, feeling it tighten and flex under the weight of his captive as the bag continued to swing.

David began to unwind the knot. "You won't be able to run away, so don't try. I've prepared for that." He struggled with the last knot for a moment, but then the tension in the rope disappeared and the canvas bag fell to the floor with a *thud*. David grabbed the broom and stood back near the stairs.

The canvas flapped violently in the middle of the circle of white powder as the captive struggled free. A sinewy, black arm wound through the hole at the top of the bag as clawed hands pulled away the yellow rope. A dark, lithe figure slipped from the canvas into the light of the kitchen.

David froze.

The creature stood just over four feet. It was covered in matted black hair and two twisted horns projected from its head, curling above a terrifying, animal face. It glared at David with blood red eyes and lunged toward him.

David threw his arm across his face to protect himself and squeezed his eyes tight.

But there was no impact.

David opened one eye.

The creature was still standing in the circle. It looked surprised and angry. It lunged again.

David flinched, but the creature fell back into the circle as if colliding with something invisible. It tried again with the same result. After several attempts, it stood in the center, panting and looking around in confusion.

David leaned against the bench and let out a long breath. "So, it does work!"

The creature eyed him suspiciously.

"The circle," David said, indicating the roughly scattered white powder on the floor. "You're not who I was expecting, but you're still trapped!"

The creature hissed.

"What are you?" demanded David, brandishing the broom.

"Krampus," the creature growled.

"Krampus? Never heard of you!"

"I've had other names," Krampus said in a deep, guttural voice, "*zwarte Piet*! *Schmutzli*! *El Hombre del Saco*!"

"What are you doing here? And where is San—"

"Ah!" Krampus interrupted, "you were expecting my brother!"

"Your brother?" David said, turning the idea around in his head.

Krampus nodded. "Yes, but he only visits good children!"

"I'm not a child!" David shouted.

Krampus shrugged. "And yet, you still believe in us?"

"I believe in him! Not you!"

"Well, he's the Saint and I'm the claws! You can't have one without the other." He laughed horribly. It started deep in his throat and bubbled up to end with a snort.

David stared at the strange creature, shaking his head in disbelief. His plan had worked—the trap had been sprung—but not with the result he had hoped for. He couldn't show this creature to Bobby, could he?

While David considered what to do next, Krampus pushed the remains of the canvas trap to the edge of the circle and examined his surroundings. David could now see that instead of feet, each of Krampus' legs ended in a shiny hoof. It reminded him of animals at the carnival.

"What now then, little Imbiss?"

"My name is David!"

"Is it?" A long, red tongue flicked out of his mouth and slithered across his black lips.

"You can entertain me!" David said brightly, the image of the carnival animals still in his mind.

Krampus looked surprised. "Entertain you?"

"Yes."

"Why would I want to do that?"

"Because you have no choice. You're my prisoner!" David shook the broom to confirm his threat.

Krampus raised his eyes to the ceiling. "Won't we wake your parents?"

"They're not here!' said David, returning to his stool. "They've gone to a party!"

Krampus settled onto his haunches in the middle of the circle. "All alone!"

David didn't like the way Krampus' eyes had flashed as he spoke. "Listen! I'm not letting you out of that circle unless you entertain me."

Krampus sneered. "And what shall I do to entertain you?"

"Magic," said David eagerly. "Can you do magic?"

Krampus grinned and ran a clawed hand across one of his horns, like a cat bathing. "I am good at making things disappear, but not from inside this circle." He considered David, and then his eyes flared. "I will tell you a story, little Imbiss."

David pouted. "Boring!"

Krampus ignored him and closed his eyes. "This is the story of a clever girl named Annica. She was the daughter of a wealthy land owner who lived in a grand estate with rolling gardens."

"There's a girl called Annica in my class!"

Krampus opened one eye. "Is there?"

David wasn't sure if Krampus sounded surprised or not. He rested the broom handle across his knees and listened.

Krampus closed his eye again and continued. "Annica was mean and exceptionally cruel. One day, her mother's servant girl lost a silver teaspoon. She searched the house high and low for the spoon. Annica helped her look."

Krampus opened his eyes and thrust his head forward, making David jump and drop the broom.

"But it was Annica who had hidden the spoon," said Krampus, his words running over each other, "and while the servant searched, Annica took it to the servant's room and hid it there. The next day, she repeated the game, taking another spoon and hiding it while the panicked servant searched."

"She doesn't sound that clever! If all she does is steal spoons," David interrupted, retrieving the broom from the floor.

Krampus ignored him and continued with his story. "Of course, the master soon noticed the missing spoons, and it wasn't long before someone found them. The servant girl begged the master of the house to let her explain, pleaded with him to give her a chance." Krampus wagged a clawed finger in the air. "But she was sent away."

"What happened to her?" David asked, leaning forward on the stool.

Krampus' tongue slithered around his lips. "Oh! That's the best bit, little Imbiss." He grinned, showing sharp, stained teeth. "One day a beggar came to Annica's house and asked to see her. He told Annica his sister had worked as a servant at the house. Annica didn't care! He told Annica his sister had died. Annica didn't care! He told Annica he knew she had hidden the spoons. Annica didn't care!"

"Wait! I thought you said no one knew she had done that?"

"Don't interrupt!" roared Krampus, his eyes flashing.

The force of his anger was unexpected, and David nearly fell backward off the stool. He quickly regained his balance and watched the creature in silence.

Krampus grunted in irritation, and then, as if recalling

his place in the story, nodded before continuing. "That night, the beggar stole into the house and put the sleeping Annica into a sack and took her away." Drool hung from his mouth. "He ripped out her pigtails and drowned her in ink." He roared with vicious, hissing laughter.

David swallowed, unsure if he should speak.

Krampus wiped the drool from his cheek with his arm and leaned close to the edge of the circle. "Entertained?"

"No," David said quietly, shuddering at the proximity of the creature. He remembered that Krampus was his prisoner, and it didn't matter how much he raged, he was still trapped. "That was awful! The beggar was more evil than Annica!"

Krampus straightened up. "That's only because he saw her for what she was." He turned on the spot, his eyes rolling around the room until they settled on David. "You haven't done anything naughty, have you?"

David licked his dry lips and hopped off the stool. He felt Krampus' gaze follow him around the kitchen as he leaned the broom against the bench and filled a glass with water from the tap. He wondered if the creature knew what he had done.

"Are you going to let me out of this circle now?"

"Not yet," David said between mouthfuls. "I don't want a bag of coal again this year. I want something fun!"

"But coal is good," hissed Krampus. "It keeps the family warm."

David put down the glass. He was deciding what he could get the strange creature to do next when he saw a bundle by the back door. He crossed to it, moving around the powdered circle in a wide arc.

Krampus' head swiveled, keeping his eyes fixed on David.

The bundle was a large hessian sack. "This is yours?"

asked David, prodding the sack with a foot. "What were you bringing me this year?"

"Not coal!" Krampus said with an edge of excitement in his voice. "You only get coal once."

David knelt down beside the sack. It was large and looked full and heavy. He unwound folds of the rough hessian material at one end and several thin branches sprang out. Their wood was yellow and a few dried leaves were still attached to the fraying ends. "What are these?"

"Ruten!" shouted Krampus, waving his arms in the air.

David ran his fingers over the ruten's surface; they felt smooth and were slightly flexible. "What are they for?"

Krampus ignored the question. "How did you trap me, little Imbiss?"

David pushed the ruten back into the sack. "My name is David!" He stood and walked back to the bench.

Krampus followed his every step with fiery eyes and put his head to one side. "Must have been very clever."

"Yes, it was clever!"

"How? How so clever?" pleaded Krampus.

"I found it in a book," David said. He could show this horrible creature how clever he had been. He checked the circle again before collecting two dark, leather-bound books from a shelf in the study. He raced back into the kitchen and held them in front of him proudly. "I found it in here."

"Found what?"

David flicked through the musty pages and held up the book to show Krampus the spot. An illustration of a fat man with a sack glaring at a steaming cauldron filled the yellowed page. David thrust a finger on the writing below the illustration. "Wolfsbane and salt! Says here, he doesn't like it. We spread them in the traps."

Krampus nodded. "Clever? Yes." He looked at David questioningly. "We?"

"Yes, me and Bobby. He lives next door!"

"I'll scrape my fingers inside your skull," whispered a hoarse voice across the kitchen.

David glanced quickly around the room. But there was only Krampus, and the creature hadn't moved.

"What... What was that?" he asked nervously.

Krampus didn't appear to have heard the voice. "I have another story for you," he said, licking his lips.

David found himself nodding, but was still looking about the kitchen for the source of the strange voice.

Krampus sat on his haunches again in the center of the circle and closed his eyes. "This is the story of the son of a weaver. His name was Patrick." He opened one eye and glared at David expectantly.

"There's a Patrick in my class, too," said David slowly, putting the books down on the bench and sitting on the stool.

"Was there?" said Krampus, closing his eye again. "Patrick was also a cruel child. Although he had plenty of toys and was well fed, Patrick would steal from the family next door. The family was poor; they didn't have many toys, and sometimes they couldn't afford food, but Patrick didn't care. He stole from them anyway."

David didn't want to hear another story. He was thinking desperately now about how to get Krampus out of the house. He couldn't leave the creature here, and if he removed the circle, he was certain it would attack him. The voice had also worried him. Was there someone else in the house?

Krampus continued, as if oblivious to David's concerns. "One day, while Patrick's parents were away, a young woman came to the door. She said she used to live next door. Patrick didn't care! She said the rest of her family died. Patrick didn't care!"

David shivered and checked the circle again. Although the powder was intact, he still felt uneasy. He considered getting Bobby to help him get Krampus out of the house.

Krampus' voice seemed to get louder. "So, she put Patrick in a sack and took him away." He grinned and opened both eyes. "She ripped out his tongue and tricked him off a cliff." Krampus used his hands to demonstrate the action and snorted back another laugh.

David clenched his teeth and edged toward the door.

"Going somewhere, little Imbiss?" asked Krampus, looking up with a frown.

"Just next door. I'll be back."

"Oh! Didn't I say," Krampus said, sliding up to the edge of the circle and narrowing his eyes. "I already visited Bobby."

It knows, thought David, fighting a desire to run. If it has already spoken to Bobby, it must know what he had done. "Where is he?" he asked in a voice that didn't sound like his.

"His trap wasn't as effective as yours."

"Where?" David's voice was a whisper.

Krampus' eyes stared at him darkly.

For a moment, David thought he could see a reflection of fire in them. Then a thought occurred to David. It wedged uncomfortably into his mind, and no matter how he reasoned with it, it refused to go away: you can't fill a sack with sticks! He glanced at the chalk circle again and walked back toward the sack by the door. Without looking at Krampus, he knelt down and gripped its top. He could feel the beat of his heart in his hands. Carefully, slowly, David moved the ruten aside and widened the sack's mouth. The inside was shiny and wet, and a lumpy mass bobbed in the blackness. Tentatively, he reached out a trembling hand and touched it. The mass felt soft and slightly warm. He pulled his arm away in disgust, feeling the sticky black residue on his fingers. It was like ink.

"I'll rip out your tongue," said the hoarse voice.

David spun around, but there was still only Krampus in the kitchen, and he was staring intently at David.

"It is true you are clever, little Imbiss."

"David!" he said, feeling hot. "My name is David!" He wiped the ink off his fingers and stood on unsteady feet.

"But it doesn't matter how clever you think you are." Krampus lifted one of his legs and placed the hoof outside the circle.

David felt his blood turn to ice.

"You didn't really think you were clever enough to trap me, did you?"

"But... the books," stuttered David, unable to take his eyes from the hoof.

"What? These books?" said Krampus, the two volumes suddenly appearing in his claws.

David's eyes searched the empty bench on the other side of the room and he nodded dumbly.

"Yes, they are quite good, aren't they?" purred Krampus, turning them in his claws. "Some of my best work."

"Your best work?"

Krampus laughed. "But of course, little Imbiss! I am the one who set this trap, not you! Couldn't you tell from my stories?" Krampus shook his head. "Perhaps I shouldn't always be a beggar or a young woman."

"I'll be missed," David whispered, his heart racing in his chest.

"Oh, no! That's not how it works. Another boy will take your place." Krampus inhaled deeply and snorted. "And your parents won't even notice. You may be able to hide what you do from others, but I always know." He barred his teeth in a ferocious grin. "I know what you did to Iris Fernun's cake!" He moved forward, and a second hoof left the circle.

David's mind screamed. It knew. It had always known.

"I know what you stole from Mister Green." A pitchfork appeared in Krampus' claws.

David fought down the rising panic and tried not to look at the pitchfork, but his face muscles had stopped working.

"I also know what you did to poor Brian Hogling behind the bike shed."

David could feel himself shaking. His mind was screaming at him, but he couldn't move. He could only watch as Krampus stalked toward him, a snake-like tail thrashing wildly behind.

"You have done some truly evil things. But now you will be my little Imbiss," Krampus whispered, closing in on David. "And I will scrape my fingers inside your skull." He loomed above David, his eyes flashing and his body shaking with glee. "And I will rip out your tongue." He was suddenly holding the hessian bag.

David watched, helpless, as Krampus slowly unfolded the bag, its black maw gaping and dripping wet.

"Now, my little Imbiss, you will entertain me!"

David felt hot, rough claws handle him into the darkness and itchy hessian across his skin.

"I have another tale to share with other naughty children now!" Krampus' voice was muffled through the sack's thick material, but David could hear it echo in his head. "About the boy named David, who tried to catch Saint Nick."

David felt the sack lifted, and his body slid into the ink. He felt the warm mass press against him. He wanted to scream, but his mouth felt tight and would not move. The ink covered his legs and arms and oozed around his neck and face, burning his lips. The liquid choked as it trickled down his throat and filled his lungs. And as a different, heavier dark-ness filled him, he heard Krampus' voice as a hoarse whisper.

"Darkness bleeds for all dark deeds, and I'll always catch

you in the end."

Killing Christmas

Mark Parker

"Blessed are those who thirst and hunger for righteousness, for they will be filled."

— Matthew 5:1 (from the Sermon on the Mount)

This is gonna be some kinda Christmas, Doug Connolly thought as he eyed the fuel gauge of his Dodge Ram pickup. It felt like he'd been driving for weeks and still he wasn't any closer to his destination. *Bethlehem, Pennsylvania.* Fuckin' family! It was always the same. It was always him going to them, never the other way around. But he had to admit it would be nice to see his brother and sister again. He hadn't been home in five years; they had a lot of catching up to do. Hell, at this point, it would even be good to see his father. And it'd been a very long time since he'd been able to say that.

His father had spent the last ten years in and out of rehab, tending to his chronic alcoholism. Of course he never seemed to think it was *him* who had the problem. But it sounded like he'd at least made some headway in the past couple of years. When they'd last spoke, his brother Dean and sister Chloe had both attested to how much their father had changed. And neither of them were pushovers, so if they said the man had changed, he most likely had.

Doug wasn't as easily convinced though. What did the specialists say? It was *consistency* in a person's behavior that mattered most. He followed that school of thought for sure. He didn't want to crucify the man for no good reason, but they'd had their share of knockdown fights over the years, so he was reserving his praise for proof. He'd spent the last five years in Tallahassee, working on a crew that assembled pre-fab homes. "One step up from a trailer living," he'd always said. But it was a job and he was grateful to have it. Even if it'd meant him moving to the opposite side of the country to get it.

The job had given him the out he'd been wanting. It also afforded him a decent enough income, so he couldn't complain. When things had gotten particularly nasty between his father and him, the move to Florida had been his ticket out of Dodge, so he'd taken it. Back then his father had been a miserable drunk—and a mean sonofabitch to boot!—always ranting and raving that life hadn't dealt him the cards he felt he deserved. When he was on one of his binges, he would go around punching and kicking holes into pretty much everything without any care for what he damaged or who he hurt.

One night when Doug had ducked out the front door to miss his father's swinging fists, he'd climbed into his then beat-up Ford Bronco and started driving, and he didn't stop until he'd crossed the Georgia/Florida line. Of course he'd felt shitty about leaving Dean and Chloe alone to suffer their father's onslaught, but there was only so much he could do. Besides, he never treated his siblings the way he treated him. Even his mother had left a year after he did. Apparently she'd packed up and moved in with her sister in Hershey. Far enough to put some distance between her and the explosive insanity of an alcoholic husband. And who could blame her?

Doug had never been particularly close to his father, so being on the far side of a long-distance relationship suited him just fine. Dean had been his father's favorite, then came Chloe. As the middle child, Doug had always felt like an afterthought. Taking himself out of the family equation seemed to make the most sense at the time, and did even more so now. Of course the blast-furnace heat of Florida had taken some getting used to, especially after the bone-numbing winters he'd lived through in Pennsylvania, but it was a fair trade to be away from his father's unpredictable bullshit. Now that he was drawing closer to his hometown, he could feel the tension knotting his insides.

As he slowed down to round the upcoming turn leading to Route 80 in the eastbound lane, he saw a green highway sign appear across the black horizon ahead. He let out a deep sigh. "Please tell me this is my exit!" He hadn't seen a rest area for miles and desperately needed to take a leak. As the glowing green rectangle drew closer, he saw the words that confirmed his hope: BETHLEHEM PENNSYLVANIA – 20 MILES.

Peeling off the highway, he was grateful to see what came into view next. It was another sign reading: REST AREA – NEXT RIGHT. He stayed in the right-hand lane when the turnoff came into view. The closer he got to the dimly lit parking lot, the more he needed to find a restroom. And *bad*. His bladder felt like it was about to explode. He'd stopped at one of those gas station Burger Kings earlier in the day and had downed more coffee than he probably should've.

He pulled in next to a dark red minivan with SANTA'S WHEELS stenciled on the side. *Lame*, he thought, turning off the ignition. Climbing out of the truck, he locked the doors, and all but ran across to the front door of the octagon-shaped building that had WELCOME CENTER painted on a bright blue sign above it. It felt good to stretch his legs. He'd been driving for almost six hours straight and was glad for the break.

As he crossed the parking lot, he breathed in a chest full of much-needed fresh air. Overhead, the night sky was teeming with stars. All signs pointed to Christmas being near.

Once inside, Doug's nostrils were immediately assaulted with the astringent odor of bleach and pine disinfectant. The smell was so intense it made his eyes burn and tear up. Squinting against the glare of the overhead fluorescents, he headed toward a propped-open door reading MEN, which had a fully stocked cleaning cart standing in front it.

Stepping into the restroom, he nearly ran into a wall of red and white fur. Standing just inside the doorway was a big guy dressed in a Santa getup. He surmised this must be the owner of the red van outside.

"Um… excuse me," Doug said, doing his best to navigate around the man's girth. He had no clue why the guy was standing so close to the door. Maybe he'd just finished washing his hands and was on his way out. But it somehow didn't seem so. The big guy appeared to be absorbed in thought. He was just standing there staring down at his gloved hands, like the riddle to the universe was somehow hidden there.

Doug walked over to the urinal furthest from the door and unzipped himself. He stood there for what felt like a solid ten minutes, emptying his bladder and wondering what Santa was doing at a rest area men's room in the first place. On his way in, Doug thought the parking lot had looked surprisingly empty. He would've expected there to be much more traffic on the highways this close to the holidays. It would appear that Old St. Nick needed to take his share of bathroom breaks, as well.

Reluctant to have to walk past the guy again, Doug stood in front of the urinal for a few more seconds before zipping up and turning in the direction of the sinks. As he did, he saw something glint out of the corner of his eye. When he looked up, the man was staring directly at him with an odd look in his eyes. The man's face was almost as red as his suit, and a thread of glistening drool stretched from his lower lip to his chin. This was certainly no Santa he would want delivering toys to his kids, if he had any.

Trying his best to finish up and get the hell out of there, Doug held his hands under a stream of ice cold water and did his best to crack a smile. "Someone's in the holiday spirit," he said to the man's reflection in the water-splattered mirror. The man just kept on staring at him, not saying a word. With his luck, the fur-dressed bastard was probably some kind of sick pervert, waiting to pounce on unsuspecting travelers as they came into the Welcome Center to relieve themselves.

Doug felt a chord of fear run up his spine. Except for the two of them, the place was empty. If there was a janitor on duty, he was certainly nowhere in sight. Doug figured if this guy *was* some kind of sicko, he needed to get the hell out of there as quickly as possible. He didn't even bother to use soap. He turned off the faucet and wiped his wet hands on his jeans, then headed for the door, careful to cut a wide arc around the man's substantial body.

Just as he did, the man's enormous head turned in his direction.

"Would you happen to have a phone I could use?" the man said.

His voice sounded dry, like sandpaper on stone.

"Don't they have phones here?" Doug asked.

"They do, but none of them seem to be working."

Doug didn't know what to think—or *do*. Even though their voices were low, the sound echoed off the tiled walls like rumbling shouts.

"I don't mean to be a bother," the man said, "but my van's broken down. I was fortunate enough to make it safely off the highway before the damned thing crapped out on me."

Doug wanted to say something silly about reindeer and all, but he swallowed the comment and instead offered a half-hearted smile. "Yeah, I suppose that is lucky. You can use my phone, to call Triple-A or whatever."

"That would be helpful," the man said.

Doug handed the man his phone and walked sideways past him, out into the lobby of the Welcome Center. Even though he was probably only making a call to an auto service, Doug figured the guy deserved at least some privacy, weird or not.

Staring at a wall of illuminated vending machines, Doug thought the place had a kind of *Twilight Zone* atmosphere to it, especially with it being as empty as it was. He felt like he'd stepped through some kind of wormhole and was now trapped in a parallel universe that was a bizarre altered version of his own. Walking around the deathly quiet place, he was relieved to see a car pulling up to the curb outside. After a few seconds, a college-age guy walked through the double doors and smiled in his direction.

"Boy, am I glad to see this place open!" the kid said. "I've needed to piss for a friggin' hour!"

"I know what you mean," Doug said. "It was the same

for me a few minutes ago."

"Headin' home for the holidays?" the kid asked.

"Yeah," Doug said. "A decision I've been second guessing every bit of the way."

"Where you coming from?"

"Tallahassee."

"Holy shit! That's one helluva drive!"

"Tell me about it," Doug said. "Thankfully it shouldn't be much further now. I just saw a sign for Bethlehem. Only twenty more miles."

"The holidays can be a pain," the kid said, "but it sounds like you'll be there soon. I'm sure your family will be happy to see you!"

Doug didn't want to tell the kid he had a recovering alcoholic for a father and a mother who'd left when she'd had enough of his abuse.

The kid smiled again and walked past him, heading in the direction of the men's room.

Anxious to leave, Doug flipped through a display of maps and flyers for local attractions. After a few seconds, he walked over to the front door and pushed it open. He breathed in the cold night air, which was fresh and smelled of snow. The cloying scent of bleach and disinfectant still clung to the still air inside the building, which made him feel flushed in the face and queasy. He looked down at his watch. Apparently Santa was calling the fucking North Pole with as long as it was taking him. Doug headed back toward the men's room but was stopped dead in his tracks when a series of horrible sounds echoed out into the lobby. First, there was loud shuffling. Then, a bloodcurdling scream. And then a span of the most awful silence.

What the fuck—?

Against his better judgment, Doug ran to the open doorway of the men's room and stood in shocked bewilderment as he crossed over the threshold. He expected to see a wall of red from the old man's fuzzy suit, but instead was confronted with a different shade of red — a much darker one.

On the floor in front of the urinals, the kid was sprawled out face down, and the wall above him was covered with a horrid spray of what could only be blood. Doug felt like he was about to faint. His head was spinning, and a heavy wave of nausea washed over him.

He grabbed the doorframe to steady himself, but it did little good. He'd never seen anything like this.

So much blood…

After a few seconds, adrenaline kicked in and helped to focus him on what he should do next. He quickly searched the men's room for the man in red, but the sonofabitch was nowhere in sight. Doug stepped over to the kid's body. He needed to check for a pulse. Instinct told him there wouldn't be one, but he went through the motions anyway.

He pulled on the shoulder nearest him and nearly wretched when the kid's face came into view. The boy's mouth had been slashed wide open. From ear to ear there was a gaping gulf that was beginning to coagulate with blood. It looked like a ghastly, wide-mouthed smile.

Doug let go of the kid's shoulder and quickly got to his feet.

He kicked the door of each of the stalls, knowing the sonofabitch couldn't've vanished into thin air — not at his size — but his search came up empty. Doug didn't know how it'd been possible, but somehow the man had found a way to get past him. *But when?* The only time Doug had been distracted was when he'd been looking through the rack of maps and travel brochures, then again when he opened the front door to get some fresh air. But both incidents had happened

317

before the horrible sounds had emitted from the men's room. There was no way the sonofabitch could've gotten past him. *No way!* Doug hadn't heard footsteps or any doors opening or closing.

Just then, he noticed something he hadn't seen before.

In the far corner of the room was what looked to be a janitor's closet. He walked over to it and pulled on the door-knob. The metal door opened with a loud creak. The small space was dark and cluttered with cleaning supplies—a bucket filled with dirty water, a mop, push brooms, a shelf of cleaning solvents, a couple boxes of toilet paper rolls, paper towels, and garbage bags—and at its back was some-thing rather unusual. *Another door.*

He kicked the door and it flew open without resistance. A gust of frigid air blew in and Doug's eyes were met with a haze of gauzy light. He stood there for a few moments while his eyes adjusted to the low-lit space beyond. The door opened onto the Welcome Center's back parking lot, which stood empty except for a bright yellow DOT truck filled half with sand and half rock salt. Doug took a step forward and searched the lot for any sign of the man, but not a soul was there. The DOT truck's front seat was empty and the engine was off.

After a few more moments, Doug pulled the door closed behind him and stepped back into the blinding light of the men's room. At least now he knew how Santa had made his stealthy escape. And with *his* phone!

Slamming his fist against each of the stall doors again, Doug searched for any sign of his cell. He knew he should've already called 9-1-1 by now to get the police there, but the last few minutes had played out in a sluggish blur of panic-induced detachment. When he came to the last stall, Doug saw his cell sitting in the half-filled basin of the toilet bowl, floating amid a sludge of deep brown urine and feces.

"You've gotta be fucking kidding me!" he shouted. Under any other circumstance, he would naturally leave his phone to rest in the rancid swill, but this was far from a normal situation. He knew if he left his phone behind, once the cops did make their way there and discover the kid's body lying in its own pool of blood—along with *his* phone resting in a stew of shit—they would know he'd been there and link him to the kid's murder.

Running back to the janitor's closet, Doug grabbed a trash bag from one of the boxes, shook it open, and thrust his fist into it. With the plastic lining for protection, he walked back to the last stall and snatched his phone from the toilet. He slammed his booted foot down on the handle of the toilet to flush the goddamned thing. Then he turned and tossed his shit-streaked phone into one of the sinks.

Once the running water had washed it as clean as it was going to get, he pulled the plastic bag off his hand and tossed it into the trashcan next to him, then tugged a fistful of paper towels from the wall dispenser hanging above it. He turned off the faucets, then laid the stack of paper towels on top of his phone, folding up the whole bundle. He returned to the janitor's closet for another trash bag to toss it all into.

Knotting the open end of the bag, Doug set it in the sink furthest from where he'd rinsed off his phone, then used the next sink over to wash his hands. Protected by plastic or not, the mere thought of shit and urine made his stomach turn. The whole time he kept glancing up at the large mirror over the sink half expecting to see Santa with his leering eyes and drooling chin—and the glint of a razor raising up to lay his own face wide open. He felt terrible about leaving the kid where he was, but without a phone there wasn't much else he could do. As soon as he found one, he would call the police and alert them to what'd happened.

Stepping outside, the night air felt as if it'd dropped twenty degrees in the short time he'd been indoors. The lot out front was empty except for his truck. He ran across the open space and jammed his hand into his pocket, fingering the keychain fob to open the truck's doors.

Climbing in, he pushed the auto-ignition, and the truck rumbled to life. Doug tossed the bag with his phone in it onto the passenger-side seat and threw the truck into reverse and peeled out of the parking lot without as much as a glance at his review mirror.

Once back on the open highway, he realized he'd been holding his breath since exiting the rest area's on-ramp. He exhaled and tried to breathe deeply. His lungs felt like they were filled with cement. He desperately tried to regulate his breathing as best he could, slowing his inhalations. Soon the throbbing in his head gradually subsided and his breathing returned to normal. In an effort to distract himself, he turned on the radio. Luke Bryan's southern strains filled the cab—and his mind—with something other than the gruesome scene he'd just witnessed. How could that Santa-son-of-a-bitch have killed that kid and fled into the night like some crazed, oversized elf? He still couldn't fully comprehend the enormity of it all. At times, life with his father had gotten brutal, but nothing as violent as this. He wasn't used to seeing such blatant cruelty.

All that blood...

The kid's face split wide open...

He couldn't believe any of it. It all had the weight of a terrible nightmare. But one he'd actually lived through. He felt relieved when he saw the sign reading BETHLEHEM PENNSYLVANIA. If anything could pull him back to some semblance of normalcy, it would be his family.

As he took the exit that would let him off nearest his

father's house, the dread he'd been feeling at the prospect of going home was gone. Instead, he felt oddly comforted by the thought of being around his brother, sister, and father. After the horrible incident he'd just experienced, *anything* would be a step up. And if what his siblings had said was true, things with his father wouldn't be so bad. In fact, they might even be pleasant. Only several more minutes and he'd be there. Driving into his hometown, Doug was struck by how nice everything looked. Downtown Bethlehem was nothing like where he lived in Tallahassee. Here, the streets were lined with potted Christmas trees decked out with colorful lights and garland. There were wreaths with crimson bows and *Season's Greetings* banners strung with lights stretched across the main streets from opposing streetlamps, giving the place a warm, welcoming atmosphere.

It was odd, of course, that things were so quiet with the streets all empty, but he'd pulled into town a bit later than originally planned. The insanity of what'd happened at the Welcome Center had gobbled up some of his travel time. But that wasn't anything compared to what that poor kid had gone through. Doug wondered if anyone had found the body yet and called the police. He was going to stop and make the call himself, but figured it might be better to wait until he got to his father's house. When he arrived, he could let his family know what'd happened, and together they could sort things out. It was still so unthinkable. The horrible images of the gruesome scene came flooding back into his mind, like rushing streams of ice cold water shocking his system. The terrible truth of it was all but paralyzing.

Doug pulled his truck to the curb in front of one of his mother's old shopping haunts and took a moment to pull himself together. He was surprised to feel tears sting the corners of his eyes. He didn't care. It felt good to let go of the tension he'd been holding onto. After he had a few minutes to regain his composure, he pulled back onto the main road and headed in the direction of his father's house.

Pulling into the driveway, Doug was shocked to see the stretch of asphalt empty.

Where is everyone?

The house stood in total darkness. Gone were the shimmering holiday decorations he'd just driven past. His father's house couldn't've looked anymore glum. It was downright depressing. Not even a fresh coat of paint would've dispelled the shadowed gloom. Doug felt like putting his truck in reverse and heading back the way he'd come. After the night he'd had, he didn't need any more bullshit, family or not. Instead of being welcomed home, he was sitting alone in his truck, feeling completely out of place in a way that probably shouldn't've come as any sort of surprise to him. Especially where his father was concerned. Dean and Chloe had probably just been trying to make him feel better by telling him their father had made so many positive changes in his life.

It surely doesn't look that way to me! Doug thought.

Not knowing what to do next, he remained sitting in his truck for almost twenty minutes before putting it into reverse. It wasn't easy to remain in a place he didn't feel like he was wanted.

Just as he was about to leave, he heard a familiar sound coming from behind the truck.

Barking.

Glancing at his rearview mirror, Doug caught glimpse of a welcomed sight. It was the family dog, Gretchen. She'd been his constant companion in the few years before he'd left. She'd never left his side once. In the years he'd been away, the sweet girl had never left his mind either. In many ways, it was Gretchen he'd missed most.

He opened the driver's side door and climbed out. "Hey there, beautiful girl!" He crouched down and gave the dog a big hug. Excitedly wagging her bushy tail, Gretchen trotted over to him and began licking him all over his face. Animals had a way of showing unconditional love and loyalty no matter what. Certainly in a way that no human ever could. "How've you been, girl? I sure have missed you!"

The dog continued to lick him all over, wagging her tail wildly as he held her close, rubbing his hands all over her squirming body.

"Damn, man. I thought you were never gonna get here!"

Doug looked over his shoulder and saw his brother walking down the drive.

"I almost didn't... It's been one helluva night."

He gave Gretchen another hug, then stood up. "You were just about to miss me. When I got here and saw the house all dark, I thought you guys had bailed on me."

Dean grabbed his younger brother by the shoulders and shook him. "Why on earth would you think that?"

"Well, you never know. I thought maybe you'd changed your minds about my coming home for the holidays. Or maybe dad had fallen off the wagon again."

"Nope," Dean said. "Chloe and dad went over to St. Michael's to help get the church ready for tomorrow night's midnight mass. I told them I'd bring you over once you got settled in."

"Bring me over? Where's your car?"

Dean laughed. "It's in the shop. The transmission's shot."

"So I guess we're taking my truck?"

"If that's okay," Dean said, putting his arm around his brother's neck and kissing him on the cheek.

"Dude! Your beard feels weird." Doug laughed. "I'm just glad to see I'm not here alone. Gretchen's barking kept me from leaving."

"Good thing. She's a good girl!" Dean said, scratching the dog behind her ears. "Dad would've been bummed if you'd missed his concert solo tomorrow night."

"You've gotta be kidding me! Dad doing a solo? When did he take up singing?"

"Chloe and I told you he's changed."

"I know you did. But I wouldn't've thought *that* much."

On the way over to the church, Doug told his brother about the kid's murder at the Welcome Center.

"Holy shit, dude! You called the cops, right?"

"Well, actually... no. The son-of-a-bitch in the Santa suit tossed my cell into a shit-filled toilet before he left."

"Oh, jeez..." Dean said.

"Yeah, I wasn't about to use it after that. I'd planned on calling them once I got here, but when I arrived and the house looked empty, I didn't know what to do. I figured maybe I should leave, then Gretchen started barking and you came out. I guess I just lost track for a second."

"It sounds like that guy who's been all over the news," Dean said.

"What guy?" Doug asked.

"There has been a rash of murders in the surrounding area. Not all of them have been as gruesome as what you described. Although several were pretty bad. A prostitute from Allentown was found with her legs cut off at the knees. That was probably the worst. Then there were some elderly folks at a nearby nursing home over in Easton who had their meals poisoned. And a couple of farmers in Quakertown and Ewing were found dead in their tractors with motor oil poured down their throats." Dean stopped. "Shit... I guess they were all pretty bad!"

"Damn," Doug said. "And I thought life in Florida was

crazy."

"It's horrible to think they may somehow be connected." Dean shrugged. "But who knows, maybe they are. What kind of evil sonofabitch would do such things—and this close to Christmas when it's supposed to be all about good will toward men and whatnot?"

"I'll tell you, man," Doug said, "I nearly lost it at that Welcome Center. I've never been so freaked out in my life."

"Well, it'll only get better from here on out. Dad's been doing really well. He goes to daily AA meetings and has started to go to church. I think it gives him hope that his life really can get better if he focuses on the right things. He's been sober for over a year and a half. He spends all his free time doing charitable things for others. I guess he figures it's his way of making up for all the bad stuff he's put us through."

"No wonder the house looks shitty," Doug said.

"Yeah, he's more about tending to others right now. Rather than focusing on his own needs, he runs at the first mention of someone needing help. Maybe now that you're home, you can give me a hand sprucing the place up a bit."

"Ah..." Doug said. "So that's why you wanted me to come back to Pennsylvania. So I could take up the slack around the house."

"Well, it sure wouldn't hurt," Dean said with a wink, then he pointed out the window. "It's up here on the left."

"What is?" Doug asked.

"The place we're going. You know, St. Michael's."

"Oh yeah, that's right!" Doug said.

St. Michael's was a large, white, clapboard church that looked more Quaker than Catholic. So many of the churches in this area were difficult to discern in terms of denomination. They varied in design from gothic behemoths of granite and marble to much simpler houses of worship used by the local

Amish farming community. Doug's mother had been baptized Catholic and had vowed she would bring up her children in the Roman Catholic faith no matter what. Even if their father wanted to live his life as a non-practicing heathen.

Doug had never been sold on the whole *one true religion* thing, but he knew it was important to his mother so he never made a fuss about going to mass on Sundays, or on holy days of obligation throughout the year. Although he never felt religion should be a matter of *obligation,* he tried to see it from his mother's perspective. Many people considered faith an obligatory thing—like not eating meat on Fridays, or doing some sort of penance during the forty days leading up to Easter—but he believed someone should worship God out of love, not a sense of obligation. A love that was freely given made more sense to him than doing something because the alternative would lead to an afterlife burning in the fires of hell. That wasn't any sort of belief system he wanted to be part of. Since living in Florida, he hadn't been to church once. And hadn't felt any different for it.

Inside the church, a group of people wearing Santa hats were stringing fresh garland laced with bunches of holly from pew to pew. Someone was on top of an enormous ladder, replacing the lightbulbs in all of the hanging fixtures, which were wreathed in sprigs of pine and holly. Certainly no one wanted the lights to go out during one of the most important masses of the year.

Doug had to admit the place looked great. A life-size Nativity had been set up at the front of the sanctuary, to the left of the altar, with a gleaming silver star suspended high above it against a deep-blue velvet backdrop. On the right side of the altar there was an enormous Advent wreath with tall pillar candles—one white, at its center, surrounded by three pink candles and one purple—denoting the four Sundays leading up to Christmas. Each of the six-foot tall brass candle holders had been wreathed in fresh garland and bunches of holly, along with glitter-spayed pinecones woven throughout, which really brought all the decorations together in a truly tasteful way. The only sign of any *secularity* was the tall decorated tree at the back of the sanctuary, situated next to the holy water font where the church's baptisms were conducted.

Chloe and his father smiled broadly when they heard the back door of the church open and saw the two brothers walk in.

"Praise Jesus!" their father said smiling, as he all but ran down the center aisle of the church to greet them. "I am so happy you're both here," the man said. "Especially you, Doug. I hope the drive up from Florida wasn't too hard on you."

Doug's father threw his outstretched arms around him. Then Dean and Chloe joined in, when she approached a few steps behind him.

"This is going to be an awesome Christmas!" Chloe said, kissing both her brothers. "Especially now that you're here!" she said, shooting Doug a wink. "Holidays are meant to be shared with family."

"It's good to see you all, as well," Doug said, "but first I need your help with something."

"What is it, son?" his father asked. "Do you need help carrying something in from the car? Have you had anything to eat? You must be hungry after such a long drive."

"No, Dad, it's not that… Unfortunately, it's something much worse."

Doug spent the next few minutes relaying his encounter at the Welcome Center to his father and sister. Caught up in the gruesome details, Doug broke down, crying against his brother's chest.

"My God, son, I'm so sorry you had to witness that. We'll call the authorities, but first let's at least get some coffee into you. I don't think we have anything stronger."

After sending Chloe to the sacristy, where the parishioners had set up a small coffee pot to keep them all energized throughout a long night of decorating, the three men went into one of the two crying rooms at the back of the church, which were fitted with telephones. After pulling up some chairs for them to sit in, Doug's father dialed 9-1-1 and handed the phone to him. "Just tell them what you saw, son. We're here for you. Things will be fine."

Doug gave an account of what'd happened to the officer on the phone. How he'd encountered the big man dressed as Santa. And the horrible event of the kid's murder. He relayed what'd happened to his phone when the officer asked why he'd waited so long to call. He told him how the man had told him none of the phones were working, and that's why he was asking to use his. Even as Doug heard himself say the words, he knew they sounded a bit suspect, but he also knew what he was saying was the truth. The officer on the line asked for a number he could be contacted at, and Doug gave him his father's cell phone number.

"I can't believe the night you've had, son," his father said, pulling him close in an awkward embrace. "I know we've had our problems over the years, and most certainly have our share of fences to mend, once everything's said and done, but as soon as we finish up here, we'll head home and get you settled and something to eat. Then you can get a good night's rest. Things will look different in the morning. I promise. Now that you've called the police, that should be at least one weight off your mind. What an awful way to have to start the holidays."

"I do feel better," Doug said. "I just hope they don't think I had anything to do with that kid's murder. "

"Son, we're in church. There's no need to swear."

"Whatever..." Doug said, defensively. After a minute or so he continued. "On the way over here, Dean was telling me about the murders that've occurred in the area. You think they could all be connected? It could be likely that they're all connected, but who really knows for sure? If so, the police probably know much more about what's going on than any of us do."

"You're probably right, son," his father said.

Dean smiled, rubbing his brother's shoulder for reassurance. "For the moment, let's just try to put it all out of our minds and enjoy our time together. It's almost Christmas Eve."

The door at the front of the church swung open and a large man dressed in clerics entered the sanctuary accompanied by a gust of wind.

"Boy, it sure has gotten cold out there!" the priest said, rubbing his hands together briskly. He smiled broadly at the group of parishioners who were helping get the sanctuary ready for the following evening's mass. "You're all doing a wonderful job. And here I thought I'd have to do all this decorating myself!"

"When have we ever let you do it all on your own, Father?" one woman asked. "You know we're happy to help any way we can. It's an honor to prepare the church for the Nativity of our Lord."

Doug thought the last words the woman spoke sounded a bit disingenuous, but who was he to judge? He knew millions of people who spoke the same way about Christ— as their Lord and Savior; the very center of their lives.

Chloe walked into the room holding a tray with three steaming cups of coffee and a bunch of sugar packets, along with some powdered coffee creamer and stirrers.

"Sorry, but there wasn't any real creamer left."

"No worries, honey," their father said. "As long as it's good and hot, we'll be fine."

Doug warmed his hands around his cup of coffee and drank it black. It wasn't a steak dinner, but hopefully it would at least take the edge off for the time being. The hot liquid felt good going down.

"Dean," their father said, looking at his oldest son, "I was thinking maybe you and your brother might want to head on home. Your sister and I can finish up here. We shouldn't be much longer. At least you both can get comfortable and grab something to eat. There's no need for us to all be here. I'm sure your brother would like to get settled in."

Dean nodded. "I was thinking the same thing. What about you, bro? Wanna grab something to eat?"

"Sounds good to me. I wouldn't mind taking a nice long shower, as well."

They all stood up and shared another group hug.

"We'll be right behind you," Chloe said. "We're almost done here."

As soon as Doug and Dean walked into the house, Doug made a beeline for the bathroom. He wanted desperately to wash the night off of him. He could still smell the stench of bleach, pine-scented disinfectant, and blood on his clothes. A steaming shower would feel great and help to wash the night's horrors away.

"I'll make us a couple sandwiches," Dean shouted down the hallway.

But Doug had already gotten out of his clothes and was under the steaming spray of the showerhead.

"Feel better?" Dean asked when his brother walked back into the kitchen wearing black sweatpants and a dark red *Buccaneer's* t-shirt.

"Much," Doug said.

Looking at his brother's shirt, Dean couldn't help but razz him. "Dude! When did you cross over to the dark side?"

Doug laughed. "There *is* football beyond the *Steelers*, you know!"

"Traitor!" Dean said.

"When in Rome..." Doug joked.

Together, he and his brother shared light conversation and hungrily gobbled down two roast beef sandwiches each, made on home-baked white bread, accompanied by heaping mounds of potato salad and baked beans.

Dean kept the conversation going by asking his brother all about his life in Florida. Did he like his job? Was where he was living nice? Were all the girls down south as hot as they looked on TV? He was happy to speak about anything *other* than murder!

Doug was grateful for the break in tense conversation. It was awesome just to be shooting the shit with his brother around the kitchen table like old times. He was surprised at how good it felt to be home. There were comforts to be found there if he remained open to them. In some ways, after having seen his father over at the church and how different he seemed to be, Doug's worries had been lightened some. He now thought he just might be able to have a nice Christmas after all.

It was like no time had passed between them; Gretchen was curled up at his feet beneath the table, with her head resting on his bare toes. He was incredibly happy to see her again. He'd often joked that she was the only woman for him, and in many ways he still felt that way.

"So..." Dean chided, "how are those *Buccaneers* of yours doing, bro? Clearly you haven't been watching the *Steelers*, who are sitting pretty at 10 and zip."

"I have the NFL channel at my place in Florida. I've been keeping track. What do they say? Once a *Steeler* always a *Steeler*?"

Dean chuckled. "Yeah... Something like that."

When their father and sister got in a little before 10:00 pm, Doug was already sound asleep on the living room couch in front of a roaring fire. Dean was reading a Jonathan Kellerman book in his favorite recliner.

"He's out like a light," their father said. "No doubt he needs the rest."

"Yeah, he had a shower the minute we got in. And then we ate and came in here to watch some TV, and after a few minutes, he was snoring away. He was out before I could even bring up what he wanted Santa to bring him this year. Under the circumstances, I figured it was best to leave *Santa* out of our conversation altogether."

"Good idea," his father said.

"Have either of you eaten?" Dean asked. "Do you want me to make you a sandwich or something? I picked up some cold cuts and potato salad on my way home from work today. And there are still a couple cans of beans up in the cabinet."

"Actually, that sounds great," Chloe said. "I'm sure we could both use some sustenance. Who would've thought decorating a church could expend so much energy?"

"If you don't mind, I think I'm gonna grab a shower first," their father said, taking off his coat.

"Not at all," Dean said. "Chloe and I can talk smack about you while you're gone."

"Nice..." Chloe said. "Don't pull me into your ruse!"

The next morning, Doug woke to the wet warmth of Gretchen licking his face.

"Hey, love of my life..." he mumbled. His throat felt as if he'd swallowed a handful of sand.

LICK! LICK! LICK! It was clear which family member

was Gretchen's favorite, even if he had been gone for five years.

Doug grabbed the TV remote from the end-table next to the couch and pressed the ON button. The TV sprang to life with a BREAKING NEWS story from Channel 69 out of Allentown.

"It would appear yet another body has been found," the newscaster reported somberly. "And just one night before Christmas Eve!"

On the screen, a WFMZ cargo van was set up in front of the rest area's Welcome Center, bringing the previous evening's carnage into sobering view. Staring blankly at the reporter's face on the TV screen, Doug once again felt that parallel universe thing from the night before.

The male newscaster relayed the details of how a youth had been found slain inside the men's room of the rest area. He was careful to not give too many of the grisly details. Rather, he reported the event with a kind of respectful detachment. But clearly the old news adage was being adhered to—*IF IT BLEEDS, IT LEADS!* Glancing at his watch, Doug saw that it wasn't even 7:00 am yet.

After sharing a leisurely breakfast of pancakes, bacon, and steaming, fresh-ground coffee, the four of them got washed up, dressed, and headed out to Chloe's Honda CRV. Chloe told Doug they had wanted to wait for him to get home before picking out this year's family Christmas tree. Doug had to admit it was a nice gesture. Clearly they were all doing their best to make him feel as welcomed and as comfortable as possible.

"Nah," their father said. "It's just that Dean didn't want to have to lug the tree into the house all by himself."

They shared a laugh, and for once Doug felt good just to be doing normal things. So much had happened in the past twenty-four hours—not to mention the history he and his father shared—it was a welcomed relief to see that Dean and Chloe had been right in their assessment of how much their father had changed. It was clear he was an altered version of his old self. A much *nicer*, accommodating one.

At Unangst Tree Farms in nearby Bath, they picked out a beautiful, seven-foot Frazer Fir that they all knew would look perfect set up in front of the large bay window in the family room.

"She's a beauty," their father said.

"Doug gets to put mom's angel on top of the tree this year," Chloe said, kissing her brother's cold-reddened cheek.

"He sure does," their father said. "I know your mother would be pleased."

"She sure would be," Dean said, bringing up the rear as they walked their purchase to the car. After securing the tree to the luggage rack on the roof, they were ready to head home when Doug heard someone shouting across the gravel expanse of the tree farm's parking lot.

"Are those some of my parishioners?" the lumbering man said, swinging a large wreath in one hand and a pine swag in the other. Both were decorated with emerald-green Christmas balls and laced with a string of clear lights. As he got closer, they saw that it was Father Meechum from St. Michael's.

"Guilty as charged," their father said as the man approached. "Father, this is my son, Doug. He's visiting from Florida for the holidays. Doug, this is Father Meechum, our pastor over at the church." It was the same priest from the previous evening; the one who'd come into the church about a half hour after he and Dean had arrived.

"Yes, I saw you last night. It's nice to meet you," Doug said politely.

This man's eyes were watering, most likely from the frigid, pre-Christmas temperatures. "I hope you're going to be joining us for this evening's mass," the priest said, smiling broadly.

Doug felt a knot form in the pit of his stomach. There was something oddly unsettling about the man, but he couldn't put his finger on it. Something about the way he was looking at him. But also something *else*. His watering eyes, perhaps. It made Doug's skin crawl for some reason. Then he caught sight of what it was. When he reached over to shake the priest's hand, he saw a thread of glistening saliva hanging from his lower lip.

"Sorry, the man said, swiping at his face with his coat sleeve, with both of his hands filled as they were. "It's abominably cold out here. You're smart to be living where it's warmer. Florida's bright and sunny even when it's winter."

The glistening strand of saliva shot a jolt of panic through Doug and caused him to rock back on his feet.

It couldn't be…

"Father," Dean said, "if you don't mind, we really should get this tree into some water. We'll see you tonight, okay?"

The priest smiled. "I understand. Chloe, were you still planning on stopping by the rectory to help me get things organized for after mass? Nothing major, just a few snacks, and perhaps some libations." He said this last part with a wink.

Doug watched the man's every move. How he formed his words. The wandering look his eyes took on as he spoke Chloe.

"Of course, Father. I'm more than happy to help."

"Good then," the priest said. "I'll see each of you later."

He turned and walked toward his car, swinging his purchases as he went.

Climbing into the backseat beside Dean, Doug watched as the priest put the fresh wreath and swag into the trunk of a black Volvo. He was half surprised to see the priest wasn't driving a dark red van with SANTA'S WHEELS painted on its side. The whole way back to his father's house, Doug sat in silence as the forgotten hills of his home state rolled quietly past.

Something continued to tickle the back of his brain. He couldn't help wondering if the pastor of St. Michael's and the man dressed as Santa from the previous evening were one and the same. It was just a feeling, but he wasn't certain how he could be sure. It wasn't the kind of thing you could be mistaken about. Calling somebody a cold-blooded killer undoubtedly came with its consequences. If he were wrong in his assumption, any number of things could happen. Maybe even some irreversible things involving the law. Doug knew there was no way he was going let his sister go to the church rectory alone. That much he *did* know.

"To help me get the snacks ready for tonight's reception after mass," the priest had said.

"OVER MY DEAD BODY!" Doug screamed inside his head.

Chloe would be there as planned, but he would be there right alongside her, to offer whatever assistance he could. He might even ask Dean to come along—for backup—in case his gnawing feeling was correct. Once there, he would be able to determine whether his sinking suspicions were justly founded. If so, Doug thought he might just kill the psycho son of a bitch with his own bare hands.

At a little before 9:00 pm, Doug and Chloe drove over to the rectory to help get things ready for that evening. As they approached, Doug felt like driving his truck right up onto the rectory lawn and through the enormous leaded window that looked out over the decorated side yard separating St. Michael's from where the pastor lived.

Pulling into the driveway, Doug said, "I'm glad you were okay with me tagging along. As long as I'm in town, I might as well help out."

"You and I both know why you wanted to come along," Chloe said.

"Oh? And why is that?" Doug said.

"Because you wanted me all to yourself, silly! There's only so much of Dad and Dean a person can take." She smiled and wrapped her arm around his neck.

"You caught me," Doug said. "Now that my secret's out..."

"You brought back up!" the priest said from the open doorway of the kitchen. Once again there was an odd kind of familiarity to the man's voice. Doug *knew* something about the guy was off, but it still eluded him as to what exactly it was.

"You know it!" Chloe chimed, winking as she and her brother made their way up the short flight of stairs that led to the small kitchen side-porch. The pine swag from the tree farm was hanging on the outside of the kitchen door, its crystal-line lights playing festively off the emerald-green Christmas balls the swag had been decorated with.

On the surface, most folks' lives looked charming and un-eventful, but appearances could be deceiving. Doug had learned to trust his instincts over the years, and his instincts were telling him now to *RUN!* To grab his sister and get the hell out of there. But he wasn't about to leave without trying to get to know more about the man. If there was something about the man that would connect him to the kid's murder from the previous evening, Doug would find it. Even though Chloe didn't know it, his being there was definitely more for *him* than it was for her. His presence had nothing to do with canapés and spiked egg nog.

If there was any way he could be certain the priest was the same guy from last night, he would catch the sonofabitch red-handed, and then decide what he should do about it. Somehow calling the authorities didn't seem to be enough. It didn't have enough *sting* to it. If the priest and the killer were one and the same, he would find a way to turn the tables on the miserable bastard and beat him at his own game. But first he had to be certain he had the right guy. If it really was, the grief alone that the man had caused him was enough to send him to an early grave.

With the kid at the rest area dead, someone was going to spend their holidays mourning him. Family... Friends... Any number of people. It just wasn't right. If he could help get justice for the kid, he wanted to. If his suspicions were right, midnight mass or not, all hell was going to break lose. That much was for sure.

As the priest welcomed them both into his home, Doug took in his surroundings as nonchalantly as possible. When the man spoke, he smiled back at him. He did his best to appear interested as the man went on about all he had planned for the night's festivities.

The kitchen was your standard setup. There was an oak table surrounded by chairs beneath the window that looked out over the driveway, while the rest of the space was taken up by an L-shaped countertop, separated intermittently with top-of-the-line stainless steel appliances.

Only the best for Father, Doug thought ruefully.

After insisting they both join him in a glass of Christmas Cheer, the pastor walked them into the rectory's formal dining room, where platters of extravagant foods had been laid out, along with an electric urn for brewing coffee and an elaborately carved crystal punch bowl, which would most likely be used for the special egg nog recipe the priest claimed was a concoction that'd been handed down from his great-great grandfather.

"Wow, there's enough food here to feed an army!" Doug said, showing mock-interest. "Late or not, folks are definitely going to want to hang around for all this after the service."

"One can hope..." the priest said, eyeing Doug with lingering interest.

As they were shown around the rest of the rectory, Doug saw something sitting on the pastor's desk in his book-lined study that caused him to stop dead in his tracks. In a gilt frame, there was a glossy photo of a man dressed in a Santa suit, with a sea of smiling children all around him and fake snow strewn everywhere.

Doug presumed the children must be some of the younger members of St. Michael's parish family. Although less unkempt than from the previous evening, it was undeniable; this guy had to be the same sonofabitch from the Welcome Center murder.

As the parishioners and their families began filing into the church at a little before 11:30 pm, Doug and Chloe connected with their father and Dean before deciding where they were all going to sit. Doug was happy doing what he had in the past whenever his mother would bring them all to church. He would plunk himself in the very last row, knowing it would make for an easier exit once mass was over.

Instead, his father led them up toward the front, where he said they'd all be able to see better. He no doubt wanted to make sure his kids got to see him up close and personal when he was called up to sing his solo.

"Dad," Doug said, "is it true that you are going to sing for us tonight? Or was Dean just pulling my leg?"

"Yup!" his father replied. "*Oh, Come All Ye Faithful* is all mine!"

They shared a laugh before Doug excused himself and headed toward the front of the church. He made like he was going to the bathroom, but once he was passed through the church's left-side vestibule, he took a quick detour and found exactly what he was looking for.

Doug stood before a heavy oak door that had a brass plaque on it reading: SACRISTY. Doug knew of all nights, this was undoubtedly the worst night he could be confronting a priest, as he was preparing for the one of the two most important masses of the year. But it was clear he didn't have any other choice. These people had to know about the wolf in their midst. From what Doug had seen the night before—in the way all the parishioners had flocked around the man they faithfully trusted to lead their congregation—he knew they needed to know just how much deceit and treachery had infiltrated their masses with the psychotic man's presence.

Without a sound, the sacristy door opened onto a group of young altar servers helping prepare for mass. And of course, the good Father himself, who was struggling to get dressed.

Bright faces turned in Doug's direction as he anxiously entered the sacrosanct space. Each of them all but gasped as the stranger entered their midst.

"Can I help you with something?" a deacon, already dressed in his alb and stole and ready for the night's celebration, asked Doug. Remaining silent for a moment, Doug watched a few altar servers assist the pastor in donning his full regalia—alb, chasuble, stole, and cincture—of course all on top of his crisp, formal clerics he'd had custom made in Rome.

"I need to speak with Father," Doug said, feeling his face flush a hot red.

"As you can see," the priest said, "now isn't the most opportune time. We're busy trying to prepare for midnight mass."

"Yes... I know what tonight is," Doug said. "But this is something that can't wait."

Father Meechum turned back toward him and smiled guardedly.

"Is there something wrong with the trays of food you and your sister were kind enough to bring over? Our coffee urn isn't acting up again, is it?"

"No. This has nothing to do with the coffee or food."

"Everyone," the pastor said, "please give Mister Connolly and me a moment. We have plenty of time before we all need to go take our places at the back of the church for the procession."

He then turned to face the tallest altar server in the room. "Justin, would you kindly take the censer with you? And make sure you get all three cakes of charcoal good and hot this time. We want to make sure the incense is nice and strong, so it's sure to deliver our prayers straight to heaven!" The priest smiled warmly.

In unison, the group of altar servers followed the deacon out of the sacristy, leaving Doug and the priest alone in silence.

"What seems to be the problem?" Father Meechum asked Doug, obviously put out by this sudden intrusion.

"I know who you are," Doug said flatly. "And I know what you did, you sick son of a bitch!"

"Excuse me...?" the priest said. "I won't have you coming in here defaming the house of the Lord with your senseless ramblings. What in God's name are you talking about?"

"My *ramblings*?" Doug repeated. "Trust me when I tell you, *Father*, why I'm here has nothing to do with rambling..."

"Well, then," the priest said, tugging at his Roman collar

341

like a petulant child, "…get on with it. In case you forgot, our time is running short, I've got a mass to celebrate!" He said this with a look of displeasure on his face, which was growing redder by the second.

"Well, at least *your* time is," Doug said, shortening the distance between them by inching up a few more feet. "Seriously… You don't think I know who you are? Or the unthinkable truth of what you've done?"

The large man flinched as Doug approached.

"I'm sorry, but I'm no good with riddles. What nonsense are you prattling on about?"

Before Doug could give any thought to his actions, he slammed his clenched fist against the side of the priest's beet-red, bulbous face. Looking much like the fights he'd watched on Pay-Per-View, the pastor's face jerked to the side—nearly in slow motion. His impeccably groomed hair now stood out in thick, unruly patches.

"You insane sonofabitch!" Doug spat. "Surely you remember me from last night? You know… When you were at that rest area twenty miles out of town, slicing that poor kid's mouth before leaving him there die and *me* to take the rap for you. You in that ridiculous looking dark red van with SANTA'S WHEELS painted on its side! As if you're some great, selfless deliverer of *hope*. Which we both know is a fucking joke! It's undeniable just how full of shit you are. Just like what was in that crapper you tossed my phone in!"

Doug stepped forward and kicked the priest squarely in both knees, causing him to double over in pain. "And now your entire congregation will know you for the blasphemous, sinning son of a bitch that you are. Do you really think such a weak disguise—a fucking *Santa* suit, for crissakes!— would be enough to keep me from recognizing you in this getup? I mean, how *stupid* do you think I am?"

Not waiting for an answer, Doug threw himself at the priest, who was still bent over nursing both knees. Reaching down, Doug roughly grabbed the man by the wrists with both of his hands and began pulling him toward the door of the sacristy. In a matter of seconds, they would both be out in the sanctuary of the church, which Doug suspected was now *packed* with parishioners gathered to celebrate the birth of their Lord.

"I can't believe I have to do this on a night like this," Doug said frowning. "But I'm afraid you've left me no choice. Do you expect me to let your parish go on without knowing what an evil, twisted piece of shit you really are?"

Dragging the heavy bastard through the side vestibule into the brightly lit space of the sanctuary, Doug could hear gasps coming from over his hunched shoulders.

"Yes, folks..." Doug shouted over his shoulder in order to be heard by everyone present, "I'm afraid you'll see the program for this evening's service has been altered quite a bit. The celebration of the Nativity that we all came here for tonight will most likely need to be held over until next year's mass."

Several linebackers from the back of the church, doubling as ushers, ran up the center aisle with clenched fists at their sides.

"No sense in charging me, gentleman," Doug said calmly. "Once you hear what I have to say, you'll be grabbing this son of a bitch by his feet." Although the two men continued to lumber toward where Doug was hunched over the thrashing priest, they'd both slowed their pace a bit, not sure what was really happening here.

Pointing to the presider's chair behind the candlelit altar— enormous poinsettias flanking it on both sides—Doug looked down at the pastor and swept his left arm in a dramatic gesture toward the large, carved chair that was decked out with emerald-green brocade cushions and holiday greens.

"By all means, Father, take your rightful seat—one last time—before the authorities cart your sinful ass off to prison for the atrocities you've committed."

The man struggled to get to his feet. The deacon and altar servers who were standing near the Advent wreath stepped forward to see if the man needed their help.

"I'm sorry, but I'm not going to stand for anymore of this!" the gaunt deacon said. "Someone call the police. This man is clearly crazy! Yet another sad case of the apple not falling far from the tree."

Doug's father stood up and headed toward where the deacon was standing. "One more word out of you, Norman, and I'll be happy to show you just how *crazy* I can be!"

Dean got to his feet and followed his father up the thickly carpeted aisle.

With the priest now situated in his presider's chair, Doug walked over to stand behind the lectern, roughly tapping the microphone to see if the thing was working.

"I'm assuming this thing's on," he said into it.

For the next few minutes, Doug relayed the events of the previous evening to a church full of gaping faces. When he was done, he could hear a number of the female parishioners crying into clenched handkerchiefs.

"Now, I know you're not going to believe me when I say how truly sorry I am to have to share this deplorable information with each of you," Doug said. He stepped out from behind the lectern and headed toward the lower step in front of the cloth-draped altar. "But please trust me when I tell you, I know all too well what a terrible shock this may come as—especially on as important a night as this is for all of you."

"Father Meechum has been an amazing shepherd for our parish!" one woman said from the back of the church.

Doug couldn't help but laugh. "While that might be so, ma'am, he's also a cold-blooded killer. If you don't believe me, perhaps you'll want to watch the nightly news. If the reporting is correct, there's a very good chance *all* the recent murders that have been taking place around here have been committed at his hand. Sliced faces, poisoned senior citizens, and God only knows what else the news hasn't reported on. I'm afraid we may have only seen the tip of the iceberg when it comes to what your dear Father Meechum has been a part of."

"What the *fuck* would you know of any of this, you simpleton?" the priest shouted from where he was seated. "You don't live here anymore, remember. You chose to leave town when things got difficult between you and your dear, old dad. Some son you turned out to be, huh? You weren't even strong enough to help your father in his darkest time of need."

Doug didn't allow himself to take the bait. Instead, he turned back to face the congregation. "And now I'm sorry to say, you're beginning to see your wonderful *shepherd's* true colors for yourselves. Now I suppose I can rest my case."

"Block the doors!" a parishioner called out from one of the side pews. "I don't know about any of you, but I'm calling the police!"

At that, Father Meechum stood up and ran to the altar.

"How *dare* any of you people judge me! I've given twenty years of my life to this parish. I've seen you through all sorts of sin and depravity. You wouldn't believe the things I hear in the confessional. Incestuous relationships, homosexual activities, orgies among married couples. No one takes the covenant of marriage seriously anymore! God forbid any of you should curb your lustfulness. And don't even get me started on the all the rest of your despicable deeds! You name it... Child abuse, domestic violence,... *Bestiality*, for God's sake! And you think *I'm* the abomination. Really?

"Each of you think you know me, know my motivation for doing the things I've done. But I can assure you, I did those pathetic retches a favor by ending their dismal lives. You all come in here every Sunday claiming to love the Lord and asserting that you follow his Commandments to the letter. But then I hear what you tell me in the confessional, which I can assure you, is a far different story. You act all sanctimonious, as if each one of you has been delivered to us directly from the Lord on high. What an absolute joke! In the end, you do what you've always done. You leave it to me to absolve you of your sins, as if being anointed with oil and making the sign of the cross is somehow a magic spell that erases everything. Not to mention what you blame on God himself! The list is long. The church's stance on premarital sex and abortion, masturbation, same-sex marriages, and any other number of things. We all want to play God with the lives we've been given, but then blame Him for when things don't turn out as we'd expected them to.

"Well, crucify me if you want, but I can assure you that I'm the bigger man. At least I'm taking custody of my actions, even if it's after the fact! I'm not like each of you, sitting in judgment, sniveling over a few ended lives. Really? Are my actions truly any worse than anything any one of you has done? I wouldn't say so. You should all be ashamed of yourselves!"

The two ushers who had started to rush Doug earlier when he dragged Father Meechum into the sanctuary now took off running directly at the priest as if they were both working off the same brain. The pastor was still standing behind the altar in abject deference against his congregation of sinners. Both men charged him like twin bulls in an elaborately decorated china shop, while Meechum stood there, glaring in every direction.

As they went, one of the men shouted, "You don't think I know what my son says you did to him, you sick prick? And you wonder why he only served *one* of your masses as an altar boy. That's all he could take of being around you with your inappropriate groping and leering glances. I didn't believe him when he first told me. I didn't even report it to give you the benefit of the doubt. But now I see he was right. You made a fool of me, but it won't happen again!"

The other one was shouting, "You told my daughter she was going to burn in hell for all eternity because she made the decision to have an abortion after being raped at her prom! Now who's gonna burn in the fires of hell, you holier than thou, smug son of a bitch!"

As the red-faced priest was roughly knocked to the floor when both men collided with him, he absently reached for the edge of the altar, and when he did, he ended up taking the heavily starched altar cloth—and the two *lit* brass candle holders—down with him. The second the flickering candles met with the heavy weave of the dark tan carpeting, the candle flames caught and the entire altar was suddenly engulfed in flames.

"Oh my God!" one of the parishioners shouted. "Someone get the fire extinguishers from the back of the church."

Someone else yelled, "Call 9-1-1! As old as this church is, the whole place will go up in no time!"

Within seconds, people were running in every direction, looking for ways they could help without getting seriously hurt. In a moment of panic, you could see everyone mentally going through a planned route of escape in their heads in the event things got quickly out of hand. Thankfully the church doors were unlocked because the mass was supposed to have been in full swing by now. But of course they wouldn't want to open them until absolutely necessary. Any draft could set the fire burning out of control. An open door could easily have these flames reaching the ancient rafters in a matter of minutes.

While some of the male parishioners took off toward the back of the church to gather as many fire extinguishers as they could find, the flames began to skitter across the newly installed carpeting. Within seconds, the crackling flames grew taller and quickly ignited the pine boughs and holly branches that were all over the sanctuary. They all watched as the Advent wreath and its glitter-sprayed pine cones went up in a bright flash.

In a dizzying swirl, the entire church was nearly engulfed in flames.

Screaming parishioners ran toward the exits, but the black smoke was dense and stifling, which made maneuvering through the packed pews nearly impossible. Most did as they'd been taught, and as soon as they made their way out of their seats, they dropped to the floor where the smoke would naturally be thinner. But it was no use. In an all-out state of panic, people were trampling blindly over one another. The congregation milled about in confusion like passengers on the sinking *Titanic* while cries and shouts for help filled the toxic air.

With a loud series of crackling sounds, the life-size Nativity, with its intricately painted, wooden statues—Mary, Joseph, the Three Wise Men, and of course the Baby Jesus in his hay-filled cradle, was the last to go. But *go* it did! The only objects left in the wake of the devouring flames were a few stone farm animals, recent additions to the Holy family that had only been added the year before.

As a small group of choking parishioners made their way outside—staggering to get as far away from the infernal heat of the church's interior as possible—the loud wail of sirens could be heard quickly approaching.

Pushing her way out of the church through a cloud of blinding smoke, Chloe choked and gasped for air, searching the scene for her father and brothers. She was elated when she saw her father bent over a group of crying children huddled on the church lawn.

Chloe looked at her father in disbelief.

She threw her arms around his neck and began crying. "I can't believe any of this is happening!"

"I'm just thankful you made it out okay. Have you seen either of your brothers?" Tears quickly filled his eyes.

"I know they're both outside. I think they went back into the church once to see if there was anyone they could help to safety. But then I heard them shouting once they both made it out again, wondering why the fire trucks hadn't made it to the church sooner."

"Praise Jesus," he said. "At least they're both okay!"

They were still hugging and crying when Dean and Doug threaded their way through the crowd.

"We don't have to wait until the fire's been put out, do we?" Doug asked, soberly. "I've really had all I can take for one day." He ran both hands through his unruly, soot-streaked hair.

"No, son. Of course, we don't. Now that the police and Fire Department are here, there's really nothing else we can do, but wait and see who was blessed enough to make it out of this unbelievable night alive. I'm all for getting the hell outta here!"

"Sounds like a plan to me," Dean said.

With flames climbing higher and higher into the freezing night air, Chloe, not wanting to think of who might not have made it out of the church before it went up in flames, walked her father over to her car as the two boys headed in the direction of Doug's truck.

Following their father and Chloe out of the church parking lot, Doug looked over at Dean in total disbelief. Just when he'd thought he'd seen the worst incident of his life with the kid's murder at the rest area, now there was this. He thought he would confront the priest and the cops would be called and they'd take him away. End of story. Never in a million years could he have imagined things turning out as they had, with St. Michael's going up in a sea of flames during one of the highest holy days of the calendar year.

"Dude, why didn't you tell me about Father Meechum?" Dean asked, slapping him on the arm. "You went over to the rectory with Chloe knowing you were going to confront him, didn't you?"

Doug shook his head. "Not at first. At least not completely. I was pretty sure he was the same guy from last night, but I needed to get a bit closer to him to make sure my suspicions were rightly founded."

"So when did you know for sure?" Dean asked.

"When I saw a picture of the son of a bitch dressed like Santa! When I felt the bile rise in my throat, I knew my hunches were spot on."

"Yeah, I guess that would do it for me, as well," Dean said. "Despite the unbelievable insanity of all this, I really am glad you're here."

Doug sighed heavily. "Under any other circumstance I would feel the same, but after what we've all been through, I can't help thinking my visit might not have been the best idea. Not that seeing you guys hasn't been great, because it has."

"I understand," Dean said reassuringly. "I just hope you'll stay a while, at least until we've all had a chance to visit."

"I don't know how long I'm staying," Doug said, shaking his head. "I'm doing my best to push all this shit out of my mind, but it's not every day I have to witness a gruesome murder, then watch a church and many of its parishioners go up in flames."

"I know..." Dean said, looking out the passenger side window, unable to think of anything else to say, still in a state of shock himself. Beyond the truck's windows, festive Christmas lights blurred as they drove past, making everything seem as if all was as it should be in their closely knit home town. But, of course, Dean knew better than that. After tonight, he knew nothing would ever be the same again. There was no way they could lie to themselves and act as if things hadn't played out as they had.

"Some visit this has been, huh?" Dean said finally, glancing over at his brother. "It'll be a miracle if we ever see you again after all this."

"It sure hasn't been what I was expecting, but if it's any consolation, it has been a hell of a lot more manageable with you guys here to support me through it all."

"Well, at least that's something," Dean said. "I just thank God mom wasn't here. She would've had a heart attack on the spot."

"No doubt."

As they drove the rest of the way home, Doug spotted something out of his rearview mirror he knew he hadn't seen on his way into town the previous evening. On the side of the tall, light blue water tower that usually read WELCOME TO BETHLEHEM someone had climbed up and spray painted a line through the B and added an A after the E, leaving the sign to now read: WELCOME TO *DEATHLEHEM!*

Shaking his head, Doug laughed out loud.

Dean said, "What's so funny, bro?"

Doug shrugged and said, "Dude, you wouldn't believe me if I told you." Then he smiled a truly sincere smile. "What do you say we hurry and get our asses home. At least there we have a better chance of making it through the night alive!"

Dean looked down at his watch. "I hate to say it, my friend, but it's already morning. Merry Christmas, little brother. I think you're gonna like what I got you."

"Let's hope so!" Doug said with a wink. "If you spent less than five-hundred bucks, you know you're going back out shopping tomorrow."

They both laughed.

For the remainder of the drive, Doug was sure to take the shortest way possible back to his father's house. This was one Christmas Eve he was more than happy to have *far* behind them all.

ABOUT THE AUTHORS

JP Behrens has been a storyteller most of his life. He has weaved an intricate web of bold faced lies, some of them in the form of stories. Everything in one's life is a learning experience, and he's tried to learn from both wondrous successes and miserable failures. Though JP has managed to fib less often, he still tells the occasional exaggerated tale here and there. Get updates at JPBehrensauthor.com.

Steven Bigwood is a retired attorney and former newspaper reporter and magazine editor who lives in Southern California's High Desert. An inveterate night owl, he typically watches the sun set behind the area's boulder-strewn hillocks and the outstretched arms of its Joshua Trees before he starts to write. His upside-down Christmas tale, No Sugar Plum Fairies, is the first imaginative fiction he has published.

Rose Blackthorn lives in the high mountain desert with her boyfriend and two dogs, Boo and Shadow. She spends her free time writing, reading, being crafty, and photographing the surrounding wilderness. She is a member of the HWA and has appeared online and in print with Necon E-Books, Stupefying Stories, Buzzy Mag, Interstellar Fiction, Jamais Vu, Eldritch Press and various anthologies including *The Ghost IS the Machine, A Quick Bite of Flesh, From Beyond the Grave, O Little Town of Deathlehem, FEAR: Of the Dark, Equilibrium Overturned, Wrapped in Black: Thirteen Tales of Witches and the Occult,* and *Cranial Leakage: Tales From the Grinning Skull Volume 1.* More information can be found at the following links: Twitter: twitter.com/rose_blackthorn; Blog: roseblackthorn.wordpress.com/; Facebook: www.facebook.com/RoseBlack-thorn.Author; Amazon: amazon.com/author/roseblackthorn; Goodreads: www.goodreads.com/author/show/5758684. Rose_Blackthorn.

Chantal Boudreau is an accountant by day and an author/illustrator during evenings and weekends, who lives by the ocean in beautiful Nova Scotia, Canada with her husband and two children. She writes and illustrates horror, dark fantasy and fantasy and along with her *Fervor* series and her *Masters and Renegades* series, she has had many of her stories published in a variety of horror anthologies, online journals and magazines. Find out more at: chantellyb.wordpress.com

Kevin G. Bufton is a thirty-something father, husband, and horror writer (in that approximate order) from Birkenhead in the UK. He has been writing short horror fiction since 2009 and has appeared in over forty magazines, anthologies, and websites worldwide. One day, he hopes to be able to scare people for a living. What he really wants for Christmas is world peace... and beer—plenty of beer.

Alyn Day is an active member of the New England Horror Writers living outside of Boston, MA. She is an avid horror enthusiast with an inclination towards zombies. Publications include *So Long and Thanks for All the Brains, Daily Frights 2012, Women of the Living Dead, Zombie Tales, Here Be Clowns, Horror on the Installment Plan, Zombies For a Cure, Quick Bites of Flesh, Let's Scare Cancer to Death, Phobias* and Brian Keene's *Operation Ice Bat.*

Nicole DeGennaro currently works as a copy editor for a science publisher and lives in the Hudson Valley area of New York. Although she studied journalism at Purchase College, her heart has always belonged to fiction writing. Her short and flash fiction stories have been published in the anthologies *Scared Spitless, Gothic Blue Book III: The Graveyard Edition, Gothic Blue Book IV: The Folklore Edition, The Grotesquerie* and *100 Worlds.* You can learn more about Nicole at her blog: nicoledegennaro.wordpress.com/.

David J. Delaney is a registered nurse from Australia writing when and where he can. He's written short stories and is currently finishing off a novel. He write across all genres, with inspiration coming from life experience through to stories he has read.

Gerard Griffin was born in Oadby, Leicestershire, where he still lives with his partner of twelve years, and a trio of beagles. Twenty years working in one of the region's illustrious pork pie factories has desensitized him to most forms of horror. He hopes that his own fiction will mirror the nightmare of his day job to some small degree. "Crack!" is his first published story.

Vicky MacDonald Harris lives in Lincoln, NE. In print, her poems have been published in the NaPoChapBook collection published by Big Game Books, The Lincoln Underground, and in *Try To Have Your Writing Make Sense: The Quintessential PFFA Anthology.* Additionally, her writing is online at Poets and Artists, Hobble Creek Review and several pop-up Tumblr poetry events like the24project, and Women Poets Wearing Sweatpants. She blogs at pageofwoeabsolved.blogspot.com when she isn't finding time to work on revisions on her first novel.

Susan Jay is a native New Yorker who works as a school psychologist by day and a writer of fiction by night. She tends to shy away from all things horror, admitting she's easily scared, and prefers to focus her creative energies on romance. However, when she saw the Call for Submissions and saw it was for a charity she strongly believes in, she felt the need to contribute something. She's glad she did, as this is her first published piece.

Geoffrey K. Liu is a writer living in the navel of civilization between Baltimore, Maryland and Washington, DC. When he's not trudging across the corpse-ridden, apocalyptic landscape of customer service, he's procrastinating on various writing projects, including an epic series of horror/fantasy novels that he swears are going to be awesome when they're finished... someday. Geoff's other short stories have appeared in various publications. Geoff is deathly afraid of scorpions, white sauces, and failure. You can follow his brain dribbling online at geoffreyliu.weebly.com.

Kerry G.S. Lipp teaches English at a community college by evening and writes horrible things by night. He hates the sun. His parents started reading his stories and now he's out of the will. Kerry's work appears in several anthologies including *DOA2* from Blood Bound Books and *Attack of the B-Movie Monsters: Night of the Gigantis* from Grinning Skull Press. His story "Smoke" pioneered The Wicked Library podcast's explicit content warning. KGSL blogs at www.HorrorTree.com and will launch his own website www.newworldhorror.com sometime before he dies.

Steph Minns has been a keen reader, writer, and artist since childhood. Originally from the suburbs of London but now living in Bristol, UK, she works part time as an administrator and spends her spare time writing. Her dark tales range from stories set in dystopian realities to ghost and horror. She is a member of *Stokes Croft Writers*, a small Bristol-based fiction writing group. Steph's publishing history to date (including *Bloody Christmas*) runs to seven short stories and a novella; *Any Old Iron*, a dark fantasy, published by author Chris Fielden in the competition anthology 'To Hull and Back,' October 2014. *Tiny Claws*, won the *Dark Tales* March 2014 international competition and is due out in a winners story collection in 2014/15. *Dreg Town*, published in an anthology on dystopian futures called 'Broken Worlds' by *Almond Press*, December 2014. Gothic ghost novella, *The Tale of Storm Raven*, published as an e-book by *Dark Alley Press*, April 2014. *The Flight of Horses*, appeared in the sixth *Darker Times* horror/dark fiction anthology after receiving an honorable mention in their November 2013 competition. Ghost story, *Watcher from the Woods*, published as an e-book by *Alfiedog Publishing*, August 2012. She also has a website—stephminns.weebly.com—where there are short stories readers can download for free, plus links to interviews and reviews.

Christopher M. Morgan is a New England native transplanted to Jacksonville, Florida, where he became trapped by life and still believes he will one day return "home." For now he lives in denial, yearning to see a season change or even a single snowflake fall. His mundane job is in communications engineering which is every bit as imaginative as it sounds. Morgan spends his limited down time appeasing the voices by venting his psychoses into the laptop, conjuring and cajoling them into story form. His long suffering wife and daughter are relieved he no longer vents these horrors aloud to them...

Mark Parker is Owner and Managing Editor of Scarlet Galleon Publications, LLC, with *Dead Harvest—A Collection of Dark Tales,* as the company's inaugural publication. Mark is also the author of several short works of fiction, including *Banshee's Cry, Way of the Witch, Biology of Blood, Lucky You, Halloween Night,* and the forthcoming *Spinster, Burzum,* and *Way of the Witch II – Sticks & Stones.*

Jordan Phelps lives in London, Ontario, where he spends much of his time being forced by daydreams to write things down. When he's not doing this, he can often be found playing with bumblebees. More of his work is featured in the anthologies *Dead Harvest* from Scarlett Galleon Publications and *A Chimerical World: Tales of the Seelie Court* from Seventh Star Press.

After several different careers, **Mike Pieloor** finally gave into the demands of his writing muse and in 2012 published the dark fantasy/supernatural novelette, 'Dark Water.' He is a little too excited by steampunk and gaslamp fantasy and is currently working on a series of novellas set in an alternate Victorian era. When the hourglass allows, he is also working on the sequel to 'Dark Water' and his first novel. Mike lives in Australia and is a member of the Australian Horror Writer's Association and the Canberra Speculative Fiction Guild. He grows orchids and loves all things dark and fantastic. Connect with Mike at www.facebook.com/MikePieloor or www.mikepieloor.net. au.

Joel Reeves is a teacher, author, and an avid collector of pulp science fiction and fantasy. He is the author of several short stories and his rollicking fantasy quillogy, *Of Quills and Kings, Walpole Unbound, Dreams, Schemes, and Spiny Machines,* was recently published by Double Dragon Press. He lives in a small Michigan town with his wife, children, and pet cat, Penguin.

Philip Thorogood is a writer born and raised in Peterborough, UK. He started out writing fan fiction for Games Workshop's subsidiary publishing company, the Black Library, and has since branched out into other avenues.

DJ Tyrer is the person behind *Atlantean Publishing* and has been widely published in anthologies and magazines in the UK, USA and elsewhere, most recently in *Amok!* (April Moon Books), *In Creeps The Night* (J.A.Mes Press), *State of Horror: Illinois* (Charon Coin Press), *Steampunk Cthulhu* (Chaosium), *Tales of the Dark Arts* (Hazardous Press) and *Cosmic Horror* (Dark Hall Press), as well as in *Sorcery & Sanctity: A Homage to Arthur Machen* (Hieroglyphics Press), *All Hallow's Evil* and *Undead of Winter* (both Mystery & Horror LLC) and *Fossil Lake* (Sabledrake Enterprises), and in addition, has a novella available on the Kindle, *The Yellow House* (Dynatox Ministries). DJ Tyrer's website is at djtyrer.blogspot.co.uk/. The Atlantean Publishing website is at atlanteanpublishing.blogspot.co.uk/.

Jay Wilburn lives with his wife and two sons in Conway, South Carolina. He left teaching after sixteen years to care for the health needs of his younger son and to pursue full-time writing. His sons enjoy Christmas time very much and tend to believe that it starts once the decorations go up in the stores in October. Follow his many dark thoughts at JayWilburn.com, on his author page on Facebook, and @AmongTheZombies on both Twitter and Ello.

ALSO FROM GRINNING SKULL PRESS

If you liked *Return to Deathlehem*, why not check out where it all started…

O Little Town of Deathlehem — where

Krampus, not Santa, brings the holiday cheer…
… the lights on the tree, so festive and bright, skitter and crawl and possess a lethal bite…
… malicious little elves, not a jolly one, know if you've been naughty—or nice…
and
… family gatherings often turn deadly.

An otherworldly artist finds beauty in man's depravity…
One woman's therapy session frees more than just memories…
A fertility ritual delivers more than just an abundant harvest…
The ultimate hot sauce proves to be too much for one man…
An obsession with dreams pushes one woman over the edge…
… and many more!

For some, death is not the end. There are those who are doomed to walk the earth for all eternity, those who are trapped between one plain of existence and the next, those who, for whatever reason, cannot or will not let go of the lives they left behind. These are the vengeful spirits, the tortured souls, the ghosts that haunt our realm. Welcome to FROM BEYOND THE GRAVE, a collection of 19 original ghost stories.

Available in print from Amazon.com and Barnes and Noble, and in digital formats from Amazon.com, Barnes and Noble, and Kobo books

We survived *The Beast from 20,000 Fathoms.*
Then came *THEM!*, *It Came from Beneath the Sea*, and *The Deadly Mantis.*

They were merely practice runs.

Now prepare for
ATTACK! of the B-Movie Monsters:
Night of the Gigantis

Rampaging Rodents!

Terrifying Tentacles!

Bone-Crushing Claws!

Scientific experiments gone dreadfully wrong!

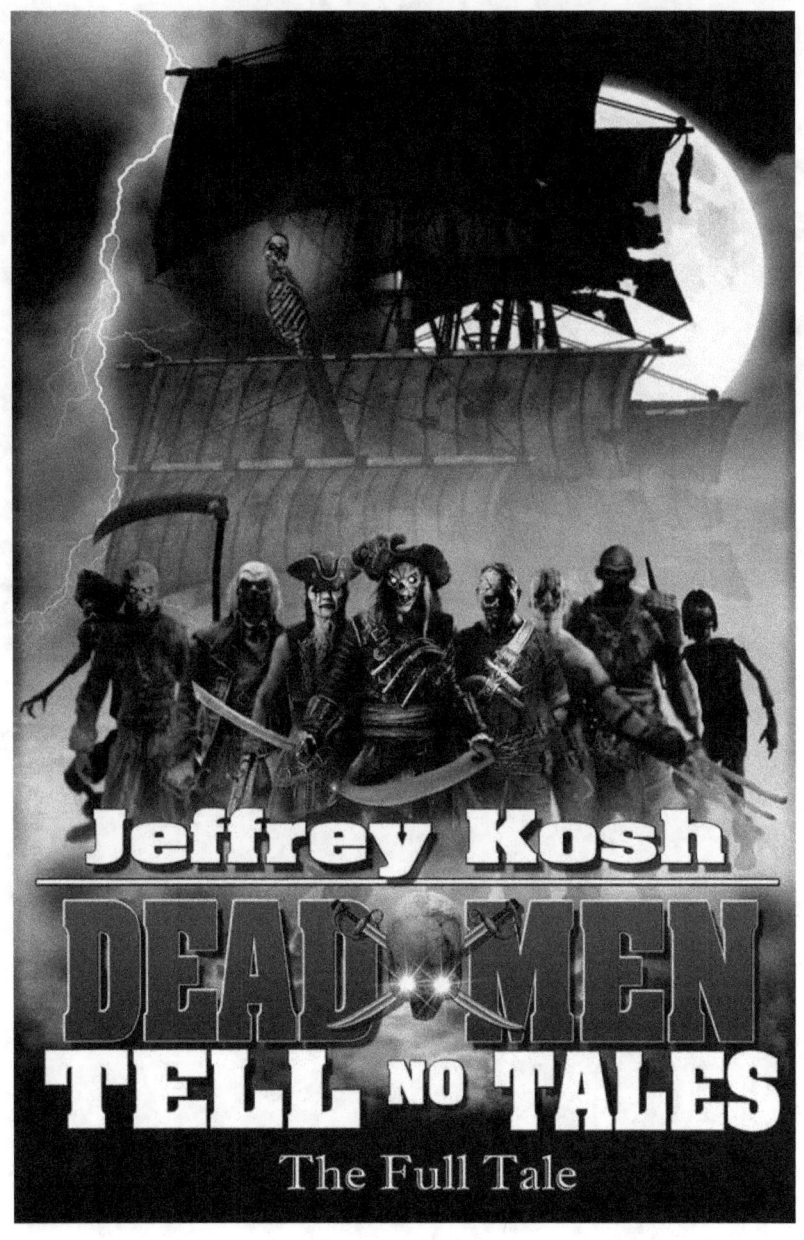

www.ingramcontent.com/pod-product-compliance
Lightning Source LLC
Chambersburg PA
CBHW050656290626
47170CB00015B/300